Charlie never tells anyone he was once married. He's removed the ring, although a raw channel has worn into the skin it once covered. If they happen to ask he simply tells them he is single, without explanation. Now and then the thought¬less remark, the "I guess you never found the right woman," remains unanswered.

Like most modern clocks, his bedside alarm displays these large segmented numbers, but makes no ticks. Some nights he stares at these numbers for hours, following the silent but rhythmical rearrangement of digital segments as 10 becomes 11 becomes 12. And some nights that's when the sound of the other breathing begins, a strained gasping, a rattle transitioning into a congested growl at the bottom of his wife's throat, as if all the ticks of time have congealed together in their haste to be done.

His wife had lived that way, on the other side of their wide bed, for days it seemed, although it had probably been only a mouthful of hours, her still hands folded insect-like on top of the covers. Only her mouth moved, really, the spastic power of it nodding the head and jolting the chest: automatic, muscular inhalation and exhalation, her body's final act.

He'd stayed with her most of that evening, then gone to the guest bed because he couldn't sleep with that future memory unfolding there alongside him, and then he'd come back. Back and forth, up and down, all night.

All that was a lifetime ago, but that was the way they passed their last minutes together, as these stiff bits of time appeared and disappeared across the face of his silent clock. And then their marriage was gone, swallowed up by the sound escaping with her final breath.

From "Breathing"

THE NIGHT DOCTOR

AND OTHER TALES

BY STEVE RASNIC TEM

CONTENTS

BREATHING

He wakes up to the sound of his own breathing. This is not unusual, although each morning it seems louder than it did the morning before, and the sound occupies more of his day. He lives far from any highways, and far enough from his nearest neighbor, that sometimes his own breath is practically the only sound he hears. When he was a child in bed he was sometimes terrified by the noise of his blood pulsing in one ear—as if his heartbeat were trapped somewhere inside his pillow—and this new obsession with breath feels much the same.

It has been this way for months: his breathing, the turn of a page, the exhalation of a cushion, the creak of the bed, his breathing, his hands preparing food, the click of the fork against china, his cup knocking the wooden table, his breathing, his breath. Now and again he sighs for companionship, but it brings back only a vague recollection of being held.

He comes to believe that the rest of the world is breathing with him, as a breeze lifts the curtains and stirs the pages of his book, as he unscrews the cap of the milk jug and smells the cold, as clouds float past his windows, as the trees glide back and forth within their anchored locations, as the shadows outside creep and multiply and eventually swallow everything he sees. Breathing occurs everywhere. Respiration is universal.

His mother, who spent her last few hours chasing her breath and never quite catching it, would admonish him about his inaccuracies, insisting that the difference between breathing and respiration was some essential distinction whose significance he hadn't yet grasped. "Breathing, Charlie, is what happens when you expand and contract your ribcage. You have to use your muscles in order to breathe. Respiration is a chemical reaction. Oxygen and glucose are converted into carbon dioxide, water, and energy. Human beings and animals breathe, plants do not. Plants respire. Insects don't breathe either. They obtain their oxygen through diffusion." Although Charlie learned to appreciate the way his mother's mind worked, he didn't care for her distinctions. He much preferred metaphor. "The world breathes," he told himself when alone. "And I am flying in its breath, so fast sometimes all the details blur."

Ten, and eleven, and past midnight and he still hasn't fallen asleep, as he is waiting to hear the breathing that is not his. It is certainly not something he wants to hear—just the anticipation terrifies him. But he can't fall asleep knowing it might be coming, and he has convinced himself these sounds of another's breathing might come at any moment. He has heard them a few times now, quite distinct from his own, but he was so tired at those times he might have been confused.

Sometimes the open bedroom door moves, ever so slightly, even when all the windows are closed. Sometimes that glass bird hanging in the bathroom swings on its invisible fish line, jerkily, as if batted. His wife had loved the way it caught the light in the morning. Sometimes water streams from the tap, even though he is sure he squeezed the handle shut. Sometimes he doesn't feel alone here in the house, even though he has become alone everywhere. Sometimes there is this intimation of breathing that is not his own, and as much as it frightens him, something about that breathing is unaccountably precious.

Charlie never tells anyone he was once married. He's removed the ring, although a raw channel has worn into the skin it once covered. If they happen to ask he simply tells them he is single, without explanation. Now and then the thoughtless remark, the "I guess you never found the right woman," remains unanswered.

Like most modern clocks, his bedside alarm displays these large segmented numbers, but makes no ticks. Some nights he stares at these numbers for hours, following the silent but rhythmical rearrangement of digital segments as 10 becomes 11 becomes 12. And some nights that's when the sound of the other breathing begins, a strained gasping, a rattle transitioning into a congested growl at the bottom of his wife's throat, as if all the ticks of time have congealed together in their haste to be done.

His wife had lived that way, on the other side of their wide bed, for days it seemed, although it had probably been only a mouthful of hours, her still hands folded insect-like on top of the covers. Only her mouth moved, really, the spastic power of it nodding the head and jolting the chest: automatic, muscular inhalation and exhalation, her body's final act.

He'd stayed with her most of that evening, then gone to the guest bed because he couldn't sleep with that future memory unfolding there alongside him, and then he'd come back. Back and forth, up and down, all night.

All that was a lifetime ago, but that was the way they passed their last minutes together, as these stiff bits of time appeared and disappeared across the face of his silent clock. And then their marriage was gone, swallowed up by the sound escaping with her final breath.

He is awakened again in the middle of the night by the breathing: as ragged as his attempts to find the meaning in it, as persistent. He reaches for her as if forgetting, as if the hard facts of the event could ever slip his memory. That part of the bed is cool and unruffled, the sheets smooth and polished. He waits there with his hand still on her side of the bed, banking on the possibility that this is simply another dream. When it comes again, a distant intake of air followed by the beaten gasp, he swings his feet out of bed and sits there on the edge.

Sometimes it begins this way—he is aware of his own breathing, and then he is aware of the other's. Sometimes it is so loud and insistent inside his skull he develops a rhythmical headache, the pain creating sharp flashes of light at the corners of his eyes. Sometimes that illumination stays, and everything he sees appears viewed through a filter.

Tonight the tortured sounds of this breath are so loud and distinctly distant Charlie feels compelled to investigate. He travels the dark house with a flashlight, his slippers whispering across the hardwood floors. He is reluctant to switch on the lamps, afraid their glare might hide more than they reveal.

In the living room he stumbles over a pair of shoes left out.

He can't remember taking them off, or when. A tide of magazines and newspapers spills across the floor to the left of the couch. He remembers sampling them, gazing at pictures, now and then reading a stray description of things he no longer cares about. On the coffee table a glass lies on its side, the wood beneath it marred by a ghostly film. Under the table is a package he'd received in the mail, the corners and sides smashed, the encircling tape shredded but never breached. He doesn't remember trying to open it, or what made him abandon the attempt. Since his life changed he has done a lot of things he cannot remember, or understand.

He gasps for air, having held his breath for too long during the search. He listens to the way the sound of it scatters and fades into the mess his house has become. He waits for an echo, or a repetition, and realizing he hasn't been hearing that breathing for some time prepares to return to bed.

But that's when it returns, rising out of the shadowed corners and spreading across the walls: the gasp, followed by the choked return of air, too loud for anything normal, making his eyes flash with pain.

The door to the coat closet is open, the hangers jammed to one side, a tangle of coats and shoes and old camping gear fallen onto the tiled entryway. He'd been desperately seeking something, he remembers, although he has no memory of what it might have been.

A sharp inhalation shakes him, and a pained sigh pushes him deeper into the house. His own breathing becomes more difficult as he fixates on its awkward mechanics. The inside of his mouth is painfully dry. He finds he can hardly breathe when someone else breathes with so much pain.

In the kitchen he pauses beside the refrigerator and listens. He is convinced he can hear that other breathing struggling inside. And when he opens the door he is sure what comes out is some kind of exhalation, but it is not the breathing he's been looking for.

His eyes flash again from the pounding, and the dark hall is highlighted with a kind of ghostly bioluminescence. He catches only a glimpse of what passes him: a bare arm, the side of a shoulder, and he can't remember the last time he smelled his wife's hair, and yet he can smell it now.

In the dining room everything lies hushed beneath a heavy drape of darkness. Even with the flashlight he finds it difficult to apprehend more than a few inches at a time. There are dirty dishes on the dining room table. He can't remember when last he ate there. He moves slowly, feeling anxious for his own breath, his own heart. Something is wrong with both of them, he thinks, and he feels disappointed. The arrival of this word surprises him, but he is convinced it is the correct one.

Going from one doorway to the next he is suddenly captured by vertigo, and no matter how much he shakes his head it will not let him go. He can feel the rest of the world pushing him around as if he were spinning inside a great emptiness. It was a mistake to have ever left his bed. What had he really expected to find? The imagination always promises everything, both the wonderful and the terrible in unending supply, but at the end of the day it all goes away, leaving you alone in bed with the lights out and only the compulsive and enigmatic movements of the air to accompany you.

He crashes face-first into glass, embarrassing himself with a humiliated cry. He slides open the patio door and cool air drifts past him into the room. The breathing is out there—softer than before, but still distinguishable from his own anxious wheezing. The paving stones shine with damp, and fearing he might fall he kicks off his slippers. He steps outside in his bare feet, listening carefully as he pads across cold stone into wet grass. There are woods behind the house, and a border of opulent green embraces and shields it from prying eyes. Animals are frequent visitors, and he cannot deny the possibility that one may have gotten inside the yard, or maybe even inside the house. He understands how a bird with a damaged wing can somehow sound like a soul lost and confused by concluding events. Or how a starved animal's hungry activity might mimic an attempt to deliver a final speech. Their last day together she said nothing to him, not a single word.

Charlie has been unable to look at animals since his wife died. He finds their darting eyes, their cautious grace, too painful to contemplate. He won't even glance at a dog being led by its owner down the sidewalk, and if a cat crosses into his yard he usually turns away. He is not sure why. He knows they live short and brutal lives, many of them, and he can't believe it's worth it simply for some scattered spells of freedom. His wife had loved animals, and maybe that's where the pain lies. She felt sorry for their fragility, that they died so quick and often.

Do they know that this house is his? Do they pay any attention to him at all?

His mother, if she were still alive, would scold him for his fantasies. He wonders if his wife would be disappointed to see him now, moving cautiously about his own house like a thief.

There is a soft, explosive snort, followed by those sounds of harsh but persistent breathing, of something more emotional than the simple mechanical sounds of dying. But he's no expert in any of this. He's ill-prepared for these events, or right now for anything else it seems. The breathing continues, rough and directionless, and too compelling to ignore. It seems to come from somewhere beyond the dark outline of trees, out of the darkness itself, perhaps, stubborn and resistant to interpretation.

Charlie and his wife used to talk about what they would do, if one were to lose the other. Of course they would still live on and find some kind of happy life. Of course they would connect with someone else, and make some reinvention of who they were and why they lived. They had planned it all out the way they planned to spend their money: so much for essentials, so much for treats, so much for forgiveness and a blanket permission to thrive. A haunting had never been anticipated.

As the world breathes the trees sway closer than he is comfortable with, but then pull back, breathing out and breathing in. Across the yard a head appears out of a line of heaving bushes, swaying slightly, and then Charlie sees the rest of the body.

The antelope stands nearly motionless, gliding its head back and forth ever so slightly as if undecided, as if waiting for Charlie to make the first move, ready to run if the move feels wrong.

Charlie is stunned. The creature breathes so loudly—a stuttering of ragged gasps, distorted and multiplied—that Charlie can hear nothing else. Fear makes his muscles rigid, and he waits to the very edge of suffocation as he studies that other breath.

Sometimes a predator will drive these animals down out of the foothills and into the city, but what kind of predator Charlie has no idea—it's something he doesn't want to think too much about. And once here—where could such a creature hide? He considers that it might have been in hiding near his back yard for ages.

It's just an animal, he tells himself frantically. *There's nothing it can do to hurt me.* He actually doesn't know this for sure, but the thought still reassures him.

The creature continues to gaze at him, its body stiff with focus. The hair along its neck appears slightly frosted from the cold, the hair on its lower jaw white, with black on top of the muzzle leading back to the large eye sockets high on the skull. Its chest heaves, appearing stained. Suddenly it charges him, moving faster than any animal Charlie has ever seen. He has no time to move, and covers his head protectively.

It stops only a few feet in front of him, reeking of musk. It's much larger than he expected. The sounds of its labored breathing are thunderous. Charlie raises his head and tries to look at it directly, thinking that perhaps that's what you're supposed to do with a threatening animal, assert your human superiority.

The animal's face has been ravaged, the skin torn and hanging here and there in flaps, with one eye blinded, a dull pale stone wrapped inside a network of scar tissue. He looks barely able to hold up his own weight. He nods drunkenly, as if ready to collapse. His nostrils pulse rapidly, struggling for more air.

A male. Charlie is somehow surprised by this. The horns rise too tall above the skull, and they have that barb. And it isn't an antelope, but a pronghorn. His mother would have been pleased by the accurate reclassification. Although this one is much larger, and broader than average, an authentic force of nature. Enormous heart, enormous lungs. It's the fastest mammal around. Why the pronghorn is still standing here Charlie has no idea. But he has started to breathe with it, dragged into its painful rhythm—it seems he has no choice. His chest begins to ache, and there are sharp pains along his ribs, and he begins to seriously wonder if he's having a heart attack. But there have been so many times the past few months he's thought this—he's been in so much pain—and every time they say it must be emotional, and that he should try to relax. "You should talk to someone"—he's heard this again and again.

The animal continues its struggle for air, taking Charlie with it, to the edge of consciousness and a failure of normal eyesight. That earlier apprehension of bioluminescence returns, and Charlie is swarmed by the faint glowing outlines of hundreds of people, wandering aimlessly through this limited space, searching for whatever they might be searching for, but unable to say. There is no way to find any remnant of his wife inside such confusion, but he is compelled to try, and twists his head around, and says her name, and goes blind from weeping.

The pronghorn snorts explosively and blood pours out of its mouth. Charlie follows the blood down to the massive rusty mat across the animal's chest, and finds the leaking wound around the side, a jagged fragment of wood protruding, and bobbing with each arduous breath. A piece of a fence post, he thinks, or a branch from a tree.

The spastic breathing, the nodding of the head, the jolting chest, and the last gasps attempting to eat the air. Charlie can see that it's about to run again, and once it's gone there will be no recapturing it. There's nothing to be done for it, but Charlie can't help wondering if he got it to a vet if for once a miracle might be possible.

It springs at the same time Charlie grabs, and once he has his arms around its neck he locks his fingers and won't let go, and is dragged for a while, his mouth full of hair and blood, until this magnificence finally shakes him off, and disappears into the dark.

He lies there attempting to catch his breath, and wonders if this time it's even possible. He can't hear himself breathing; he can't hear anything. Back there in the house behind him a challenging silence waits, and after he checks himself for damage that is where he intends to go.

APARTMENT B

Tom chose to bring very little from his old life into the new apartment. A few clothes, a few random artifacts, but most of his clothes and furniture were new. "I hope you won't take that the wrong way," he told his adult son. He knew that might sound as if he didn't care about his son's feelings, which wasn't true, but he didn't have all the language he needed to explain himself. The reasons were complicated and hard to understand, even for him. But if he were to greatly simplify he would say that he needed to avoid pain. He didn't want to feel haunted anymore.

Of course he still kept photos of his son and his dead wife, and he hung some of them in his new bedroom in a place of importance—on the wall just above a sock drawer in his new chest of drawers, so that he might look at them as he dressed each morning. But they had no real relevance in his new life. His son lived hundreds of miles away, and his wife—he no longer had his wife. Over the three years since her death that had become somewhat easier to say. He was in this new life and in this new life he was unmarried. The only sane thing to do was to accept that. You shouldn't live in the past—people always said that, didn't they? Living in the past was something everyone did, but everyone seemed to agree it wasn't healthy.

He had never lived in an apartment before. He had gone from his parents' house into a small house with his new bride and from there into increasingly larger houses until their son had left home and their interests had stopped expanding. His wife had liked to sew and play with clay. He'd liked to read, and tinker. Now no one did any of those things. Whatever life was left to him was unusually free of distraction. Someone else might have used the word "empty," but Tom refused to.

His new second floor apartment had two bedrooms—one he would sleep in, and one he would put things into until he could think of a better place for them. The living and dining rooms were combined, and relatively small. The kitchen was an island of sorts in the middle, small enough to discourage a long stay, which was fine with him. He had never really understood cooking, and intended to eat pre-prepared meals and salads from the local deli, or perhaps some soup or stew from a can.

Off the dining room there was a small sliding door and a balcony beyond—something he had never had before. He ventured out onto this narrow platform his first evening in the new apartment, and saw that his son had placed a lawn chair from the old yard as furnishings—something he hadn't asked for but could see the sense in. He sat there for almost an hour and looked out and down on the large back lawn of the complex. He was glad he didn't have to mow anymore, or plant, or worry about how people felt about the outside of his house, and what they therefore might assume about what went on inside his house. What they might assume about him.

Other people were out on similar balconies and one or two of them waved. He did nothing to encourage them, and they stopped. Here and there were traces of a lit cigarette or an illuminated phone screen. Tom let the darkness swallow him, and when he went back inside doubted anyone noticed.

The first few nights sleeping in his new home felt like overnights at some lower-priced motel. This was a good thing— he felt it relieved him of any responsibility for the experience. By week's end, however, he was feeling critical of the bed and the color of the walls, and wondering why people cared so little anymore about standards and good service.

He did dream, but not about his dead wife or his distant son. He dreamed of trips never taken, cities never visited and yet oddly familiar, meetings with strangers who were so like friends from his past he felt like he had known them forever. They were inviting him on a journey, it seemed. They didn't promise he would like it, but they made it clear he had no choice.

He had taken early retirement and so there was no particular plan to his days. He usually woke up when the sun came up, but his new bedroom window was shaded unpredictably so sometimes hours would pass while he debated whether it was a new day or not. He tried a simple clock to fix the problem, but he finally had to get rid of it. He didn't like the way it sometimes sped up, sometimes slowed down, and sometimes didn't appear to change at all. He decided he didn't really need it—his body and his circumstances would somehow tell him what to do.

He didn't leave the apartment the first several weeks. He didn't even open the front door. There was no real necessity—he had plenty of food and other supplies—but he recognized the strangeness of it. He'd never been in the least socially adept, but he'd also never imagined himself a hermit before.

But he had been unable to shake off a peculiar sense of instability since moving into the apartment—an oddness of proportion or geometry. As if he were slightly too tall or his legs slightly too long to move around the space comfortably. And it seemed as if his lungs could never quite take in enough air. He didn't want to go outside until he had solved the puzzle of his environment—he didn't feel safe. He thought he might fall at any moment, and he knew what sometimes happened to elderly men who fell. Was he actually elderly? If he had the thought then perhaps he was.

So the first time someone knocked on his door Tom felt slightly frightened, especially since the knocks seemed to have some urgency behind them. He wondered, briefly, if the building were on fire. But wouldn't the smoke detectors have gone off? There were smoke detectors, weren't there? He knew there had to be, but he'd never noticed them.

The woman at the door appeared young, with her dark black hair. But she had the skin of someone older. He'd never been good with ages, and that lack of skill seemed to become more evident every year. Why did he even care about her age? He felt embarrassed, and he hadn't even said a word. She brushed past him and sat down on the couch.

He hesitated, not sure whether he should close the door or not, but fearful that someone else might force their way in, he shut and locked it.

The woman sat on the edge of the couch fiddling with the hem of her skirt and squeezing her knees together. "A family used to live here, the Blakes? Did you know them? Well, of course you didn't. That was years ago. They were a very nice family."

Tom couldn't imagine why she was here. But even if she were crazy she must have a reason. "I didn't know them." What else was there to say?

"No, I said that—there was no reason you should know them. They were a very nice family—that's all I meant to say, really. Is it just you here, by yourself? No family?"

"I have a son, but he's an adult now—he lives in another city." No need to tell her which city. No need to tell her he was a widower. He still wore the ring, and he saw her looking at it. But he'd put on weight since he first married and now the ring was too small to get off—he hadn't taken it off in years. He wasn't trying to be mysterious, or to convey a false impression, but taking his hand somewhere, getting the ring sawn off—that was a major step, wasn't it? He didn't even understand all the implications of such a deliberate decision. And wouldn't that be a bit of a betrayal, to deliberately damage the ring that way? He should put a Band-Aid over it until he could decide what to do.

"A lot of unattached people live here. I'm unattached. You'll fit right in."

Tom doubted it. When was the last time he'd fitted anywhere? He couldn't remember. "I haven't met anyone yet. I'm just getting—acclimated."

"Well then, I'm your first." She smiled, but it was a weak smile, as if she were somehow ill and simply trying to be brave. "But I'm not going to tell you my name. I'm going to let you guess it."

He avoided the couch and sat down in the burgundy armchair opposite her. Was she flirting? Tom couldn't remember what flirting was like. "That's alright," he replied, although he wasn't at all sure.

She smiled broadly, but said nothing. She seemed to be waiting. Was he supposed to ask for clues? Finally she said, "So what do you do?"

He did nothing. He'd been spending all his time in his new life trying to figure out how to do more than nothing. "Retired," he said. "I ran an office. I had a staff. They did all the work, I guess. I kept them busy. Sometimes it was a challenge. People will just sit there, you know, if you don't give them something to do. I guess they call that purpose. People feel they require a purpose or they won't do anything."

What was this nonsense he was saying? His "staff" was two co-workers in the research department. They all did the same work—he was simply the contact person. Most of the time they had no idea why they were researching the subjects they were researching.

"It sounds important."

He nodded. He said, "Yes." This could not be farther from the truth. He apparently wanted to impress her, but he had no idea why. Had he been this way before he was married? He couldn't remember.

"It's good to take charge of things," she said. "Too many people just let things happen to them—do you agree?"

"Taking responsibility," he said. "That's what you're talking about."

"Exactly." She crossed her legs and adjusted the top of her dress.

"Will you excuse me?" He got up and went into the bedroom and shut the door. He pushed the knob in and twisted to lock it. He sat down on the edge of the bed with the lights out.

Without a clock he couldn't tell how much time had passed, but it seemed like a long time before he heard footsteps coming down the hall. The steps stopped in front of the bedroom—he could see two shadows in the narrow strip of light just beneath the door. Her shoes, he supposed. The doorknob turned back and forth and there was a rattle as she tried to open the door. After a few minutes the shadows vanished and he could hear the footsteps in the hall and then in the living room, and then the front door opening. He held his breath. Then the sense of the room itself exhaling as the front door closed.

After a few minutes he crawled further up on the bed in the darkness and put his head down on the pillow. The lights were still on out there, but he decided that was acceptable.

Sometime in the middle of the night he grew cold and crawled under the covers, but he didn't open his eyes. He dreamed of walking in darkness, and every now and then a faceless voice would say hello, but he was always too afraid to answer back.

The next morning Tom got up and cleaned the apartment. Theoretically there wasn't a lot to clean. Since he'd moved into the new apartment he'd meticulously picked up after himself. His meals were pre-prepared and promptly disposed of. No stray ingredients or evidence of preparations to erase. And since he hadn't gone outside there had been no dirt or other debris to track in. His guest from the night before might have brought in something on her shoes, but if so it wasn't obviously detectable.

But Tom understood that dust was always a concern. Particles drifted through the windows, filtered down from the ceilings and even from the apartments on the third floor, an unknown amount traveling upwards from deep within the fibers of the carpeting, and there was always a certain percentage of dead skin cells—his and those of previous occupants—although the exact percentage appeared to be a figure of considerable debate.

The world renewed you, or replaced you—depending on your degree of optimism—at its own rate. He did not know how to feel about any of it. He scrubbed the floors and cleaned the surfaces as best he could—tried to rid himself of contamination. But he was haunted by the approximations of memory, by the unsupported promises of the imagination. His imagination suggested he might have everything, and yet he knew nothing was there, no matter how much that nothing clamored for his attention.

The next morning, she let herself back inside, although Tom was positive he hadn't given her a key. He'd been sitting outside on his balcony again, following the comings and goings of strangers, and wondering if there might come a time he'd consider introducing himself. Even this tiny glimpse of an outside world was discomfiting. There were couples out walking their dogs, there were all those children playacting an actual life, there were all the legions of the dead, and the tantalizations of their laughter, the transient evidence of their happiness that dissipated in his scattered spells of reason.

She smiled at him as he entered his own living room. Her skin was as pale and as unblemished as the promise of sleep. She sat on the couch with some awkwardness, as if waiting for his next move.

"I'm sorry," he said. "I don't know what this is, but I'm not ready for it."

"I assumed you were lonely. I assumed you wanted some company."

"But I don't know how to do this," he said. "Is there someone I can call to come get you?"

"Could I just use your restroom? I know where it is—I found it while I was searching for you last night."

He nodded, said, "Please take your time."

She paused just inside the bathroom. "You know, the Blakes were much nicer neighbors." Then she slipped inside and shut the door.

Tom went into his bedroom, grabbed a pillowcase, and slipped the photos of his wife and son inside. He'd made a terrible mistake. He went back into the living room and looked around. Nothing here was his. He didn't recognize any of it. He opened his apartment door and left, carrying the pillowcase with the pictures close to his chest. He didn't bother to close the door behind him.

Once Tom reached the lawn of the apartment complex he turned around and gazed at it. It didn't look much like the brochure he'd received in the mail nearly a year ago, the one that had made him decide on this purchase sight unseen. It resembled a stack of concrete slabs, with stress cracks showing in the corners. The bushes around the garden level units appeared yellow and sickly. Not that it mattered a great deal, he supposed—apartments, houses were all pretty much the same—they were boxes for people to put their things in, and then to climb in afterwards and shut themselves off from the wind and the rain and the ones that might do you harm if they ever got in. At least the old house had had his history, however painful that history had eventually become.

He started down the sidewalk with no particular plan. He had some cash in his wallet and a credit card. He could always access his bank account if he discovered something he wanted to spend it on.

A variety of restaurants and other businesses lay on the other side of four lanes of highway. Their signage was incredibly bright and colorful. He passed a number of people on the sidewalk and their clothing was incredibly bright and colorful as well. Desperately so, he thought. Desperate reds and desperate blues. Desperate greens. Their eyes looked tired and pale, as if worn out trying to make sense of all the bright colors. Even the younger ones looked weary. Even their newer outfits appeared poorly cared for.

He hadn't paid adequate attention and brushed against a large man in a soft gray suit. The man stank of stress and a poor diet. Tom felt immediately embarrassed by his knee-jerk judgment when the man stopped and said, "Are you all right? Can I help?"

Tom had no idea why the man thought he might need assistance. Was it really that obvious? There was a looseness about the man's skin, as if it were a poor fit. "Thank you, I'm fine," Tom said.

The man went on his way, moving awkwardly as if in pain. It seemed to Tom that everyone he had seen today appeared ill.

A couple crossed over the highway to his side of the street holding hands. The way they clung together—Tom wondered what they feared, what they imagined might happen to either of them. They were really too young to know all the things that might happen. When they reached the sidewalk they gave each other a sloppy embrace, lips slipping off lips and then inhaling skin, makeup, whatever aftershave the man used. They appeared drunk, inebriated, but also intoxicated on themselves, and on the fact that they had each other. He wanted to give them some money, but when he approached them they ran away, laughing. Whether at him, or at the fun they'd found in each other, he couldn't say.

He didn't know how far he was from his old house. He'd stopped driving years ago, and since then had developed a poor sense of direction and distance. Not that it mattered in any practical sense. He'd sold the house and disposed of all its contents. That act was done and could not be undone. It was a terrible mistake, he realized now, but it had seemed like a good idea at the time. He had wanted to both escape pain and force himself into a new and useful life, or if not useful at least reasonable. The problem with such a strategy is that if you find you cannot complete the course you've laid out, if you come half way down the path and you discover it is the wrong path but you have given away all your resources, what do you do?

You die, Tom supposed. Such people died, or they wandered around in some kind of untouchable limbo.

It must have been close to lunchtime because there seemed to be a great number of people out on the sidewalk now and in the crosswalks. Tom couldn't have said for sure but this seemed like a reasonable guess. Singly and walking in groups, sometimes, many with nametags clipped to their pockets or hanging from lanyards. Some of them walked while eating—a sandwich or a protein bar in one hand, sometimes with a drink in the other, sucking through a straw or sipping or gobbling liquid down a long-necked bottle.

Some of them made pained noises when they ate or drank. Some of them gasped for air. Tom saw more of that loose skin he had seen before, loose and too pale and sometimes with dark shadows over where the blood vessels ran, where the blood pooled or where there was an old weakness or injury. Some had scabs or scratches. Some walked with the awkwardness characteristic of pain or injuries new or old. Some looked longingly for companionship and some of them actively avoided it.

Tom had nothing to say to any of these people. Tom had no idea how to make them feel better or provide even a moment's relief. He supposed he was like many of them but to identify too much, to accept that his experience was all too common, was to take away some of the validity of his pain. He should never have left his old house. He shouldn't even be here.

Without being aware of it he had entered one of those great stone and concrete plazas that stretched between buildings.

Here was this seemingly endless plain of paved world anchored by monuments to technology and commerce. Populated by hundreds of people, perhaps thousands, milling about as if purposeless but of course many of these figures had their purposes timed down to the last minute.

Many were getting too close. He couldn't be sure if they had him exactly in mind or if simple space restriction were forcing them all together.

"No," he said plainly, and one or two nearby stopped in their tracks. "No," he said again, as a young man in a hurry ran right into him.

Tom went to his knees as more gathered around him. He held the pillowcase with the photographs inside up to his face. Several people were approaching. One of the women resembled his neighbor from upstairs.

He was very hungry. He hadn't eaten all day. And they kept coming closer to him, wanting him to rejoin the human race. But he wasn't having any of it. He wanted to do something, something else. He took out the photographs of his dead wife and his faraway son and began eating them.

RED RABBIT

He found her on the back porch again, watching the yard through the sliding glass door. He didn't want to spook her, so he made some noise as he left the kitchen, bumped a chair, and made a light tap with one shoe on the metal threshold that separated the porch from the rest of the house. Then he stopped a few feet behind her and said, "What are you looking at, honey?"

"The rabbit. Matt, have you seen that rabbit?"

"That was yesterday, Clara. Remember? I went down there, and I scooped it up with a shovel, and I dropped it into a trash bag. Some wild animal got to it. Rabbits can't protect themselves very well. That was yesterday."

"But it's back." Her voice shook. "Can't you see it?"

He followed her gaze to the lower part of the lawn, where it dipped downhill to the fence. Shadows tended to pool there, making the area look damp even though it hadn't rained in almost two months. Beyond were a field of weeds and wildflowers, and the line of trees bordering the old canal. Beyond that was the interstate. You couldn't see it, but you could certainly hear the traffic—a vacillating roar that you could pretend was a river if you really tried.

The skinned and bloody rabbit had appeared there yesterday at the bottom of the yard, eased out of the shadows as if from a pool. And here was another one, its front legs stretched out toward the house, its body gleaming with fresh blood. This must have just happened. They must have had some sort of predator in the yard.

"I see it," he said. "Something got another one."

"Something terrible is happening," she said. "I've been

feeling it for weeks. And now this rabbit—I see it every day. Sometimes just after sunrise, sometimes just before sunrise. I thought I was going crazy, but now you see it too. What do you think it wants? Can you tell me what it wants?"

Matt looked at her: her eyes red and unfocused, lips trembling. She was somewhere else inside her head. She was wearing this old green tube-top thing. She'd never looked good in it. Her back was knotted, her shoulders pushed up, her arms waving around as she spoke. He figured she must be crazy tense if he noticed it—he never noticed things like that.

He felt sorry for her, but he also felt scared for himself. The woman he had loved had been gone for years, and now he was left with this. He wasn't a good enough person to handle something he hadn't signed up for.

"It's not the same rabbit, Clara. There must be a predator loose in the neighborhood. Probably just a big cat or maybe a dog. It's just a dead rabbit. I'll go get the shovel and take care of it. There's nothing to get upset about."

He didn't really understand how her mind worked anymore. But maybe his being logical helped her. No one could say he hadn't tried.

"There's blood all over him," she said. "He's all torn up. Can't you see that something terrible is going to happen, that something terrible *is* happening? Can't you see it?"

She continued to stare at the rabbit in the yard. She wouldn't turn around and look at him. It felt creepy, talking to her back all the time. He didn't dare touch her when she was like this, like a fistful of nerves. He didn't think she'd looked at him full in the face in days.

"It was a wild animal. It had a savage life. And something got to it. It's not like a cartoon, Clara. Rabbits can't protect themselves very well. Real rabbits in the wild, their lives are short and cruel. "

They hadn't had sex in a long time. He'd been afraid to touch her. You can learn to live with crazy, but you can't touch it. He couldn't let her drive, and when he left her alone she called him at work every hour to complain about some new thing she'd suddenly realized was wrong. Their GP kept prescribing new pills for her, but he was just a kid, really. Matt was sure the fellow had no idea what was wrong with her.

"I haven't been feeling right, Matt. Not for a very long time. Something terrible is going to happen—can't you sense that?"

"I know that's what you feel, but just go lie down. Let me take care of this, and then I'll come join you." But he knew she wasn't hearing, the way she stared, glassy-eyed and the edge of her upper teeth showing. He stood in front of her and whispered, "Go inside now. Please." When she didn't respond he stepped closer to block her view of the yard and put one arm around her, gave her a bit of squeeze.

"Honey, just go inside and lie down. I'll join you in a few minutes. Maybe I can even figure out what's killing these rabbits, and I'll deal with the thing. You just go inside." Hopefully she'd be asleep when he was done. When she was asleep he could grab a drink, watch some TV, relax and unwind for once.

He grabbed a shovel and a trash bag and some gloves and started down the slope of the lawn. He'd generally neglected that part of the back yard. The ground there had always been mushy, unstable. He didn't know much about ground water, septic systems, any of that stuff. But he figured it must be some sort of drainage issue, maybe because of the old canal, or maybe because of an old broken septic system, something like that. It didn't smell too bad, just a little stagnant most of the time, a little sour. Only sometimes it stank like rotting meat. But they couldn't afford to fix it whatever it was, so he'd just tried to ignore it.

The carcass wasn't where he had seen it. In fact he couldn't find the rabbit anywhere. He thought about that mysterious predator, and went back to the house and grabbed the rake that was leaning against the wall by the sliding glass doors.

He stood still, the rake held in both hands in front of him, raised like a club. He still didn't see the rabbit. He felt unsteady, and shortened his grip on the handle. He imagined that the predator, whatever it was, had dragged the body off somewhere. Some of the more dangerous animals in the region—coyotes, a wildcat or two, once even a small bear—had been known to wander out of the foothills and follow the canal into the more populous suburbs. He crept down the lawn toward the fence, afraid he might lose his footing. The grass looked shiny, slippery, as if the earth beneath were liquefying.

He detected a subtle reddish shadow as he got closer to the fence, and then saw that it was a spray of blood. The body had been pushed up against one of the fence posts, eviscerated, but still clearly some version of rabbit. He was glad Clara couldn't see this. It must have suffered terribly, ripped and skinned alive, all gleaming, bright-red muscle, damp white bone, strings of pale fat. But the muscle had no business being bright red like that, like some kind of rich dyed leather. He'd skinned squirrels with his dad—he knew what a dead, skinned animal looked like, so dark and bruised. But this? This looked unreal.

He bagged it and trashed it, then brought out the hose to wash away the blood and any loose pieces of meat. That's what you did with this sort of thing. That's how you handled it. You cleaned up the mess and then you went on with your life. Later he grabbed his binoculars and studied the field and the trees beyond, checking for any signs of movement. He saw nothing. If he had been ambitious he would have climbed over the fence and walked through the field to the row of trees that bordered the canal. He could have followed that canal into some other place. The water might not be running through the canal anymore, but it was still a passage to something, wasn't it? But he wasn't ambitious. And he didn't want to go there.

Matt drank and watched TV until about midnight. The house was a mess—Clara hadn't cleaned in weeks. He couldn't abide a messy house, but he worked all day—he didn't have the time. But if he had the time he knew he'd do a great job. It wasn't that hard keeping up a house—you just had to understand how to manage time and not let it get away from you. He hadn't signed up for this. He'd tried—and you owed your wife at least to try. But everybody had limits. You couldn't expect a man not to have his limits.

She didn't wake up when he crawled into bed with her. Good thing—she'd ask about the rabbit, and he didn't want to talk about that damn rabbit anymore.

He woke up once and saw her standing at the window,

looking out onto the back yard. He started to say something, started to ask her what was wrong, but he stopped himself. He was tired, and he knew what was wrong.

He woke up alone. He didn't like waking up alone, but he didn't want to answer any of her questions. He fell back asleep, and when he woke up again the room was bright from the sun coming through the window. He'd overslept, but at least it was the weekend. Nothing important ever came up on the weekend. They'd stopped doing the important stuff a long time ago.

"Clara, you up here?" She didn't answer. "Clara!" Nothing. He got his pants and shoes on and went downstairs. He still couldn't find her. He felt a little panicky, and he was mad at himself for feeling a little panicky. He made himself be methodical. He went back upstairs and searched each bedroom as he went down the hall. He wasn't sure why they had all these bedrooms—they didn't have any kids. They had way too much house, but he'd gotten such a good deal on the place.

He felt a pressure building behind his eyes. He tried to shake it off. He went back into their bedroom and looked in the closet and in the master bathroom. He got down on his knees and looked under the bed. There were several socks, another larger, unidentifiable piece of clothing. He made a note to sweep under there later.

He called again from the top of the stairs. "Clara! Are you in the house?" Nothing. No steps, no rustle, just the soft hum of the refrigerator. He went downstairs and jerked open the front door, a little too hard. It banged against the rubber bumper mounted on the wall. He hadn't realized it before, but he was beginning to feel pretty angry. Maybe she couldn't help it, but this was ridiculous.

She wasn't lying on the front lawn again, thank God. And the Subaru was still there, which was a big relief. Matt thought about getting in his car and driving around looking for her. But she could be anywhere, and besides, he knew that once you started chasing after someone like that it never ended, not until you'd given yourself a heart attack. She was a grown woman—he shouldn't have to be searching for her. He made himself stop. Most things got better that way: taking a break, waiting. People needed to be patient, not make such a big deal out of everything.

He went out to the porch and sat down. That's when he saw her kneeling down at the bottom of the yard, her back turned to him. Just like she always did. Her shoulders were heaving.

He slid open the door and stepped outside. "Clara?"

She didn't speak, but he could hear her crying. Then he saw the blood streaks on her sleeves. He started running. "Clara!" Not again. Not again.

He came up behind her and grabbed her by the shoulders, twisting them to stop her from whatever she was doing. He grabbed both of her hands and raised them, trying to get a good look at her wrists. Her forearms, his hands, everything slick with blood. "Where's the knife, Clara!"

She looked up at him, wide-eyed and dull. "No knife. I didn't see a knife."

He couldn't find any cuts on her wrists, her arms, her hands. He looked down at her knees, and then the grass, and then the bloody bits he was standing on. He jumped back in alarm. It was another rabbit, skinned and gutted, its flesh weeping fresh blood.

"It's *back*!" she said, her voice rising. "It's back!"

"Dammit, Clara. It's not the same rabbit!"

She stared at him, her face tilted. "But how can you tell it's a different rabbit? How do you know for sure?"

He started to explain, but what was there to explain? "Because this is real life. We live in real life, Clara! Just stay right here. I'll get something to cover it with, and then we'll go wash you up, okay?"

He ran into the garage and grabbed a drop cloth, and on his way out he grabbed the rake, too, just in case of, just in case he needed it. But when he got back Clara was gone. The rabbit was still lying there, but there was no sign of Clara in the yard. How could she have moved so quickly? He stared down at the rabbit. It looked like all the others, as far as he could tell. One huge eye, pushed almost out of its socket, stared up at him.

He looked around the yard, the edge of the house, inside the house. He couldn't find her anywhere. He gave up. He imagined her walking around the neighborhood, her shirt bloody, her arms and hands bloody. Somebody would call the police. Well, the hell with it. He'd done everything he could.

Matt left the rabbit and went back inside. At least he could clean himself up. At least he could get that much done.

After his shower he grabbed a jar of peanut butter out of the fridge and stood at the kitchen window digging two fingers into the jar and eating the peanut butter right off them. Looking through the window into the porch and then through the sliding glass doors made the yard seem a pretty safe distance away. He could still see the fields and the line of trees beyond, and he was sure he'd be able to see any movement out there if there was any. But there wasn't any. After a while he collapsed into that old chair on the back porch and sat watching the yard for a couple of hours. It was midafternoon by then and he hadn't had any lunch. He supposed he could find something in the fridge to heat up, but then maybe Clara would come home. Fixing him something might occupy her, keep her mind off things.

He was actually pretty surprised she hadn't shown up yet. If the police had picked her up they would have come by now. He was used to her being anxious, but she usually snapped out of it after an hour or so and managed to get going on whatever needed to be done. He'd call some of her friends but that woman Ann had moved away six months ago and he didn't know any of the others, if there were any others. Clara never made friends easily, at least not since he'd known her.

He couldn't get over those damn rabbits. Whatever had gotten to them, it must have wiped out an entire den. Why had the thing left its kills in his yard anyway? Like a house cat dropping the mouse it slaughtered at your feet. But you had to trust your eyes—most of the time it was the one thing you could trust.

Clara needed to be back soon. She'd always been this timid thing, couldn't protect herself worth a damn. Terrible things happened to timid creatures like that. She knew. That's why she kept saying that. Well, terrible things do happen, Clara. It wasn't too hard predicting that.

He must have dozed, because the back yard suddenly looked dimmer. That shady bit down by the fence had grown, spread half-way up the yard toward the house. Lights were popping on over at the neighbors'.

He sat up suddenly as a chill grabbed his throat. "Clara!" he yelled as loud as he could to scare it away. Still no answer. He listened hard now. The refrigerator still hummed. It was like he was living by himself again.

He could check with all the neighbors, but the last thing he needed was for everybody to know his business. He could call the police, but would they even take a report? Maybe if he told them Clara was a danger to herself. She'd cut her wrists more than once, but she'd always botched the job. Timid people like that, he reckoned they intended to botch the job.

He thought about talking to some young policeman, trying to explain how Clara was, trying to explain about the skinned rabbits, how they must have a predator in the neighborhood, and how the cop would act deliberately patient, and condescending to this older guy who had just called in about his missing wife, who'd only been gone a few hours, probably on some impulsive shopping trip. Matt couldn't bear it.

She'd been a lovely girl when he'd met her—pretty, and shy. She'd made him feel like he was about the greatest man in the world. Then she got nervous, and then she got old, and surely she was crazy now. Maybe if he was truly a good man he could handle that—he'd stick with her and make the best out of a sad situation. But people had to be realistic. Good men were few and far between.

Flashing red lights broke through the trees on the other side of the field. They made it look as if parts of that line of trees bordering the old canal were on fire. But then the wind shifted the branches a bit and he could see that he was mistaken. There were scattered fires on the interstate beyond. And many more lights and faint, but explosive noises. People shouting maybe. Or cars being pried open like clamshells to get to the meat inside. The Jaws of Life, that's what they called them. But only if the people inside were still living. If not, then they were the Jaws of Death, weren't they?

The radio was right by the chair, so he could have turned it on. But he'd rather wait until Clara showed up and then they could learn together what terrible thing might have happened over on the highway. Matt supposed it was an unhealthy thing in people, how listening or watching together as the news told the details of some new disaster tended to bring couples and families together.

He sat and watched the red flashes and the burning and listened hard for the noises and the voices until it was dark enough for the automatic yard lights to come on. The gnawing in his belly was painful but he had no interest in eating, assuming eating was even the sort of remedy required.

He could see everything, except for that shadowy region down near the fence. He could see the rake where he'd left it, and the folded-up drop cloth. But there was no sign of that rabbit. Something had moved it, or maybe—and the idea made him queasy—it hadn't been completely dead. Skinned, but not dead. Crawling around suffering.

As Matt's eyes grew weary he found himself focusing on that area of shadow. It had always seemed odd that the longer you stared at a shadow the more likely you were to find other shadows swimming inside it. Something moved out of the edge. In the border between dark and light a skinned body lay in the slickened grass. Bleeding heavily, and this one much too large for a rabbit. Stripped to muscle and bone, it was an anatomical human figure made real. The skin over part of one breast remained. And when it reached its scarlet arms toward the house it called his name.

THE HANGED MAN

His wife came home earlier than usual. Perhaps. He was no longer a proper judge of time. Time had gotten away from him, had hopped into a red convertible with a beautiful woman and roared out of town, time's mouth open and wailing so harshly even the most practical were driven to tears. Time was a manic depressive, as was the street they lived on, as was Roger, before he'd hanged himself.

"Roger? Again?" she said from the doorway. She hugged two paper grocery bags to her chest, one soaking through the bottom, something translucent and goopy dripping onto her yellow shorts.

He began to speak, but his tongue got in the way. He straightened his head within the crude noose, his neck muscles straining to hold the broken vertebrae together. He opened his mouth and wiggled the tongue a bit. It felt like a large pickle attached by a bit of membrane to the floor of his mouth. He tilted his head back and let his tongue fall into place.

"I didn't know....you'd be home," he said, distracted by the way the tongue flogged at his teeth. "I'm sorry. It helps me relax."

"You don't look....relaxed," she said. Of course people couldn't know until they'd actually tried it, he thought. All your life you fight against gravity, the struggle wrecking your joints, your posture. But to give in to gravity, to just let everything fall into its gravitationally-determined place, to give up and to give in, was more than satisfying.

If only the neck didn't hurt so much. And the way the vertebrae ground together, the sound was a constant backdrop.

His kids came in then, the three of them rushing past

Angela before she had a chance to block them, squealing and grabbing each other in that mock-aggressive way they had. They didn't look up at him, but ran around his dangling legs, knocking against the scraped edges of his boots, making his body begin to spin on the rope that suspended him from the light fixture. He could feel the neck skin folded over the edge of the tightening noose begin to tear, and a rain of plaster pattered his head as the light fixture loosened.

"Whoa! Whoa!" He felt ridiculous about the word choice, but he was starting to panic.

"Kids! Stop!" Angela shouted. She'd put her bags down and was striding toward them. Roger could see the egg carton slipping from the top of one, beginning its slide toward the floor. There would soon be a terrible mess, and of course once again he was the one who had caused it. "You're hurting your father!"

He really wished she hadn't said that. Jamie and little Alicia stood at stiff attention in front of him, arms straight and quivering at their sides, but eyes cast down, unable to look up at him. Only Matt looked, staring with hooded and somewhat feverish eyes. Roger couldn't tell whether his son was angry or sick or both.

He was pretty sure he was damaging them. It was a knowledge he suspected most parents had. But he let his inability to see into the future be an excuse. In any case, he wasn't sure he could stop now even if he tried.

After Angela hustled the kids out of the room Roger managed to ease his head out of the loop and drop to the floor. Enough time had passed since the initial break that the neck had stretched somewhat, the tendons and the layers of skin softened, so that it was as floppy and wobbly as a piece of cooked pasta and as difficult to control. But the head fit neatly into the dip in his left shoulder so he left it there.

He'd been unforgivably foolish. Life was all unintended consequences, it seemed, for those who lived unconsciously. He couldn't even remember why he'd hanged himself initially. Some disappointment, or some experience he felt he needed to avoid. He'd lost the exact reason along with most of his college level calculus. And now he repeated that fatal act of hanging because the strangulation and the resulting nothingness comforted him. He could not help himself.

Dinner was quiet and awkward, but hanging always made Roger hungry. He finished his mashed potatoes and went back to the serving bowl for more. Alicia, the baby, was watching him, studying him like a bug on her pillow. Actually she wasn't a baby anymore—she was past three—but it annoyed Roger whenever Angela pointed it out.

He was self-conscious about eating in front of the kids. He had to twist the spoon at the very last moment and slip it between his lips without spilling it. Sometimes it took some effort to get the food to move into his esophagus and down. Sometimes it stuck there in the bend and caused swelling.

"Daddy's head is like a bad balloon," she said and pointed.

He had to think a moment, then remembered how when balloons lost air they sometimes flopped over into the horizontal. "Clever girl," he said. She climbed onto the table and poked his mouth. He realized then his smile was a growing vertical crack in his sideways head. He kissed her finger and she giggled.

No one else said a word. He and Alicia might have been alone at the table.

After a period of silence his wife said, "Time to go to bed. It's a school night, kids."

"We get an hour of TV!" Jamie said in outrage.

"Not tonight. Please, just cooperate for once!" She rubbed her temple a bit too vigorously for comfort. Jamie looked down at his plate and Alicia got quiet again, slipping slowly back into her chair. Matt hadn't said a word all evening. Roger looked into Angela's face. He didn't blame the kids for being scared. There was something broken about it.

He supposed it was a measure of the tension in the house that the kids settled in quickly to the earlier bedtime. They all allowed him to hug them, but only Alicia hugged him back. They brushed their teeth wordlessly and changed into their pajamas. They looked exhausted as Angela marched them into their rooms for tucking in.

Roger wandered around the house during their final preparations. There had been changes over the past few weeks he had been unaware of: new curtains in the living room, a new rug in the main bath—it was circular with an enormous sunflower head in the center. Angela had apparently rearranged the guest room so that the bed rested against a different wall and the vase on top of the side table now held fresh flowers. Was she expecting company?

The coffee table in the living room might have been new. His memory was that it had had several chips in it, but this one appeared perfectly smooth. Had she had it refinished? The magazines spread across the top of it were recent, fashion-oriented (Since when had she become fashion-oriented?), and arranged into a semi-circle as if for a photograph. Why had he never noticed these things before? He felt merely a visitor in the home they'd lived in for nine years.

When he went up to their bedroom he found Angela already asleep, or pretending to be. He stepped closer to the bed, thinking that at least he could lean over and kiss her on the cheek, but when he bent forward his head slipped off his shoulder and dangled down in front of him like a football in a flimsy sack. He picked it up and balanced it on his shoulder again and stepped back.

"I'm really sorry. I know I've ruined everything," he said to the back of her head. Then he realized there wasn't really much more to say that mattered under the circumstances. "It's no excuse, but I'm sure it was an impulse thing. I have no idea why I did it." She lay completely motionless. He was sure she was acting now. He felt humiliated. "Of course I'm not the first to do something they'd dearly love to erase. One ridiculous moment—that's all it was." Still nothing. As he was leaving the room he said, "I don't remember when it happened, when you stopped being on my side and I stopped being on yours. I just know I never expected that."

Roger went downstairs and out the patio doors, perhaps a bit too urgently. His head bounced on his shoulder to dizzying effect. It was a clear night, the stars a glorious curtain.

They lived in an older development where almost every house was exactly the same—dark brown brick, smallish casement windows. Most were two stories, but there were occasional single-level houses they sold for retired people, which Roger thought too much resembled mausoleums, because of their shape and smaller size.

The development spread across a broad hill on the west side of town. Their house was one of the first ones built, at the bottom. From their back yard Roger could see overlapping arcs of the development, so like strata as they moved up the rise to the newest homes near the top. Viewed sideways, these arcs appeared as a mass of poorly architected high rises and terraced homes, their own gravity ripping them apart to reveal the distant and unreachable star fields beyond. The vision inspired awe, but also a kind of sickness. He felt too tired, too old to be looking at such wonder, too spent. He had a sudden urge to go wake up the kids, drag them down to come see this, but thankfully stopped himself from acting on the impulse. It would have been a further compounding of the disastrous father he had become.

He needed to sleep. He needed to find a place to lie down. He could feel the tiny rips progressing from the deep ligature crease around his neck, so like that proverbial dotted line where since childhood he'd been trained to fold. Shadows had begun to bleed into the corners of his eyes, and if he did not rest soon he feared he might go blind.

The next morning, he stopped Angela as she was hustling the kids out the door for school. "Let me take Matt. It'll save you some time if I take him to his school."

"What? You can't drive...not now."

"I've been practicing in the Honda during the day while you're gone. Short trips to the park, that sort of thing. I'm *fine*, just had to get used to a new way of looking, and reacting."

"I'm not sure he'll let you. Has he spoken to you about, about what you did? Because he hasn't said a word to me."

"I'll ask him." Roger tried to speak with minimal movement. She'd say no if his head was flopping around. There appeared to be a slight smell now. He wondered if she was aware of it.

Matt had his backpack and his lunch ready. Roger sank onto the bed beside him. "Feel like playing hooky today?" Matt's eyes went wide. "You just can't tell your mother."

Breakfast seemed to settle his son down a little. At least he no longer stared at his father as if terrified. Roger did see the embarrassment in Matt's face when they entered the fast-food restaurant and some people stared and others obviously tried not to stare. Besides the looseness of the head, and the vague stench of it, Roger had discovered that morning that his mobility was increasingly impaired. His right leg had gone loose in its sockets and was prone to an undesirable wobble. He almost fell over going through the door.

Breakfast was a pair of breakfast sandwiches and a cake of hash browns, washed down with what Roger assumed to be acid, but Matt appeared to have no trouble with it. They hadn't had such sandwiches when Roger was a kid. If they had he'd have weighed four hundred pounds by the start of fourth grade.

"How about the zoo afterwards? I always intended to take you, but I never seemed to get around to it."

"Why?"

Roger found he could hardly look his son in the eyes. And his son didn't seem to want to look at his eyes, either, at least as they were currently placed. "What do you mean? Don't you like the zoo?"

"I mean why are you being so nice to me now?"

Roger felt punched. "I love you son."

"I guess you do. I guess I love you, too. But you were never this nice to me."

Roger looked at his hands. They were dry, resembling scarred ground. The edges of his fingers were gray, and they appeared to leave grayishness wherever they touched.

"You're a lot like me. You always were," he said, "That's always scared me." Matt's eyes looked large. "Not that I wasn't proud. But you shouldn't be like me. You know when you put that towel around your neck and jumped off the roof of the garage?"

Matt nodded. "I was playing super hero. But I was just a little kid."

"That was just over a year ago, Matt. That's the kind of thing I used to do. Anything that popped into my head, I'd do.

Seeing you be like that, it terrifies me." Roger realized he was crying then, but there was something wrong about it. He put his fingers to the skin below his eyes. It was perfectly dry. He probed the corners by his tear ducts—still dry. He could feel himself crying, but no tears were coming out.

"Dad, what are you doing? People are looking."

"Don't be like me, Matt."

"I won't. Why would I want to be like you?"

"Just don't."

They went to the zoo, and Matt seemed to have a good time. He especially seemed to like the elephants. At least he wanted to stay there and watch them for a very long time. Roger didn't like the big cats, the way they stared at him. Everywhere he went they stared at him, until finally he grabbed Matt and they left the area.

Matt had never been to a 3D movie before. "The first one you see, it should be with your dad," Roger said. The sequel to 300 was playing, that one about the Spartans. But it was obviously too violent; Angela would have a fit. So Roger settled on *Stalingrad* instead. 3D *and* IMAX. Historical, too, although so was 300, supposedly. Sub-titled, but that was good, too, even if it went over his son's head sometimes, it stretched him. He could always say that the first subtitled movie he ever saw was with his dad.

Roger discovered that when he looked at the subtitles sideways they separated into two different images of the words, like an echo. From time to time the words behind the front subtitles said different things, terrible things. Matt and Roger left the theater after the scene in which all the soldiers caught on fire, but they kept attacking even though they were in agony. They appeared to be screaming, but the sound of the roaring flames drowned out everything and became their new voices.

"I'm sorry." Roger couldn't think of anything else to say.

"It's okay, Dad. I didn't want to see any more of that, but it was still, I don't know, it was something, wasn't it?"

"It sure was, son."

When they climbed into the Honda, Roger discovered he no longer had the ability to drive. His gray hands kept slipping off the steering wheel, and he couldn't control his eyes enough to see what he was doing, where he was going. Matt helped him onto a bus. People whispered. Roger was relieved to overhear the word "drunk."

The bus dropped them off at a stop a couple of blocks from home. Roger encouraged Matt to walk ahead a few steps while he fell back and let the shadows take him.

"Don't be like me," Roger said.

"I won't, Dad," Matt replied, still walking, not looking back.

"Don't be like me," Roger repeated, not quite knowing what else to say.

"I said I won't." Matt kept walking.

"I don't know why I did it," Roger said. "I was a little sad, but not that sad. No impulse control, like when you jumped off the garage roof, remember? It was just a one-time thing, you know, son? And then this other happened, the way I keep doing it, like I can't stop myself. It was just a one-time thing. But see what happens? Do you see?"

Matt said, "I see," and walked up their front steps.

"Tell your mother I'm sorry. She knows I'm sorry, but tell her again."

Matt went inside, but didn't reply, shutting the door behind him.

Roger didn't turn around then—there was no point. He wasn't going anywhere. His skin tingled all over from the tiny rips that spread, and dissolved in the presence of a greater rendering. He gazed at the closed door of his home and thought, *please. Don't go back on the roof. One wrong move, and you step into sky.*

THE FISHING HUT

A bad accident on the highway snarled traffic headed into the river valley. Bishop had heard no account of it, but suspected it had something to do with the fog, the milky clouds having thickened the closer he'd driven to the water. Its whiteness was an unhealthy shade, like drowned flesh.

He had no patience for delay once he'd decided to do something, even if it was something he had no desire to do, like fishing. "It can be a form of meditation," his doctor had said. "It'll relax you." Bishop hadn't been fishing since childhood.

He had started to say "Couldn't I simply buy some fish?" when he noticed the specimens mounted on the doctor's wall. Flat, gaping-mouthed things. They reminded him of those carol-singing fish trophies you could buy in the shops during holidays. His doctor was serious about this.

In the next car a man in a fisherman's hat and vest was leaning forward, intently gripping the steering wheel. He looked anything but relaxed. Bishop had his own vest, recently purchased. It was a terrific garment—seven small pouches of varying sizes mounted on each side of the sturdy metal buttons. He had his old Boy Scout compass jammed into one of them— the rest were empty. It would be useful to wear this, he thought, on long plane trips, or during boring meetings.

Irene wanted him to change doctors, as this one never told him directly that he should lose weight or exercise more. Bishop liked that the man didn't treat him like a child. He hoped he could go back to him. But at the end of this last visit, while shuffling the latest test results into Bishop's file, his doctor had said, "One more thing. My receptionist says you make her uncomfortable. She says you stare a bit too long. She's good at her job. I could never afford to lose her. Check back in in six months or so, we'll see how you're doing." Then he'd been dismissed.

Hadn't he gazed at her as he would at anyone else? He hoped they wouldn't tell Irene. Long marriages sometimes ended over a small bit of misinformation.

Traffic loosened up as he passed the scene of the accident. He didn't look. People always wanted to look, and it was rarely a good idea.

Cars were parked haphazardly on both sides of the gravel road. Men and women were trudging in the direction of the stream, burdened with poles, nets, equipment boxes, bags, lunch boxes. He'd had no idea fishing was still so popular. Perhaps it was the economy. Perhaps they needed the fish for food. Whatever it might be, none of those involved appeared to be taking pleasure in it.

Something fluttered in his stomach, or perhaps it was in his bowels. Bishop had a poor sense of anatomy, his own or anyone else's. He tapped the dashboard impatiently. He'd agreed to this because he was open to anything that might improve himself. But he hated wasting time. He could smell the chicken salad sandwiches Irene had made for his lunch. The unmoving line of cars into the camping area was a mile long. All of that traffic going in, and none of it leading out. The opposite lane was perfectly clear.

The purpose of this trip was to relax. It wasn't to catch fish. If he wanted to eat fish (which he did not), he could always order some at a restaurant.

Bishop pulled into the opposite lane and sped up the car. As he passed the long line of vehicles two or three honked their horns, but most of the drivers appeared to be obliviously settled into their seats. Within a few minutes he was past the officially designated camping and fishing areas, speeding down a gravel road which veered away from the river after only a few hundred yards. As he wondered whether he might have gone too far he saw the old man in worn overalls approaching from the other direction. He seemed harmless enough, so Bishop pulled alongside and rolled down the window.

"Is there a place around here I can fish?"

The old man looked up, his eyes strained, watery, as if he were about to cry. It was a look Bishop saw in the mirror nearly every morning. It meant nothing, however—Bishop hadn't cried in years. "You've passed the campgrounds. That's where most of them fish. Up ahead there's a turnaround. Don't try to turn before then—you'll wind up in the ditch."

"Thanks, thanks for the tip." He didn't know what he would have done if he'd driven into the ditch. Out here in the boonies you were at other people's mercy. "But is there some place ahead? Some place quieter I can go?"

The old man looked down the road in that direction. He rubbed his eyes. Then looked back at Bishop, leaning forward, as if examining Bishop's face. "I guess there's the old fishing hut. Some still use it, I reckon. It's quiet, and it's shady enough, if that's what you're looking for."

"It sounds perfect. How do I get there?"

"Perfect," the old man said slowly, as if examining the word. "I don't know. Good enough for some. Depends on what you're looking for, like I said. Go about a mile past the turnaround. The next wide spot in the road. There on the right, between the bushes—that path will take you down to the river, and that there hut. If that's what you want. God bless." The old man turned his head and continued on his way.

Bishop found the turnaround soon enough, but after a mile and a half on the odometer there was still no sign of the spot the old man had described. The trees closed in on the road, some branches low enough to brush the top of the car with a rasping whisper. The margins of the road were ragged and overgrown, the ditches completely hidden, making it imperative that he stay on the gravel. Obviously the old man had misremembered, but Bishop had no choice but to continue as there was no place to turn.

In the clear stretches the sun was brutal. He smelled the sandwiches again, and again there was that flutter in his stomach, like something sliding, turning over. He wanted to eat before the sandwiches grew too warm. Were they safe after even this long in the car? But he was hesitant to stop and retrieve one, fearing some country driver would come racing over the hill without seeing. Now and then he spied a glimpse of water on his right, a teasing sharp reflection, but no more than that.

Then rounding a bend he saw a dusty brown car parked in a wide space alongside some bushes. Bishop pulled in too quickly, but managed to avoid a crash. He sat for a moment and let the engine die, staring at the other car's rear end. Ridges of dried mud layered the bumper and covered the lenses of the backup and turn lights. A frame around the license plate proclaimed, "There's Nothing Better than Fishing!" He considered that unlikely, but possible.

He climbed out and retrieved his fishing gear from the trunk, and at the last moment his sandwich bag. The path through the bushes was narrow, but well-trodden.

He caught his first glimpse of the roof of the hut as he descended the slope: a broad expanse of shiny tin with significant areas of furry rust. He didn't see the walls until he was almost at water's edge: they were gray, streaked green and a dull, damp black. The structure looked solid enough, except some of the boards going into the water had warped. The building had been erected in the near half of the stream. Square openings at each end allowed the river to flow through.

A narrow ramp on pilings led from the bank through another black opening in the side of the building. Bishop could see deep shadow inside scarred with brilliant slashes of light. He followed the hard path to the ramp and stepped up on it, testing his weight. It shook, but he continued. His footsteps made everything creak and moan. He hesitated at the black opening, tempted to knock, but that seemed ridiculously polite. If there were locals inside he didn't want them laughing at him. He ducked his head and went in.

"Hello," a man said. He was seated on the floor by the opening on the upstream side. The light there made both his face, and the board he was sitting on, reddish and warm.

"Hello," Bishop replied. "Is it okay to fish here? This isn't private property?"

"All are welcome." The man turned his head into the light. He was red-faced, bald, but looked pleasant enough. He had a beard of white stubble. "Some farmer built it forever ago, but as far as I know no one's ever claimed it. Folks have fished here without interference for decades."

The hut was longer inside than Bishop would have guessed. Now that his eyes had grown accustomed to the light he could see that there was no floor; the man was sitting on a shelf two planks wide stretching the length of the interior and supported by triangular brackets of blackish two-by-fours. There appeared to be a matching shelf on the other side, but he could see only part of it—the rest fell into murky shadow and confusing reflection. Three feet or so separated the two shelves, with no obvious way across other than to make a huge athletic step or to drop down into the stream and then climb up onto the other side.

Bishop couldn't imagine doing such a thing—what if something were hiding in the water? The gravity in his abdomen shifted as if things had moved around.

Although dark, the water didn't seem very deep in the hut, and the shelves weren't terribly high above the river. Adults of average height could sit on the edge of a shelf and dangle their feet into the stream.

Bishop wasn't sure where to sit. The stranger obligingly moved his tackle box so there was room to sit beside him. He appreciated the gesture and began walking down the length of the shelf in that direction. The boards bowed alarmingly with a liquid groan that echoed through the structure. Bishop looked down and saw rusted nails moving in their crumbling holes. He stopped.

"Come on now. It's much sturdier than it looks," the man said.

Bishop laughed self-consciously and took several more steps. "I'm Bishop," he said, but the fisherman didn't reply. He eased himself down a couple of feet away from the other man.

"There you go. Safe as houses, as my dear departed father used to say. He used to fish here. My uncles, too, when they were alive."

"So, it's a family tradition." Bishop felt almost loquacious, but not quite. He normally liked to talk his way through unfamiliar situations, but here he felt a certain degree of reticence was demanded.

"Tradition, obligation, obsession—it's all shades of psychology, I suppose. We're all onions, you know."

Bishop had no idea how to respond to such an odd comparison, so he didn't try. He smiled, nodded, and brought around his pole, carefully working one of the worms from his small jar onto the hook. He'd practiced the maneuver for several hours at home, slaughtering generations of worms in the process. A grim and bloody business. "So the fishing is good here?"

The fisherman stared at him. He was another weepy one— he had the old farmer's red, leaking eyes. "Not with that sort of bait, I'm afraid. Do you have a fly in your box or in that magic vest of yours? A Mayfly, perhaps, or a Hopper?"

The man wore a worn flannel shirt, paint-stained jeans. Bishop's fancy new vest was pristine, and almost empty except for the compass. "Pardon me?"

"You'll have better luck in these waters with an artificial fly. You know, something with some fuzz resembling what the fishies normally feast on. You can borrow one of mine if you like. I make my own in the evening." A small case suddenly appeared in his hands, opening as he slid one thumb around its edge. Inside was an array of feathery, fuzzy things. Some looked somewhat like actual insects, others more abstract, suggesting the generic idea of an insect. Bishop had seen this sort of thing on television.

At the far end were two non-fuzzy ones, unusual, elaborately-carved figures with hooks attached. They looked more like totems than lures. Bishop reached for them.

"No, not those. You're not ready for those. Pick a fly."

Bishop figured it must be obvious he didn't know what he was doing—the man had found him out. "So very kind…" he murmured. He picked one, although all the flies looked much the same—beads and wire, some feathers, some thread. The fellow helped him attach it to his line. Ready at last, he let his line drift into the dark green waters below.

"They feel safer hidden in the shade here. Most of us do," the fisherman said.

Bishop pondered this. The meaning was clear. They felt

safer, but of course they weren't. "I have sandwiches. Chicken salad if you'd like one."

"I don't mind." The fellow took one from the offered bag. "Make these yourself?"

"My wife did them up. She takes very good care of me, I'm happy to say."

"You're lucky to have a wife, a man your age."

"What? I'm only fifty-six!"

The fisherman gazed at him with swollen, wet fishy eyes. "Sorry. I'd have thought much older."

There was certainly nothing Bishop could say to that. It had been a kind gesture, but the man didn't know the first thing about him. He leaned back and tried to choke down a sandwich. He felt slightly weak, flushed, and vaguely annoyed. His gut turned, as if seeking to avoid the food coming its way. Perhaps Irene was right. His doctor wasn't tough enough on him.

The next hour crept by in uneasy silence. Something was off about the sandwich. Bishop couldn't tell what, but he couldn't finish it. Irene's sandwiches were usually so good.

Despite the fisherman's reassurances, Bishop felt uncomfortable sitting on the boards. They creaked and snapped and moaned every time he shifted his weight—he could almost feel them splintering. He pictured himself falling into the deep dark green at any moment, moss and dank liquid filling his throat. He supposed there was no real danger of drowning, but the danger of embarrassment was significant.

The light inside the hut shifted as the day wore on, but always brighter on the upstream, riverbank side, and in that two- or three-square-foot space where the fisherman sat. It appeared to be a matter of the angle of the sun, and the interfering shade trees on the bank. The opposite side of the hut was always dark. To stare into that wall of darkness too long made Bishop feel as if he were going blind.

Apparently the fisherman had chosen his spot well. Bishop imagined it was always pleasant where the man sat, and warm, and the best place in the hut for fishing. Except this day, at least, there had been no indication of a nibble.

"Have you had any interest?" Bishop asked. "In your bait, I

mean. Because nothing appears to have touched mine."

"The fish here like to defy expectation."

"Perhaps they've moved on."

"Oh, they're there. If you look closely, you can find their shadows."

Bishop stared down into the dark viridian waters. The river appeared impenetrable at first, but then his eyes acclimated. He began to see the faint outline of old stones—rectangular, like foundation or paving stones. But no sign of fish. He started to say so when something darkened the area directly beneath his feet, and then the water lightened again. "Yes! I think I see one!"

"A commitment to patience is required," the fisherman said. "This life is not meant for everyone. At least not for very long."

Bishop continued to gaze into the water. There was another world down there, a whole other life, perceivable by someone such as himself only through a veil of distortion. "I would simply like to catch a fish," he said. "Even a small one would do." He hadn't wanted to come fishing, but having done so he wanted what he came for.

"How about you?" the fisherman said. "Are they biting any better where you are?" Bishop looked up in confusion. The fisherman was staring into that deeper darkness on the other side. He glanced at Bishop. "We always think it's better over there. But apparently it's not. No, wait..." He turned his head to the darkness again. After a moment he turned back. "Apparently there have been some recent nibbles."

"Who? Who are you talking to?"

"That one. The other fisherman. He always prefers it in the dark. He's had a nibble, two actually. But then he always manages to catch something, even on the worse days. I've seen it time and again. He catches whatever he wants—he catches his limit."

"There's a man sitting over there? When did he—" Bishop stopped and gazed into the darkness. "I'm sorry, that was rude. My name is Bishop. I didn't know you were there."

"He was here before me," the fisherman said. "He's always here quite early. He was here long before me, and I suspect he'll be here long after."

Bishop nodded. The man in the darkness said nothing. Perhaps the fellow wanted to be left alone.

Bishop returned his attention to his fishing pole, the transparent line dropping into the still darkness below. He willed the fish to come. He decided he would catch one fish, just to say he did, and then leave. He tried not to look into that shadowed region of the fishing hut again, but could not help himself.

There was a sourness about the air inside the hut that came with closed-in spaces where people had lived a long time. There were sprays for that, he believed, deodorizers which never worked completely but which people had settled for. *We leave quite a bit of ourselves behind.*

The smell might have come from the river, or the damp, moldy lumber, or a combination of the two. Or from the ones sitting here fishing. What he could see of the interior was mottled in damp shadow and damp green. The patterns flowed when touched by the changing light.

By mid-afternoon Bishop had surmised he would not be catching any fish. The fisherman's luck appeared no better, but it apparently bothered him less, because he'd jammed the handle of his fishing pole into a hole in the boards so that he could spend much of his time dozing, or staring out the opening of the hut at the river flowing toward them, or the sky, or—Bishop realized he had no idea what the fisherman was looking at.

Now and then in the dark across the way he would hear a definite splash, but whether it was something coming out of the water or something going in he could not tell. Whatever it was it bothered him. Again he could feel the solid shape fluttering under the skin covering his abdomen, and he suspected seriously that it might be a fish, and if so he needed to protect it from these other fishermen at all costs.

He had decided to take his gear and leave, or perhaps just abandon his fishing equipment and walk away—infinitely better, he could just announce that he had to retrieve something from his car and never come back. Then he wouldn't have to face any silent criticisms, any invisible accusations. Not that he owed them any sort of explanation. He had always taken care of himself. He had always done what needed doing. Then it began to rain.

It was actually pleasant at first. The change began as a whisper of urgency blew through the hut, the breeze stirring the line so that for one excited moment Bishop thought he might have a fish. Then things began lightly falling onto the tin roof, leaves and seeds perhaps, twigs and other tree debris, but once the harder strikes began he recognized the accumulation as rain, the individual beats blending into a downpour of agitation.

The fisherman turned his head to gaze directly into the rain, his silhouette back-dropped by water blended seamlessly into sky, a curtain of shimmering pewter scored with thousands of shallow parallel scratches. Now and then the scratches would shift and ripple, pushed sideways by the wind, and sometimes a needle of sun would pierce through the thinner bits, and Bishop had to avert his eyes. And sometimes there would be wind and rain and sun and lightning all, a blend Bishop had never known possible.

The river ran more swiftly through the hut, carrying leaves and small branches, the level rising an inch or two until it licked the bottoms of Bishop's new boots. The fisherman turned his head slightly, murmuring, "It hardly ever rises higher than this," as if that were meant to reassure. The man's white stubble caught the dim light, and Bishop wondered if that was the kind of beard he had to look forward to. He thought about how hard it would be to shave such a wrinkled face, how many nicks there would surely be.

The debris floating down through the opening increased rapidly: vine and feathers, some nesting material, trash. Then there was that matted, furry thing, some of its fur missing and exposing the pink hide of the shoulders, the belly, as if it had been shaved or scalped. One paw or hand outstretched, the fingers or claws spread, snagging the opening as it came into the hut, which made it spin, drifting down past Bishop, fur and hide spinning, circling, so that Bishop was afraid it might be trapped inside the hut with them, and then a sudden flood of muddier water pushed through, flushing the slowly rotating corpse out the other end.

"I've been sitting in this same spot for years," the fisherman said quietly. "The same view, the same attitude, the same luck." He stood up and faced the darkened half. He leaned forward, and it appeared he might jump into the water, but then he stretched his leg as far as he could to the other side, falling headlong to bring himself completely across. He slipped into the shadows there and Bishop couldn't see him anymore.

Bishop himself stood up then and stared at the edge of the shelf, the sluggish water below, the dark on the other side. He should do something, move or leave. He should do whatever it was he came here to do.

"You're not ready," the fisherman said from the other side.

Bishop could still see nothing but darkness, even though he imagined he felt the weight of him, like an aggrieved absence. "Do you mean I lack the skill? What's so special about sitting over there? What do you mean?"

But there was no further explanation. He waited for a very long time.

Bishop would not go fishing again, and avoided that part of the county completely, but he always assumed the fishing hut was there, if he ever were to decide to visit again. He didn't want to discuss the incident, and so found another physician. His new doctor was always full of dire predictions and warnings, and Bishop began to believe that the smallest mistake in food choice or activity might put him in serious mortal jeopardy. There appeared to be no path that escaped the mysteries and vicissitudes of time.

Still, Irene said she felt better about his care, even when the bad news came.

A SUDDEN EVENT

They had been together long enough that she rarely surprised him anymore. Not that he knew what she was thinking. He'd decided years ago that everyone's thoughts were kept inside a locked box, and even when they told you they were giving you a key, they weren't.

"Did you hear that?" Ann said, pausing at the curb before crossing the street.

"Hear what?" Roger said, then smiled, "well, obviously not." But he had, hadn't he? He wasn't sure. Maybe, now that she'd mentioned it. But it had been more like a pressure change he'd felt somewhere in his head, he thought, than any proper sort of sound.

"That. Somewhere over there." She gestured with her entire head and then she fell into the street, into oncoming traffic. What troubled him most, as he thought about it later, was how he hadn't jumped in front of the cars trying to save her. It all happened so suddenly Roger hadn't understood what had just occurred. And then he had just stood there and watched as the love of his life lay in the street with cars approaching. He couldn't explain it. Ann meant everything to him—after five years of marriage he still remained obsessed with her. Wherever she went, he followed. So why hadn't he moved to help her? There was no reason, no excuse.

He tried to make up for his lapse a little every day, bringing her soup, rubbing her back, reading to her. He did all the housework now, all the cooking and cleaning. And he didn't mind—he owed her that much and more. All the cars had managed to stop as a couple of absolute strangers helped her out of the road. But even when she said she forgave him, he wasn't sure. Even when she said she was perfectly fine, she obviously wasn't.

"That thing in the corner, why is he there? Why did you let him in?" Her tone was familiar to him. He'd done something obviously foolish, and she wanted to know why. He never had an adequate explanation to offer.

He looked, even though he didn't expect to see anything. But he'd discovered that a strange thing happens when you're asked to focus on something you're convinced is perfectly mundane. It was like being asked, "What's wrong with that chair?" Then you stare at the chair for a very long time trying to figure out what might be wrong with it. And sometimes you find something.

It was like that with the corner. Roger stared at it for the longest time trying to figure out what Ann might be seeing, and there did seem to be something odd about the geometry, no doubt because of the way the house had shifted over the years, and the shadows there did not quite match their corresponding objects, as if some improbable lighting effect was at play, or so it seemed to him. But maybe he was simply looking too hard. He couldn't be sure. If you looked too hard at things you couldn't function properly in the world. You couldn't even walk across the street without falling into traffic.

"There's nothing in the corner, honey," he said, and strangely it seemed like a leap of faith on his part, even though there really was nothing there. "Just some shadows. What you must have seen were the shadows. Shadows can be tricky things sometimes."

"Huh," she grunted, which meant she didn't really believe him, but wasn't going to talk about it just then.

After her fall they'd seen doctors. Her GP at first, then a neurologist, and an orthopedic guy. She'd insisted she was fine; Roger wasn't convinced, and wanted answers. She'd stop now and then and tilt her head as if she were hearing something. Or she'd squint her eyes to stare at whatever wasn't there. When he asked her what she was looking for she'd become quite angry. "I'm not looking *for* anything!" she'd shout. "I'm looking *at* something. It's not as if I *like* seeing it—it has no business even being there!"

The doctors never found anything—and as he insisted on more and more tests Roger was sure they thought he was the one who was ill. Only her GP acknowledged any sort of problem. "Well, she doesn't *seem* herself. Maybe she just shook some things up when she fell. Maybe those things will sort themselves out over time."

"But she heard something *before* she fell. She had just tilted her head, kind of like this." Roger tilted his head in approximation.

"Well, that may have signaled the start of some internal event, whatever it might be. *Was* there a sound? Did you hear anything?"

Roger could hardly understand him. He was too busy trying to hear the other.

As the days crept on he'd catch her staring into that corner, and staring into other places which had previously seemed, at least to him, completely devoid of interest. He'd begun to resent it—he'd never be able to look at these ordinary aspects of their home the same way again.

"What if they do something to the house?" She posed the question almost as a challenge, as if his laxness were endangering them.

"What? Who are you talking about?"

"The ones there, the ones who do that sort of thing."

"Ann, there is no one trying to do anything to our house!"

"But how do you *know* that?"

He didn't know how to answer. What kind of answer is *I just do?* He could have told her that if she were in her right mind she would know that those threats, that her personal terrorists, did not exist. But he could not bring himself to say that to her. And the fact that he could not come up with a better answer seemed to endanger everything.

She slept longer every day. And when she was up and moving she'd gradually ease herself into strange postures, odd ways of moving her body through the spaces of their home, peculiar and awkward poses when she sat in their chairs. He hadn't realized it was happening at first. Then one day he saw her lean around the corner at a precarious angle, leading with her head, her eyes alert, vaguely predatory. And a few days after he came down in the morning to find her lying on her back on the couch, her head hanging almost to the rug. In both cases her eyes appeared to be searching, as if using the difficult position to gain an improved angle for observation.

"Meow," she said, and he left the room quickly, sensing he was about to see what he could not un-see. The sensation seemed to follow him, and he ran back up the stairs.

After several months he could not stand to be in the same room with her. When he was forced to pass her he did so quickly, occupying his mind with some random, meaningless tune.

And then theirs became a house almost completely without sound. She was in bed most of the time, breathing so shallowly, so noiselessly, he would sometimes hover over her, staring intently for signs of inhalation, ever-so-slight indications of movement. Finally when there was the vaguest indication of life he would leave, feeling released from his vigil.

Of course his footsteps still made the floors creak, and there was the sliding sound of drawers, of clothes dropped into a hamper, a refrigerator door opening, water released from a faucet, a gas flame hissing in a burner, soup rising into bubbles. But all of it so muted. To help the quiet along he turned off the phones, ignored the radio and television, took time off work so he wouldn't have to start the car, held his breath from time to time.

After eight or nine months the quiet began to deepen, to solidify, until Roger could feel the breadth and distance of it, how it was an ancient thing that might take them with it when it decided to leave. Thinking about it exhausted him, and he became convinced that when sound did return, it would be the sound that Ann had heard that day, the sound that had started everything.

For the first time in a long time he decided to sleep in the same bed with her. He couldn't hear her breathing but he was sure she was still breathing, just so slightly it was as if she were in hibernation. Weeks of minute-to-minute paranoia must be incredibly tiring, he thought. He stood there in the doorway dressed in his pajamas, searching for a gentle rise and fall of covers on her side of the bed. The effort brought back a yearning he'd forgotten he had: to be next to her, to feel her warmth spread out and envelop him. She looked as she always had. He was the odd one, the one who could not accommodate, the one who could not adjust to change.

He could feel the distant pull of it, the way it made him tilt his head. It was almost unbearable waiting for the sound. In order to escape the tension he slipped beneath the covers, pulling them up until he was buried completely under their folds. Still, he remained on his side of the bed, afraid to touch her.

Her whisper was so soft he could not make out the words.

He used his forearm to raise the covers, making a kind of cave, the way he had done as a child. Of course it was dark, so he shouldn't have been able to see anything, but there was the pale glow of her face turned up toward him, her eyes two glassy black disks floating in pools of milk. "Can you hear it?" she asked.

"No, no I can't," he lied.

Her lips approached him, and before he could say another word her dreadful gravity had pulled him down as she forced him to hear.

PAULA BREAKS

Paula had not left the house in weeks. Every time she'd asked permission her husband said no. "Things have changed since last you were out," he told her. "All the sidewalks are starved. They'd never be able to resist feet like yours."

"You like my feet?" she asked, hoping for a compliment.

"They're like dying fish, the way they flap," he told her. "You ought to take a gun and put them out of their misery."

Before he left for the day, he broke off her hands and locked them in his safe. This had happened so many times before they came off relatively easily, with not as much pain as she'd initially experienced. For the rest of the day, the only way she could open doors was to kneel and turn the knobs with her forearms.

She attempted this with the front door, but of course it was locked. The telephone squalled but then burst into flame before she could figure out how to answer it. It was probably him, checking up on her. He would be furious because she didn't answer.

She did not dare gain weight—he weighed her periodically—so she fed herself with long gazes out the window. She could hear children playing, somewhere, and somewhere an ice cream truck was gliding down a shaded street, its jangly music like a broken dream. She could see the top stories of an apartment house on the next block, and in one or two of the windows women sat and stared. She wondered if they noticed her. She wondered if anyone remembered who she was or where. A black bird tumbled out of the sky and landed on the grass below. Paula watched as a cat dragged it into the bushes.

A woman was running down the sidewalk, and before

Paula could cry out, the woman had been chewed to bits, her remains a warning to the others.

"At least she *had* remains," the ceiling fan said, loose and working itself away from the ceiling. Paula moved to another room before she lost her head.

When she heard the key in the lock, Paula ran to the front door to greet him. Her body bounced eagerly even though she told it not to.

His head moved up and down like a security camera, swinging away from her for a slow evaluation of the room. Still, she bounced. "That looks ridiculous," he said, "without hands. Did you even bother to clean, or were you staring out the window again? Where's my drink?"

"No drinky," she said with a baby's mouth. "No hands." She made an exaggerated sad face, her lower lip pouting like a drunken clown's.

He swung his briefcase into her face, and for a moment she smelled a field full of cows spontaneously combusting. He stood over her, his chest heaving, and she was worried he might have a heart attack. Then what would she do?

"You know you might think about taking care of *me* for a change." He blinked, looking at her bare, splayed legs. "You didn't even bother to get dressed today, did you?"

She felt the words rushing up her throat; she was ready to vomit them. Instead she bit them off. They turned to salt in her throat, gagging her.

The next thing she knew, he had her in his arms. "I couldn't live without you," he whispered into her ear. "You know I love you, don't you?" She could tell he was waiting for her answer.

"I know," she managed, staring at her handless arms, not knowing what to do with them.

"I couldn't do this, any of this, without you," he murmured, and she raised her head and watched as electrical cords wriggled and tried to yank themselves from their outlets, as metal combs ran up the wallpaper and unzipped it, exposing the apartment's pale underbelly.

He spent the next hour tidying her up, apologizing, and reattaching her hands with duct tape and glue. "It's horse glue," he said, "and there's nothing stronger than a horse."

She wondered if horses were so strong why they didn't stop men from making glue out of them. But perhaps that was a ridiculous thing to think about when your husband was giving you back your hands.

"From now on you get to keep your hands," he said. "That was really pretty ridiculous of me—how can I expect you to clean house and fix dinner if you don't have your hands?" He kissed her on the neck, lingered, and gave her a little nibble. "Oh, I could just eat you up," he whispered, biting just enough to hurt. She stared at the kitchen counter until the corner of it melted, dripping red goop onto the white tile floor.

He graciously ordered Chinese, which they ate on the couch in front of the TV. Then he started drinking, and the more he drank the angrier he became, and the drunker she became, even though he hadn't shared it with her.

He suddenly shouted and everything hit the wall, including her. She sat in the corner and watched him, all by himself in the empty center of the blast. He looked like a sad little boy who had broken all his toys. "I wish you wouldn't make me lose it like that," he said. "After a long day at work it just takes everything out of me."

"Maybe if you took a nap?" She'd forgotten that she should never suggest things. She pushed herself more tightly into the corner, until the geometry of the wall began to separate and she could feel herself falling through the sky.

She could hear him ask from the ground below, "You do love me, don't you?"

She didn't know why he bothered to ask. He didn't believe anything she had to say. "Of course—" but she didn't finish.

"I couldn't live without you," he said again, so softly it was more to himself than to anyone else. Still she heard it, and felt weakened by the statement.

Still falling through the air, she closed her eyes.

"I don't want to have to teach you a lesson!" he shouted from the street. She got off the bed and looked around—the apartment was on fire.

It had been a whirlwind romance. He'd said he loved her on

their second date. She should have jumped out of the window right then and there. She jumped out of the window now.

A little bird flew up to her. "Just keep your mouth shut!" it warned. She smiled, feeling just like a Disney princess.

Her mother used to say (her lips squirming around a broken cigarette, her eye swollen shut and as black as Daddy's toast she'd burned that morning) "Let your smile be your umbrella, Sweetheart."

She never could figure that out. Wouldn't a smile just fill with water?

Paula's last, desperate hope was that she wouldn't bounce. If she broke, if she broke into a thousand pieces, at least some of those pieces might escape.

LOST IN THE GARDEN
OF EARTHLY DELIGHTS

Where to begin?
I'm as bad with beginnings as I am with endings. Where do things start? Events go on, blending one into the other, and for some reason we remember them out of sequence. Moments cluster, and within that cluster we try to figure out how we got there, find our way out, arrive at some meaning, some temporary but safe destination.

Strange events have occurred in my life the last few years, or perhaps they always have and I'm just now beginning to notice. Often they begin with a dream, where I suppose most strange events begin. I go through periods where it seems each night I'm in a different world, walking around, conversing, sitting at an outdoor table somewhere sipping tea. In all of these worlds of my dreams I seem to function much better than I do in my waking world (I refuse to call it "real" because that would only make me despair.) I mean, at least I'm talking to people in these worlds. At least I'm participating.

My favorites are those worlds which seem sparely furnished, where each object in the world functions well and there is no need for a lot of approximations, practice objects which aren't quite as good as they should be. That doesn't mean there still can't be a lot of variety. But isn't most architecture, invention, and especially legislation a kind of rehearsal for something better? We keep trying because we know we still haven't got it quite right.

I wake up from these dreams, and I must admit most mornings I wake up in a rage because I'm not in that other world and I'm pretty sure I can't get back there. I throw things around. I break things, I'm sorry to say. I have a real world problem with anger.

I, too, am a rehearsal. Every day I live tells me that.

But strange events have been happening. Let's start with this one. Black mold in a shower, a full-sized outline of a person on my shower wall. Clearly it's my dad, but then this was Dad's shower. This was Dad's house, this was Dad's car, pretty much everything I own was once my dad's. I was still living like a college kid with all my possessions in one room when my dad died. I was his only living relative, and so I inherited Dad's world.

It wasn't easy at first. We didn't have the same tastes, but then at that point in my life I really hadn't come up with that many tastes of my own. I took a few pictures down, put a few up, and got rid of that really old gold shag carpet. That was about it.

Oh, and I got rid of Dad's clothes. Okay, that was pretty much a lie. I got rid of some of Dad's clothes, actually not too many. See, we were approximately the same size and I hated letting those clothes go to waste.

And then ten years after his death my dad's shadow comes to me in the shower in this outline made up of oily, black mold.

It reminded me of one of those worlds in my dreams. I called it the world of skin and shadow, because people walked around in it mostly nude, but they weren't troubled by questions of modesty because all that was wrong with them, all that they might want to hide beneath clothing, was also walking around in the form of these thin shadows stripped from their own bodies so that they didn't have to feel bad about them anymore, given to their negative twins, these angels of corruption whose apparent function was to walk around and remind them that they shouldn't get so full of themselves because this was what they once had been.

So I've been thinking that maybe this shadow of my father is the sum total of all those things that killed him: the poisons and diseases and bad habits and negative attitudes that took him from me before his time was due, now stripped from him and alive on the shower wall.

I've scrubbed it off several times—careful not to actually touch any of it with my hands, of course—and each time it's come back again, but just a bit fainter, a bit less well-defined. With enough scrubbing and re-scrubbing maybe it won't come back at all.

Here's another strange event.

Faded letters on an old T-shirt. I can't read it at first. Three nights a week I help a local rescue shelter pull homeless people in from the cold. Weekends I do a little work with alcoholics— nothing therapeutic, just a volunteer assistant sort of thing. I'm not really that nice of a guy, not the kind you'd expect to do something like this. But this thing I have about anger, this getting angry a lot, this cycle of getting disappointed and then getting really angry because of the disappointment? Helping other people seems to break that cycle for a time. Besides I figure if I wasn't helping these people out these would be the kind of guys I would be hanging out with all day, the kind of women I would be dating. Like I said before, I don't have that many tastes of my own. I borrow other people's, or I let them press their tastes onto mine. And I really don't need that in my life right now.

I never ask these people anymore why they live on the streets, what kind of lives they had before, what they think might have gone wrong. I used to—out front I think wanting answers to those kind of questions was one of the things driving me to do this work. But it quickly became apparent that these were the last things these fellows wanted to talk about, and to continue to try to pry this kind of information out of them was simply cruel. I knew some might say they'd chosen this world, but it was simply because they could not imagine choosing anything else.

What I really wanted to know, of course, was if this could happen to me. If I lost my job and remained out of work long enough. If someone I loved very much died. If the world I'd dreamed about shifted its details too far one way or the other. Sometimes it takes all our effort to keep the anxiety of simply being human at bay. If you lose focus you can be swept off the curb right into oncoming traffic.

It is considered acceptable somehow that the terminally ill may lose focus and so disconnect from the rest of the world. My father lost all coherence as a human being toward the end and everybody understood and did not hold it against him. But for people like my friend here in the faded T-shirt, or like myself if I were in the right circumstances, the world offers no special dispensation. We are expected to simply deal with things, and maintain.

Don't think I feel sorry for myself. My life has no more room for sorrow. It simply makes me angry.

This older guy, hippie-looking guy, probably my father's age when he died or a little older, is wearing this T-shirt, with this sixties sort of lettering. "Be Here Now" it says. I vaguely remember the phrase from books, from songs, from protest rallies that didn't really protest anything, just protested everything. It was a Buddhist kind of thing, a Yoga kind of thing, Zen or something like that. It basically meant what it said. Be in the now, don't let the past drag you down. The future takes care of itself. It's all good. That kind of thing. It went out with bell-bottom pants and miniskirts; disco or something replaced it. No surprise there, I guess. I mean, even the sixties didn't last all the way through the sixties. But I gather it was real popular for a while, on T-shirts and posters. Be Here Now, forget about the past, and don't worry about tomorrow.

This guy looks like he's been wearing this T-shirt ever since the sixties. It's practically glued to his skin. It falls apart when we peel it off him, which is really too bad. Be Here Now. He's been wearing it so long the words have transferred to his chest, stained his skin, along with the angry infected red rash that has the doctors worried. We have to scrub him down and apply all kinds of creams, disinfectants. He won't speak to us. He refuses to tell us his story.

In the back of the shelter I find some new clothes for him. Then we make sure he can shower on his own. He's shaky, but at least he can stand. Then the fellow surprises me. He asks me if I'll sit by his bed until he falls asleep.

"I don't like sleeping in a strange place is all," he says.

I look at him a minute trying to figure out what he really has in mind, but nothing comes to me. His feet are sticking out from under the end of the blanket. He's wearing slipper socks I found with Daisy designs on them, yellow on blue. They're a little small for him, and around the edges I can see the tears and dark bruises on the exposed skin.

He gazes up at me. "You know sometimes I'm afraid this might be Hell," he says. "But I'm even more afraid it might be Heaven."

I sit on a stiff-backed chair and watch him struggle with the sheets and blanket, struggle with his eyes. His face twitches. I've long believed that everyone reminds you of someone else, whether you're aware of it or not. This fellow does remind me of my father, miserable for all those years in a job he hated and a loveless marriage. He blinks at me as if reading my mind.

"I like to read in bed," he says. "Except I don't see so good no more."

"Do you want me to read you something?"

He nods and pulls the covers up to his chin.

Again, something in that gesture so like my father his last year. Like a little boy under the weather, tucked in and waiting for his bedtime toys. I thought that picture hideous at the time— my dad was dying hideously.

But still I watched over him, sat beside him.

In too many relationships we reach this point: waiting for things to end, or waiting for them to die. Nothing left to keep us interested in this other person, so now we're just biding time. It seems they're no longer part of our world. I've always thought there was something shameful in that.

"The paper would be good," the fellow mutters from the bed. I'd forgotten I promised to read to him. I go over to the reading rack and grab a newspaper. They are all old, long outdated. What they chronicle might as well be another world. But I hope this fellow won't notice or care.

"So," I sigh. "Do you want the headlines? Sports?"

"Something about cars," he says definitely. "If that's okay."

"Sure, why not? I like cars." Which is a lie. Just a small one, but I often wonder why we always feel we have to lie to these people about our own feelings. Then it strikes me that that is in part what separates us from them. We lie out of politeness. People like this fellow don't always have the wherewithal to be polite. "There's a piece on the new Volkswagen Beetles."

"I used to have a Volkswagen," he says. "Had it for years. Now they won't let me drive anymore."

"Looks like they've included some of the original Beetle's design features. Internal grab rails, the flower vase on the dashboard. But in the new Beetle you'll find a built-in radio cassette, sixteen-inch alloy wheels, twin air bags, ABS brakes, and air conditioning as standard."

"Can I get an orange one?"

"Orange?"

"You know—like a school bus?"

I search through the article. "Dark blue, green, red, silver, bright blue, black, white. There's something called Reflux Yellow, a limited edition. But no orange."

"Oh, okay. I like orange. It makes me think of oranges."

"Well, yeah. I guess I like green myself." His mouth curls into what appears to be disgust.

Then a narrow lizard's tail appears above his right ear, flicks the lobe and draws a line of blood. The man blinks rapidly, eyes tearing as if in sudden pain, but he betrays no other reaction.

I find myself little more concerned than he. Like I said, strange events have been happening. And here's another strange event: what just occurred hardly bothers me at all.

"I like a green car," I say to the guy. "I really do. Like a big green pepper. Or a melon."

"Okay," he says, with the lizard crawling up his head to the hairline. But the lizard doesn't have a lizard's head—it has a red-and-blue-striped devil's head whose eyes blink and blink and blink at me, this devil-headed lizard that apparently lives in this fellow's body and comes out now and then. "Could you maybe tell me a story?" he asks.

"You mean like a bedtime story?"

He nods. I don't know any bedtime stories, actually. My dad never read to me. Of course I was exposed to them in school—*Hansel and Gretel, Rumpelstiltskin,* and the like. But most of the details didn't stick.

"OK," I say. "This is a story called…'The Prince of the Kingdom.' Once upon a time…there was a prince, except he'd never known he was a prince before. Some fellow in a fancy suit just came to him and said, 'You're the prince now.'

'Of what?' the new prince asked. 'You mean of here?'

'Well, no,' Mister Fancypants admitted. 'Not *here*, exactly. Can I get back to you on that?' And Mr. Fancypants left."

"That's not the end of the story, is it?"

"No, no, not at all," I tell him, but I'm really not sure because I'm making it up as I go along.

"Is there a princess? Does she come?"

I think about it. "No, there isn't. At least I don't think so."

"Can't you just imagine one? A princess that comes and tells him what kingdom he's the prince of and then takes him there and she makes him happy and at last he will never be lonely again?"

I consider the idea for a very long time and then I say, "No, I must admit I cannot imagine that at all. I really wish I could."

"Then how about this," the old homeless fellow curled up like a child on the bed says, his face flickering in and out, going from a suffusion of exertion to the sallow shades of human remains, hope and despair, flesh and bone, like a distress signal sent from some distant world. "The newly-made prince returns to his home where he begins imagining, designing, and building his new kingdom, because all he really needed was an official title, you see. He just needed to be *told* he was a prince."

I'm frankly surprised, and a little ashamed of myself to be so surprised. "That's actually pretty good."

"I really like your world," he replies.

And I'm not sure if he's referring to the world of the story we've just told together, or some other world that might be mine. "You do?"

"Well, yes. You take care of people and you tell them stories. I bet you have a nice, peaceful house, don't you, with lots of books? What better world could there be?"

The journey out to the street takes but a few minutes, and

when I arrive there, where the shadows of the buildings that were overlap the ones that will be, where roads disappear and new paths resolve from nothing, I am overcome with possibility.

BLATTIDAE WINE

Fatigue would craft a yellowish haze by the end of the work day. Sometimes he could taste it coming. Shadows arrived unexpectedly at the corners of things, in the shallows of a face. They thickened, or multiplied, and he felt a kind of intoxication, followed by a sickness that could not be settled. His skin had gradually developed an oiliness, and although he was sure everyone at the office noticed, no one said anything. He must be seriously ill, he thought, but that kind of paranoia was to be expected under the circumstances. He also found the experience almost pleasurable. If he were ever cured of this, he would no doubt feel better, but he'd be disappointed.

As he left the building, a peculiar sort of blurriness always occurred. Everyone Scott looked at appeared to be leaving their bodies. He'd shake his head, and shake his head, but it failed to fix anything. His perceptions could not be reset. He'd think it was raining, but it was not.

Scott was always the last one out of the office for the car pool home. He'd find something necessary to do before leaving— something to file, some message to send, some bit of clutter to straighten or eradicate. He couldn't leave if his desk were in any small way out of order. He hadn't always been like this. But now everything had to be in its place, and anything unnecessary, or ugly, removed.

The others tried to treat his tardiness as a joke, a personal idiosyncrasy, but Scott could tell it annoyed them. Their manager Bryan never let the teasing, or the complaints, go too far. They hadn't been good friends before, but apparently Bryan had decided to take Scott under his wing. He appreciated the gesture, but the price was listening to a great deal of advice he couldn't use.

"You should start dating again—you're not too old. She's the one who left. If you stay home all the time, she wins right?" Bryan saved his advice for the two days of the week he drove the pool. He'd drop the others off, and then Scott and Bryan would be alone in the car for at least a half hour, depending on traffic. "You just wait. You get out there, find yourself a new lady friend, she'll come crawling back. Then you'll be in the catbird seat. You'll have all the choices, all the power. Screw her."

Scott felt anger rising to his lips, and bit into the lower one to keep it safely inside. To say nothing was to betray her, and this was his fault because of the story he'd fabricated. He'd had to tell people something, the neighbors, her co-workers, his co-workers. He'd needed some sort of explanation for her absence. Maybe he could have come up with a less offensive lie if he'd had more time. This was embarrassing, and shameful. But now he was stuck with it, and Bryan's unwanted advice.

"Well, at least you never had kids. Believe me, this kind of thing is so much harder with kids."

Scott turned and gazed at Bryan. His vision was blurring again. Bryan's arms looked too thin, his fingers too long and too stiff to grip the steering wheel properly. One of Bryan's hands was fluttering in the air. An unpleasant jitteriness had taken over the car. Scott wiped at his eyes. It was as if he were wearing dirty glasses. Sometimes people had been rude enough to ask why they'd never had kids. He'd always tell them, *she already has her hands full with me.*

"Tomorrow night the guys and I are going drinking. Maybe we'll meet some females—you should come. We can pick you up. But you really should start driving again, don't you think? I don't mind driving you around, and the guys, well, we all understand that you're taking this hard. But it's about time to get back in the saddle, just in general, you know?"

A yellow smear of insect parts drifted across the outside of the windshield. Bryan cursed and hit the wipers. Scott followed Bryan's arm from the steering wheel to his shoulder. He watched as a similarly yellow soup oozed from Bryan's hairline and down his face. Bryan's skull suddenly appeared smaller, as if being consumed. "Thanks," Scott said quickly. "I know, but I'm not ready yet. I'm working on it. But I probably shouldn't be drinking right now. Actually, I'm not safe to drive."

"What, your doc put you on tranquilizers?"

"Something. Yes, tranquilizers."

"You should have told the guys. They might have understood better."

Scott hated that he'd sacrificed more of the truth to this ordeal. But it was certainly true he was far from steady. He was far from all right.

After a few more minutes they turned onto Scott's street. He and Lisa had moved there three years ago—an inexpensive, quiet neighborhood where they figured they would eventually retire. They never wanted to move again. Lisa, at least, had gotten her wish. "I see you're keeping the place up," Bryan said as they pulled in front. "That's a good sign." Scott got out and thanked him.

The grass was trimmed, the flowers blooming, the landscape uncluttered, the concrete swept, and the front of the small white house clean and commercial ready. Scott hired a fellow twice a month to maintain the parts everyone could see. The curtains, as always, were closed.

Easing open the door reintroduced him to the smell: a grainy aroma reminiscent of dog food, and underneath something oily, petroleum-like, suggestive of automotive lubricants and bug spray. It wasn't exactly a foul odor, but it was unpleasant. The worst thing about it was that he was getting used to it.

The living room looked normal enough, maybe even cleaner and tidier than when Lisa had taken care of things. Pillows squared neatly against the overstuffed chair backs, side tables dusted, the carpet still showing vacuum lines. But he never used this room. It had become something innocuous for the postal carrier, or a nosy neighbor, to see from the front door.

He stopped and listened. He'd learned every sound the house made: the particular creaks that occurred fifteen minutes after the furnace cut off, the soft popping noises along the ceiling of the east-most bedroom during a strong wind, that odd sound from the kitchen floor when the freezer went off-cycle. Nothing troubling about those sounds anymore. Then there was that soft whisper and scratch of movement that reminded Scott his life had changed.

He had to push aggressively on one side of the French doors to get into her bedroom. It had been Lisa's idea to move into the old dining room, at least for sleeping, because of her intermittent moaning, her sudden panics in the middle of the night. "You won't be able to sleep. You'll be late to work every day. I'll wear you out." She was also in pain, although she would never talk about how much. At the height of her illness her doctor had given her as many pills as she wanted. She was rarely moved to scream. Discarded plastic amber medicine vials followed her through the house and decorated the floor by her bed.

He'd resisted separate bedrooms for a week or so—they'd slept in the same bed for decades. But he was so tired, his eyes burning, his fingers shaking. Sudden noises made him weep. But didn't she need him now more than ever? And yet he was desperate for sleep, and that's why he'd eventually given in, and let her down.

Finally he pushed the door open enough to squeeze inside. Papers and trash were gathered against it, and a large rock of hardened, yellowed material which might originally have been paper, or cloth, or chewed up bits of wall. It was impossible to tell. There were new rules in his life, an extraordinary physics, and he didn't understand most of it.

That same hardened material had dripped and scattered through other parts of the room. Like candlewax, but with a foul smell. The rest of it—and it was all a mess, with no actual furniture visible anymore—was a pile of shredded paper, a pile of shredded bedding, a variety of nibbled trash, and—recognizable from their colors and patterns—disintegrating fragments of Lisa's clothing stolen from her closet. Nesting material.

He didn't see her, and he didn't see it, and he felt shamefully hopeful that both were gone, and he could now clean this room, shovel it empty, and get on with his life. It would be a devastated life, but he would piece it together, and at least this chapter would be done.

But then came a small movement in the middle of everything, a vague pulsing, a flutter of paper and stiffened cloth. Something opened and the movement was suddenly larger, and then the giant insect extended itself, rotated, and stood up amid a shower of crumbling debris until it was at least four feet, maybe five feet tall. It rested its rear end with the wicked looking pincers into the corner.

It wasn't any variety of bug Scott was familiar with. It looked much like a roach, but he thought its head was proportionately larger, its mandibles too long and broad, and there seemed to be way too many parts attached, but he didn't really know because he'd never studied one under a magnifying glass. Its antennae were like skinny black tree branches with many more segments. And if the huge eyes were compound he wasn't able to see their facets. They appeared liquid and deep, and too dark to see into.

The insect was chewing on a pale, linear bit wedged into its mouth parts. It looked like a french fry. The last few weeks Scott had brought in bags of fast food for dinners and weekend lunches. He'd eat some, and the insect would snatch the rest. Lisa didn't eat. He was surprised there was still some left.

"So, did ye bring me nothing?" the insect asked. The accent was vaguely British. It had an annoying habit of imitating bad accents from time to time—bad British, bad Australian, or maybe South African (Scott wasn't really sure). Yet another reason not to trust this creature, or listen to its lies.

"Nothing now. I'll be going out for food later. But maybe something a little healthier. All this grease...."

The insect tilted its head rapidly, finished off the pale fry. "Grease is smashing. Don't bother me with that health nonsense."

Scott looked around for her. He sometimes thought maybe he'd already let her go, that he was ready to make the change, but he felt panicky when he didn't see her. "Where?"

"Don't worry your head. Still with us, safe and sound." It gestured with one of its many legs.

Scott pushed his way through the garbage toward one corner of the room. He moved some large strips of foam and cardboard. She was sitting on the floor, leaning against the wall. Still tightly wound up in a stained and leaking bundle—like a bed sheet, but thinner, stiffer. Purplish stains dotted the upper edge. He peeled away some of the top to reveal her soft gray hair, her pale forehead, a sliver of her closed lids. She was snoring, still making that wet rattling sound. "Oh, sweetheart," he said, tearing up, "please don't do this." He kissed her head as best he could.

"Here, mate," it crooned inhumanly behind him. "Come have some of my wine."

Lisa had stopped eating a few months before. Not by choice at first—her stomach simply wouldn't accept it. But after a while she wouldn't even try. Even the smell of cooking food, or a taste of water, made her stomach cramp.

"It's back," she said.

"You can't know that without a scan." It had been his role during her illness to keep what they knew separate from what they didn't know, but were afraid of. "Try not to make guesses until you see the doctor." She'd smiled and patted his hand. That was her way of comforting him—she suspected him of denial. He suspected himself of denial.

Her GP diagnosed gastroenteritis and said it would go away in a few days. She just needed to drink plenty of fluids, which she couldn't do. Eventually she retired to her bed and refused to get up. After a few days he begged her to eat. "How are you going to get better if you don't eat?"

"I can't. You don't understand." He hated hearing that. He had to understand.

Over the next few weeks the house gradually grew darker. That was when the yellowing began. It was a subtle effect, and occasionally he thought he must be imagining it, but if he sat with it, and stared into the stained air, it became unmistakable. No, he really didn't understand. He called the power company and told them there'd been some kind of malfunction—all the lights in the house were dim. He suspected a power leak—was there such a phenomenon? They sent someone out and he guided the man through the house. When Scott took him into the bedroom he simply explained that his wife was ill. "It's the fellow from the power company," he whispered to her. "We'll just be in here a minute." She may have acknowledged him, but her voice was so soft he couldn't be sure.

The fellow said he could find nothing wrong, but they would "monitor" the situation. He suggested that Scott try higher wattage bulbs. On his way out the man asked "your wife an invalid?" Scott didn't know what to say. He felt vaguely insulted, but he didn't know why. "Mine too," the man said without waiting for an answer.

Scott went back into the bedroom and sat on the edge of the bed. "He couldn't find anything." She didn't respond. "Honey, can't you just try to get up and eat something?" She may or may not have said something then. "I could wash your back. Would that feel good?"

He went into the bathroom and got some soap and a damp cloth. He slipped one hand under her neck. "I'm going to pull you up into a sitting position, okay? Try to help me if you can."

As he pulled her up she glanced sideways at him. She moved her lips but nothing came out. He noticed that her lips were seriously chapped and he berated himself for not noticing earlier and doing something about it. As he raised her from the bed her nightgown tore away and adhered to the bottom sheet.

He hugged her to him and shifted her for a glimpse of her back. The skin there looked dry and darkly discolored and swollen in parts. It was peeling away from the center into an expanding blister and the border of that blister had edges which were now separating from the rest of her skin.

The discolored skin suddenly fell away, unfolding into something impossibly three-dimensional, wriggling its lower body as it freed itself from beneath her buttocks. Scott could not quite comprehend what he was seeing and wanted urgently to let go but was afraid Lisa would tumble out of bed. The thing rose up and peered down at him and tilted its head, reaching out something—Antennae? Foreleg?—to touch his face then to caress and probe his ears, mouth, and eyes.

The head was huge, brown and black, and was covered with hairs of a sort. The eyes were liquid, and suddenly appeared to quake. More like a human's eyes, or at that size, a cow's eyes, but shiny with intelligence. Scott closed his own eyes involuntarily and felt a scraping against his cheek. He opened them again as the huge insect passed over him and stood by the bed, looking down on them. Its expression was unreadable, if it was any kind of expression at all.

It slowly moved into the corner with its back to them and began ripping the wallpaper off the wall.

Scott laid Lisa down quickly and reached for the phone. Her hand stopped his arm. "What could you possibly tell them? What would you say?"

He stared at her. Her eyes were open, alert. "Am I crazy right now?" he asked.

"It helps," she said. "If you call someone, I'll have to leave here, and I'll never come back. Can't you see that? They'll keep me somewhere, and they'll try to help me, but they won't be able to. I want to be home."

"But that *thing*?" He glanced into the corner. Paper and bits of wall were rapidly disappearing beneath the insect's aggressive movements of head and legs. It made a sharp grinding noise unlike anything Scott had ever heard before. He tried to look at the parts of it, find a place for it in his head somehow. It wasn't like anything—brownish, yellowish, blackish—and he thought it had too much of everything. It was disgusting the way a roach was disgusting. When he was a kid the family would come home, turn on the lights, and they'd be all over the kitchen floor, black and skittering around with their foul legs. It was the only time he ever saw them. They were like some sort of dark, nasty miracle.

"I can't explain it," she said, closing her eyes and swallowing with a painfully dry, rasping noise. "I know it's disgusting, but somehow it's helping. It makes me feel drunk, like I'm already somewhere else and there's something soothing in that." She clutched his hand. "Or maybe I've already died. Have I already died, Scott?"

A stinging sensation in his chest made him wince. "Of course not. You just need to see the doctor. I'll load you into the car and we'll find out what he can do."

"I can't. Not now. Maybe later, but right now I just need

to sleep, okay? Don't worry about that thing. Go into the old bedroom—get some rest. I'll be okay. I just need to rest, too. Could you please do that for me?"

He pulled the sheet and the blanket back up around her and tucked her in. He paused at the door. The thing had stopped moving, standing motionless in the corner with its back to the rest of the room. Lisa was also motionless, all wrapped up like a package with her eyes closed.

Scott went into the living room and sat on the couch for a long time. If he was thinking of anything he did not remember it later. The bedroom was quiet for the most part, except for now and then a scraping or a rustling noise. He stared at the phone. She was right, of course. People would come, and that thing wouldn't be there. Maybe the wall damage would be, maybe not. He wasn't sure. But he was sure they'd take her away, and she didn't want that. Maybe they'd take him away as well. Eventually he lay down, and after a while he went to sleep.

Scott was aware of Bryan watching him as he was eating his lunch. They were down in the break room, no one else around. It was awkward and uncomfortable, especially since Bryan wasn't saying anything.

Finally Scott couldn't take it anymore, looked up and said, "What?" A couple of pieces of food fell out of his mouth but he didn't care.

"Sorry. I just hate seeing you eating that stuff day after day."

Scott stared at his burger, bright threads of melted cheese lacing the pale green lettuce. Grease dripped onto the yellow wrapper he'd spread open on the table to act as a plate.

"I know it's bad for me..." He stopped, made himself swallow when he saw the look on Bryan's face. "Sorry. But it's fast, it tastes good, and it fills me up."

"I got you, I got you. We all do it. And I know it's worse for some people—some people just have to be with someone or they don't function correctly. I think maybe you're one of those people. But what you're doing, isn't that what they mean when they say somebody's 'eating their feelings?'"

"Maybe, I don't know. I don't know that I understand

psychology that well, especially my own." Scott looked at his burger with regret. He didn't think he could eat it anymore.

"I'm not saying you need therapy. Just somebody to talk to. Do you have somebody to talk to?" Scott thought Bryan might be hinting around that that somebody could be him. Scott hoped not.

"Yeah, I do," Scott said. "I have someone to talk to."

"What are you?" It was the first question Scott was able to ask the insect. It had taken him awhile to get there. Initially the insect didn't speak, and so there was no answer. But Scott kept asking the question again and again. He didn't know what else to do. Lisa didn't want him to call anyone, or to make any attempt to remove the thing. Apparently it helped Lisa to have the creature around. He couldn't imagine how, and didn't want to know.

But eventually, it did begin to speak, and Scott and the thing would talk, even though Scott hated those conversations— talking made their circumstances seem unspeakably normal.

"I'm an unknown species, as far as you're concerned," it said one day. "But there are some vague resemblances to Family Blattidae. Cockroaches, you would call them."

So at least Scott's first impressions had had some accuracy. That was the beginning—defining things, naming them so that they could talk about them. Then there were the requests for food—always something fast and greasy. Then the pronouncements. The insect tended toward the philosophical, and would make these statements spontaneously and out of context, and usually at times Scott did not want to hear them.

"Believe me, there's nothing more intoxicating than entropy, when everything is sliding away from you, and there's nothing you have to do about it."

Most of the time Scott had no idea how to reply. And as the evenings wore on, and he tried to think of new things to say to Lisa, about how he felt, and what she meant to him, and troubled himself over whether what he said was helping, or hurting, even though she probably couldn't hear him at all— he grew so tired of it all, and the pain that came from holding his face perfectly, unreadably still could only be assuaged by a certain liquid that came from the insect's body. Scott could never hold on to the memory of how it was delivered, but once it was delivered, everything felt as it should be, as if everything in their life together had become inevitable now.

It had been a draining day after a mostly sleepless night, and when Scott got home from work he sat down on the couch in the front room and stayed there. It hadn't been that long ago when, arriving from their separate jobs, he would make some tea and Lisa would grab some water or juice, and they would sit there enfolded together, and talk barely above whispers about what they had seen and what they had heard and how they felt about it all. The subject matter would change according to the vagaries of that particular day, but often it would come back around to how lucky they felt, and they would wonder how such luck had come to them, and how it was vaguely embarrassing to be talking of such things.

This night it was as quiet as it had been on those evenings, and Scott thought he would just sit there and wait until he heard something, and once he heard something he would get up and check on her, and go into that dreaded room, and stay in there because he felt he owed it to her, and he would look at that terrible thing, and he would be in that terrible world, until he was too tired to stay awake any more, and could give himself permission to leave.

But this night he heard nothing for a very long time, and he tried to equate this quiet with the quiet life they had had in the past, and he could not. This quiet grew heavier the longer he waited. This quiet spread out and filled the room with such weight that soon he wasn't sure he could breathe. This quiet grew denser and fuller, until eventually he had to kneel down on the floor, and fold his arms around his head in order to keep himself from crying out in pain as he was crushed by its gravity.

Then finally there was the slightest of whispers. It might have just been a draft. But he took it as his reason to get to his feet and go into her room.

The insect sat motionless and silent on its mound of sundry trash, its many legs folded with such complication it resembled an intricately carved statue. It had yet another fry shoved into its mouth parts, but at that moment was not chewing.

Scott looked around at the room and believed that it had changed. There was obviously lesser of it—he could see parts of the floor now, and a great deal of the trash had been compacted into these hard little yellow lumps, and much of it eaten, he supposed, since none of it had actually been taken out. He could now see more fully into the open closet, and her hanging clothes, which were fewer now than he remembered, and a great deal of them obviously chewed.

He should have taken better care of her things. He didn't know what he'd been thinking. He'd moved her best clothes into this closet assuming she'd eventually need them, but of course she wouldn't need them. They were completely useless to her—she'd been wearing only sweats and pajamas and night gowns. And now all her best things were ruined.

Scott himself had made some changes to the rest of the house. He'd packed up her sewing room, and her collection of books. He'd been getting them ready to give away, figuring she would never use them again. He'd marched through the house methodically, picking out her things, moving them, putting them away, throwing them away, and fixing things into a kind of order. He'd thought at the time that he was taking care of things for her, dealing with things so that she wouldn't have to. Now he considered himself both a thief and the worst kind of traitor.

He couldn't find her in the corner where she had usually been hiding. He scuffed the debris back from the wall with his shoes and found nothing, not even pieces of that bundle thing she'd been wrapped in.

"She's over there beneath the window," the insect said suddenly. "In case you really need to see her. But I would recommend against it. She is greatly diminished, I'm afraid."

Scott had noticed the smallish package earlier. He stared at it now, but could not force himself to go any closer. It was made of that stiffened, paper-like material, and it was roughly the size of a small potted plant—about a foot tall, about six inches wide. The bottom part looked heavier than the top—it had spread some, and there was a roundness to it. There was a dent on the side near the top, and the bundle appeared to lean away from that dent. The stiff material had darkened along its upper edges, into something of a rose color, where it looked as if numerous petals had come together to make a relatively tight seal, like a closed bud.

"There is nothing here that should distress you," the insect said. "It is all part of nature. You are not feeling sorry for yourself, are you? Perhaps you should drink something?"

Scott stared at the insect. The fry kept bobbing, trapped in its complicated mouth. He wished the thing would eat it already—it frustrated him, although he wasn't completely sure why. "Where do you keep finding fries? I would have figured all those fast food bags would be empty by now."

The insect stopped its chewing and fixed Scott with a motionless stare, its head tilted. Scott could see that it was molting, something he'd been unsure of before. Hard, translucent skin hung from the back of its neck and several legs. It had lost one of the shorter legs—the discarded member was lying in some trash a few feet away. Scott wondered how long it would take the insect to grow it back.

Then the insect spit the fry out. It landed right in front of Scott, who leaned over, and touched it with his foot. He decided it wasn't a fry after all—it was a finger.

Scott made a noise he did not recognize and moved toward the insect, which made itself flat as a sheet of paper and drifted under the door. For a moment it looked like a pool of filth, spreading.

The next morning Scott called in sick. A few hours later he called back and resigned. It wasn't a considered move—he didn't have any back-up plan, or much money in savings, and this would end his insurance coverage. But he couldn't imagine himself going into the office anymore. In fact he could imagine very little beyond the immediate walls around him, and how he needed to simplify things, clean up, disinfect, and throw out. He thought about this for a week, sitting on his couch in that uncluttered front room. He got up only to go to the bathroom, or for a quick snack. When mail accumulated beneath the door's mail slot he'd pick it up and throw it in the trash without examination. When he was too tired to keep his head up he'd stretch out and let himself sleep, and dream about the house and its walls, and Lisa's absence. When he wanted to wake up he simply opened his eyes, but there appeared to be no difference between eyes open and eyes closed. He needed a plan to get him moving, but the act of planning felt delusional.

A subtle change in the house told him it was finally safe to get up and do what needed to be done. He couldn't have said for sure if it was a shift in temperature, or a minute transformation of smell, or a whisper in one ear. He roamed the house with a large trash bag hanging from each hand—avoiding Lisa's bedroom for now—and he put into those bags everything that did not belong. By the time he had filled the bags he discovered that most of the objects he'd put into them were his own. Lisa's personal things were largely untouched, and prominent in every room. He went around with more bags and disposed of Lisa's items as best he could, as much as he could bear. It took several rounds and most of the day, but finally the bulk of the house was as fresh and empty as it had been the first hour they'd moved in.

In Lisa's bedroom the clothes hanging in her closet were torn and chewed beyond repair. He boxed them and stuck the box in a corner of the garage, unable to carry them out to the curb. There appeared to be little trash left, and the little there was cleaned up quickly. The room still possessed that strange aromatic blend of pet food and oil. He imagined he'd have to get rid of the carpet in order to remove that fragrance.

A small insect crawled out of a rent in the carpet. He stepped closer, looked down. It was exactly like what he had lived with the past several months, but infinitely smaller, and Scott was suddenly spiraling through the possibilities: if that creature had shrunk, or had offspring, or had never been that large in the first place.

A flood of them poured out of the hole in the carpet, massed together into a momentary afterimage of Lisa's face, her mouth drifting, and then everything he remembered about her scattered.

He'd gotten quite cold the past few minutes, sitting on the examination table with no shirt on. He wasn't going to tell anyone, however. He'd learned to tolerate it. At home he'd recently dispensed with wearing shirts altogether—he'd become intensely bothered by the friction of cloth against skin. The nurse had offered him a gown and he'd refused it. He'd gotten more stubborn, more unreasonable as he'd grown older. He hadn't intended to—it just happened.

He reached into his back pocket for his wallet. The maneuver sent a pain across his side, as if a muscle, or a bit of intestine, had caught on a bone, or something else. He didn't know. He'd tried very hard to be ignorant of his own anatomy.

Now the pain spread up into his chest. A certain space within his torso began to fill with the inflammation. It had an outline, an almost physical presence. It had weight.

He managed to flip open the wallet and look at her photograph. He did this several times a day. It was never very satisfactory because the image in the photograph never quite matched the image in his head. The image in his head was more alive, but it had lost much of its sharpness over the years. He was afraid that someday it might vanish altogether. Slipping the wallet back into his pocket brought him more pain.

The doctor came in, his head bowed over the folder in his hands. He looked up quickly and nodded before speaking. "I don't like these numbers. We'll see what the X-rays show us, and then we'll decide where to go from there. I hope you can wait a bit?"

Scott shrugged. "My days are largely unscheduled." The doctor continued to study the papers in his file. Scott wondered what might happen if he asked to see those papers, but he didn't ask.

"So, do you drink?"

"Not really."

The doctor smiled without looking up, and busily jotted something down. "That's normally a Yes or No question."

"Why, do I look like I've been drinking? What do your 'numbers' say?"

The doctor gazed at him for a moment. "Nothing definitive, actually. I don't believe you've had anything this morning, if that's what you're asking. There's something about your eyes, but there could be a number of explanations for that. Men your age, living alone, widowers especially, sometimes fall into bad habits—drinking too much, lying around, eating badly, letting the housekeeping go..."

"I keep an orderly house," Scott said. "I make a point of it."

The doctor left before he could ask him if he could get down from the table. So he stayed, folding his arms to gather more warmth. The pain crawled quickly down his back and dug into his lower ribs. Scott could feel his skin begin to shift, as if it were separating from the muscle underneath. He had come to hate his skin, and every useless thing it hid from the outside world. A fetid odor permeated the air as things began to detach, and something substantial slipped out.

"The doctor, or a nurse, could walk in any minute," Scott said. "How would you explain yourself? Because I'm not going to."

He could feel the insect behind him, moving around. The metal cabinet on the floor in front of Scott, the shiny faucet, part of the window reflected fragments of it. For some reason he thought it taller, slimmer, than what it had been before, if it was the same one. But then *why* would it be the same one? Nor did he know if it would actually be visible to someone who didn't know him that well. Perhaps someone had to love you before they could see it. Scott decided people weren't meant to know the rules.

The insect said nothing, but touched the back of Scott's neck. Scott's body tightened up, but nothing happened. He tried to reach for his wallet again, but discovered he couldn't move his arm. "I'd like to look at her photograph one more time, if that would be alright with you? You see I keep losing the specifics of her face. I forgot her voice a month after she died—did you know that? It just slipped out of my memory one night while I was asleep, and no matter what I tried, I couldn't make myself hear her voice again. But her face—I couldn't hold on to it exactly—there was always some aspect missing that would have made that memory come substantially alive, but at least I've held on to the major details. But I'm afraid I'm beginning to lose those too. So if you could just let me..."

The insect touched Scott's shoulder then, in a way that felt almost parental. And then it did that thing it did to relax him, leaning over as if to kiss, and delivering its wine. Scott closed his eyes as the delicious cold flowed through him, and took him across into that other place.

"So if you could...if you could..."

But the insect was so busy now, touching here and touching there with unanticipated gentleness, stretching its claws from one point to the other, taking Scott's measure, as if fitting him for a suit.

HALF-LIGHT

Elaine began hearing voices several days before. She'd been here too long; she'd outstayed her welcome. The infusion pump was the worst, with its constant sighs, and obsessively repeated words. "Old … old … old …" and "gone … gone … gone," and others, some in different languages. Sometimes it blended its words into the whirs and hums of the other machinery, as if to deliberately disguise its statements, so she had to listen so carefully in order to glean its messages it gave her a headache. "Remember me? It's Bill," one of the voices said. "I'm going to kill you, and you won't even know for certain you're dead."

Of course, she was in the worst possible place for voices. The hospital corridors were fragrant with the cries of the dying, the confused, those with too much pain to bear. How could people stand to work here? What was wrong with them?

All around the hospital souls tapped at the windows, begging to be let back in.

This morning, uncharacteristically emboldened, she'd asked a nurse, "So, how many people have died in this room?"

"Oh sweetheart," the young woman said, "People die everywhere."

She objected to being called 'sweetheart' by young professionals—it was condescending. Yet it was comforting as well, so she'd allowed it during her stay here. It had been a long time since she'd been anyone's sweetheart. Longing was like a disease, and some never recover.

"Where am I now?" she asked, as she asked every day. Because she'd forgotten, just that moment.

"You're in the hospital, dear," the nurse replied again. "And we're going to take very good care of you."

Again the same response, as if scripted, as if to cover up the murder happening everywhere. But she still felt they cared here. The problem was there were only a limited number of answers to go around.

"Sometimes I think you're all trying to kill me. But most of the time I know that's not true. At least I don't think it's true. Could you remind me, when I think you're trying to kill me, that you're really not?"

The nurse looked sad. "Oh, sweetheart. We're all trying to help you here. Sometimes the sickness, and the pain meds, they make you think things that aren't true. Just tell me when you're having those thoughts, and we'll talk about it, okay?"

Elaine nodded. She was a good nurse, but she left Elaine's door open too often. People would pass by, and some would invariably look in, civilians. She was of an age they all talked about, but didn't want to be. They possessed none of the clandestine knowledge reserved exclusively to patients and staff, the secret handshakes of death and disease.

Someone down the hall was weeping. What was happening to them? They must have gotten to him, or her, first. She kept looking, but it was all occurring too far away for her to see. Events were rapidly distancing themselves. Very soon she would not be allowed to participate at all.

She'd watched for ghosts since she'd been admitted, but felt there were so many she'd probably never be able to single out an individual spirit. Ghosts were enmeshed in the walls here, the furniture, and the very air. Ghosts illuminated and ghosts obscured. Ghosts permeated everything. No wonder she required supplemental oxygen—the ghosts must be crowding her lungs, stealing her breath before it could do her any good.

"I just need to check your vitals." It was a confusing statement. Elaine wasn't vital anymore—that was the problem. She'd gone from being an active working woman, an administrator, to an old woman lying in bed and attached to tubes. "Are you doing okay?"

"I used to travel every night," Elaine replied. "Now I travel all the time."

The nurse smiled and clipped things on her, and wrapped her arm in a band—it was soon so tight against her skin she thought the bone would snap. She felt herself go, and then something brought her back from the brink again. Was it this nurse? Probably not, even though she seemed quite nice. Death was out of their hands and beyond their ability to cure. "Your blood pressure is a little low," the nurse announced, but sounded not at all concerned. She pricked Elaine's finger to read her blood sugar, but Elaine was sure there'd be nothing more interesting in its pages than numbers. It may have hurt, but Elaine was concerned with much bigger pains.

Elaine held her hands up in front of her eyes to see if she was fading. "I can get you some lotion, dear, if you like," the nurse said, not understanding.

"That would be very kind, dear," she replied, pleased that she could still play this game.

The nurse went away in search of lotion, but never came back. Had she really been on Elaine's side, and so they had to get rid of her? Elaine slipped out of bed, climbed on top of her headboard, and sat there on her haunches, knees sticking straight up in the air and her butt touching the backs of her feet. Elaine remembered sitting that way as a child. It was a treasure to be small enough to fit almost anywhere.

Perched so high, as in a tall tree, as on a cliff, she could imagine herself a predator, winged and taloned and ready to swoop down and take what she wanted, even steal a life if that was her whim. All things were possible.

The blinds were down as she'd requested. She hated seeing outside when she couldn't be there. Half-light filled the room with a thin fog, graying in the corners, the in-between and under places. But still thick enough that the breath from a whisper might leave a trace. The nurse came in but didn't see her hovering there. She gently applied the lotion to Elaine's still hands and then to her still arms. The nurse checked her breathing: steady and without distress. *Not dead yet*, she whispered from her perch. The night's small triumph.

The Elaine on the headboard watched the Elaine in bed sleep, stir, struggle within the grip of some dream. She made her observations with a cool, unemotional, indifferent eye, as if the woman's pain had nothing to do with her. The woman's skin was paler than she remembered, and there were more wrinkles under the chin, and less fat inside the cheeks. She'd also acquired a nervous pulse above one eye. This was clearly not her best self, but she was owed a certain fealty, of course.

Disturbances slipped into the half-light. Their ripples traveled gently around the bed, paused at the window shade, and dissipated. Elaine could hear their tiny complaints in her sleep, their heartbreaks. She would have dearly loved to see their faces—maybe next time. The Elaine up on the headboard blinked, and fell back into her. It wasn't safe here, Elaine thought, but she couldn't keep her eyes open.

She'd lost too many days it seemed—to sleep, to inattention. She had had too many dreams, too many strange notions, too many fears. She had limited time, but she had no idea how to use what she had. She was apparently determined to waste her life.

Someone tall was standing over her. Some past doctor, some passed patient, or someone intent on murder. She attempted to raise her arm in his direction, and although she saw her arm floating off the bed, she couldn't be sure if she'd actually succeeded.

Sometimes the nerves could not believe the illness of the flesh, and so plotted their escape, dreaming invisible shapes in the air, of an adventure outside the body. Elaine could feel her nerves pull and stretch inside her, their movements causing her pain. She begged them to stop, but they had created a mind of their own. It floated there in the half-light at the foot of the bed, completely uninterested in her plight. Was this the source of those murderous thoughts? Other minds drifted by, a mind field. They filled the air like grim party balloons. She rose into the air and the higher she rose the smaller she became. She poked one of the minds and it drifted away.

Another of her doctors came in. He stood over the bed and watched her silently for a time. "Can you tell me how you're feeling?" he finally asked.

Elaine was surprised to hear herself answer. "I'll be fine as long as they don't kill me first."

If the doctor was surprised he didn't show it. "Who are they?" But as she didn't know she couldn't tell him. "The end is blended into everything—you may not recognize it." She looked up at him in alarm. Why would he say such a thing?

A few minutes afterwards the young nurse came in and adjusted Elaine's fluids and left. Of course by then she knew what she should have said to the doctor. Why did you always come up with the perfect answer later?

"When work is done, when love is done, the soul can wander what remains, but the one thing it cannot do is explain." She could not say that, but she could think it. Of course she realized that did not answer his question, but it was what she wanted to say.

She gathered herself on top of the headboard again, gazing down at that poor woman lying in the bed below. She felt vaguely guilty—she had abandoned ship. But she also felt impatient with this woman who would not let go. No one wanted to stay with the dying anymore. Where was her gothic entourage, her sad-faced hangers-on?

The half-light swam with lazy shapes, as if she were an ingredient in some soup. Was this the ectoplasm she'd read about? She admonished herself not to name things, because naming led the mind astray.

Beneath her transparent feet her body suddenly wailed its loss of future. In extremis, she rose to the ceiling, sailed through the spaces between the spaces, and down the long corridors both architectural and spiritual. She passed rooms containing patients sleeping and awake, and for the ones who turned to watch her it did not matter if they were sleeping or awake.

Down below, the nurse's station murmured with farewells and changing shifts, a rhythm of small vicissitudes and losses, all too busy to notice the slight alteration in air. She'd become an expert in brevities. She should have felt something then, but her feelings were racing far ahead of her. It was a familiar notion— all her life she'd been unable to keep up.

All around her doors were opening and closing as she was carried along by invisible currents. Would she recognize the one meant for her? When the fissure finally appeared, would she understand what she was seeing?

At least she was capable of acknowledging the others, these fellow travelers, these separated selves. Most were too focused to give her the time of day, but now and then one would startle as they came face-to-face. But faces were now a momentary thing that dissolved with the minutest shift in the light.

Finally deep in the bowels of the building where things were sent and things were stored when there was nothing more to be done she reached that place where she felt a large number of them had gathered. There was nothing to see, so why did entering here fill her with that terrible sound? They did not exactly welcome her, but they seemed happy, or at least satisfied, that they were once again one more.

She waited for it all to end, and was disappointed when it did not. The rest of them turned to her, beckoning her forward, insistent that it was time to go. But the Elaine back in her bed was calling, and she screamed as she was jerked back through the corridors like a struggling bird at the end of a fowler's snare.

Her doctors and nurses had gathered there, around the body in her bed. She was the center of attention at last, half in light, and half in the darkness of the end.

She'd taken so long to build this life; naturally she would resist its disassembly. But she coveted that time when she would no longer be an object to be prodded or even seen. She hovered over and around them, not quite able to see the stubborn self that still held her fast.

But something stirred in the sheets, and the professionals quickened their pace, closing in, hands and instruments out to save her.

But because she was already one step into the half-light, she passed unnoticed between them, and stretched her hand out to touch that Elaine, whose eyes opened wide as she at last recognized the face of her murderer.

She grabbed what was left of the brightness, and finished it.

Silence lay there in the bed, and the air quaked with absence.

MISTER AINSLEY

He'd been alone for almost ten years. It felt a great deal longer. He'd almost forgotten what it had been like living with his wife, all the small kindnesses she had done for him which had made him feel like a member of the human race. But now that she'd been gone a decade it was easy to think of that period as a very lucky dream he once had, from which he would wake up filled with optimism, until he remembered that it had in fact been only a dream.

Now he spent his time in solitary activity or, when necessary, in a series of actions meant to limit human contact. It was unfortunate that he had to waste his energy with this. Active avoidance meant ignoring, or turning away as quickly as possible, the random people who came to his door. It meant spending too much time studying his caller identification display to determine whether he should answer the phone or not. It meant for the most part avoiding all forms of social media, even though he used his computer as his chief source of information on current events and societal trends. The nation was entering the end of an election cycle, a risky time both for the country and his notions of well-being.

Mister Ainsley had no more interest in politics than he did in religion. The results were always based on wishes and lies, it seemed. Political questions rarely resolved, and became an excuse for an endless recycling of grudges. His rare peeks into social media to take the temperature of the culture revealed a cesspool of inconsequential resentments and confusion. People could be so dismissive, so cruel to one another. They clung to their fleeting hatreds as if their lives depended on them. He supposed this was inevitable—the true consequences of actions rarely revealed themselves during a single person's lifetime. Human beings, by nature, lacked perspective.

He had sympathy for the outsiders in such a system, whether due to gender, or race, or some combination of traits which shoved them outside the parameters of the favored class. He, too, was an outsider. But he had no desire to participate.

The current autumn had been more despairing than usual. The trees were apparently reluctant to compensate with their customary colorful display, with more grays and dying browns and surrendering blacks than he could remember from previous seasons. Several early snows had suffocated any struggling green, melting only for the annoying scatter of campaigners for the various contenders and causes stopping by his home several times daily: ringing his bell, beating his door, interrupting his thoughts concerning more enduring dilemmas.

If ensconced in his too-hot study he could ignore them until they went away. If passing through the house on a quest for tea or to relieve a buildup of agitation he might stop and answer the door.

This young man wore a cinnamon-colored sweater vest festooned with buttons and ribbons signifying a variety of positions and proposals. He was also very pale and had red hair and freckles. Mister Ainsley could not remember the last time he had talked to someone with red hair and freckles. Intrigued, he stood and listened, even though the glare of sun, and this young man's scarlet mane, hurt his eyes.

"I won't take up much of your time, sir. Are you a registered voter?" Mister Ainsley was not, and never had been, but he must have nodded distractedly, because the young man continued. "I just wanted to know if you'd heard the good news about..."

After a moment's confusion—was this a religious spiel, or a political one?—Mister Ainsley allowed the words to pass around him, the repetition of key adjectives occasionally stirring his ragged sideburns, or the hair dangling over his collar. It had been awhile since he'd been out for a haircut, but he couldn't decide if he could still tolerate a human being's nervous fingers on his scalp. He made an effort to focus on the pale boy's watery eyes, the soft lines of the face wobbling and losing definition, the freckles beginning to wander off the skin. Before Mister Ainsley could react appropriately the young man had fainted part way into his entrance hall. Not sure what to do now, a stranger having entered his home for the first time in years, he dragged the figure the rest of the way in and shut the door. He slapped the lock lever into place with belated anger.

He did not think of himself as particularly strong, but his muscles had rarely been tested. He felt uncomfortable leaving this earnest young man lying on the floor. He stooped and grabbed him beneath the armpits and lifted. Mister Ainsley could feel some irregularities in his pelvic region as he began to move with his burden, some gravitational shifts as his spine attempted to alter its alignment in response to the unaccustomed stress. He considered it fortunate that the young man was unconscious and unable to witness as Mister Ainsley, by means of a few dozen backwards waddling steps, got first the fellow's shoulders and buttocks, then his feet, up on the couch. He examined the shoes now propped up on the antique cushion—his guest had stepped in something creamy and fibrous and unidentifiable. Mister Ainsley pulled a rag from his coat pocket and used that to remove the shoes.

The campaign worker was very still, but not dead. Mister Ainsley stared at the freckled face, almost expecting those freckles to shift position, to take up residence in another region of the young man's face, but they did not. He could see the shallow rise of the chest, the intermittent flare of nostrils, sometimes accompanied by a sudden, deeper inhalation, as if the young man were smelling something. Of course. It had been so long since he had entertained visitors he had forgotten how certain scents affected people. He had a spray he could use. It wasn't particularly effective but it might do.

He glanced around the room looking for elements which might disturb. He could only guess of course—although he tried to keep up with trends in sensitivities it was difficult to decide what might be deemed unacceptable when he himself accepted it on a daily basis very well. Was it the specimens? Taxidermy was a great deal less popular than it once had been, but it wasn't unheard of. The gray glops of half-digested paper?

He retrieved a trash bag from the closet and scraped up the more obvious bits.

As an afterthought he grabbed any potentially trypophobic-inducing objects—of which he had quite a few—and hid them. In deference to his late wife he'd never displayed them, but since her passing they'd naturally crept into his furnishings and decoration, along with certain long-standing biological stress relievers. He'd always found a wide variety of hole patterns to be soothing.

The young man stirred, groaned. He would have to wrap things up, but he hated being rushed. No doubt this young man's world was a world of rushing, but Mister Ainsley was physiologically incapable of this trending pace. He went into the kitchen and he grabbed the spray, a gray liquid in a clouded plastic bottle. He misted some into the air around the living room as he moved, finally stopping over the couch and spraying an extra amount there. The young man's freckles looked darker, like tiny insects or flecks of dirt. Mister Ainsley resisted the urge to reach out and touch them. Going back into the kitchen he thought to spritz a copious amount onto his own chest and into his hair before returning the bottle to its hiding place.

"Hello?" The voice sounded both groggy and panicked. He returned to the living room just as his guest was sitting up, shaking his head. "How? How did I get here?"

"You fainted, I'm afraid. Have you eaten today? Or perhaps you're exhausted from the day's labors—when was the last time you slept?"

"I…" The young man's mouth hung open, languid and wet. Mister Ainsley paused a moment and stared.

"In my observation politicians, preachers—notice how the lips come together in those words, as if the mouth wants to push them away—they take advantage of young people. You are their source of free labor. For the cause, they say. Causing irreparable harm, I suspect."

The young man stared at Mister Ainsley as if too exhausted to blink. But the blood was easing back into his face, flushing the paleness from his neck and ears. "I smelled something." He raised his chin, but instead of sniffing the air he awkwardly stuck out his tongue. "Tasted it, too. But I don't *now*. I'm sorry, but it was *awful*, I think. I can't really remember what it was like, but I know it was awful, and then everything was gone."

"So terrible it was for you, you left the world. Is that what you're saying?"

The young man finally blinked. "I'm sorry. I don't want to be rude."

"Of course not. But when something in our environment goes awry, when we're introduced into the alien, a shutdown can sometimes occur. Purely involuntary. I sympathize. I would say you were fortunate. Some might sleep for days after such an encounter. Some might even die."

The poor fellow shook his head in response. "Wait, wait. What are you saying to me? Just please stop, until I catch up. I don't know what's wrong with me, but I just can't quite catch up." He tried to stand, and immediately sat down again.

"Take your time—you've had a bit of a shock," Mister Ainsley said. He genuinely understood how the young man felt. After all, hadn't he been there himself? A fish out of water? Yes—that was the expression, and so he said, "It's the fish out of water phenomenon. As if you might drown in my air. There's no hurry about this. You can leave when it's time, but not before. You mustn't. I can't let you. I … it wouldn't be correct."

"I have a lot of houses to get to today."

"Your campaigning? Yes. I understand that you are quite dedicated to this nonsense. Sorry, I do not intentionally offend. But politics? All this spouting off about things they have no intention of fixing anyway? All this upset about some condition that will have changed in a few years, if not in a few months? Humanity lacks patience—that's your *real* problem."

"It's … it's *important*." The young man looked around. "Like Wilson, for governor. You've heard of him? He'll *restore* things to what they once were. Surely someone like you, you must admire his … his conservatism."

"You believe I am conservative?" Mister Ainsley took a step closer to the couch and the young man drew back, pressing himself into the cushions, looking pale again. "I do not even understand what you people mean by that word. Perhaps,

perhaps, but I assure you I am capable of the most *radical* behavior."

The campaign volunteer struggled for words, eventually making a surprising barking noise. It was a kind of self-defensive gesture, apparently, against Mister Ainsley's approach. The young man opened his mouth and started again. "This house, the way you dress ..." He looked around, and stopped speaking, as if trying to reinterpret what he saw.

Mister Ainsley glanced down at his outfit. Like most days, he was wearing one of his deceased father-in-law's old suits. He'd never met the man, but his wife had kept a closet full of the dead man's clothing. In all likelihood it was an old-fashioned look—perhaps even antique—but Mister Ainsley did not think in those terms. The suits kept him warm, which was better than the alternative. As he had aged he had grown sensitive to the cold, as he had to heat, and to many common household chemicals.

The house was a collection of antiques: wall to wall bookshelves filled with fine old hardbacks, art works from the Victorian era, the occasional small-scale replica of some bit of classical sculpture. All that had been his wife's, accumulated over the decades of her spinsterhood. His contributions were the artifacts, the found objects (from beaches and trash heaps, midnight wanderings through the town) and the specimens— in jars, or mounted on boards using his primitive taxidermy skills, triggers for old memories and forgotten instincts.

The young man had managed to stand, and was desperately gripping the back of an old chair, but at least he wasn't teetering. He was looking at some of the portraits hung up on the wall behind the couch.

"Generations of Ainsleys," he told the lad. "Some of them quite important, I gather. My wife came from an extensive family."

The young man turned, closed his eyes, opened them again. He was frowning. "Your wife's family? Then you ..."

"I took my wife's last name. I know it isn't customary. But we all do what we have to, and sometimes only one option is available."

"I knew a friend, of a friend," the young man said. "He did that, but he was much younger. I think it was a political thing, a statement. But I've never heard of, well, someone from your generation ..."

"My *generation*, yes. The word lacks precision, don't you think? I mean it's all so *relative*. Most of what you see here— anything of measurable value—belonged to my late wife. She had a large collection of books, a few of which I have learned to read, as I have learned to read newspapers, magazines, internet text—although the many visual cues have helped me. My wife taught me a great deal—she once taught children. She was quite good at it, always generous with her time. I have learned a great deal in her house, although now I suppose it is technically my own—but I don't believe it will ever be fully mine."

"She sounds—you know, I really *must* be going—she sounds like a very fine lady."

"Oh, she was. Although underappreciated by your lot, certainly. It used to make me quite angry, in our early days together. I think you people thought she was quite plain, but then you are obsessed with appearances, aren't you? To your own detriment, I'm afraid. You completely misread both the beauty, and the danger."

"I think, I think ..." The young man appeared to be determined, but he was "losing the thread," as people now were prone to say. Mister Ainsley liked the expression, but thought it a shade optimistic. After all, it assumed there was an identifiable thread to be lost. "I'm ready to go. I want to *go* now."

"Oh, but you cannot leave without first seeing the garden. You like gardens, don't you? She was so very proud of it, and I've managed to make some interesting additions of my own."

It took little effort to nudge the young man toward the back of the house and into the kitchen. He could barely stand, which made him no match for Mister Ainsley, even with his aging joints and increasingly confused architecture.

The poor fellow was staring into the sink. Mister Ainsley looked down in dismay—he had forgotten to clean that bit up.

Pieces of an animal's desiccated corpse lay spread across the cast iron surface. Fur and bone and spoiled flesh made a kind of goulash whose original form Mister Ainsley could no longer remember. Worse, teetering on the lip of the sink was a fork with dark pieces of the animal's meat still speared on the tines.

"I do apologize for this," he said. "I tend to be an impulsive eater. I can never predict what might taste good, so dining has become a trial and error affair I'm afraid."

The young fellow's eyes darted. His cheeks appeared polished to a high sheen. The freckles were like a mottled pattern buried under a warm, transparent shellac, providing a bit of tasty texture to the tender skin. Mister Ainsley looked away in embarrassment, and pushed the young man out the back door before he could respond. The setting sun was still bright, but the tall plants tended to filter it.

"It is an impressive sight, if you will forgive the braggadocio. Glorious colors and smells, do you agree? My wife was very proud. I always thought it a tragedy that a woman with such a keen interest in gardening should suffer from congenital anosmia. My poor dear was born with no sense of smell at all. Of course, if she hadn't, I'm not sure our relationship would have been possible, much less last as long as it did."

The young man stared at him, then struggled to turn around, reached for the door. Mister Ainsley batted the hands away, and turned his guest back around. "No, no. None of that. Enjoy the garden, if you will. Drink in the day. Just let me show you what you are missing."

Mister Ainsley proceeded to guide the young man around the garden, nudging him along step by step like a reluctant bride. Many of the plants had broad, enormous leaves, and were far taller than the norm. They had a fleshiness, a substantiality, which he found reassuring. "For years my wife dumped my bath water out here, can you imagine? She was quite ecologically minded—she hated the wastefulness she saw everywhere. Initially I had no interest in the garden—I had little interest in anything, really—but then it began to remind me of all that I had forgotten."

There was a slight rise in the ground near the back fence. Mister Ainsley took his guest to the top of this subtle elevation, and pointed. "You can see the beach from here, most days, and some suggestion of the ocean beyond. That was where she found me, washed up into that debris-embellished sand, barely breathing, my flesh shredded, the trip having worn my memories almost to nothing. She was a small woman, but determined. She dragged me through that field, and up that incline, there. She had a history of collecting things, but I believe I was her greatest prize."

Mister Ainsley continued the tour, although it seemed his guest had lost interest. He pushed him around and around that yard, with each revolution featuring some new thing—something bloomed, something turned to display a new angle, something receded, something shyly brought forward. Eventually they came to that specimen whose extent was now the farthest, and the most spectacular. It was tall and pale and the main portion of its body was shaped like a gigantic rounded star fruit (which supposedly Mister Ainsley had only seen in photographs, but he believed this was not the full truth of it). Its legs were like the cabriole legs on classical Greek and Chinese furniture, serving more like a stand for its body's support, since that wasn't its primary method of locomotion. For it had wings as well, enormous, transparent, fan-shaped combs on several sides, their surfaces wrinkled like cabbage leaves. And the head of this flower—if it could have been described as a flower—were stamen topped with these eye-shaped structures. The slits along its sides were reminiscent of gills, but they were looser, and filled with what appeared to be eggs. Its aroma, its atmosphere, was all inclusive.

"That, that's a *plant*?"

Mister Ainsley turned to the young man in surprise, because he hadn't really expected to ever hear from him again. "I actually don't know. I've always thought of it as a kind of reminder of a life I once had, of a life that perhaps no longer exists."

His guest tried to run, but he obviously suffered from diminished capacity. After a few steps he fell to the ground, and Mister Ainsley bent over him to apologize.

Those freckles proved impossible to resist. It was all genetics, really. Mister Ainsley couldn't help himself—his manners had always been instinctual.

THE LONG FADE INTO EVENING

Simon had nowhere to live until his cousin offered him a house in a run-down development on the outer edge of town. All he had to do was stay there to discourage vandalism. The development was almost empty, scheduled to be torn down.

"You're not suicidal are you?" Will asked as he handed him the key.

"Angela left me years ago. I haven't been successful in years. Why would I kill myself *now*?"

Will, pretending to shuffle papers, didn't look up. "I know it's been rough, and you're not getting any younger. It's just that a few of the families that are left have kids, teenagers. I'd hate for them to find …"

"Old fellows like me, we don't have the energy to kill ourselves. We usually just fade away."

Will stared at him. "I see. Do you need directions?"

"I lived in the neighborhood when I was a kid, in one of those old Victorians before they built this awful thing. Now here it's a wreck as well."

"I've read about that. There was some trouble wasn't there? Overcrowding, and some violence? Something about a fire?"

"What didn't burn they bulldozed. Everybody scattered, went their ways. Now here I am with nowhere else to go."

"I've arranged for someone to drop off a sleeping bag and supplies. I'm working on a bed."

"I'm deeply grateful," Simon replied. And he was. He'd just never understood who decided what goes, what stays, and where people got to live.

"By the way, we've had a problem with cats. Feral cats, running all over the place. Best not let one of them scratch you."

Simon examined the keys as if reconsidering. "I hate cats," he said.

On moving day he rushed to finish his final shift at the corner store and get his belongings—everything stuffed into a cardboard suitcase and a patched laundry bag—from behind the counter to the bus stop. Most of the shelves were empty. As ordered, he kept rearranging what remained from the "Going out of Business" sale for more appeal, while restlessly waiting for his replacement to arrive. Julie, always out on a date with no consideration for anyone. By now he'd lost everything of importance, but at least Simon held on to his manners.

A pack of twittering girls burst through the door and raced each other for the drink machine. He used to tell the teens to slow down but the way even the young ones would turn on you these days he no longer dared. Further evidence of how the new world was eating the old. "The girls are worse than the boys," someone he worked with once said. The sexism embarrassed him, but he worried it might be true. All he needed was a broken arm, or a deep scratch from a dirty fingernail.

He watched as they poked their phones, took pictures, and mixed different sodas at random into a single cup. Apparently they would share. They all appeared to have too many fingers, different colors on too many nails. The new world was raising them strange. Perhaps if he had a child of his own...but Angela always feared he would drop or lose it.

One caught him staring and flashed her tiny tit. The others screamed madly. He blushed and turned away, looking down at his things. He prayed the gigglers would be gone before he tried to haul it all to the bus stop. He hated when he had to pretend to ignore their catcalls.

His possibly future caretakers ran out the door without paying. He was relieved not to have to ring them up. Julie came in after, smiling knowingly and smelling of booze. Simon gathered up his life and stumbled for the door.

The bus contained a few more broken types like him, an older woman in a nice dress, and a figure bundled in its oversized coat. Its head, wrapped in a scarf and topped with a watchman's cap, appeared too small for its torso. Its eyes were buried. The bus sped down the block passing the girls with their surplus of fingers, their writhing clump of shadow hungry and hideous on the greasy brick wall.

The bus struggled up the hill past bars spilling their last patrons, who hailed and cursed the driver who was too wise to stop. At the peak where the lanes grew wider he sped past abandoned storefronts, lots jammed with ancient equipment, the iron skeletons of dead buildings, the rows of silent warehouses with rusted doors flush to the road. There was the rare bus stop, the random passenger standing with one arm waving, but the driver never slowed. Simon believed this part of the city need never exist.

The route would not take Simon all the way to the development. The bus dropped him at a darkened stop to stand beside a crumbling, heavily-graffitied bench. Some words were almost recognizable, but lay obscured beneath mindless exhortation. The ground rose steeply before him, and somewhere beyond that rise of shadow the aging development began. Smoky grayness drifted down from the low clouds and seeped out from the overgrown embankment. The hill's silhouette was deceptive, suggesting primeval forest more than cultivated landscape.

Instead of taking the road around, he pulled the flashlight from his laundry bag and sought a shorter path. He followed a trail of broken, grass-invaded sidewalk through the unkempt greenbelt and up the hill. He had to struggle through tall-weeded fields, ignoring unidentifiable animal sounds in the underbrush, the occasional glimmer of a red or yellow eye. Man-shaped spaces opened up in the dark vegetation a few feet away, but no one approached. He tried to remember what, if any, of these features had been here when he was a boy. It had been wilderness then, too, although even less controlled. He and his friends would venture there after sunset. He vaguely remembered the darkness, and the dreadful confusion of echo, but nothing else.

He was nerve-exhausted by the time he entered the murky blocks of identical one-story ranch houses and sodden lanes of the development. The neighborhood of his youth had been a crowded slum but at least it had some grandeur in its height and architecture. A sea of bright holes identifying downtown shimmered in the distance behind him. Ahead were the squat rectangles of unlit homes, and houses with few lights on, and houses half-gone into ruin, a handful of dried-up gardens and trashed-out back yards, their wire fences plastered in random trash.

In an abandoned playground a shattered teeter-totter sprawled like a sacrifice across its steel pipe center. The swing framework still stood erect but rusted, its seats and slide gone without a trace. So where did the remaining children play, or were they too old for something so innocent? One was crying now, he thought, although it might have been one of those stray cats.

Simon had no way to determine which houses were actually empty, and which were occupied by people who just wanted to keep to themselves. Without knocking on doors, perhaps peeking through windows, which he wasn't about to do.

In the old days, in that other neighborhood of taller and less uniform homes, he heard a great many things: the voices of friends he hadn't seen in decades, music playing from a record player in a neighbor's upstairs window, misunderstood whispers from lovers hiding themselves in the shadowed strips near walls. All of that had been torn down and bulldozed, the old neighborhood beheaded. It occurred to Simon he now had more memories than life. It was an uncomfortable way to travel.

Several houses had yellow police tape stretched across their front doors and around their near-identical porches. He assumed the police actions had something to do with drugs; in the news it always had something to do with drugs. That and gang activity. A lot of these poorer teens fell into gangs.

When Simon was young a bike ride to and from this neighborhood had been nothing. He'd fly down the steep curl of road and although the trip back up was a challenge he accomplished it without too much difficulty, feeling like a star athlete afterwards. Not anymore. He should have kept in better shape. Once here, he didn't expect to leave often. He supposed that was how older people became trapped.

He found the house Will was providing—low and dark and indistinguishable from the others. The newish lock looked inexpertly installed, the hasp mounted crookedly, and rattled as he fiddled with the key. Simon slipped inside and slapped the switch, lighting up the messy interior. He gasped involuntarily from the stench: human waste and aromas both sweet and sour underneath. He reminded himself that his cousin was allowing him to stay here for nothing.

Houses weren't built to last anymore, nor did it make sense to. Technological expectation changed so quickly it didn't pay to invest in building for the long term. People moved on, although not necessarily up.

When he first glimpsed the living room walls he imagined a crowd of onlookers, but the arrangement of shadows proved to be stains. Studs and nail head patterns were clearly visible beneath the thin paper.

Cleansers and chemicals and various old tools were stored in a closet with random junk. He couldn't tell how old any of it was, or how dangerous, but he did what he could, sweeping the foulness out the back door and dumping chemicals on the hardwood floors where they'd been deeply stained, windows open to the cold air to get rid of the smell. He just needed to get his situation clean enough so that he wouldn't mind sleeping on the floor. The revealed boards were scarred as if from games or ritual. Or maybe from cats. Cats can do a lot of damage if locked inside by themselves.

On several walls sprays of relatively fresh graffiti obscured older layers of scribbling, and here and there certain words and symbols were emphasized by means of deep cuts. He could make no sense of it, although the patterns of marks created an emotional effect not unlike music, so he wondered if some of these marks referred to songs. Over the days to come he painted over the graffiti, but with no confidence it wouldn't return.

Long threads of dust floated through the rooms. The remnants of his old life were hardly more substantial than these. With most of the people he'd ever known gone, the fabric of day to day reality seemed thin.

That old house where he'd grown up had probably been

less than a hundred yards from here. It had a screened back porch where on late nights the adults filled their drink cups and the children consumed their allotted portions of sugar and ran mindlessly around the yard. This house and the ones around it had no back porch and he wondered when those had gone out of fashion. No doubt around the same time as gatherings with the neighbors.

He remembered games of hide and seek that lasted for hours and covered every lot in the neighborhood. He remembered childhood crushes on young girls whose names he no longer remembered. He remembered he would not take a bath when a certain babysitter was on duty, the one who always wanted to help.

In one corner of the living room a sleeping bag, some toiletries, and food had been left for him. When he thought he'd cleaned sufficiently for a relatively untroubled night's sleep he crawled into the bag and succumbed almost immediately.

The morning came quickly. He had dreamed and sweated, and now the sleeping bag stank. He wondered who might have used it before. He crawled out and walked barefoot into the kitchen, splashed his face with water tinged a muddy rust color. He'd let it run until it cleared. He went to the back door and opened it for air and sun.

He was surprised not to see the sun, or even the sky. A few feet in front of him a tall brick wall with curtained casement windows blocked his view, awash in smoky gray shadow, part of a larger house that rose three stories. Looking straight up he glimpsed the old-fashioned soffits and Victorian roof. It looked somewhat like the house he'd grown up in, except larger. Turning his head he saw similar large houses out to both sides, an entire neighborhood of slummy Victorians in ill repair. He could also hear creaky music, children's voices, a cat's howl, the soft explosive echo of a distant barking dog. But he couldn't make out any of the finer details of his surroundings, not even this close.

Simon went to get his flashlight for a more detailed look. But when he came back there was the sky, and the sun just over the treetops illuminating a vista of dull one-story homes. The filth he'd scraped from the house the night before still lay piled around the bottom step. Sometime during the day he would have to bury it.

He took a breath. He hadn't been fully awake. It happened sometimes, even several minutes after walking around, a piece of dream still lodged in your brain changes the world. There were the sounds of children squealing like the damned in a nearby yard, but was that still part of the dream? The excited screams of children at play often fooled you into thinking there had been some grave tragedy.

Simon worked several hours in the bathroom and kitchen—scrubbing and throwing out the useless and the unsalvageable—not bad for an out of shape old man, he thought. He felt uncomfortably heated and propped open the back door. The outside temperature had dropped precipitously. He'd tried the thermostat but the furnace wouldn't come on. Another problem to ask Will about. Whatever sounds he heard—the whistle of a speeding car, the broken explosions as a plane pushed through the air overhead—were very far away. Whoever lived nearby was impressively quiet. "Safe as houses," as his mother used to say, but it never reassured. Some houses weren't safe at all.

Cooking smells drifted in from outside—some sort of richly spiced meat, perhaps a stew. Someone in the neighborhood knew how to cook.

He thought he heard a school bus pull up and children piling out, but the sounds faded quickly, swallowed by the increasing rush and push of the wind. It would be a breezy time for a walk, but he'd only have light for a couple more hours, and Simon wanted to see the neighborhood and some of its residents in the light of day.

The wind hitting the house made a constant groan. Simon wondered if the poorly-built structure could bear it—he imagined minute fracturing exacerbating decay, perhaps even some sort of collapse. A sick apprehension heightened his need to get out.

Outside in his coat he walked toward the broken playground. He kept his eyes open for people, but after a few blocks there was nothing, not even any toys left outside or laundry on a line.

He listened carefully for conversation or music—he was sure he'd heard some before—but all he heard now was the wind battering the shoddy roofs, and a whistling down the lanes between the structures.

There should have been teenagers out, even if the adults had the sense to stay inside. Teenagers were the adventurers and the hasty ones, those always said to be "at risk."

A sudden clamor from several houses over made him pick up the pace. But it was just a piece of roof blown off into a side yard. He wondered if his own roof was sound. He stared hard at the twisted bit of wreckage, the curly shadows trapped beneath. Then a mass of the curly shadows unfurled and escaped around the edge of the house on its too many legs. A cat with insulation tangled into its fur, he presumed, living in the house's attic. Poor thing. That's when it started to rain.

He liked the smell, like damp earth everywhere, moist dirt in the air he breathed, like a memory of his future, as if the rain had released something from the dirt of the aging neighborhood. The air grayed around him, fading everything it touched. Or was it his eyes failing? He hadn't been to an optometrist in years, afraid of what he might be told. Complete failure took a long time to occur, it seemed, but the process was relentless.

The rain was light, so he continued walking for several blocks around the complex. He saw no one, no signs that children had recently played, no signs that any of these houses were occupied at all. There were lights on in a few, but with the lack of residents he guessed they might simply be on for security. And yet he couldn't believe his cousin had lied to him—what would be the point?

"Hello! I say hello! Is anyone else here?" His voice bounced and echoed against the brick.

As if in reply a distant truck horn sounded like a large animal in distress. Simon was reminded that you couldn't always trust your senses to tell you the truth. He turned the corner and walked in a different direction, hoping for a new perspective. He peered over fences and gleaned a few new details—mud-encrusted junk, old foundations exposed between patches of unmown grass, an abandoned barbecue lying on its side like a felled animal. But nothing recent, nothing indicating current occupation.

He became gradually aware of the faint stench of invisible smoke, like the memory of an old barbecue, or when his grandmother used to lie about her smoking habit and snuck off behind the house for a drag or two before the cancer eventually took her.

He came to a wide circle in the lane with a bent and dead streetlight poised over it like some kind of giant predatory insect. When he was a boy the neighborhood kids used to gather beneath the streetlights and ride their bikes at night. He stooped down—there were warm cigarette butts beneath the crippled lamp post. He looked around, saw nothing, and the charcoal sky split open from the weight of water, beating him momentarily to the ground.

He looked up, saw the dark twisted shapes lingering nearby like a collection of corroded statues, their rude fingers pointing as they plotted their harassment. All around him the blurred outlines of the houses had added a story or two, with high roofs swaying precariously overhead. Cats encased in their wet and wiry fur took swipes at his face. Simon ran to find shelter, pushing himself against a greasy brick wall. He thought he recognized the house—someone's aunt had lived there when he was a child. But that was impossible. He looked up to find the window where she used to watch for her husband, and found slanted yellowed eyes staring at him through the rain—he thought maybe some feline's eyes, or child's. The pale face that suddenly appeared around the eyes was much like a skinny child's face, surrounded by a matted cloud of ashen hair. But he was greatly fatigued, and this was the only face he'd seen in a couple of days, and he found it increasingly difficult to see in this dimness. *This is what getting old is like*, he thought. *A long fade into evening.*

The rain began to ease and so Simon headed toward home. With each step the force of the rain lessened and the clouds of moisture dissipated, and no house was over a story again, the houses beaten down, until he reached his own house where everything was remarkably dry. Something escaped out of his back yard—a tangle of broken or too-many-segmented legs. A truck was parked out front and two squat men were unloading the bed his cousin promised.

There was a leak in the kitchen faucet, the water oozing like syrup. It had begun raining again, beating against the house like a thousand tiny fists. The house appeared to resent the abuse and issued some grumbling complaints of its own.

At least the bed made Simon feel more civilized. It wasn't particularly comfortable, though better than a sleeping bag on the floor. But now he could imagine uninvited guests hiding beneath. He wasn't a child anymore, of course, but he was feeling very little like an adult. He tried to sleep but could hear tiny tappings on the house's most distant windows, water still dripping from the rain or maybe the trapped beating of moths against the glass. Eventually succumbing, he dreamed of a small riot he'd witnessed as a child—teenagers throwing bricks, someone's mother screaming, faces washed in blood. The young sometimes simply couldn't take it anymore and had to strike out because of conditions. But sometimes when you were old you were too wrapped up in your memories to move as fast as you should—you got hurt lying in the way.

The next morning he found long strands of, presumably, animal hair coiled in the corners of the room and lying across his blanket. But he had been cleaning aggressively and couldn't imagine where these coarse strands had been hiding. As the sun rose the movement of shadow inside the house became unceasing: trees bending outside the windows, the travel of clouds across dark patches of sky, and the nearby houses rising up hazily and swaying in the wind.

He crawled from out of the covers and staggered to the back door in trepidation, but there were no big houses in the back yard today. By the fence a cluster of weeds and something else unrepentantly tangled. He looked for eyes but could find none.

He thought he heard children playing in some remote yard, bossy and excited and dramatic and now and then hurt and crying over nothing and everything. But this might have been a memory. He didn't bother to look around. He suspected he wouldn't find anything.

Gazing up at the overhead electrical lines that travelled over the back yard Simon observed their poor state of repair. Tiny bits of black insulation lay scattered like dead bugs all over the grass.

He took another stab that morning at cleaning. It shouldn't have been necessary, but dust seemed to come out of nowhere to spoil the rooms. The floorboards weren't tightly fitted—dust from the crawlspace underneath seeped through. Dust also came down from the ceiling, from the flaws at the corners and the holes where plants once hung. It came back as fast as he wiped it away. Dust also issued from the loosefitting windows and from under the front door. Many of the yards in the development had gone back to bare ground and now the wind was redistributing them.

He stayed away from the windows, not even wanting to look. Sometimes outside there were old house façades that shouldn't have been there, and slanting shadows from tall houses torn down decades ago. He could see the way the light shifted inside as the outside world impossibly changed—and if he were to look out he'd have to doubt his own sanity.

He still had seen no teenagers, no children of any kind, but he heard their feet scuffling outside, and the ragged sounds of their breath as they ran away. Where were their parents? Where were anyone's parents? No doubt hiding beneath their beds. At least the cats he'd seen had left him alone.

As if in answer his own bed creaked and something shifted in the light, but Simon refused to turn around. If he just kept his mind on cleaning he would be fine.

Early that afternoon the clouds lifted and light glared across the bedroom ceiling. He witnessed the vague lines in one corner of the heavily textured surface, the slightly depressed outline of a trapdoor into the attic.

It made sense, of course. Each of these houses would have some sort of attic. He could see a fuzz of lines along one side of this small hatch—cobwebs or insect legs or simply an accumulated string of dust hanging down. Perhaps if he removed some of the attic dust he wouldn't have such a dust problem below. And besides, there might be things put away up there and forgotten, treasures no one remembered.

He had no ladder, but he could slide the bed into the corner. From there it was a simple matter of standing and pushing the panel up and to the side, and then the strenuous but doable labor of leveraging himself up into the darkness.

He saw no treasure, but copious amounts of dust. Much of it had accumulated into furry mounds in the corners. He caught a glimpse of daylight, and shifting himself for a better view saw that a corner of the attic had been damaged, rotted out all the way to the outside air, ragged as if chewed.

Long, coarse hairs from the mounds glistened, moved. Then one of them shuddered, and a ragged gap in the middle opened wide.

Simon dropped back onto the bed, hastily fitting the panel back into place. Over the next hour he rummaged through the junk in the closet, finding a few strips of metal he could screw into the panel's edges and secure it to the ceiling. He slid his bed back into the middle of the room and lay there watching the fastened ceiling panel. At one point the metal strips might have wiggled, but that might have been his eyes and nerves fraying from staring too long. Outside the teens ran around the house— he could imagine bands of them looking for trouble, or was it the pets they'd left behind? He was too old and too nervous for this. Tomorrow he would hike out of here and visit his cousin. *Thank you and sorry and thanks but no thanks.* He wasn't sure if he'd tell him what he'd seen and heard. Old men had been locked away for less. He fell asleep pondering if there was anywhere else to go, and dreamed of being dragged screaming from his bed.

But he woke up still in his temporary house and on his temporary bed. The ceiling panel remained safely in place. What was different was the redness of the room, as if Simon were seeing it through a veil of blood. He shook his head and rubbed his eyes. The intense redness still permeated, brighter near the window. He slid off the bed and fumbled the curtains aside.

A glorious scarlet sunset had swallowed the world and retrieved the tall old grandfather and grandmother houses from his childhood. The residents were outside shouting their enthusiasm as they walked toward the center of the development where the air was brightest, as if the sun were descending at that moment into their neighborhood. He could see little more than their rapt and shiny faces, the rest looking thin and dark as lamp black. His eyesight was clearly fading. He knew he would see nothing of the new world now.

He wasn't sure what to do but couldn't bear the thought of remaining in this cramped little hovel with all that human activity going on outside. Why had they hid themselves away from him? One glimpse from their hiding places should have told them he had neither the inclination nor the ability to do them any harm. And with those things in the attic he felt safer outside. He jerked open the door and hurried out, determined to get a good look and become a part of whatever was to come.

A few of the neighboring ranch homes appeared unchanged, but as Simon followed the stragglers toward their brilliant destination he saw that the remainder had gradually warped into two stories or three or four, the walls stretched vertically thin to transparency, as if they were decaying upwards into these phantom rectangles with deteriorated regions allowing the night sky to show through. In some places a bright oblong of window appeared to float high in the air with a shouting person inside, with no discernible supporting structure around it.

He turned to the rioter next to him to share his amazement—it was an old man gone to crumbling cinders from his ribcage down.

Turning the corner he came face to face with the blackened crisp remains of youth gangs, shouting and punching those around them even as they had fingers and limbs flaking off. At the block's center a hollow building displayed a boiling fire inside, dozens of those furry bodies exploding out from its blazing core like flaming cannonballs fashioned of fur.

They had their dirty, dirty hands all over him, their sooty clothes reeking of smoke and booze and the stench of newfangled habits. He tried to reason with them but discovered he no longer spoke their language. There was nothing he could do, it seemed, and when they dragged him into the flames he found he no longer wished to resist.

DOMESTIC MAGIC

(CO-WRITTEN WITH MELANIE TEM)

Felix didn't hate his mother, but got so mad at her so often she probably thought he did. Sometimes his anger scared him, that she might be right when she said thoughts could make things happen.

That was what made him so mad—that she said and believed ridiculous stuff and she almost got him believing it, too. And she didn't take care of Margaret right. Why'd they have to get a mother like her?

He'd skipped school again today to run errands with her. She'd never ask him to miss school, she was worried he'd get behind like she had when she was a kid. But she just let him do it. What kind of mother let her son skip school? Wasn't that against the law? What kind of mother made her son worry about her so much he didn't want her leaving the house without him? At his age you were supposed to be thinking about friends and music and video games and sex, not whether your mother was capable of crossing the street by herself or taking care of your little sister. He was almost grown now; it was too late for him. But Margaret was little.

He couldn't remember his Mom ever saying no. He was the good kid, which was kind of sickening but it was easier than doing stuff that made his mother cry and chant and cook weird stuff in the Crockpot that stank up whatever crappy apartment or homeless shelter they were living in at the moment.

Margaret was not a good kid. Felix tried to tell her what to do because somebody had to, but she just ignored him or laughed or threw a fit. When she was a baby she'd cried all the time because her world wasn't perfect, and Mom had fussed and worried and chanted and rubbed goop on her chest and the soles of her feet.

When Margaret had started crawling and toddling she got into everything, Mom's stuff and Felix's stuff, dangerous stuff and stuff you didn't want ruined. One time because of a hunch he looked into the dirty playroom of the shelter and she was coloring in his school books, copying one of Mom's so-called secret designs over and over again in the margins, crossing out words and underlining other ones, and he had to pay for the books. Another time when they lived in a studio apartment he had a feeling and found her on a chair reaching into a cabinet and dipping into Mom's jars of herbs and tinctures and sticking her fingers into her mouth, and he grabbed her and yelled at her and she threw up all over everything.

Mom would explain why she shouldn't do whatever she'd just done, and Margaret listened and then did the same thing again or worse because now she had more information. Felix yelled at her but it didn't make any difference. The minute she'd started talking she'd been whining, sassing, lying, chanting, telling you her dreams whether you wanted to hear about them or not which he didn't.

So he had a crazy mother and a bratty sister who was probably crazy, too. It was like living with aliens. Everywhere else Felix felt like the alien, but he was the most normal one in this family, which was scary.

Mom patted his shoulder and said in order for powers to be most efficacious we have to meet people where they are and not wish they were somebody else. What about somebody meeting *him* where he was for a change? The only thing Felix ever got from his mother's advice was knowing what words like 'efficacious' meant in case they showed up on some standardized test.

Practically the minute Margaret could run she'd started running away. Not like she was going somewhere; more like she was just *going*. Mom would chant and throw cards and do divinations until she thought she knew where Margaret was. Then she'd send Felix to get her. Felix got mad when she was wrong because she'd wasted his time. He got mad when she was right because Margaret was such a pain and Mom wouldn't punish her. She said it was Margaret's nature and the rest of the world, including him, would just have to get used to it. Well, what about *his* 'nature'?

Wasn't that child neglect? Was there somebody Felix could report it to without having to tell everything else about his nutso family? Like that Mom really was a witch? She preferred 'seer' or 'person of powers,' so he made a point of thinking 'witch' in case she could maybe read his mind.

So far today there'd been no calls or texts from the school that Margaret had escaped. So here Felix was with his mother in a thrift store doing his best to act as if he'd never seen this crazy lady before. Being anywhere in public with her sucked. The older she got the weirder she became, and if anything bad happened to her he'd be stuck with Margaret by himself.

She talked to junk. Out loud. Who does that? Now she was holding up some old jar thing and speaking to it. "What have you held inside you? If I put some quarters for the laundromat into you, will you help me make them multiply?"

Great. Felix had been saving quarters for a couple of weeks so he could wash his and Margaret's clothes. He almost had enough. Maybe the jar would cough up a couple more. If they walked around much longer in dirty clothes somebody would surely call Social Services. Maybe that would be a good thing. Maybe not.

When the tone of Mom's voice told him she was about to start chanting, he walked over to the other end of the store and pretended to be looking at men's shoes. He needed shoes. So did Margaret. But who knew where this stuff had been, who'd touched it, what they'd used it for? Felix didn't believe in evil spirits but he did believe in germs. Donated clothes like from churches and clothing banks were safer but still embarrassing.

His mother bought the jar for herself—for the family, she'd say—and a long curved knife for Margaret. A knife for an eight-year-old? One more thing he'd have to get rid of, preferably before Margaret saw it and thought it was cool. Nothing for him. He didn't want anything, but it was another reason to be mad, along with the fact that she'd wasted $2.78 they didn't have.

Sometimes people paid Mom for tomatoes or rhubarb, spells or potions or readings, and she got food stamps and checks from the government, but it still seemed there was never enough money for good food. Nobody should live like this, especially a kid like Margaret who didn't have a choice. But Felix was almost old enough to have a choice.

Next stop was an organic grocery where everything cost a fortune. Mom had been sick a lot lately, and she said it was because she had to wait for money to come in before she could buy what she needed. But obviously it was the crap she ate from places like this and from her garden and the woods and streets. He wasn't going to put any more of that crap into his body no matter how Mom tried to hide it in orange juice or disguise it as real food. Give him burgers and fries any day. "The government removes essential nutrients from our food," she told him cheerily for like the thousandth time as they went into the store. "Who knows what they replace them with?"

It was one thing to practice voodoo medicine and hoo-hoo eating on yourself. But not getting real food or health care for your kids made it other people's business. What would've happened if he'd told the school counselor that time Margaret had a fever for days that made her blue eyes shine like wet lilacs and Mom had refused to take her to the ER but she'd made her dolls dance?

When Felix came home from school that day every doll in Margaret's room, every figurine, every picture of a human or beast, even stuff that only vaguely looked like it had a head and legs was gyrating, hopping, waving, dancing. Margaret was laughing, and then she was out of bed and trying to make them dance the old-fashioned kids' way, moving them with her hands and pretending. She got frustrated and Mom wouldn't do it again because she said it wasn't right to be frivolous with your powers, and Margaret threw a fit. To shut her up, and because he was happy she wasn't sick any more, Felix played puppets with her and showed her how to put life into them or pull it out of them or whatever. The puppets had tugged at his hand and Margaret's hand, and she'd hugged him and said he was the best big brother in the world and he had to teach her how to do that, and he did his best but she never did learn.

So maybe Mom had cured her, but maybe Mom had made her sick in the first place. Felix never got around to telling the school counselor and pretty soon they'd moved anyway.

Margaret had the only clean, relatively nice room in their new house. Every other space, including half of his basement man-cave, was full of the witch's projects. Her clay sculptures and things that looked like body parts floating in colored liquids had mingled with and seeped into his ships in bottles and crushed leaves and sketches of things he knew about but couldn't name yet, couldn't quite make move, and everything got ruined. He'd given up having projects after that.

Seeing her plop another grape into her mouth, he whispered, "Mom!" She raised her eyebrows. The produce guy was heading their way (again) to tell her to quit shoplifting. What kind of role model was this for Margaret? Felix hurried around the corner and pretended to be interested in free-range eggs. More than once Mom had explained to him what 'free-range' meant, but he refused to remember it and picturing the top of a stove full of brown eggs running around free like hamsters out of their cages made him laugh.

Mom chatted away at the bored checkout clerk. Felix just wanted to get out of there before she did something else embarrassing, and he almost made it. He had picked up the grocery bags—why was it his job to carry the bags?—when Mom reached over, stroked the bananas, and sang out, "Thank you, my little curved friends, for letting us eat you." The clerk stared at her, then stared at Felix, the poor kid with the crazy mother. Maybe somebody would call the authorities. Could you lose your kids for talking to bananas?

Mom wouldn't quit until she'd checked out at least one used bookstore. Felix wanted to tell her to carry her own damn groceries, but her back or shoulder or arm was giving her trouble. He thought about leaving her there and going to what they were calling home this week in order to be there when Margaret got out of school. Wasn't it illegal to leave a little kid alone? But when he compared who was more likely to get into trouble on her own, Mom or Margaret, Mom won by a landslide.

He thought about pulling a Margaret and walking away as far away as he could get.

But he'd never do any of that because he was a wimp and a mama's boy and her enabler, and somebody had to watch out for Margaret, which made him mad at both of them. Too bad he couldn't just think Margaret into a safer place. Mom could probably do that, so why didn't she? Personally, Felix didn't have any magic.

Mom and the bookstore guy said hi to each other like they were buds, except that Felix heard the OMG! in his voice. She got out her list, longer every time because nobody could ever find any of the books she wanted. The bookstore guy tried, or pretended to try, until a couple of actual customers came in. Then Mom wandered around. With the bags Felix couldn't fit between the shelves unless he turned sideways. The plastic handles dug into his hands. There were chairs but they all had books on them, and even though the bookstore people always said it was okay to move the books if you wanted to sit down, Felix couldn't bring himself to do that, and it would be embarrassing to sit on the floor. He leaned against the end of a bookcase, willing it not to roll, and tried to think about things other than his mother or his sister.

She'd be here for a while, looking up weirdness like the fourteenth word on the sixty-seventh page in twenty-one different books. She'd write those words down in a tattered notebook and study them for weeks. She never bought anything—on her way out she'd grab some random book out of the freebie bin. When he edged around the towering books crowding the apartment he'd pretend to cast a protective spell so they wouldn't collapse on Margaret, but it was just making fun of Mom. Every time they moved there were more boxes of books to carry, except you couldn't bring extraneous stuff like that to a shelter, which was the only good thing about being homeless.

Feeling like a homeless person again with all the crap he was carrying, Felix almost wished for a grocery cart. The thrift store bag had the name of the store in enormous letters so there was no way to disguise where they'd been shopping, and the jar was heavy against his leg and who knew what would be released or destroyed or pissed off if he dropped it and it broke. Naturally the natural-foods store wouldn't use plastic so he had to deal with a flimsy cloth bag, and something in it smelled weird. The not one but three books Mom had grabbed out of the free bin without even looking had slick dust jackets and kept sliding out of his grip. He couldn't reach his phone to see what time it was, which at least meant he didn't have to deal with Mom's dumb comments about how cell phones introduced foreign energy into your brain.

"You about done?" he asked her. "Margaret will be home soon."

But she was communing with the spirit of a piece of trash out of the gutter. Felix didn't want to know what it was or what she thought she was doing, but as she gently deposited it into the bookstore bag he couldn't help hearing its voice and seeing that it was a piece of broken pink plastic with sharp edges that would probably tear the plastic so everything would fall out and he'd be the one who had to retrieve it all and figure out how to carry it. "What is that?"

"That's Tinkerbelle. A piece of Tinkerbelle. You know how your sister loves Tinkerbelle."

He had no clue what Tinkerbelle was or if his sister loved it. "What's it for?"

Mom smiled. "I don't know yet. But it told me it could help us."

"Right." He didn't sound half as sarcastic as he wanted to. She reached up and actually patted his head. He hated when she did that. She was the one who didn't understand the world and had to be taken care of and have things explained to her but wouldn't listen. He might be the kid, but he was the grown-up around here. "If you have a talent you should use it," she told him, like he hadn't heard that a million times. Like she was talking about a good pitching arm or being able to fix cars. "Sometimes there's just a thin line between survival and disaster. Sometimes it's so thin you can't even see it. Remember that, son. My abilities help this family stay afloat."

"Terrific, Mom. That's really nice. Can we go? Margaret will be home and I gotta take a leak." The second part was very true. He hoped the first part was.

If he started off first there was a good chance she'd get distracted and stop following him and he'd have to go looking for her and Margaret would either be at home alone or not at home and wandering around somewhere by herself. Finally they were heading more or less toward the apartment. Felix sometimes worried that Margaret would forget where they lived today, or that he would. Mom seemed at home everywhere, which was really annoying and kind of creepy.

He was tired of walking but most of the time they couldn't afford bus fare and he couldn't get a job to buy himself a car because he had to watch out for his sister and his mother. When he complained Mom just twirled her fingers at him and said walking was good for your mind and your soul. She had her arms stretched out and her head thrown back, singing high and loud, and people on the sidewalk were detouring around her, even the homeless people. She actually squatted by one of them and invited him to sing with her, and he swore at her and walked off. Too crazy for the crazies. Felix trudged along, lugging her bags of junk and worrying about Margaret and hating it that he had to lug and worry.

They could be wearing decent clothes, eating good food, living in a nice house—still living in that house where he'd actually had a little space of his own. But no. She'd rather shop in thrift stores and wear smelly old clothes and eat obnoxious things and mumble under her breath. "Why can't we have a better life?" he'd say.

"It's a resource," she'd say. "Like clean water. You have to be careful or you might use it up."

"Why do you let people think you're crazy? Just *show* them what you can do—it'll shut them up!" Never mind that she *was* crazy.

"It's an art, that means it's personal, and nothing you can really explain. You don't know why it works, it just works. And what may work for me, may not work for you. That's what people don't understand. They try it out, it doesn't work for them, and they stop believing."

"Why do we have to live this way?"

"It's all about luck. You try to line everything up proper, and the luck runs your way. But when it runs your way, you got to remember that means it runs against somebody else. So you have to be careful. You have to be responsible. You don't want to hurt people, but sometimes you have to just to survive, just to make do for you and yours. And sometimes maybe you let go of the luck so that it'll work for somebody else, because that's the right thing to do. You'll figure it out, Felix. I have faith in you." Just what he needed.

Could you go to the media with a story about a mother who was a witch and had special powers but wouldn't use them for the betterment of her children? Devising what he'd say and quietly rehearsing the interviews he'd give to the press occupied his mind so he could tolerate the rest of the walk back to the apartment.

Where Margaret was not.

Felix knew she wasn't there before Mom opened the door. Something about the energy. He didn't like noticing energy. He also knew Margaret was in danger. He didn't know how he knew that. Maybe he was wrong. Maybe he was just imagining the worst, and that would not make it happen. He wasn't the witch of the family.

Just as he dropped the bags onto the already-full couch, the handle of the health-food bag broke. It wasn't his job to chase after the bottles that rolled across the floor. Mom talked to them as she gathered them up. She didn't seem worried about Margaret. She seemed kind of excited or something. He didn't have time right now to try to figure her out.

On Margaret's bed in the corner, her lunch bag was open on top of homework papers. So she'd been home after school. She hadn't been doing her homework, though. Toys were out of the trash bag she kept them in. Crayons and colored pencils were scattered around, and papers with drawings on them of her stuffed animals and dolls with legs going this way and that, kicking at the big empty spaces on the page.

"She didn't eat her sandwich." Mom was digging through the bag.

He took the neatly-wrapped sandwich away from her. "Mom, she *never* eats her sandwich. And nobody will trade with her. She throws it away at school or on the way home. Maybe today she was—distracted." Maybe she was kidnapped. Maybe she was—

"Why not?"

He unwrapped it, took it apart, spread the halves like a biology lab dissection. "Look at this—broccoli, grapefruit slices, and what's this paste made out of—honey and hummus? And I used to think this was bean sprouts, but it's that weed from the backyard, right? Gray bread, like chunks of paper mâché. Who eats like this, Mom?" He thought about keeping it for evidence.

"It's full of essential nutrients! What has she been eating, then?"

"I give her money. From little jobs I get. And sometimes I just take it from your purse."

"Stealing is bad karma." She was looking at the floor.

"Like you never steal. And starving your kid—I bet that's bad juju too." He'd heard that word in an old Tarzan movie on TV and had just been waiting to use it on her. "She's gone, Mom. We've gotta go find her."

She didn't try to pretend Margaret might be at a friend's. Margaret didn't have any friends, because she didn't want anybody coming here. Felix had been the same way, so by now he didn't know how to make friends. Once Margaret was back safe, he might just point that out to Mom.

Mom said suddenly, "You look around the room, think about where she might have wandered to. You're smart, you'll figure it out before I can. I'm going out to get a tattoo."

Felix stared at her. "Mom. Margaret's gone *missing*."

"And we'll find her."

When she rolled up her left sleeve Felix realized it had been years since he'd seen her bare arms. It was covered by a series of mostly geometric tattoos, some maybe professional and a lot of them obviously amateur—it wouldn't surprise him if she'd done it herself with a sewing needle dipped in plant-based ink. Gross.

"Look." He didn't want to, but he looked. There was a tattoo of a sailing ship. "Look," and there was a fairy with a wand. "I've been tattooing pieces of your and your sister's lives, your passions, your dreams, maybe a lot of things you aren't even aware of, onto my body since before you were born. It's my map to my children. Once I add her disappearance, I'll know right where she is."

He found himself focusing on her tattoos, or they focused on him. They were changing, developing, growing longer and thicker, joining and crossing over to display twisted passages and dance-like movements.

He jerked his gaze away. "Aren't there some practical things, more *normal* things we should be doing? Like walking down the street, searching the park, knocking on doors? Maybe even calling the police?"

"No need for that. Don't you understand that the authorities poison us against the natural magic of the world? But go ahead and do that 'normal' stuff. Watch and listen. Pay attention to your feelings and let them guide you. I have great faith in you, Felix." She hurried out.

For the next few minutes he searched the room. He picked things up gently and put them back where he thought they'd been. Tearing things apart would've just made him more scared, and Margaret would be furious when she came home. Books facedown to hold her place didn't tell him anything. None of her zillion unicorn and castle and enchantress and Harry Potter posters had anything to say to him, either. Real magic was a sham—hard to access, hard to control, crazy and arbitrary and unfair. It promised everything but never gave you what you really needed.

In her lunch bag he found a slip of paper. Mom used to leave notes in his lunch, too—stupid advice like YOU CAN DO IT! AND REACH FOR THE STARS! This note had a silly fairy sticker on it that said Tinkerbelle, plus a lot of weird designs, circles mostly, with various spokes in them, and scribbles connecting them. If he glanced at them a certain way the circles turned, and the scribbles danced. Right beside Tinkerbelle, under the glow of her tiny wand, was GO FIND THE MAGIC! in Mom's one-of-a-kind handwriting.

Tinkerbelle told him what it meant, which was a clue to how upset and out of it he was. Mom had sent Margaret away on some impossible quest.

One of his sister's drawings crinkled under his hand, tingling his skin. He pulled the drawing up against the light and watched as the lines of the furiously dancing doll vibrated.

Felix had no idea what he was doing. Like his mother always said, he let himself be led. With various pencils, pens, crayons, he extended the lines on the paper so that they wrapped, cocooned, buried the dancing doll in a hard shimmering tunnel. Then the spiral spread off the paper to contour the folds of sheets, comforter, pillow, until he dropped everything, hands shaking, and stood back.

Vaguely he recognized the park by that shelter they'd stayed in for a few weeks last year, elaborate slide system with a tower where kids waited their turn. On the wall of the playground was a mural he couldn't see in the drawing, wizards and fairies, gnomes in fur coats like rats escaping a sewer, that had always creeped him out when he'd taken Margaret there. So had all the old guys hanging around like wizards who'd lost their powers, or who'd just hallucinated them, now convinced all the tasty magic was there in the bodies of the playing kids. Margaret had always wanted to say hi, and Felix hadn't let her. The lines didn't show anything but the dancing of the kids and a space of no-dancing, no-motion, watching.

The deep-shadowed tangle behind the playground hid the entrance to a secret cavern, or something more every day. The sewer. He'd yelled at Margaret to keep away.

When Felix got into the park it felt like dusk although he didn't think it was that late, hoped Margaret hadn't been left alone that long, didn't stop to check the time on his phone. Homeless guys were sitting on the wall. There was the mural, more faded and dirtier than he remembered, layered in a graffiti of filthy, hysterical requests. The opening of the sewer pipe was huge, protective mesh broken into fringe. It quivered like it was singing.

Margaret was in there. Looking for a magic place. Because she was a kid, and magic could be anywhere her mother said it was.

Felix dropped onto hands and knees and, without allowing himself to think about it, started into the pipe. Then the darkness detached into a ragged bulk of shadow backing out. The man grunted, hit his head and swore. The seat of his pants was muddy. He had Margaret. Her pale face popped up on one side and then disappeared.

Felix's first impulse was to block the exit, trap the guy inside the pipe and call the police. He fumbled for his phone. Then he thought he might have a better shot at saving his sister if he moved out of the way. The guy kept coming, dragging Margaret, his fist swallowing her hand. Felix grabbed at the guy's shirt and was about to throw himself at him when Margaret yelled, "No! Felix! He's my friend!"

The big, red-faced, dirty guy was all the way out, and he reached back into the pipe with both hands and pulled Margaret out. She hugged him before she hugged Felix. The homeless guy growled, "You better tell somebody, dude."

Into Felix's neck Margaret said, "I'm scared, Felix."

"Of him? What'd he—"

He felt her shake her head. "Of Mom. She makes me do stuff. She doesn't take care of us. My friend says it's not right, kids shouldn't be treated like that."

"Felix, you found her!" Mom went to hug Margaret but Margaret turned away. "I knew you could do it—I've always had faith in you." To the homeless guy she said, "Thanks, Woody," and kissed his cheek.

"You sent her out here, right?" Felix didn't care who heard. "A test for me."

Mom looked at Margaret and lowered her voice. "She loves magic but she didn't inherit my abilities. You did."

"I want it!" Margaret wailed. People were looking at them. Woody patted her head, told Felix again to tell somebody, and shambled off to find saner company. Felix finally found his phone.

"You have great talent, son. And if you didn't find her, I was your back-up." She was actually proud of herself.

She'd think he hated her, but he didn't. He just didn't have anything more to say to her. He waved his hands once, twice, and the lines danced around them. He didn't know if Mom couldn't see them, but she definitely couldn't see him or Margaret. He called 911.

THE SECRET LAWS OF THE UNIVERSE

Ed thought the toaster had a disapproving aspect. "Have you told your wife yet?" It was difficult to tell which part of the toaster the voice was coming from.

Ed sought to avoid eye contact, but had no idea where not to look. "I don't want to worry her."

"Human beings like to be prepared, or at least to have the illusion. It's characteristic of your race."

"They're not my race." When the toaster began to harangue him, demanding some sort of explanation, Ed left the kitchen. He'd been speaking emotionally, not logically of course. Often he didn't feel like part of the human race, and he didn't expect anyone to understand this, but he wasn't about to be embarrassed in his own home by an appliance.

Behind him, he heard his toast pop up with a ding, done. The toaster sighed.

"It'll get cold if you just leave it there." His wife glanced over the paper at him. She had her own breakfast spread out over her end of the dining room table—ham and scrambled eggs, a carafe of black coffee, bagel and cream cheese, and a bowl of freshly-sliced fruit, all the colors artfully arranged.

"I don't like my toast hot. Cool is fine with me."

"Well, nobody likes it cold."

"I said cool, not cold. And with a little bit of strawberry jam on top, it tastes great."

"I'd be happy to fix your toast when I make my own breakfast, however you want it fixed, Ed. I'll even stick your toast in the freezer, if that's what you really want."

"Well, I appreciate that." It was a marriage lie, and marriage lies don't count. "But you have a job to get to. And I have to be able to do a few things for myself."

Jillian gazed at him with her head slightly tilted. "I guess I can't argue with that."

The coffee carafe said, "Tell her you're going to kill her, Ed. You owe her that much, for all she's done for you." Or perhaps it was the chandelier. One of the bulbs blinked and buzzed, sending painful pulses directly into Ed's brain.

They all acted as if he *wanted* to kill her. Clearly no one understood. He went back into the kitchen and retrieved his cooling toast from the top of the toaster. It caught on the edge of the slot until he ordered, "let go, dammit." He slapped it on a plate.

Back in the dining room he stared at his plate with the burnt square of bread. He'd forgotten his table knife.

Was it okay to put the jam from the serving spoon directly onto his toast if he hadn't touched the bread with his lips? He reached over and took the spoon out of the jam, loaded it, and deposited the bright red spread on the edge of his plate, cognizant that Jillian was watching him, waiting for any mistake so that she might instruct him in some fine point of etiquette. He guided his toast across the protruding jam, being careful not to let any of it spill onto the table.

Of course he knew this convoluted methodology couldn't be the way things were normally done, but at least he hadn't contaminated anything or messed up the tablecloth. She couldn't call him on that. Sometimes he had to jump through hoops simply to avoid the tiniest of mistakes. The jam wasn't evenly spread but at least he'd achieved some coverage.

"You're calling your doctor today, right?" She sipped her coffee, gazing at him unblinking.

"That's the plan."

"Those headaches aren't going to go away by themselves."

Ed didn't say anything. His toast was frowning at him. Whether that meant the toast agreed with Jillian and was expressing its disapproval, or the toast wanted Ed to say something back to Jillian, anything that meant he was a man with his own voice, Ed did not know, because unlike the toaster, the chandelier, and the carafe, his toast apparently had no speaking apparatus.

But the displeasure of the toast was palpable, even more so because of its silence. Unable to eat anything so disapproving Ed picked up his plate and the jar of jam and returned to the kitchen.

"I'm hardly surprised you're not hungry," the toaster said. "Guilt rarely whets the appetite."

In response Ed pushed the unhappy toast into the garbage disposal and turned it on. The toaster cried out in alarm.

Ed stood with hands on either side of the sink and stared out the window. It was a bright morning, the sun lending its glow to flowers and lawn. It was the kind of day he would have loved to just lie down in the grass and take it all in, letting the warmth spread through his limbs and set fire to his blood. That was one of the few perks available to temporary life forms, experiencing that interchange between air and sun and flesh, one's body a soup of cells thriving and cells dying. A toaster could never know this pleasure, or a chandelier, and yet a toaster could be repaired endlessly, if one ignored practical economics, or its bits recycled into some other machine. And that chandelier might hang in the house for the next family, or the one thereafter, long after Ed was gone. Longevity had always been unfairly distributed. Shouldn't his life be worth more than a stone's?

He should have been out there, enjoying his temporary time, but that would have been irresponsible, and impossible to explain to Jillian. "She really has done everything for you," the jar of jam said from the counter. "She's been very patient. Not everyone would put up with your eccentric behavior."

Ed found a sharp knife and stabbed it down into the sweet strawberry goodness. The jam attempted to expound further, but Ed churned the knife blade, eviscerating the aborted speech. He heard the TV go on in the living room. Jillian enjoyed watching a few minutes of television every morning before going into the office, usually programs recorded the day before which she fast-forwarded between the more interesting segments. She liked the shows about "real people" the best, a kind of programming which appeared to have completely taken over the airwaves.

A young woman was talking about becoming a professional singer. She said it was her dream and she refused to have a backup plan. Ed felt badly for her. Everyone he knew, practically, had been forced to live their backup plan, and all too often it was not of their own design, but handed to them. "Here," the world said. "Go do this instead."

Someone was trying to talk over the young woman. People could be so rude sometimes, so callous and uncaring. There was even laughter in the background. Then Ed realized it was another soundtrack laid over the first.

"Now would be a good time, Ed," the TV said. "She's watching some of her favorite shows, enjoying herself—what better time for her to die?"

"But she has to get to work," he offered lamely. "She's going to be late."

"Do you really think she wants to be at work? Wouldn't she rather be famous? Wouldn't all your kind much rather be famous?"

"She loves her work. She says it all the time."

"She's learned to make do. If you kill her now, it should make the evening papers. Don't you think she would like that? And if you continue, if *you* become famous, then she will as well. Famous people, they live forever."

"I don't think she'd rather—"

"You have the knife in your hand already, Ed. Now why don't you use it?"

Ed looked down at the knife clutched in his right hand, strawberry jam melting off the blade and dribbling onto the clean white tile floor. He backed away from the sound of the television, turned and ran to the back door, jerking it open with his left hand, confused about what he should do with the knife.

The man from the dairy was bent over the milk bottles on the back porch, replacing the empties with full ones of an impossibly white color, the milk so bright in hue it could only be a motion picture effect. The man straightened up, his white suit so perfect with nary a wrinkle, and when he saw the knife stained with still dripping strawberry jam he looked as if he would scream, and if he were to scream Jillian would come out there, and she would miss her shows and be late to work, but most of all she would be so terribly disappointed in him, when all she'd ever done was her very best for him.

The milkman looked down and Ed's gaze followed. The knife was embedded slightly above mid-abdomen, at an upward angle. And all that red couldn't possibly be jam. The dairy man fell back against the railing and toppled to the ground.

Ed waited anxiously as Jillian gathered her purse, keys, briefcase, and a compact, fashionable lunch tote with flower designs which looked a bit like eyes elaborated with fanciful makeup. Several of these eyes now looked up at him in despair. The jangle of her keys said "Do it, do it when her back is turned!" He had a hammer he'd retrieved from the closet hidden behind his back for that very purpose, but he knew he would not be doing it. Not this time.

"I don't know why these people waste their time on these impossible dreams," she was saying with a kind of aimless annoyance. "Even if they're talented, well, what difference does that make anyway? Most people are unlucky, or they lack the connections. You have to know how to work the system, you know."

Ed was anxious for her to leave, but the conversation had veered so closely to what he pondered each and every day he couldn't quite let it go. "So how do they learn how to do that? How do they find out?"

"How should I know? Do I look like a success to you? Some doors close, you leave them closed. You can't reopen them." She was obviously furious now, and he didn't know why. She frightened him when she was like this—he couldn't have swung the hammer at her even if it had been the right time. "I'm just a working girl, remember?"

"I'm sorry, I—"

"Just call your doctor, make an appointment, okay? And make a few job contacts today—you can do that for me, can't you?"

"Of course," he said softly, also annoyed now, stepping back so she could leave. He could have swung the hammer as she turned, but he would not kill her in anger. No matter what, it could not happen like that.

As soon as he heard her car pull away from the front of the house he returned to the back yard where he'd stashed the dairy man beneath an old quilt. He went to his knees beside the body and started to cry, but then furiously wiped his tears away and began to roll the quilt up with the body inside. He had a little bit of old twine—he didn't think it would hold—but he wrapped it around the legs and head anyway. Then with considerable strain he began dragging the awkward package toward the garage along the side of the house, the head-end snagging on the edge of bushes and flowerbed fencing, forcing him to stop now and then to wiggle things free. At least the overgrown bushes around the edge of the yard shielded him from the neighbors. Jillian had nagged him for months to trim them back—perhaps he hadn't gotten around to it for a reason? Could this be working the system?

"Where are you going with that?" the house said.

Ed knew it was the house because of the weight the words made in his head, and because something along the lines of the foundation had shifted and shifted back, even though it hadn't been visual exactly, but more like a movement between dimensions, like traveling through time. In any case it frightened him, because of the depth of structural instability it suggested.

"I'll put it into the trunk of my car. Then I plan to drive it somewhere, get rid of it somewhere."

"Good, I wouldn't want it just lying around here. Is that Jillian in there?"

"No. No, it's someone else." Ed was slightly surprised at the house's ignorance of what had recently occurred in its own back yard. Is that what happened when you lived longer? Your perspective changed so much you didn't even notice the daily tragedies?

"I thought the plan was to kill Jillian, and that would open up some doors, some possibilities for you to have a different life?"

"It's not that cut and dried, but yes, obviously if the life you're living goes away there will be room for a different one. You don't even have to think about it—it will just happen."

"And yet you've killed someone else?"

"It was an accident."

"You're avoiding what you know you need to do to get that other life—you don't want to kill her. You'll kill everyone else in the world first to avoid killing her."

"Of course I don't want to kill her. We have some problems, but I've always loved her, still do. But I don't know what else to do. This *can't* be my life."

"The secret laws of the universe are a conundrum. Why do some get what they want and some do not? The laws mean even less to a house. We are simply here, and then one day you people make a decision to tear us down."

"I have no such plans." Ed was thinking he had no more control over such decisions than over anything else in his life.

"You could travel to her place of work and kill her there. It would be most unexpected," the house said.

Rather than answer (Could he? Would he?) Ed replied, "I have no problem with rules per se—rules, laws, principles, that's what makes mathematics, chemistry, physics, work, right? And without those things the world would not function."

The house appeared to have fallen back asleep, or into whatever meditative state architecture is prone to. Ed did not want to discuss things further anyway, instead busying himself getting the body into the trunk of his car, and his car out of the garage. The vehicle ran sluggishly. Ed had not driven it in weeks.

Body disposal was actually not a topic Ed had seriously considered before. He certainly wouldn't have tried to dispose of Jillian's body—you don't do that kind of thing to someone you love. Although he hadn't thought it completely through he'd always assumed he'd claim an intruder had killed her, or that she'd fallen down the stairs. Faking grief would have been no problem because his grief would have been completely genuine. In fact he'd always thought that killing her might fall under the general category of natural causes. Anticipated, certainly, but hardly desired.

So he drove around awhile, hoping to see some options. "I thought we were going to your wife's office," the car said. "I thought you were going to kill her there."

"You've got a pretty good radio. It's been awhile since I listened to it—let's turn it on. Full volume."

"You're changing the subject."

"There are people at her office. They would see."

"But have you thought about trying to live in that house after having killed her there? That would be stressful, don't you think?" Ed hadn't considered that. "You didn't think about it because you never seriously thought you would go through with it."

Ed leaned forward and switched on the radio.

"You're not going to be able to avoid this," the car said from the radio and from everywhere else. Ed turned the radio off to kill the echo.

He gradually began to realize that he was in an unfamiliar neighborhood. It was an older suburb with mature trees, the houses built in the late sixties, maybe early seventies. Split levels and tri-levels mostly. Not very expensive—he supposed they'd be called cheap by some, but very well kept. Perhaps too well. When he considered all the painting and countless specific repairs to old wood and siding and plywood, the effort to keep casement windows usable, all the lawns mowed and hedges trimmed and leaves raked, and the incremental landscaping improvements—the borders and gazebos and fountains and walks and statuary—the time spent keeping up these doll houses, these pleasant appearances, it boggled the mind. Wasn't there a better way to spend your time than devising temporary façades in order to put the best possible face on your world?

The street was quiet, empty. The kids would be in school, he supposed, the adults off at their jobs. There would be a few retirees, no doubt—this was the kind of neighborhood some would retire to—the top of the ladder, the end of the chain, the penultimate destination and the final goal. For some, this was what life would amount to.

An older fellow—dressed in a furry rust-colored sweater and corduroys, a bit warmly for the weather—shuffled down one of the neatly paved and edged driveways toward the street, leaf rake in hand. He didn't look happy or particularly sad, but there was fatigue in the way he began to rake at the few leaves spilling off his lawn into the gutter. He used short, deliberate strokes precisely overlapped so that every bit of lawn was covered, his almost aggressive focus tiring to watch. Once he got all the leaves into the gutter he herded them toward one particular pile along the curb. For what reason Ed could not imagine.

His property seemed to be the most perfect, the most refined of any of those very refined properties on the block. It must have taken him days, a lifetime of days, to obsessively groom his realm, this relatively tiny area of the universe. "He's got it all sorted," the car said. "At last he thinks he's got it all figured out."

"I understand the impulse," Ed said. "During these spells of unemployment I'd go out and work in the yard. Not just because Jillian nagged me to do it, but because that way I could show all my neighbors I actually had things to do. It was the only time I ever talked to any of them, really. We'd talk about the weather, and what needed to be done, and how good it would all look if we could only get it all done, but we knew we couldn't get it all done because it was so constant. It made me feel like one of them, but it was depressing. I kept asking myself, 'Is this what it's really all about? Is this what a human life amounts to?'"

The car began to roll forward. Ed never could decide if the car did it on its own (surely a car that talks was capable of driving itself), or if he had deliberately put it into gear and stepped on the gas pedal. In fact, he couldn't even remember if he'd pulled over and parked in order to observe the neighborhood more closely, or if he'd been driving the entire time, but cruising slowly.

As the car came upon him the elderly man looked over his shoulder in mild surprise. Not fear, really, and not true surprise. It was the kind of surprise you experience at the moment even though this was something you'd really been expecting all along.

The man went down quickly, and the bump the left front tire made as it rolled over him was much smaller than Ed would have expected.

Ed drove along in silence for a time, out of that neighborhood and into another, another still. The car appeared to have nothing to say. Then, as Ed searched for the on-ramp, the car spoke up. "See how easy that was? Quick and painless."

"We don't know there wasn't any pain."

"I didn't hear any screaming, did you? You could have done the same thing with Jillian—it could have been finished by now."

"I don't think I could handle it if Jillian looked at me the way that old fellow did. His last sight was me behind the wheel. I'd hate for the last thing Jillian ever sees is me behind the wheel."

"It's only a moment. A second. She might even think she was hallucinating it."

"That doesn't help any."

"That old man should have been Jillian. Are you going to kill everybody in this city before you get around to killing your wife? I thought you wanted a different life for yourself. I believe you once said *this* just couldn't *be* your life."

"I'm going to her office now. We'll just have to see what happens."

"You have to *choose*, Ed," the car said plaintively. "I know you love her and it's a terrible thing, but you only get *one* life. People get trapped because they settle for feeling *just a little* happy, or being *just a little* successful." The car horn blared suddenly, painfully. "Wake up, Ed!" the car screamed unmercifully. "Wake yourself up!"

If he drove the car head-on into the next tree would he feel any pain, and for how long?

He found the on-ramp to the interstate bypass that led downtown, a narrow single lane hidden behind a row of trees, as if this part of town wanted to pretend it was out in the country. The highway was rather full for a Thursday morning, and he found himself veering close to the other lanes, sometimes crossing lines, as he attempted to get a good look at the other drivers, and assess in some way their purpose, their intentions, or at least their mood. Periodically someone would honk their annoyance, and the car would honk back in kind, on its own and independent of Ed's wishes. It occurred to him that this might be a dangerous strategy, and indeed some vehicles made their own incursions into Ed's lane.

"Look at all these people with nothing to do," the car said.

"Some of them drive for their jobs, and some of them have important errands to run, I'm sure."

"And some are just driving aimlessly around," the car said. "I'm an expert at this, remember? I can tell when a driver has no business being out on the road."

"I don't know that you can say they have no business..."

"They can't stand or sit still. They find their own little patch of ground, the area beneath their shadow, an intolerable place to be in. They'd rather do anything than fill their own space. They can't be satisfied anywhere. If they could jump out of their own skin, believe me they would. Traveling around aimlessly in a car is simply a substitute for jumping out of your own skin."

Ed had been paying so much attention to the car's speech he hadn't noticed their relative position in the lane. He looked out the driver's side window and saw the man in the next car, just a few feet separating them, as he mimed a performance of the radio's latest hit single. The man turned his head suddenly, as if now aware of being watched, and stared at Ed with his mouth open.

The side of Ed's car rubbed the other vehicle. "Scrape!" the car said, followed by a high-pitched metallic chuckle. The other car went up onto the concrete divider and flipped over just as Ed passed it. He watched in his rear-view mirror as other cars crashed into the first, spinning it on its rapidly-crumpling hood.

His car took the next exit, accelerated down the off-ramp and trundled over two homeless people stationed there with their cardboard signs. One of the wheels caught and spun, damp red debris spraying out from the wheel well. Ed began to scream.

"Calm down! I'm trying to drive here!" the car said.

The car took side streets and alleys, cutting across the occasional parking lot. Bits of metal and other trash dropped off here and there. Finally they pulled behind a building near a service entrance.

"This is Jillian's building. How did you..." Ed began.

"You've taken me here before, remember? Now go do what

you have to. I, unfortunately, won't fit in the elevator." With that the car sputtered and stalled out.

Ed climbed shakily from the car. Clearly, at least in this small part of the universe, there had been a rule change. He walked around his old automobile, now silent except for the steam escaping from the engine compartment. The paint was scraped off the length of it in several inch-wide, wavy silvery stripes that shone white hot as they reflected the sun. They might even have been called "cool" under some new system of rules. Blood was spattered here and there with that randomness that never looks entirely random, but more like an artist's interpretation of random.

Clearly he'd have to kill Jillian now. Better to kill her than to have her see what he'd done to the car.

He came into the building through the janitor's entrance, which they never locked. Will, the security guy who'd once been a grocery store manager until he retired and then gone back to work in security because he couldn't survive on his small savings, dozed soundly at the front desk. There was no one else down in the lobby—most of the companies here conducted their business by phone or over the internet. Ed reached down and removed Will's gun from its holster. Will started, opened his eyes and looked at him. "Whoa," he said. "You're—you're Jillian's husband, right?"

"Shoot me," the gun said. Ed was confused. "Shoot me," the gun repeated, then Ed understood.

"You want me to *fire* you, right? Fire you and shoot him," Ed said patiently. Will sat up quickly. "Are you even loaded?

I feel loaded," the gun replied, "but I always feel loaded."

"Will, is this gun loaded?"

"Don't, don't point that at me!"

Thinking that probably answered his question, Ed now wondered if he could even shoot a gun. He never had before. He looked for the safety—he'd seen pictures. He flipped it off.

The recoil jerked his arm, so he missed where he was aiming. But he was so close, he took off part of Will's head.

He expected a great deal of alarm when he stepped off the elevator into the office where Jillian worked. Surely they'd heard the explosion downstairs? But everyone walked around as if nothing were wrong. Didn't they understand that there was always something wrong? Several people nodded and smiled, no doubt recognizing him from an appearance he'd made at the last company picnic. He'd gotten quite drunk and Jillian hadn't spoken to him for days.

They didn't even notice he had a gun hanging from his hand. Didn't say a word.

"Watch this guy, he's coming too close," the gun said, raising its long neck, staring up with its singular, deep dark eye. The fellow almost stumbled into Ed, and the gun shot itself, or rather fired itself, somewhere into the man, who fell screaming, and the bullet continuing, blasted through the desk of one of the secretaries.

Now everyone noticed, and ran and screamed, and Ed continued down the hall toward Jillian's office, feeling vague and headachy and a little sick to his stomach. "It's not supposed to happen this way," he told the gun. "Now she's going to know everything."

"Secrets are a bad thing," the gun replied. "Better to get everything out in the open and clear the air. Time to empty the gun, Ed."

Ed made a right at the corridor and walked briskly toward the end to where his wife's office was. He held the gun out limply in front of him despite its admonitions to "Get a grip on that handle! Straighten out the barrel! A *child* could knock me out of your hand the way you're holding me!" But he didn't think he could withstand *anyone's* attempts to disarm him, however firmly he held the weapon. He felt as if he could hardly walk as it was.

With a last burst of energy (and bolstered by the gun's cries of "Charge! Charge!") Ed indeed charged the door. Then stopped short of its surface and knocked, none too loudly.

"Come in," muffled. He knew the tone. Jillian was occupied with some important business or other, unwilling to spare more than a sliver of attention.

He opened the door gently and slipped inside, pulling it shut behind him. The gun banged against the door and he stiffened, but Jillian didn't even look up from her papers. "What was that noise out there, do you know?" She was looking down and busily writing. "Did someone knock over the water cooler again?"

"Jillian." He held the gun out, his finger trembling against the trigger. She looked up.

"Jesus Christ, Ed!" She jumped up and scattered the papers everywhere.

"Sorry, sorry," he said, going to pick the papers up off the floor, the gun dangling loosely from his thumb.

"That's no way to hold a firearm," the gun grumbled.

"Ed!" He looked up—she'd run into a corner. "What are you doing!"

"I love you, Jillian. You know that, don't you?"

"What are you *doing* here?"

"I love you but sometimes two people can't live together even if they do love each other. Sometimes one person can't be who they should be, live the life they might have, as long as they're in that relationship with the other person."

"Ed, are you saying you want a divorce?"

"No, of course not! It's just that sometimes two people are so close, or at least one of them feels so very strongly about the other, that that person can't *be* who they should be if the other person even exists, anywhere on the planet."

"Ed!"

"You're always taking care of me, Jillian. You're always giving me great advice even if that advice isn't always so great for me, personally. So I'm, I'm trying to think that maybe this—" He waved the gun at her. "This whole thing is just another way you can take care of me. I'm sorry, but I think maybe that's just the way the universe works. Not much we can do about it."

"Less talking, more shooting," the gun said.

Ed took aim at the corner where Jillian was standing. He was pretty sure he couldn't hit her from that distance. He was pretty sure he would have to advance on her, get much closer, before he had any chance at all of hitting her. Which he did not want, to be so close he could see the fear in her eyes.

He glanced at the huge window behind her, and then the

other huge window along the adjacent wall. He'd always known Jillian was important to her company—he just hadn't realized she was *this* important.

But beyond the fact that she had such views it was the city itself, seen not quite as he had seen it before, all those windows, and behind those windows a countless number of secret rooms where people lived, breathed, died, as if their lives had been swallowed whole by this immortal creature, an immortal creature, of course, which all these mortal creatures had given up their lives to create, and in thanks it had stared at them all their lives with its universe of eyes, and eaten them, and condemned them to anonymity.

"I would give anything to see you reach your dreams, Ed, whatever they might be, even if they didn't include me. Don't you know that?" Jillian said behind him.

"I know, I know," Ed said, and began firing, thrilled as all that glass began to shatter and fall into the downtown streets. He heard the blare of the car horns, and the screams of the people, and Jillian's own pleas behind him, and it was as if they were all cheering him on, as he threw the gun out the pane-less window, and he himself moments later tried to follow it into the tumult below.

THE MAN IN THE ROSE BUSHES

HOMAGE TO M.R. JAMES

Lunch on that particular day of the Essex bus tour was to be at Westfield Hall, an immense old manor house with a stone and red brick exterior. Elaine had planned this part of the trip to be a bit more restful after all the British castles and museums and ruins of the first two weeks, and with only a few days left before their departure for Victoria Station, Heathrow, and then back to the States. Still, even at a reduced pace the week had been almost too much for her: the ghost walk in Maldon, the Castle Museum in Colchester and the Bourne Mill, Rainham Hall. Only Leigh-on-Sea had been relaxing—she caught herself daydreaming of someday living in such a place. But Roger had thrived at every location along their journey.

They were a bit off schedule and the parking lot by the dining hall was already full of the coaches of a half dozen different guided tour companies. The guide/bus driver appeared only marginally harried, however. Elaine supposed this happened frequently. He pulled to the side of the narrow lane leading into the grounds and announced, "I'll simply pop over and check inside. If we can't get our lunches immediately I'll talk about the Hall beforehand. No rush—a bit of talk, a bit of lunch, back on the bus and Bob's your uncle."

Roger giggled at the expression. He'd been collecting Britishisms since the first day of their trip and feeding them back to her at meals. There were grumblings among the others after the guide stepped off the bus—too tired, too hungry, too bored—but not from her son. Roger was in love with everything *old*. "There's nothing like this in Texas, Mom. Our old is their *new*, except maybe for the Alamo." They'd visited the Alamo a half-dozen times. "We should move somewhere where *everything* is old." Elaine didn't understand his fascination for the antique—not in such a young child—but his curiosity about historical things, and his impressive capacity for remembering large amounts of information, made her so very proud. She didn't have the heart to tell him that they really couldn't afford to move anywhere—she'd be paying for this extravagant vacation for years. It had all been for him, of course—she'd never been adventurous enough for travel. But the way he had blossomed satisfied her that it had been all worthwhile.

"Okay, then." The guide stepped up into the bus, slightly out of breath. "Westfield Hall. There has been a structure on this site from 1062, used as a residence, a hunting lodge, and as of ten years ago a stop for ravenous tourists. The dining hall was added then, designed to blend in with the rest of the building. Not terribly successfully, I'm afraid—such additions seldom are.

"The façade you see now is relatively new—and when I say 'new' I mean it was added in the early eighteenth century." He paused then as if waiting for a reaction he did not receive. Elaine glanced at Roger, always so very attentive during these rehearsed speeches, but he was staring out the window, distracted. She followed his gaze. The grounds on this side of the dining hall were covered with a glorious array of rose bushes of all types. An ornate metal sign marked this as *The Mary Anstruther Memorial Rose Garden*.

"Mommy, there's a man," Roger said softly.

"What man, dear?" It surprised her to hear him say "Mommy". He'd switched to "Mom" more than two years ago.

"In that broken, in that sick part of the garden. His face— he's like that Guy Fawkes man."

Roger had been quite fascinated by Guy Fawkes. They had seen the bonfires two nights before, as the bus travelled across the countryside to the next stop. At a small food shop he'd begged her for some coins to give to some children carrying a stuffed figure. "*Mom*," he'd pleaded. "It's for the *Guy!*"

She looked where he was pointing. There was one area of the rose garden which appeared to be in shade, the ground there dark and greasy-looking. The rose bushes were smaller in this area, and their colors subdued—no doubt because of the additional shadows. Even the grass appeared thin and failing and threaded with shadow. Britain in general had far too many shadows, in her opinion.

It was apparently some sort of problem area. A flimsy yellow plastic fence had been propped up around it, and she could see where holes had been dug. "I don't see a man," she said.

"He went back into the rose bush," Roger whispered, glancing around at the guide who continued his narration. Elaine could see the conflict in her son's face: not wanting to miss another second of the tour, and yet believing what he'd seen was more urgent.

"You mean between the bushes?"

"No—he went into a rose bush. He walked right into it."

Elaine put the back of her hand against his forehead, feeling the heat there. It was worrisome, how sometimes he could work himself up so. "Well, dear. He doesn't appear to be visible now."

After a moment or two she could feel him making an effort. He turned around and gazed at the tour guide. "Oh, I forgot to say that long before the addition of this southern façade," the man was saying, "the original structure was torn down and rebuilt in red brick by Sir Brian Tuke, secretary to King Henry VIII, following the Dissolution. Eventually of course it was home to the infamous Sir William Scroggs, Lord Chief Justice of England under Charles II, after he left office."

"Excuse me?" Roger had raised his hand.

"Yes, lad?"

"What was the Disso....?"

"Dissolution," the guide supplied. A few on the bus laughed softly, but not in a mean way. They were used to her nine-year-old's questions, who did not let the things he did not understand slide by. She was sure many of the Americans on the bus had no idea what the "Dissolution" was—she certainly didn't—but they rarely admitted their gaps in knowledge, or if they did so they made it sound as if the information wasn't important enough to know. "Henry VIII broke with the Catholic Church and established the Church of England. Afterwards he disbanded Catholic monasteries, priories, convents and friaries in the British Isles and seized their wealth. We refer to those actions as the Dissolution."

"Does Guy Fawkes—did he have anything to do with that?"

"All these *questions* and here we're *starving*," someone mumbled from the back. Elaine turned around furiously looking for the culprit. A gray-haired woman sitting next to a sour-looking gentleman smiled at her apologetically.

"Fawkes comes along about seventy years later, but there *is* a relationship." The guide smiled broadly, clearly warming to the subject with a favored pupil. "These events demonstrate the great distrust between Catholics and others in these Isles, culminating in Guy Fawkes and the Gunpowder Plot to blow up Parliament. Did you enjoy Guy Fawkes Day, lad, and all the bonfires?"

"Oh yes, they were great."

"My two youngest love the bonfires as well. Now William Scroggs, as I was about to tell you, who lived in this very house after his career ended, hated the Catholics, and his part in that lie which we call the Popish Plot, led to the martyrdom of Thomas Pickering, who was...."

The guide stopped suddenly, having finally noticed Elaine's urgent gestures. She'd spoken to the man privately about this earlier in the tour, how her son was a child of a sensitive imagination, and if he could just limit the detailing of some of the more violent bits in British history that would very much be appreciated.

In fact she never talked to Roger of politics, and had no intention of doing so in the foreseeable future. How to explain to such a sensitive child that the world would always have people above him determining his fate, distant, wraith-like politicians (mostly male, mostly white) making decisions that might change his life irrevocably? It didn't matter whether you called it democracy, socialism, or communism—there had always been a group who decided, and those forced to deal with the consequences.

"Well, Pickering died, unfortunately," the guide said in a soft voice. Then more loudly, "And on that sad note I do believe they're ready for us inside. Please exit the coach carefully."

"Oh, definitely dead, old Pickering," came that same, grumbled mumble from the back. "In them days hanged, drawn and quartered."

Elaine twisted around and gave the elderly man a withering look. He stared at her, blushed, and looked down. At least Roger appeared not to have heard. He hummed happily as he led her off the bus.

Because the parking lot was still crowded they had to walk through the grounds alongside that expansive rose garden. Elaine suspected the lunch venue was not actually "ready for us inside"—it had been the guide's way of changing the subject. Almost immediately he told them to enjoy the gardens while he checked in with the restaurant.

She could tell things were still not exactly right with Roger. When she asked him a question he looked up at her with a distracted gaze, his eyes always on something else, but what that something else actually was she could not determine. They wandered among the large varieties of roses, and sometimes he would read from one of the identifying signs, but it seemed to be his attempt to wake himself up more than anything else. "Perhaps we could get permission to look around inside the hall," she suggested.

He focused on her briefly and said, "Oh no, Mommy. He said we should remain out here. This is where I'm supposed to be." Then he turned away from her and contemplated that section of the garden blocked off with the yellow plastic fence.

It occurred to her that he was acting like someone who had been drugged. She'd always been glad she hadn't gone along with his doctor three years ago about giving him some medicine to control his behavior. She had seen some children on that medicine—they walked around like ghosts, as if their minds were somewhere outside their bodies. The way Roger appeared to her now—was it possible he had taken something, been given something?

Elaine tried to control herself. She'd always been prone to runaway fantasies. It made it difficult to determine when actual alarm was warranted. Obviously Roger came by his sensitivities naturally. She herself, when she had been a child, whenever she became upset, would find that her hearing was affected—she would hear things as if they were very far away. Her father used to become quite upset with her due to the delayed nature of her responses.

But her parents had adored Roger, especially her father, thinking him so very bright. Roger had loved him greatly. On their summer visits the two had been inseparable. And they'd shared that passion for old things—her father had taught him about the Indians, and they'd often gone arrowhead hunting.

"Perhaps he should go have a rest. Sometimes they get so worked up."

"What?" She turned—it was that older lady from the bus, the one with the awful husband.

"We have a grandson that way. Does the child take some kind of medication for it?" The woman looked off to the side. Elaine turned and gasped when she saw Roger, now standing on the edge of that blocked-off part, staring into those withered-looking flowers, holding his head, pulling at his hair.

She rushed toward him. Brushing too close to one of the rose bushes her sweater snagged, and she could feel the thorns tearing into her skin. Tears brimmed her eyes and for a panicky moment she could not see him, or anything else.

He'd been doing so well, not like those early years, when she was an abandoned mother with a child who "acted out". But she'd managed to resist his doctor's—in her opinion— overly stern advice. He had been one of those men who was perfectly sure of everything he had to say. It was a quality Elaine distrusted. Her father had been like that. Then during last spring's rainstorms he had driven her mother and himself through a flooded road he doubtless thought would be no problem. But he hadn't noticed the sides of the road where the pavement was being rapidly undermined—that dreadful word the police officer had used. Both her mother and father were swept to their deaths.

Now she could see him again. Roger, of course. But a tall man stood over him, his face in shadow, bent over her son and whispering into his ear. She ran toward them.

"Roger!" She hadn't intended to, but she practically screamed it.

The man turned. His face was heavily lined, his eyes almost shut against the glare of the sun. "Sorry, Miss. I'm one of the gardeners. I was just warning the young master about them holes."

"He's not the one from the bushes," Roger said. "I thought he was, but he isn't."

"You *can't* wander off like that! Certainly not in a foreign country!" Roger just looked at her, expressionless.

"Look 'ere, child," the gardener said, and then glanced at Elaine apologetically. "You'll excuse me, Miss, if I give the boy some advice?"

"By all means," she said, not really thinking it was okay at all.

"Well, child, it's just that I wouldn't be wandering about here alone, I was you."

Roger said nothing, but he nodded his head slightly.

The gardener cleared his throat, suddenly looking unsure of himself. "It's an unpleasant spot is all. Surely you can see the dankness and the dreariness of it."

"Thank you for finding him," Elaine interrupted, grabbing Roger's hand and leading him away to the dining hall.

He seemed better at lunch, although his cheeks were still quite flushed, and his head too warm for her liking. But he liked eating in Britain, even though he didn't always like the food. He enjoyed the very *differentness* of it, the new brands and kinds of condiments, the different ways of preparing things, the fact that you didn't order just fish & chips the way you did in America—you ordered a specific *kind* of fish, and he was determined to try every kind before their vacation was over.

At Westfield he ordered the shepherd's pie, something she had tried to make for him at home, but it had always turned out too soupy. After he was half done he grinned at her and said, "Yours is just as good, Mom." Of course it wasn't at all true, but it made her smile. "I need to go to the WC now." A waiter pointed him to the back of the dining hall and he ran off in that direction.

It was good to see him run, and Elaine felt herself relax for the first time since the bus stopped here. The tour was to visit another castle during the afternoon, another supposedly *haunted* castle, and although she could not imagine how she could bear one more, she knew Roger loved that sort of thing, and if it cured whatever discomfort the rose garden had caused him then all the better.

They'd always been close, the two of them, but she hoped her own childhood fantasies and anxieties had not rubbed off onto her innocent boy. It always upset her to consider it. As a little girl she'd felt consumed by energies she could never quite understand, and once trying to explain it to her mother had said "It's like my thoughts are on fire."

The noise level in the dining area had increased considerably over the past few minutes, and she couldn't determine why. She looked around at the tables, and although people were conversing, no one appeared to be shouting, and certainly she saw no signs of anger. But there was an angry energy in the air. She could feel a peculiar prickliness in the skin on her arms. And she *heard* the shouting—so loud it suppressed all normal conversational sound—a series of almost owl-like exhortations, and the exclamations of dangerous and noisome animals, and the agonized protests of someone unjustly accused.

She stood up then, staring at the room around her, her head pounding as if it were inside a bell. Where was Roger? He had been gone much too long.

The old gardener burst through the front door carrying Roger in his arms. "Miss!" he cried, and set her boy down against a wall. Elaine, the guide, and several others rushed in that direction.

"I found him lying there among them old bushes, by the holes you see. I tried talking to the boy but I wasn't getting much sense out of him."

Elaine dropped to her knees and pulled Roger into her lap. He was almost too big for such a maneuver and she fell against the wall. He sobbed then, and clung to her tightly. His head was hot to the touch, and his mouth curled into this awful scowl. He didn't look much like her own sweet boy, but more like a sick and distressed old man.

"Pull, pull. I'll *push*, Mommy! You *pull*!" He kept babbling nonsense. She could barely hold on to him as he shook his head side-to-side.

Out of the corner of her eye she saw the gardener suddenly back away. He started to leave and when someone from the staff tried to stop him they had a furious conversation and then both left together.

"I'm a doctor. Please, just let me take a look."

She would not let go, but she allowed the physician to slide in beside her with his bag. She couldn't quite make out what he was saying, there was so much noise in her head—the shouts and the pleas for mercy, and all those people standing around watching, sounding so much like angry birds, and Elaine wondered if the birds in England might be so much bigger than those in America.

Roger would be fine, the doctor kept telling her. The others reassured her too—the guide, that woman with the terrible husband, and someone representing the Hall, although she could never quite determine who.

Exhaustion. Over-excitement. An active imagination. People kept saying those words again and again. Those could all certainly be applied to Roger, but unfortunately they were appropriate terms for her as well.

The guide apologized, but they obviously needed to rest, and he needed to take the remainder of the tour on to the castle, but he would swing the bus back around to the Hall on the way back and pick them up. Roger would be so disappointed, she thought, but perhaps he would forget. She could only hope he might forget this entire day.

Elaine and Roger were taken to a private hall away from the dining area to wait for the tour's return. She sat on a padded bench facing a row of windows overlooking the rose garden, Roger lying beside her, his head in her lap. On the wall behind was a gallery of portraits and artwork related to the region. She'd been looking at a very nice drawing of a church in a gold frame, signed "M. Anstruther". She remembered from a tour earlier in the week the guide saying that the ability to produce a decent drawing indicated that a British lady was educated and accomplished, more capable of running a household. Elaine still wasn't sure if she was capable of running a household, but she had no choice in the matter. She was all Roger had.

There was also a portrait of Sir William Scroggs, according to the attached brass plate; the man the guide and the others had been talking about. She thought him an ugly man, particularly because of his superior look, but maybe that was just because of what she knew he had done—many of the British portraits from those times made their subjects appear arrogant, based on what she had seen on their trip. She didn't want to judge people on the basis of their looks, but she also thought there were those few whose sins were mirrored in their faces. Scroggs might be one of those.

The light had dimmed considerably in the past hour, with shadows easing out from among the rose bushes and seeping into the surrounding landscape, everything fading, she thought, into what she'd come to think of as "English grey". There was something quite peaceful about it, but mildly unsettling. The scene bore the suggestion of time rolling back, reaching some pleasant nostalgic point, but then continuing a bit too far.

She did not have her son's love for the old. As bad as the current period might be, she'd always believed that the present was better than the past, when such a high percentage of the population suffered unjustly. In a home this old, she could only imagine the number of appalling memories it must contain. Houses like this were a kind of Pandora's Box.

Not that she believed in every ghostly yarn she heard—she was quite convinced most were nonsense. But they *all* couldn't be nonsense, could they? The odds seemed against it. She had a vague notion that some events were so horrendous, some emotions so strong, that echoes of them must linger for a very long time. Periodically they must regenerate their details for the right audience or circumstance, until that age when their influence wore so thin they were naturally forgotten, as would happen with everyone in this world, and eventually the world itself.

Roger whimpered in his sleep then, and Elaine gently stroked his brow. She couldn't stand it to have her child in pain, or unnecessarily upset, and this *certainly* was unnecessary— they were simply visitors in a foreign land, attempting to enjoy a very special, and unlikely to be repeated, vacation.

She gazed out at the rose garden. She had a clear view of that dreary, damaged patch. A breeze had picked up, and some of those arrested bushes appeared to wave, their branches vibrating.

But she could plainly see that none of the bushes in the better areas of the garden were swaying, and there was no movement in any of the surrounding trees, no sign of a breeze at all.

A pale oval appeared near the top of one of those stunted rose bushes, and at first she thought a lost balloon was snagged there. But it wasn't a perfect oval, so she wondered if it might be a plastic bag, or a piece of cloth. And then a gap opened up within the face of it, a kind of anguished mouth, and several of the branches began to thicken, so that a semblance of a tormented stick figure was formed, which shook, and shook.

She considered it might be one of those remnants of memory caught on the thorns of the bush, but she couldn't tell exactly what it was that was being portrayed. "Torture" was the word that had come immediately to mind, but she wondered if this were physical or mental or perhaps both.

Roger moaned again and she attempted to soothe him, although she felt inadequate to the task. The distant clouds had lowered, darkening as if before a storm, and the shadows framed the figure so as to convince her it was lying in an enormous bed, sleeping, or rather dreaming, of something that had been done and could never be forgotten.

Then on the ground between the rows, just for a moment she thought she saw a form lying there, stretched out as if tied or held, and as she gazed at it she was filled with an anxiety so severe she didn't think she could endure it. She desperately wanted to turn away, but for some reason could not. And then at the peak of her anxiety that vision disintegrated, scattered in several directions as if pulled apart.

Beyond the garden and through the trees she saw the

approaching gleam of the bus, gathering the last remaining light of the afternoon and smearing it across the hills, so that she could not be sure if that coach were actually some distant memory, and these bushes spread before her, and the anguished dance of these shadows, her terrible now.

THE NIGHT DOCTOR

Elaine said the walk would be good for them both. "We don't get enough meaningful exercise these days. Besides, we might meet some of the new neighbors." Sam couldn't really argue with that, but he couldn't bring himself to agree, so he nodded, grunted. Although his arthritis was worse than ever, as if his limbs were grinding themselves into immobility, it hurt whether he moved them or not, so why not move?

He would have preferred waiting until they were more comfortable in the neighborhood—they'd been there less than a week. Until he had seen a few friendly faces, until he could be sure of their intentions. People here kept their curtains open most of the time. He supposed that was meant to convince passersby of their trusting nature, but he didn't like it. Someday you might see something you didn't want to see. You might misinterpret something. Since they'd moved in he'd glanced into those other windows from time to time—and seen shiny spots back in the darkness, floating lights with no apparent source, oddly shaped shadows he could not quite identify and didn't want to think about. He was quite happy not knowing the worst about other people's lives. He could barely tolerate the worst about his own.

Not that he had justification for much complaint. He'd always known the worst was somewhere just out of reach, so it shouldn't have affected him. Like most people, he supposed. Human beings had a natural sense for it, the worst that was just beyond the limits of their own lives. The worst that was still to come.

What with one minor annoyance or another—finding pants that didn't make him look fat, determining what pair of shoes might hurt his feet the least, deciding on the correct degree of layering that wouldn't make him wish he'd worn something else as the day wore on—they didn't leave the new house until almost eleven. Sam worried about getting his lunch on time. If he didn't get his lunch on time his body felt off the rest of the day.

"I'll buy you some crackers at the drug store if you need them," she said. "Don't fret about it."

"Crackers? What kind of meal is that? You're always saying I should eat healthier."

"For heaven's sake, Sam, let it go. Crackers to tide you over. Wheat, something like that. A lot of small meals are better for you anyway. That's the way the cave people ate—they grazed all the time."

"Cave people," he repeated, as if reading some absurd road sign. He didn't say anything more. He didn't want to whine like Bryan, thirty-four years old and he still whined like a little boy. They'd done something terribly wrong for Bryan to be that way, but Sam still had no idea what it was. Parenting was a mystery, like diet, like exercise, like how to still keep feeling good about yourself in this world.

Sam felt uncomfortable most of the time. Physically, certainly. And as much as it annoyed him to think about it, emotionally as well. A walking mass of illogic, and that was no way to be.

After they left the house they turned onto the long lane that meandered through the neighborhood. When he realized how long the street was, and how far away they were from the tiny mall—not so bad if you were driving, but Sam had stopped driving two years ago—he felt on the verge of tears. Just like some kind of toddler. Humiliating.

As they were starting out a large black bird landed in the street beside him. It threw its head back, shuddering, something struggling in its mouth. Sam glanced at his wife to see if she had noticed this. But her eyes were fixed forward, and he decided not to mention it. He twisted his head around to look at the bird. Still there. Was it a crow? It looked too big to be a blackbird. In fact it might be the biggest bird he'd ever seen up close. Its beak was so sharp. It could take your eyes out and there was nothing you could do about it, it would happen so quickly. Just like they were grapes.

His knees were hurting already. There were tears in his eyes, but at least they weren't yet running down his cheeks. Birds didn't cry. He should be like the birds.

He wasn't sure how it had come to this—he'd always been such an optimist. And he'd always been healthy—no, it was too late in life to exaggerate, relatively healthy. But relatively healthy still meant you could drop dead at any time. So he walked around sore much of the time, each step like a needle in his heels and a crumbling in his knees, and attempted to think about everything but death.

They passed another older couple. Elaine would have said "elderly" but Sam hated that word. Elaine smiled at them and said hello. The couple nodded and said hello back. They had already passed the couple when Sam managed to speak his delayed "nice day!" The man said "oh, yes," awkwardly turning his head to Sam in order to be polite, but staggering a little, almost falling off the curb. Sam could feel the warmth flooding his face. He'd caused that distraction, and the resulting stumble.

"We should have introduced ourselves," Elaine said a few minutes later. "They may have been neighbors." Sam hoped the couple didn't recognize him the next time they met. "Sam, did you hear me?"

"Of course I heard you, you're right here."

"Then why didn't you say something?"

"I don't know. I didn't know it needed answering, I guess."

"I don't talk just to hear myself."

"Maybe they're not neighbors. Maybe they're just passing through, taking a walk. They might live several blocks away—they look pretty healthy. They could probably walk that far."

"Uh huh," she said, her head down, walking a little faster. It hurt to try to keep up with her. *Too late.* That's what she would have said if he asked her what was wrong, so he didn't. She deserved better—he didn't understand how he'd gotten so fuzzy-headed. There was probably a pill for that, something to erase a certain percentage of your thoughts, clear out some space so you could pay better attention to the people you loved. So much for the benefits of exercise. Sam was feeling worse and worse.

By the time they reached the drug store Sam was ravenous. He sat on the padded bench and devoured two packets of crackers while Elaine got her many prescriptions. He'd already filled his last week before they moved. The lady across from him frowned. He looked around—he was spraying cracker crumbs everywhere. He didn't know what to do—he couldn't very well get down on his hands and knees right there in the store and sweep them up. He closed his eyes so he wouldn't see either the lady or the crumbs and continued to eat.

When he was small his mother would drag him all over town on her errands. She took him along even if he was sick, but that was just what you had to do when you were a single mother. The worse he felt the more clothing she put on him; he supposed it was meant as a kind of protection. Sometimes he'd get so hot his head would swim. She'd sit him down somewhere in a chair, or in the shopping cart, or even in some out-of-the-way corner of the floor and let him nap. He'd dream he was a bug in a cocoon, waiting to be someone else. That night she'd reward him with a long bath before he went to bed.

"Sleep is what you need," she'd say, stroking his forehead. "Go to sleep and let the night doctor take care of you."

Over the years he'd tried to make some sense out of it. Plentiful sleep, of course, was bound to help, to lower stress, to permit the body to bring its own healing. However it worked, he almost always felt better the next day. He didn't even have to wait until the day arrived, he could take a nap in the middle of the day, and then the night doctor could come. The night doctor didn't necessarily require night, he simply required that you be asleep so that he could properly do his business on you. All that was needed was that it be nighttime inside your head.

Had he really believed that the night doctor was an actual person? He'd never believed in magic, exactly—a person or a thing had to act, had to do something. So as a child he'd believed in Santa Claus because he was a person, sort of, this larger-than-life thing, an *agency*. He didn't believe in the Easter Bunny because he knew a kid who had a rabbit who'd smelled and bitten him once.

It had been oddly reassuring, and yet not reassuring at all. Because if Santa were a person, then he was fallible. He could be late, or if you moved he might not find your house. The same with the night doctor. And he had had proof—he'd once visited his grandparents for two weeks and he'd been sick the whole time. The night doctor obviously couldn't find him.

It had all been a great cause for anxiety. The fact that no one but his mother ever talked about the night doctor had only made it worse—he'd never even seen a picture of the man. Or woman, or whatever.

"Sam, darling? Are you ready to go?"

He blinked. Elaine was looking down at him, smiling. Had he overslept? Suddenly he felt lost, outside his body and not quite knowing the way back in.

"I fell…" He yawned. "I fell asleep waiting. Sorry."

"You must have needed it," she said, helping him to his feet. "I'm sorry, sweetheart. Maybe I've pushed you too hard today."

"Exercise is good for me. I don't get enough," he said, moving slowly with her arm in his as they rocked their way down the aisle, Elaine's bag full of pill bottles rattling at her hip. He willed the blood to flow; his feet were numb. By the time they got out of the store they were better, he could feel them tingling. He supposed the day would eventually come when they didn't get better, when they didn't start tingling but remained as dead as fallen logs. But not today, thank God. Not today.

It was strangely dim outside, and Sam wondered if they could have been there at the pharmacy all day. How long had he been asleep? Then he realized it was simply the clouds rolling in, and he hoped they could get home before it rained. He never liked getting rained on, not even as a child. He usually got sick afterwards. There must have been something in the rain, not just water.

They were at the highest point in the road, the remainder of the neighborhood receding gradually below them. Had they really climbed such a hill? Maybe they were lost—they didn't know the neighborhood well. They could wander for hours and not find their way back. Sam gazed around in a futile search for recognizable landmarks. But he had no landmarks in his memory for their new home.

From here they had a clear view of the afternoon sky. The clouds were heavy, laden—it might begin raining at any moment. The dark shapes of birds were darting in and out between the banks of clouds as if knitting them together. Sam thought of the giant bird he'd seen earlier and wondered if these were more of the same. They appeared to be rising up from the roofs of the neighborhood where they'd been resting, rushing up to join the others as if in collusion.

Then he saw that larger dark shape depart an upstairs window of one of the houses, climbing onto the sill like a suicide, but leaping up instead of down, rising with a swirl of its long dark coat, the bag trailing from the skinny fingers of one hand, more claws than fingers, as the figure attempted to blend in with those other flying shapes.

Sam couldn't be sure, they were too far away, but that figure seemed so very familiar. As if sensing Sam's attention the head of the thing turned back an instant over its shoulder, large eyes staring, narrow face so pale and long as a blade.

Although he didn't intend to, Sam sat down on the sidewalk then, his knees giving way. Elaine yelled in alarm as he almost dragged her down with him. He heard the panic in her voice as she screamed for someone to help them. But there was nothing he could do, as he was too busy elsewhere. Sixteen years old and walking home in the dark from the movie with his friends. He'd just left them to turn in to his own front walk, the darkness denser now because of the trees that used to shade their lawn.

His mother had been ill for several weeks, keeping to her bed except to feed him his meals and prepare his lunch for school. At times like these he'd think a father would have been useful, for her if not for him, because she had to do everything, and Sam was very aware he did not appreciate her nearly enough. But a father had never been more than a story as far as he was concerned, a few photographs that might not actually have been the man. How could he know for sure?

As he was walking up the sidewalk he felt a change in the air. It wasn't a smell, although he felt it in his nose. It was more like a heaviness had entered the space around him, a pressure increasing in his ears, his nose, his skull, and a strong sense of vertigo as if he were looking down from a very high place.

He glanced up, cowering, feeling as if the sky were about to slide down on top of him. His mother's bedroom window was open, her twin pale curtains reaching outside the frame to the night beyond like a frantic signal. Something membranous and black flapped. He could hear her moaning from where he stood, or thought he could.

Sam ran into the house and up the stairs. He came to her door and stopped because he was afraid. He thought he should knock—she would be furious if he went inside without knocking, but that didn't apply in this case, did it? Even the memory made him feel ashamed, and he could hear Elaine's voice somewhere above him attempting to offer some comfort.

He eased open the door even as the figure crouched over his mother was mucking about with her bare torso, taking something from her, sliding some spidery thing that struggled and screamed soundlessly out of her side and into his leathery dark bag. Sam cried out and the night doctor turned his head slightly to look at him with those cold pale eyes, those wet globes glistening yellow from the dim light in the hall, and that oh so elongated face which made no sense, the lower bit coming down into a kind of open snout, the upper half curved into a kind of bony blade. Before Sam could say anything else the night doctor had slid off the bed and through the window into the night and wind with a flap flap flap and a drawn-out sigh.

For days she seemed better, and Sam had begun to think the creature had simply removed the thing that had done her harm. And then his mother took a turn for the worse. And then she was gone.

And next he woke up an old man again, in the bedroom he shared with the wife who took care of him now, who'd been taking care of him since the first day they'd met back in college. The bed stand was covered with his pills, or hers, he couldn't really tell anymore. He could barely remember the names of the pills. Not because he couldn't, but because he didn't want to be that interested.

"Sam, you scared me half to death."

He shifted his head around and saw Elaine's grey face there floating within the darkened chair, propped up by a pillow under the back of her head. The rest of the room was so deeply in shadow he wondered if his eyes were going, then saw the dark in the window and realized it was night. The window was open, the curtains stirring, beginning to flap. He held his breath and twisted his head, trying to examine the room. Things stirred there beyond his ability to actually see them, and he tried to blame it on the wind and his anxiety. "How long have you been sitting there?" he asked, trying not to search the room anymore.

"A few hours. You missed dinner. Do you want something?"

"I don't know." Was he hungry? He made himself sit up in bed. His right leg hurt—he recognized the feeling. He must have been asleep for a while, his right leg pinched beneath his left. "I really missed dinner?"

"It's been about six hours. I decided to let you sleep. Sam, do you remember anything? I thought you'd had a heart attack at first, the way you just collapsed, like you'd been hit on top of the head or something."

"I just...just had a moment I guess. What, did I black out? How did you get me home?"

"That couple came by, the one we ran into earlier? The Hernandezes. You don't remember? Apparently they live only three houses down. He ran back to their house and pulled his car around, they helped you into the seat, and after we got here he helped me get you into bed. I wanted to call the doctor but you insisted you were okay, that you just needed to rest, but that you didn't want to fall asleep."

Sam did remember some of this, but it was like an imperfectly recalled dream. He couldn't explain the lapse, which was disturbing. But he'd been distracted, hadn't he? It seemed he hadn't thought about his mother's death in years. "But you still let me sleep?"

"I couldn't keep you awake if I tried! You were so tired you could barely lift your head."

So he had slept. He couldn't stop himself from searching the room with his eyes again, straining himself, his chest beginning to hurt. He was being a whiny thing. He was going to make himself sick. It would be an open invitation for the doctor to slip in and meddle with his insides. He made himself stop, even though promising details were resolving out of the dark as his eyes adjusted.

"Sounds pretty embarrassing. I'm sorry, I don't know what came over me." Maybe he was better, maybe the doctor had already done his work. He could only hope it didn't cost him too dearly. "Did they, the Hernandezes, did they say anything?"

"Just how concerned they were. Janet and Felix. I told Felix you take blood pressure medication and he wondered if the dosage might be wrong. I'll call Doctor Castro tomorrow and tell him what happened."

You don't know what happened, he thought, but left it unsaid. "Of course. But this is all backwards. You should be the one resting. I'm putting all this extra stress on you." He glanced at the sea of medicines on her side of the bed. There were new bottles, he thought, the ones from today.

"I'm fine. We're not our illnesses, Sam. That's what you always say, remember? We're much more than that."

He couldn't quite interpret her tone. Had there been resentment in the way she'd quoted him? "I could use a ham sandwich, I think," he said.

"Fine." She got up and started toward the door, then stopped, smiled. "And if you're better tomorrow, I've invited them over for dinner."

"What?"

"Janet and Felix. The Hernandezes. They'll be our first dinner guests."

After she closed the door behind her he glanced at the shadowed incomprehensibility of the room and rolled over, turned his back to it. He'd allow himself to be healed or taken, and at the moment he wasn't sure he cared which. He waited a long time, but nothing occurred.

He did feel better when he woke up the next day, although tired and a bit on edge. The room felt empty, however. He could hear

Elaine in the next room running the vacuum cleaner. When the noise stopped he heard her singing. It had been a while since he'd heard her singing. He smelled disinfectant, furniture polish. He glanced around—all their medicine bottles were gone.

"Elaine!"

She came running, out of breath. She grabbed the footboard and leaned over. "Are you...okay?" She wheezed, paused, and then asked more steadily, "Are you still ill?"

"No, no, I'm fine. You shouldn't have run, honey. Where are all the medicines?"

"The Hernandezes may want to see the house, and it hasn't had a really good cleaning yet."

"But the medicines?"

"I put the over-the-counter stuff in our respective bathroom cabinets, depending on who uses what the most. The prescriptions, and the supplements—since we don't take the same—are in a box in each bathroom closet. But I took out a week's worth of dosages and put them into two of those weekly pill organizers—his and hers. I even split the ones that needed it into quarters and halves."

"But why? Do you want them to believe we're the super healthy older couple or something?"

"No, but I don't want them to think the opposite, either. And it was just too much—I started to realize that as I tidied up. It needed to be handled—we're both lucky we didn't grab the wrong pills one day, or even overdose. It looked—I don't know—it didn't make us look like sick people so much as crazy people."

In the bathroom Sam found the pill dispenser (blue, hers was probably pink) and took his daily dose. He pulled off his T-shirt and examined his pale torso. He wasn't sure what he was looking for, some kind of markings. Cuts or worn places, incisions or maybe even bite or chew marks. There was nothing definitive, but when had he gotten so pale? He looked almost slug-like in parts.

Elaine cleaned well into the afternoon, then she started cooking. Sam didn't like the dark half-moons under her eyes. He stepped in with the cleaning, although he suspected he didn't do it well, scrubbing obsessively in some areas and neglecting others. Before dinner he did a final sweep, jammed some random flowers from the back yard into a vase, and set the table. By this point he desperately didn't want to interact with anyone new, but he understood they were fully committed now.

From the time the Hernandezes arrived the evening became a blur for him. They seemed like perfectly nice people but he didn't understand a thing they were talking about.

It seemed that Felix Hernandez had just acquired a new car, one of those boxy affairs with a small body and high ceiling. He used it to drive to the golf course, another habit newly acquired. Janet Hernandez talked endlessly about their son, an apparently always well-meaning young man who could not hold a job. Elaine commiserated and shared stories about Bryan which Sam was sure he had heard nothing about. A fall from a tree? When had that happened? Could Elaine possibly be making these things up in order to have something to share with the new neighbors?

They sat down girl-boy-girl-boy about an L-shaped portion of the dinner table, with Sam at the top of the L's stem and Elaine at the end of the L's arm. Sam wasn't sure how this had happened, but it seemed to have been Felix's idea.

Janet Hernandez was sitting next to Sam. He hadn't realized before how tall she was—at least her torso was tall. She also seemed to have an unusually large head, although that might have been an illusion because her forehead was quite high, and white hair showered down the back of the skull to float just above her shoulders. She leaned forward over her food somewhat, as if afraid it might escape the plate. And she trembled slightly. He noticed because she was sitting right beside him. The profile of her face practically vibrated.

Sam was thinking then that the Hernandezes were older than them by a few years. He looked down the table, but his view of Felix was completely blocked. He tried to catch Elaine's eye, but she was leaning over slightly, probably talking to Felix.

Suddenly Janet leaned back, her face pale, her expression puzzled. Felix seemed blurry and out of focus on the other side, but then Sam determined that something between Felix and Janet was making him difficult to see, something smearing the air, as if Sam's vision had suddenly gone greasy.

The night doctor appeared to unfold from inside that black leathery coat of his, his shoulders going up like axe blades. He turned one globular eye Sam's way. He tilted his elongated head slightly as if inviting Sam to protest. Sitting this closely Sam could see small finger-shaped bits of flesh down around the end of the doctor's snout. They stirred slightly. Some appeared corrupted by some sort of skin cancer.

Sam felt suddenly ill, his head slipping sideways. The night doctor disappeared, and Sam now had a clear view of Felix, who appeared to be in shock. Elaine was shaking the man's shoulder in concern, saying his name. Then Sam moved his head again, and the night doctor was back in focus. Sam experimented, moving his head this way and that. He could see the doctor only at certain angles, the rest of the time the figure disappearing completely.

Suddenly Felix coughed explosively and a pale chunk of chewed-up food—at first Sam was convinced it was some damaged organ—bounced off the table and onto the floor. Sam thought he heard the cat scramble for it, then remembered they hadn't had a cat in years.

Felix was laughing, tears rolling down his cheeks. Elaine was laughing as well, but Sam recognized it as the laugh she made when she was under great stress. Any minute now she would sob. Janet was pushing something around her plate with her fork. Sam saw that it was another piece of what had just come out of Felix's mouth.

A sidelong glance brought the night doctor into focus again. He sat still and erect, as if listening, or at least sensing, things Sam couldn't even begin to imagine. The night doctor's skin was soft and translucent, slightly yellow. Sam thought he could see the sharp skeleton underneath, like a gathering of blades fashioned from bone and then covered in this somewhat transparent epidermal goop.

They all sat that way an uncomfortable period of time. Felix quietly shared his recent health issues with Elaine. Elaine shared things back, but with less detail. Janet continued to move things about her plate with her fork, but ate nothing. Sam watched them all. He wondered if he was the only one aware of the fifth presence at the dinner table—he was pretty sure he was.

Periodically the night doctor stroked the leather bag he wore hanging from his shoulder. It squirmed in various directions, as if containing more than one captive.

Felix was taken to the hospital a few days later. Sam and Elaine watched as Janet rode off with a young man Sam assumed was their son. They never saw any of them again.

For several weeks Elaine became increasingly frenetic. She cleaned the house constantly, and reorganized the medicine cabinets more than a few times. Sometimes Sam would wake up in the middle of the night and find the bed empty. He'd go downstairs and discover her at the table quietly drinking coffee or taking down notes. Usually the night doctor sat there with her.

Often she would work herself into exhaustion and sleep late the following morning. He would come downstairs by himself and find the night doctor already waiting for him, standing in a corner or staring out the window.

It dragged on this way for months. One night Elaine woke him up in the middle of the night, her pale face hanging over him. He gently lay his hand on her wet face—she'd been crying. "I don't want to leave you by yourself," she whispered hoarsely.

He glanced past her, his eyes scanning the room, finding the tall quiet figure with the large eyes and the too-narrow face, the squirming bag. "You won't be," Sam replied.

THE ENEMY WITHIN

BASED ON AN IDEA & NOTES BY JOEL LANE

The body must have been in the canal for a couple of weeks. It had been difficult to identify—parts of the head had been removed, probably before the body was dumped. The *Walsall Echo* ran several stories about the crime, eventually reporting it to be the body of one James Firth, a factory worker who had disappeared a month before. He had lived alone, and medical records were all the police had to go on.

Ian showed Paul the latest clipping. He couldn't tell Paul exactly why he saved the stories about the drowned man, although Paul certainly knew that Ian had his compulsions. He had accumulated a number of such aimless and obsessive activities: saving movie tickets, writing down his dreams, biking the canal path on weekends and the occasional evening. Such activities brought him no real joy. Perhaps someday one of them might lead to something more significant, but for now they were just ways to kill time.

"I must admit I don't particularly care for this new morbid streak of yours," Paul said, but he took the clipping anyway and read it. "He worked for your company. Did you know him?"

"Firth worked in the production section as a spot-welder. I'm in packaging."

Paul gave the clipping back, rubbing his fingers uncomfortably on his jacket. Ian smelled the new soap Paul was using—he was always changing soaps, always taking showers. Paul had compulsions of his own. "I know. You carry the boxes, you load the vans. You don't involve yourself beyond that. So you've told me. But you could do better, of course. Firth apparently had a trade. You could have a trade. But you never met him? The factory isn't that large, is it?"

"If I ever met him, I don't remember. Some of my friends knew him a little, but I think he kept to himself. They never mentioned him before and now he's all they can talk about. James Firth has replaced the pay dispute and those unexplained sackings as the conversational topic of the day. I suppose I should be grateful to him for that."

"He would have had parents, Ian. A life outside work. Show some humanity, please."

Paul's comments stung, although they were typical of their recent conversations. They were going through a rough patch. They didn't talk anymore until Paul left for his job at the hospital. It seemed Paul was always lecturing him, playing the mature, older mentor. Perhaps eventually he would decide Ian was too young for him and leave, just as Lawrence had. Of course that had been different. They'd all been friends, and then Ian had gone behind Paul's back—who'd been working long shifts at the hospital, *saving lives* (of course he was only an orderly)—and slept with Lawrence. Bad enough that Paul took the moral high ground in almost every argument—the moral high ground was something Paul had actually earned.

It was late January; rain blackened the walls, pulled down the clouds until they seemed as near as the smoke from the factory chimneys. Sunlight had become the color of dull metal, and would not warm. The rain left whitish smears on the windows. The roads near their flat were constantly busy, with lorries and vans competing for the district's business. Ian found mass transport too unpleasant to tolerate and so used his bike more and more, sticking to the canal path, which was largely abandoned this time of year. Even though the rain stung his eyes and he couldn't keep the damp entirely off his skin, no matter what he wore.

He supposed he was too sensitive; even a hint of an argument could ruin his day. Ian decided to call in sick. Then he slipped on his yellow Mac, grabbed his bike, and headed for the canal, looking to ride off some of his tension.

Paul wouldn't have approved, neither of the dereliction of

duty or of the canal ride. He said the canal path was unsanitary and dangerous, "a good place for someone to murder a pretty fellow like you." Now he had the sordid Firth murder as confirmation. Well, Paul wasn't his father just because he acted like it. Ian had only left his parents in November, and sometimes he missed the family home. At least there he'd had his own room.

The canal went right past Paul's hospital, Ian's factory as well. Paul could save himself a great deal of commute time, and money, if he only had a bike. But he thought it too 'young,' and Ian had to admit it was hard to imagine stuffy old Paul straddling a bike.

Ian actually wasn't as reckless as he wanted Paul to think. The path was narrow and often muddy, slick and wet on the paved parts, and bumpy on the brick parts, so Ian took his time. He always dinged his bell when headed into a blind corner—he wasn't a *firefighter*, constantly ringing his bell so that it didn't mean anything anymore. And he'd stopped wearing clips. More than once his awkwardness slipping in out of the toe clips had caused a *cliptastrophy*. He needed his feet unencumbered to avoid a wobble and a spill.

Just before the first bridge, Ian dropped smoothly from the street onto the bumpy ramp and then onto the towpath before it dipped into the darkness made by the road overhead. Dark as a cavern with this January weather, dark as the middle of the night—which he knew about, since sometimes that's when he would sneak out and ride. Paul slept like a drunk old man, talking in his sleep, rambling on about ridiculous, impossible things concerning flowers growing out of faces held underwater. *Just punishment*—that was one of sleeping Paul's favorite phrases. He turned into a regular sleeping Nazi, he did. But he didn't wake easily—most nights it would have taken a bomb to rouse him.

Ian had his light on—he knew the path, but a single miscalculation might send him arse over tit into those stinking waters. Maintenance of the canal was no longer what it used to be, some sections being so poorly maintained the narrow-boats rarely attempted them. Too many trips down the weed hatch to free the propeller and fill the rubbish bags meant a boat journey down such a putrid ditch was rarely worth the effort. A typical stretch included heavy patches of reeds on the one side and encroaching trees on the other, weeds in the black smelly mud along the bottom and the not-infrequent submerged object. There were barely two feet of water in parts of the channel. Even the wildlife had abandoned certain areas—he rarely saw more than the occasional duck. These were sections where only cyclists and the occasional fisherman ventured. Which of course was to Ian's liking; some days it felt as if the canal were his alone.

There was something vaguely outside geography about navigating the narrow canal path, passing under signs that always pointed somewhere else—Black Lake, Tame Valley, Gospel Oak—as if he were travelling through no place to anywhere he liked. Like the transporter on the old *Star Trek* show.

He passed under numerous bridges for cars, pedestrians, railways, or some combination, with concrete or brick or steel bases, many with the usual rude graffiti, some with a different sort of nonsensical language whose origins he could not fathom.

He passed the hospital and a while later passed the factory. Several apartment buildings in between made him wonder why Paul chose the building he did, but wasn't sure it was worth bringing up with the inevitable row. Ian shouldn't have let Paul choose. The truth was, Ian wasn't confident enough that he could choose better. He didn't know much yet about himself, or the world, but of course he couldn't admit that to Paul, who of course already knew.

The Firth body had been found somewhere between the hospital and the factory but he wasn't exactly sure where. The photos in the *Echo* showed only the gathered backs of policemen and bits of the canal. Most canal bits looked pretty much the same, with rundown, broken industrial buildings in the background. The *Echo* stated that the body had been covered with black mud. Glancing at the canal now, Ian could see several black objects in the water. How could he know one of them wasn't a body? He wasn't about to check.

He picked up speed on a long paved section running alongside a brick wall. A collection of cherry pickers parked on the other side resembled the long, bent legs of a giant tumbled insect.

He looked over at a crumbling old canal side warehouse with an overhead bay for unloading. It probably hadn't been used in fifty years or more. The canal was rich in such useless and decrepit architecture. The same could be said for the whole city—where he'd been trapped all his life—modern shopping complexes looking out of place alongside shabby empty shops in the suburbs. He needed to move someplace where everything was new but wasn't sure such a place existed in all of Britain.

Ian rode under Pleck Road and out to the M6 before turning back. He didn't see any bodies, not that he had expected to, really. He'd lied to Paul. He knew very well who James Firth was. Ian had first seen him singing in a folk club two years before. Ian had been sixteen at the time and unused to drinking; he'd spent most of that evening in a daze. He remembered trying to follow that handsome singer around and never quite getting close enough. Imagine his surprise when he got the factory job and there was James Firth in another department! Not that he ever worked up the courage to speak to him—he got that way with the truly handsome ones. But he had imagined it every day. By that time he was with Paul of course, but he always thought James Firth might be another Lawrence, only better, if he could just work up the courage to speak to him.

Good thing they'd never made the connection. He felt strangely about his death, the way you'd feel if you narrowly escaped being run over by a bus. Imagine how he would have felt if they'd been lovers?

He was tired enough on his return that he decided to stay in the rest of the day. Alone like this the flat seemed alien. Paul had selected most of the furniture. He hadn't minded at first—Paul was the one with *taste*, but at this point nothing felt like Ian's anymore. It was the ground floor of a terraced house. When they moved in the old wallpaper had been left, faded blue flowers on grey. At least in his parents' house he had been allowed to paint and put up anything he liked on the walls. But Paul had very specific and conservative tastes. It was Paul's flat, really—now all grays and tans and pretentious knockoffs. It could hardly feel more oppressive. If Ian were sacked and could no longer contribute he'd lose the little influence he had. He might as well move back in with Mum and Dad.

Paul had promised they would redecorate soon and Ian could choose some pieces, the way a parent might give a child some illusory freedom by allowing them to choose some design element for their bedroom. Ian would have to put up with so much condescension about his cluelessness it hardly seemed worth it.

He hid from the rest of the flat by sitting in the bedroom playing Tindersticks on the record player. The records and the player belonged to Paul, of course, but Ian was the more dedicated fan. He'd have them put away before Paul returned— he didn't like the way Ian handled records, and some of Paul's vinyl was rare, or at least he claimed it was.

When Paul came home he brought sushi. Afterwards Paul took a ridiculously long shower and they went out for a film— something Iranian Paul had read about. Ian had a hard time following it, and finally fell asleep against Paul's shoulder. He had a dream of flowers growing on the body in the canal. It had floated there so long plants had the opportunity to take root. The song from the film's soundtrack was "Killing Me Softly with His Song." Roberta Flack. Or was this part of the dream? It seemed a strange song for an Iranian film. Ian felt terrified as the petals began to open.

Paul woke him up after the film ended. He seemed angry. "They give you too much work there," Paul said as they left the cinema. "You're exhausted all the time. You should insist on more breaks—you have rights. This isn't the slave trade."

Ian felt guilty about lying to him but was also derisive of Paul's earnestness and gullibility. It made him nervous and agitated. Paul started to call a taxi when Ian broke off and started walking rapidly down the damp and greasy pavement. "No, let's take the towpath!" he shouted back at him and started to run.

Ian was already under one of the bridges by the time Paul

caught up to him, completely out of breath and grabbing on to Ian's shoulder. His sweat stank of marsh and damp wool. "Stop...damn you...."

Old man already, so out of shape. Ian shrugged off his hand. "It's shorter, and it's free. Take a chance." He started walking. Soon enough Paul caught up again, stony-faced and sullen beside him. Ian was happy to let him stew but after only a few minutes couldn't bear the silence and needed to make small talk. "The water levels in the canal are lower this year, but I'm not aware of a drought. I suppose it made it easier, to find that body, I mean."

"It spreads. It's the leakage," Paul replied.

"What? What do you mean?"

"The water leaks into the basements nearby, some of them. All around here—it's the leakage. And James Firth—the body had a name."

Ian ignored the comment about Firth. He didn't want to argue with Paul now, here by the canal, in the dark. "Leakage? I've never heard of such a thing—is it from one of your articles or something?"

"It's—" Paul stopped and looked around. "Did you hear something? In any case it's common knowledge. You might know if you weren't running about all the time, or staying home and playing my records. A relationship requires commitment, Ian, and sometimes that means giving up our selfish needs."

"Look, if you're talking about Lawrence, that wasn't my entire fault. You left me alone with him again and again...."

"Let the dead rest."

"He's not dead."

"He is as far as I'm concerned."

There was a sudden humming, a bee-like sound, and then something dark popped up out of nowhere and passed swiftly between them, almost knocking Paul into the canal. Ian snapped his head around to follow the sound—it was a Bike Ninja, riding around with no lights on in the pitch black. The rider had removed all reflective gear to maximize his or her ninja status. Ian felt envious—he'd long wanted to do the same thing. Maybe he still would.

Paul roared, furious. "Is that what you want to be? Is that what you do when you leave me in the middle of the night?"

Ian could see the dark shape expanding behind Paul. Another Ninja.

But this one wasn't attached to any bike. Paul's face, red and angry, dropped away inside an obscuring shadow. He hit the pavement with a dull thud.

The next day at work someone caught his hand in one of the hydraulic stamping presses. It brought the production line down. Ian watched as the medics brought the poor fellow out. He overheard someone say the entire arm might be paralyzed. Ian had the opportunity to go home early but decided to stay and help out with a few random tasks. Paul was at home, recovering from the incident by the canal and Ian didn't want to talk to him just yet.

They'd both decided Paul had simply gotten confused and fallen. He had scrapes on his hands and the left side of his face, as well as several contusions along his rib cage. Paul was the one who decided it had been a fall; Ian had been there and still had no theory of his own. It had been dark, certainly, and they'd both been agitated. Paul refused to see a doctor. He seemed more embarrassed by the event than anything else.

During lunch there was a bad smell of stagnant water in the warehouse. Ian complained to the new safety officer, who assigned Ian and three others to clean the area. Early in the job his two companions claimed they couldn't bear the stench and Ian had to work alone, sorting through boxes and bags, some of them feeling warm and damp and vaguely flesh-like. Ian had actually grown accustomed to the smell and didn't find it that bad. He found himself humming that song from the soundtrack of *The Drowning Pool*, or had it been from that dream of the body infested with flowers? "Killing Me Softly with His Song." He couldn't be sure. The words from the soundtrack echoed in his head, widening the darkness inside him. He could hear water dripping but couldn't decide whether it was inside the warehouse or inside his head. And he could smell this reek of flowers, as if they'd been cooked in some humid confinement until their sweet perfumes had become a kind of stench. He kept replaying the scene in which that dark shape had risen up behind Paul. It might have simply been a trick of the shadows—Paul thought he himself was responsible for his accident. But it defied logic. Ian replayed it again. Paul had been so angry—Ian had never seen him angry like that before, as if he might lose his mind. And then that shadow had appeared so suddenly, as if it had been ripped right out of him, enfolding him like dark wings from his back.

Ian had left his bike at home, choosing to ride the bus. He wasn't sure why—it felt like a gesture of respect for Paul, for Paul's feelings about Ian's activities. But he wasn't going to give up the bike—just for this one day, as a kind of gesture. He walked home via the canal path. Today it felt like an act of defiance. But he also wanted to get another look at the canal where Paul's so-called accident had occurred.

It was a relatively clear day for that time of year. Ian set off from behind the factory through the rusted old canal access gate at the back of the employee parking lot. He only had a short period of daylight left before twilight and the rapid fall into dusk. He reached that stretch just beyond the bridge where the incident had occurred. It was already partly in shadow because of the angle of the sun.

Of course there was nothing to see. He wasn't sure what he'd been thinking. Clues were for the movies, not for real life.

He spent the rest of the walk checking out the banks on both sides of the canal. The water level was still low. He could clearly see the dark line of stain where the foul water usually reached, like the line in a toilet bowl which hadn't been conscientiously scrubbed. Of course Paul never permitted such an occurrence in their flat. The surface of the canal was a good foot below that line.

As he walked on he looked for breaches in the old concrete and stone that lined the canal, any spots where the water might have escaped and gone somewhere else. He felt foolish about it—he was no expert and couldn't possibly know what he was seeing—but he looked anyway and pretended that he wasn't completely ignorant.

There were definite fissures in the lining of the canal. Whether they led anywhere it was impossible to determine. All along the embankment there were drops and sunken areas of varying degrees. Whether they meant anything Ian was hardly qualified to say. This was a very old part of the city—it had been built, torn down, reworked, and rebuilt numerous times over the decades. Several of the buildings along its banks were either empty or non-functional. They should have been demolished, but people here loved the old—they held on to it, embraced it, even after it had ceased being useful. Why couldn't they see that sometimes it was best just to tear things down and start over?

Ian thought about their flat. No matter how much they redecorated it and hid its flaws, he doubted it would ever feel like home.

He came up off the canal path only a short distance from the flat. He could see now that theirs wasn't the only one looking for a remodel. A number of trades people were packing up their vans and loading their trucks, construction bins were full and, as darkness rapidly encroached, it brought with it not only the usual cooking smells but the aromas of fresh paint and new plaster as well.

And something else. A certain stagnancy carried over from the canal that seemed out of place here where things were being made new. The stench made him anxious and he found himself glancing into any gaps between buildings, peering over steps going down, simply trying to be more aware of his surroundings.

Alongside the building next to theirs was a depressed place where a narrow passageway between that building and the next had sunk a bit. In the side of the building there appeared to be a damaged access door whose frame had partially collapsed. Ian had never noticed it before and wouldn't have seen it now except for his heightened, what? Paranoia? He veered off the path until he was only five or so yards away. The stench was worse here. He went up to the broken door intending only to peek, but there was just the right amount of space for him to squeeze inside, almost as if the amount of collapse had been tailored specifically to him.

He felt as if he had entered his own head. The smell of foul damp, the notion of secret growth, and that distant memory of song, *killing me softly, killing me softly.*

A few yards in he found the decaying human face with the flowers growing in its sockets. No, not growing, but put there recently. Previous offerings of dead flowers lay scattered across the water that had seeped in from below, petals and stems turned brown or moldy. He couldn't see the rest of the body as it was somehow anchored below, but even with a few chunks missing he knew the face. It was Lawrence.

"Paul! Paul!" Ian went straight to their bedroom and burst through the door. The bed was empty, the covers in disarray. The foul odor of the canal was strongly evident. Water rose from the carpet when he stepped nearer the bed. The sheets, too, appeared wet.

He followed the sound of the running shower down the hall. The shadowed figure behind the clouded glass door was humming tunelessly but Ian could still decipher the melody, *killing me, killing me.* The shadow turned, and grew broader, and became confusing in its shape.

STICK MEN

Asako took the crosstown bus over to the west side to visit her mother every Monday and every Wednesday after work. She'd never been able to enjoy the trip. At least there was an express with very few stops, with a large number of women passengers which permitted her to relax, her guard rising only when some male attempted to work his way through the crowd.

She was always at her mother's before supper, and crazy or not, her mother was a wonderful cook.

The worst thing about riding the bus was that Asako could not see who boarded after her. Possibly the caution was unnecessary. Perhaps her anxiety simply expressed an unfortunate lack of confidence which she should attempt to change. She could twist her head around to see whoever came through the rear door, but she couldn't bear to draw attention to herself that way. If the new passenger was truly a threat, wouldn't that simply anger him?

She could always take a seat at the back of the bus. Then she wouldn't have to turn around to see. She could look each man in the face as he stepped on, and search for any signs of ill will. But she could not imagine that kind of boldness, and the back of the bus had always seemed the most dangerous place to sit. If a man bothered her the bus driver might not be able to see, and if she were dragged off through the rear door what could he do? Better to sit near the middle, where more help might be available.

If she sat too near the front the men thought she was forward and wanted to talk. She knew this from experience.

She always made sure she had the exact change for her trip to her mother's, twice weekly with no deviations. That way she wouldn't have to waste time using the changing machine—she could just drop her ticket and the exact fare into the box by the driver and get off quickly and down the street before anyone could follow.

"Do not let them follow you, Asako," her mother had always warned her. "It is unfortunate, but men are the major threat to women. A young woman must measure each man she meets for his level of kyoui." Sometimes men would approach her even as the bus was moving and sit beside her. She was in constant fear that one might say things she might not want to hear. Would he make her feel dirty simply because of his proximity? Some nights she could hardly breathe until she was off the bus and walking down the street again.

If too many men boarded at the same time then Asako could not adequately evaluate the ones standing in the middle, the ones whose hands and eyes, mouths and feet, were hidden behind parts of other men. Sometimes there were so many she couldn't even make an accurate count. Sometimes there seemed to be too many hands, too many heads, sometimes a few missing eyes, or torsos bent impossibly. Somehow random parts of these mysterious men in the middle had vanished, and the men themselves had become one great sprawling creature, whose alien intent and motivations were impossible to fathom.

On the rare (but not rare enough) occasions when that happened, Asako would close her eyes and struggle through the tangle of body parts. "Sumimasen Orimasu!" she would repeat, over and over as she pushed her way to the front of the bus. "I will get off here!" She would climb down at the next stop and wait for a later bus to arrive. Her mother always said that a young woman should never take chances.

Perhaps it was unfair. Perhaps she missed meeting some very nice man who might step out of that anonymous crowd of incomplete men and come over and apologize for his temerity, and then would introduce himself, and smile with perfectly even, but sincere, teeth, but Asako was not the kind of young woman to take such chances.

"You never can tell," her mother would say. "You never can tell." And Asako certainly could not.

"It is so hard to know which ones are going to be the good ones," her mother would say, and sigh.

Her mother was now in failing health, and somewhat crazy, although Asako was not sure how crazy. Was she crazy like a fox, or crazy like a lunatic?

Most evenings when she arrived at her mother's apartment, she would find her stationed by the front window, peering down at the sidewalk and the street and the people passing by. "It is always good to know who or what is just outside your house, Asako-chan. You never can tell. What are all these skinny young men with their soft faces and their hair? These girlie boys? Is that now the fashion?"

"I don't know, Mother. Maybe. I don't keep up with things." She was lying to her mother. Asako had dreamed many times of these beautiful, skinny men with their pretty faces and even prettier words.

"Something my own mother taught me, Asako-chan. Do not trust the skinny men. Although she put it differently. Dansei sutikku, she called them. You can never tell what these stick men want, or what they might do. Your grandmother was so certain I would run away with one of these stick men she would watch from our front window at night, eager to chase them off."

Asako listened politely, but although it made her feel like a terrible daughter, she thought most of the things her mother said were gibberish. Her mother's bits of wisdom made her feel anxious even when she didn't understand them.

But her mother had never been satisfied with her own performance as a parent. When Asako was just a young girl her mother would lecture her concerning the qualities of a "good" mother.

A good mother was always patient. A good mother was always warm. A good mother was kind and cheerful at all times. A good mother met every need of her child. A good mother was an ever-watchful presence in the life of her children.

Her father had been distant like the fathers of most of her friends. A businessman of the samurai type. Her mother would draw his baths and light his cigarettes. Asako had seen him rarely. When he disappeared it made no difference in her world.

Her mother was the most important person in Asako's life, and yet her mother thought herself a failure.

"I was harsh. I could not remain calm, Asako-chan. I would lose control. I could not scold you without showing emotion. Even after regular Hansei, I still had no patience. Understanding made me no less harsh."

What could Asako say? Her mother had been all of these things. She'd been frightening, strict, controlling. "What about Father? Would you have called him a skinny man, a stick man? I don't really remember, I saw him so seldom."

Her mother pondered a moment. "No, no, even though he hadn't much fat on him. He was a fierce, ferocious man. You always knew what you were getting with him. You know the old saying, 'one should fear earthquakes, thunder, fire, and fathers'?"

"No, I don't know that one," Asako lied again.

"Well, that was your father."

"I don't remember," Asako said, but did not know if that was a lie or not.

Her mother fell into silence and continued to watch the street below. Asako stood behind her, gazing over her head, not wanting to, but seeing what her mother must have been seeing. Her own tiny apartment had no windows, but at least it was her own, and she could control what she had to see.

Darkness had flowed out of the streets and ground, out of deep wells hidden between slabs of concrete, and was now rising like water against the buildings but staying just shy of the streetlights which would destroy it. Still, it was there undermining the foundations of things, loosening the grip of civilization so that everyone would live in jeopardy come the next big storm. Beneath her feet she could feel the vague heavings of the ground, the shell-like surface of the world breaking, shifting, forcing the shadows to flee their underground city for the city above.

The long shadows seeped out of the thin trees and utility poles, out of the bamboo shafts there in the water along the edge of the park, from the vertical seams of the buildings, the skinny dark legs walking and the skinny dark arms waving, and making soft creaking noises like metal crickets every time they bent.

Asako felt herself go dizzy, and sat down, and reluctantly allowed her mother to fuss after her. Her mother brought her blankets, her mother brought her tea, but Asako kept turning her head and crying, because her mother had also brought her these terrible visions, and Asako was sure she'd never be able to look at the world without seeing it through her mother's eyes.

It was the trip coming back through darkened streets, and that half-hour stop at the old station in the worst part of town, that always made her feel like a frightened child. The bright street lights only deepened the shadows. They were like stars that had dropped too low in the sky. The neighborhoods were poorly-maintained; wind blew the trash around, and the shapes waited, hunched in doorways.

Tonight the buildings appeared to tilt, their foundations shifting on the now-liquid ground, giving the impression of broken, jumbled silhouettes as the bus thundered over the rattling puzzle pieces of damaged pavement.

The narrow shadows glided out of the doorways, climbed out of the windows and gutters, their protesting joints or protesting voices making that faint creaking sound. They raced after the bus, they slapped against the closed rear doors, their sharp edges sliding over the bus looking for some way in, skinny fingers scraping at the window where Asako sat. Sometimes the bus would pass an open space and Asako would see that it had been filled with a forest of legs.

In first year middle school, their science club adviser took them to the park where he grabbed the branch of an oak tree and shook it. Dozens of tiny twigs fell to the ground, all looking perfectly trimmed to a similar length and form. Then they'd begun moving, twitching, rising up and waving. She'd gasped so loudly it made the others laugh. They were nanafushi, stick insects, and although she had been in that park and by that tree many times before, she had never noticed these creatures.

Now she watched as the long skinny forms peeled away from every vertical shape in the city's streets and attempted to follow the bus as if it were a morsel of food dropped into their midst. None of the other passengers appeared to notice anything. They were predominantly male, the younger ones slumped in their untidy boredom, the older ones wearing unreadable masks of fatigued, pale skin.

She couldn't find a spot where she could sit comfortably. She walked to one place and then the other, holding on precariously. Then she'd sit down only momentarily. After only a minute or so she'd feel compelled to stand up and wander the bus seeking random areas of relative safety.

"Watch yourself, Asako-chan," her mother said almost every night before she left. "Hold your bag tightly to your body; do not let it hang down. That is how they steal it from you."

"Yes, Mother. I am careful with my bag."

"They will all behave poorly, if they see an opportunity," her mother explained. "It's not their fault—they've been led to believe that's what they're supposed to do. It's their male camouflage. It makes them desperate and reckless, I think."

"Mother, that's not fair. You're generalizing. They can't all be like that."

"Perhaps. Perhaps. The hungry ones are the worse. I know this from experience. They are so agitated, these stick men. They move around, they can't stop moving, I think. I've seen them do this. They don't want to be recognized. So stay away from the stick men. Then you'll be fine."

Asako believed that her mother knew things, important things about men, that Asako didn't know, but Asako had a hard time understanding what she was getting at much of the time. Sometimes she thought her mother's mission was to make her feel worse about everything.

"But how will I find a good man? The men who request my company all seem so cruel, so dishonest."

"Perhaps you draw them to you, moths to flame, ants to sugar. They believe you have what they need—warmth, light, sweetness."

Asako felt on the verge of tears. "Men are not all the same, Mother, any more than women are."

"Did I say they were all the same? There are all kinds of

animals in the world, my darling. All kinds of, how do you say, types?"

"Species?"

"That is the word. You must learn to recognize each species, Asako-chan, for your safety and happiness. You do not have to worry about the chickens, my dear. It is the foxes you have to worry about."

Asako thought perhaps she had a touch of cold. She'd waited at the stop outside her mother's apartment for over half an hour, leaning into the dark, staring at the space the bus door would soon occupy, willing it to happen.

Then suddenly the door was there, opening, and she almost toppled in. The driver obviously saw her stagger, catch herself, and Asako worried that he might think she'd been drinking and not let her on.

She'd be stuck then, for hours, unable to go back inside her mother's place because she wouldn't want to answer any of her mother's questions.

But the driver said nothing, and she found her seat somewhere safely in the middle. The bus started off with an exaggerated sigh. Asako had been gazing out the window and the movement made the buildings lean.

The night was much too vertical, that was the problem, the bus now too tall, had grown far beyond its center of gravity. She, too, felt much taller than before, and too unbalanced to walk comfortably.

The buildings had roofs that disappeared into darkness, challenging the indifferent moon. Perhaps it was her cold, some vague touch of infection and the beginning of a fever, or perhaps she was finally seeing things as they truly were. Because she had no windows in her own apartment she could not keep up with the changes in the world.

Outside the bus windows the multiplying verticals whipped by, the signposts, the lamp posts, utility poles, the tall and narrow trees. Some edges of buildings, but most had been burnished and rounded by age.

A broad-shouldered man stepped on at the next stop. She felt relieved because he was not skinny. She felt ridiculous, sizing up each man she met for the threat he might pose, but she could not stop. Yet again she would be going home to a small, empty apartment and still she could not stop.

For the rest of the ride she sat with her head down, staring at the floor. At the other end she went straight into her building without looking around, anxious to burrow into her windowless apartment and hide.

The next time she went to visit, Asako thought her mother seemed more agitated. She kept glancing out her window at the dark street below, sometimes craning her neck to see as much as possible, even though as far as Asako could tell there was nothing out there to see. The skinny shadows had calmed down. Asako had not seen them for days. Obviously it had been her nervousness, accelerated by her mother's, which had made her see these things.

"These men you meet out in the streets, they look real enough, they sometimes say what you want to hear, but I do not believe they are real men at all." Her mother was wagging her head side to side like some kind of crazed animal. "They are stick men, full of attitude and their own desires, but they have no substance. They are like ghosts. They are no good for you, I think."

Her mother kept repeating herself, over and over. The same themes, the same worries. Asako did not want to leave, but she could not tolerate much more of this.

"Go along, go along. Live your life, Asako-chan. But watch where you sit. Be careful whose hands you hold. They may not be who they seem."

Asako's return bus was quite late, and foolishly she thought she would catch one sooner on another street. She turned away from the bus stop outside her mother's apartment and marched away like some soldier into darkness.

There appeared to be too many utility poles here—too numerous and too close together. They were like giant fence posts for a fence that had never been completed, meant to separate this section of the city from everywhere else. There were also trees, stripped of their branches, leaving the tall skinny trunks pointing toward the night sky.

Her eyes had been giving her trouble because of all the pollen in the air, so that sometimes certain objects became blurry and hard to see. Either these poles were out of focus, or they had grown some kind of fringe, mold or moss. It would not surprise her—the government seemed to spend little on maintenance for this part of the city.

Some of the poles appeared swollen, as if waterlogged. As if in sympathy a thick drop of water oozed out of her hairline and traced her face like an oily finger.

She saw a sign in the distance that might be another bus stop, but it was too far away to tell for sure.

Some of the poles were in worse shape than others. Some were splintered, long strips peeling down from their sides. The long splinters caught in the wind blowing down the street and waved.

When she reached the corner she could see the bus in the distance coming her way. But she hesitated to take another step. There were very few lights here. Most of the storefronts were empty.

Something rustled behind her. The pavement was broken into angular fragments. She stretched out her left foot to test the ground's solidity and determine whether the lines were cracks or seams or merely shadows. The dark lines moved toward her leg suddenly, making her step back.

The darkness behind her rattled like a pile of broken sticks. She turned quickly and almost caught them, their long legs, their improbably-extended arms coming out of the skinny torsos, an army of hungry shadows ready to follow her wherever she might go. Right on to her bus and beyond.

She turned the corner and ran down the street to where there were more businesses, more stores, more lights. She ran into people coming out of doors.

"Shitsurei shimasu! Excuse me!" she cried desperately, feeling ashamed, but unable to stop herself as she ran to avoid the shadows, not daring to look behind her, or into any of the doorways more closely, thinking that if she didn't see the shadows they weren't really there. She turned another, more familiar corner, and realized she was running along her regular bus route in the direction of her mother's apartment.

The pavement began to shift again, the concrete walk cracked, and dark shadow oozed from the damage. Asako could see the entrance to her mother's apartment building ahead, and it was all she could do not to shout "Okaasan!" toward her window in hopes she might see her.

Asako slapped her palms against the door again and again. Her mother let her in, and Asako was shocked to see a smile on the old woman's face, as if it were all a joke.

"Mother, I...."

"It is so fortunate you came back, Asako-chan," her mother said, still smiling. "Can you believe it? Look who has finally returned to us!"

Asako stared into the room, unable to see much of anything. Then the grayness crept out of every seam, converging into the tall skinny form leaning over her. Her father's mouth made a creaking noise as it opened, then out of the depths, the drawn-out sigh of "chan..."

TOO MANY GHOSTS

He'd paid more attention to the knife, and the face he'd brought forth from the wood, than to his left hand trembling as it gripped the cottonwood branch. The blade went into the side of his thumb smoothly, and if it had been wood he would have immediately realized he'd chosen his materials poorly, because wood that soft wouldn't hold the intricate detail he required. Hector watched as his blood filled the valleys of the bark, reddening the hollows of the unfinished face, an exaggerated expression of anger that dripped onto the porch's worn boards.

He laid the knife and the branch down carefully on his small table of tools and materials. Then he said "dammit" once and evenly and attempted to close the wound with his other hand.

He wondered again if he might be too old, or at least too infirm, to carve anymore. But carving was all he'd ever wanted to do. It might be all he *could* do. He hadn't the stamina to farm anymore, or the heart to sit in an office staring at a screen. If he still had a wife he might feel differently—there might be other things he could do in the world. But he no longer had a wife, so this was how he filled his time.

"Here, Dad." Lucena dangled a roll of gauze and tape in front of him. She always kept some handy. "Can I help you?"

He grabbed the gauze, wrapping his thumb with swift turns of his other hand. "I'll manage. Thanks."

She went back into the kitchen, then called, "Are you sure you can handle the trick-or-treaters tonight? You could still come with us. We could put the candy bucket out with a sign telling the children to take no more than two."

"Please tell me you're joking." He tied the ends of the gauze with a flutter of his fingers. His wife Nekana had called the maneuver his butterfly. She had loved his butterfly. "The candy wouldn't last five minutes. Parents would be coming by tomorrow to complain about their children's bellyaches." His daughter always tried to lure him back into the church, but Hector would not be lured.

"Well, at least help the boys carve their pumpkin. They love seeing the things you come up with."

He picked up the branch again, stared at it. The old man in the cottonwood stared back. Hector thought he recognized the face from when he was a boy. The eyes in the wood shifted, avoiding capture. Hector couldn't be sure. "I don't carve vegetables, mija."

"A pumpkin is a fruit, papa."

"I don't carve those either."

He heard her move back into the dining room. She fussed at the boys. Apparently they were still staring at the pumpkin, and had not even lifted their puny blades with the colorful plastic handles—very safe, but impossible to use with any skill. She did not understand. You could not carve the face until you first saw the face in your material. The boys had watched him do this hundreds of times, and now they were copying him, although they didn't have his knowledge, and they were getting into trouble for it. They would be late for the church Halloween party, she told them.

His daughter took the boys to church every Halloween for the safe candy. Hector knew of no child who had ever been poisoned, or who had bitten into a razor blade or a pin. But his daughter always imagined the worst. Now she was angry. The boys would not get their Halloween. One of them began to cry; Hector didn't know which one—they both sounded the same to him.

This was not his responsibility. He picked up the branch again. He looked for the old one's eyes, but he still couldn't find them. Perhaps the old man was sleeping. Or hiding. Hector put his knife point where the left ear should be, but he didn't know how to carve it until he could see the eyes. A sharp pain in the web of his right hand. He turned the branch over quickly, and thought he saw tiny teeth receding into the carved mouth. There was a bite mark in his skin, or was it a splinter? He pushed his thumb into the mouth but the lips did not move. He sighed and continued to ponder what he had made.

The face in the wood looked disturbingly familiar—the invisible eyes, and the way the hair flowed with the grain—but he could not connect the visage with a name.

He would decide later if he would take this carving to the craft show the next day, or stick it with the others in the field. Both his mistakes and his finest works were out in the field.

The distant explosion was too far away to cause any vibration, but he dropped the branch anyway. A piece of beard snapped off, a corner of one ear. This one was for the field, then. Hector was okay with it—this one's destination seemed inevitable.

Lucena appeared in the doorway again. "I thought they weren't working today."

"They work every day," Hector replied. "It's a big mountain—they have lots to blow up."

"These are holy days. They have no respect for the dead."

"Perhaps the dead want the mountain gone as well. Once they open the road, the dead may find some more interesting place to go."

"Papa! That's blasphemous!"

"I don't intend to be. I know nothing of what the dead want. I can only make guesses."

She left again. He heard her fussing at his grandsons again, how she would cancel Halloween completely if they didn't get a move on.

They lived at the high end of the valley, before the gap. But the gap had been closed since Hector was little, the road there buried under landslide after landslide. Nothing could get through, and so people rarely came this way anymore, except the occasional salesman, and the children for their annual Halloween treats.

Once the mountain was removed from the road life would change, Hector was sure. But he could not imagine the details. He climbed slowly to his feet.

"Where is this pumpkin you want carved?" Hector stood in the doorway, his knife ready. Of course he could see the pumpkin—it sat in the middle of the dining table, lolling as if asleep. His twin grandsons stared up at him in amazement.

Hector stepped forward, reached in, and slipped his palm under the pumpkin, drawing it up and cradling it in the crook of his arm. As her face began to appear to him he began his cuts, highlighting and recessing planes and imagined bone and muscle, those wisps of hair, the stretch of the lips, the laughter gone except for some intangible amusement trapped in the corners. Her eyes opened and followed the graceful movements of his hand. There were folds of skin across her cheekbones, but they were tidy, and soft, and well-earned. He remembered every line, where they held fast, and where they moved. He hated the material—it was far too soft, and would not hold its shape, or its health, for long. It would sag, and it would rot, and it would run.

He held his work aloft, now fully realizing what he had made.

"Papa?" Lucena gasped.

"Lito? Is that Gramma?" one of the boys asked. Hector didn't know which one. He could tell them apart perhaps every other Tuesday.

"Your grandmother is dead," he answered them, and carried her head from the room.

After his family left for the church Hector rushed to prepare for the trick-or-treaters. He was afraid he'd waited too long. The sun was setting, and he still needed to get some lights out so that the children could find their way through the field to the porch.

Another explosion, and this one accompanied by a rain of dust and pebbles from the sky that rattled the house's rusted tin roof. This had to be the last one—soon there wouldn't be enough light to continue. A dark cloud oddly streaked with red had settled over the mountain.

"There are too many ghosts here! The dead can't find their way out!" It had been Hector's father's constant complaint. Some of the old timers believed the path to heaven lay through the gap—once the gap was closed the dead didn't know which way to go. They were trapped, both the living and the dead together. But Hector always thought that what really haunted his father was that he'd made such a bad deal buying this place. The land was poor, and the slides had cut off not just the road, but their only source for water.

He ran two dusty strings of Christmas lights on either side of the porch steps and through the field, making the hollow outline of a path which he embellished here and there with luminaria. As the sun slipped behind the serrated mountain ridges the field became vague and ethereal with a random scattering of stunted, twisted cottonwoods protruding from the white sand, some branches like desperate arms reaching for the yellowed moon. Here and there he'd planted his carvings among them. As the tiny lights blinked indistinct faces and pale twisted bodies floated momentarily out of the bark.

The cottonwoods were rough and dark and yet perfect for the art he felt compelled to make. He used up the branches one at time, and when the trees finally fell completely he carved the roots. If he lived long enough he would have no more materials to work with.

Everything was so dry even the slightest breeze picked up dust and grit making it difficult to see. All along the horizon the shadows multiplied.

The wind came up with a sudden fierceness and Hector turned his face away. For a moment it felt as if all the ground would rise and fill the air. Hoping it would die down before any children arrived, he walked back into the house to prepare their treats, one hand over his mouth. Great stretches of landscape appeared to blow past him, and several of the old trees looked out of place, but this had become a frequent illusion during these late afternoon winds.

The stinging impact of wind-blown debris, the sense of mysterious movement around him, and the fact that he had to contend with all of this alone, angered him.

He split his store of candy into numerous small paper bags, a different prayer written on the back of each just as his wife used to do. Not that he believed in such things, but it would have pleased her to know he'd continued her tradition. He sat by the front window listening for the old pickups that would bring the children in their costumes, in their swollen heads and their strangely broken bodies, loaded pillowcases hung awkwardly between their legs as they struggled up his front steps. He would then take his wife's old role, greeting them, feigning amazement at their homemade costumes, and always saying something nice to the little ones to comfort them on this scary night.

A scratch at the window startled him, a broken bit of branch clawing its way across the glass. Out in the field he could see the thinner cottonwood branches snapping, spinning into the wind like amputated fingers.

An explosion sounded somewhere nearby, so close he thought it was the house itself about to come down around him. Surely they weren't working on the mountain this late? Then he saw the lightning flashes and realized it was thunder. He wondered whether it would keep the children away.

Hector had found his wife in that small church down in the mouth of the valley over fifty years ago, courted her for less than two months, eventually bringing her here where they raised a child and built a life. Then he'd had to watch her shrink and twist like the cottonwoods hopeless for water. Still, she'd dragged him stubbornly back to that church for every ceremony and obligation. But no more.

The wind had died down a bit, but out in the field sand was still stirring, a languid scribbling movement that spread upward and into the dark. It snowed rarely here, but when it did it was like this: the air full of a fine white powder that coated the black trees, flipping the world temporarily into its negative.

Hector could see dark masses within the spectral white, individual outlines moving toward his house. The dark twists and verticals of trunks began to peek through, shapes stumbling awkwardly through those damaged trees. He started to get up, wondering if he had a good place to hide, when a dozen or more children suddenly appeared, in drooping costumes and masks turned sideways across dusty faces, dragging their sagging treat bags between the rows of lights, and up his splintered steps.

Hector got up early the next morning to clean up the field. Lucena and the boys weren't up yet—they'd gotten home late from the church because of the storm. The boys had been subdued—Lucena said the storm had scared them, although they'd refused to admit it.

He gathered up several armfuls of broken cottonwood branches, stacking them for later use. Surprisingly, all his carvings appeared to be more or less intact after the storm, although some leaned precariously over, and others had hairline cracks giving new emphasis to either age or suffering.

He pulled one of these out of the ground and cradled it in his arms. The face in the wood looked gray, asleep, and had he really carved the hair that way? He searched for some fissure in the scalp but couldn't find one. The hair looked misshapen, pulled. The face appeared to open its eyes, and look at Hector, but the sun was rising higher behind him, pushing the shadows. He jammed the carving back into the ground and turned away.

Once back inside the house he began choosing the carvings he would take to the show. He could hear Lucena talking to the boys in the next room. "Mother Lupita, she would go begging in the street to collect money for her hospital, but asking no more than was *necessary*. You see, she never felt above doing whatever the poor have to do. That is why they made her a saint. And you boys—you complain about the breakfast I cook? Think about it!"

His daughter was in a righteous mood. He hurried to get out of there before she saw him, but almost immediately she burst through the door. "I can't believe you're not going with us today. It's a day of *obligation*, Papa! What kind of Catholic are you?"

He didn't look at her, but focused on selecting pieces. He always brought too many old men, when it was the lovely ladies with the roses in their hair who sold the best. "A poor one, certainly. With two hungry grandsons to feed, and I am happy to do so, make no mistake. Why do we need to pray for the saints anyway? We're the ones who need the prayers."

"Papa! That's *blasphemy*! Mama would be so ashamed!"

"You have no idea what your mother would say. You weren't there to see her suffer. She just wanted an end to her agony, and what comfort did the priest have to offer her? 'You must bear it,' that's what he said. Oh, and 'your reward is coming. You must be brave,' he told her, as if she weren't already the bravest person I ever knew."

"I know she was brave, Papa. I know she wanted to die, but only God decides when."

Hector stared at her. "She didn't want to die," he said. "She just didn't want to live in such pain, and in the end she cursed me and she cursed herself and she cursed God for that. And that is why I am not going with you today."

She was crying. "I will pray for Mama tomorrow," she said. "When it is All Souls'. I will pray that God lets her out of purgatory."

Unable to look his daughter in the eyes anymore, Hector turned his back and began getting the rest of his carvings together. He could tell how wary of him they were, how fearful that he might chip the important details. But he grabbed them anyway, clutching them too firmly. He grabbed them and took them out to his truck and threw them in. He was aware of Lucena standing there behind him the whole time, but he did not turn around. He had been too harsh with her, he knew, but it was too late now.

The craft fair had a fall theme. Of course there were the usual Halloween items—ghosts and witches and pumpkins and the like—discounted heavily because it was the day after.

When business was slow the sellers walked around, checking out the competition, catching up with old friends. Hector never engaged in that—he had no money to spend, and even less curiosity, and all his old friends were dead.

Alvarez, a potter, had been studying one of Hector's "old men," *Gray Beard*, when he said, "Your talent grows every year, Hector. That's how I know you're a true artist. You never slack off. You always raise the bar, improve your craft." Hector grunted, not that he didn't appreciate compliments. He just didn't know what to do with them. "Take this one. *Excelente!* He's the old priest, the one who died ten years ago, right? You've captured him so well, that cast of the eye, that crook in the mouth, the untidy beard."

Hector stared at the carving. "The resemblance is coincidental," he stated flatly, and folded his arms. He did not do portraits. But he hesitated. The likeness was uncanny.

"Oh, I see. But this one? This is that butcher Emilio? He died last year? I still haven't found a roast as good as what he had in his shop."

Hector nodded uncommittedly, but stared at the hook nose, the broad cheeks wrapping around the branch. He had never liked Emilio, never patronized his shop. So why would he memorialize him? But the resemblance was undeniable.

"And Mother Adoncia? It was so sad when she died earlier this year." Alvarez held the thick branch in his hands, rocking back and forth on his feet. Hector had forgotten all about the old nun. But yes, this was certainly her.

An elderly woman stopped at Alvarez's table and he scurried off with a dramatic wave. Multiple bracelets dangled from his wrist. Hector was surprised to see that he liked the effect.

He glanced at his display. The embedded faces turned toward him, or peeked out of branch forks, crooks, knots, obscuring turns. They blinked, licked lips with tongue-like wooden chips, as if wanting to address him, or waiting for him to address them.

He thought he recognized a few more of the carvings. Oliver Sanchez. A man he'd seen hitch-hiking. Madonna Pena. He believed he might have heard about her death a few months ago. A number of them had died this past year, but he wasn't sure of the details. He should have paid more attention, and then he might have a better understanding of what was happening here. Or at least he might have a clue. All perfect likenesses. All unintended.

The ragged fellow with the floppy cap—he'd once been a neighbor, and then he'd lost his ranch. Hector never knew whatever happened to the man. Had he passed away too?

"Do you have something with a Halloween theme?"

The woman's head looked so small with the scarf wrapped

around it Hector thought at first she was one of his. Then she held up a twenty-dollar bill. "Hello, customer here. I have pesos, dinero, whatever you people call it. Anything Halloween related? I'm a collector."

Hector glanced around at his pieces. They were still moving, misbehaving. "I don't believe so," he said softly.

"Why not? It's the season. Days of the Dead, anything like that?"

"No. Just these faces. Old, dead faces."

"No? Why not?"

"Not my genre." He wished she would go away, but he didn't know how to make that happen.

She stared at him sourly. "Are you insulting me?"

"No ma'am—I just don't draw my inspirations from those subjects."

"I see." She looked around and fixed on *Gray Beard*. "How did you get the wood there so gray? Is that a stain?"

Hector had no idea, now that he considered it. He didn't use stains. "It's just the color."

She touched it. He watched as she ran one finger across the successive grooves of the beard. "This looks like you have some talent." Hector tried to smile. "The sticker says forty-five dollars. Will you take thirty?"

Hector watched the old priest's face nestled comfortably in the wood. Suddenly the eyes began blinking, the lips moving. The lady was staring at Hector, waiting for his answer, so she didn't notice.

"I apologize," he said. "I made a mistake. That one is supposed to be a sample of my work. It isn't for sale."

The woman leaned in. "I'll give you fifty for it."

"I'm sorry."

"Dammit, I'll give you seventy-five. I'm not leaving this table empty-handed."

"I'm really sorry. It was not my intention to put a sticker on it."

The woman slammed the carving down on Hector's table. She picked up the nun. "This one then. Forty dollars it says." She shook the carving over his head. The nun gasped and began to cry ever so faintly. The determined woman didn't appear to notice, but Hector heard the nun all too clearly.

"I'm, I'm sorry, madam. I'm feeling ill. The heat, you know? I'm not thinking clearly. I need to close up early. I'm, I'm very sick."

She picked up Hector's former neighbor, the butcher, and another. The last one wouldn't let go of the carving lying next to it, and the woman had to shake it again and again until one of the thin branch fingers snapped. There was a collective outcry that made heads turn all around the room, but the woman didn't take her eyes off Hector. "Two hundred for the lot!" she shouted.

"No, no," Hector said, waving his trembling hands. To his alarm he noticed he had his carving knife in his left.

"What's wrong with you? Are you crazy?"

"I'm, I'm stuck here..." He tried to drop the knife, but his hand wouldn't let it go. When she saw it, she began to scream.

Hector woke at dawn, but remained in bed. Both hands trembled; they had not stopped since yesterday. His eyes burned with a soft fire, and things floated in his vision.

"Papa, are you okay?" Lucena's head was in the door. In the darkness she looked like a figure he'd never completed.

"I'm just a little under the weather, mija. Go on, go to the church. Pray for your mother—help her find her way to Heaven."

"I will, Papa. I was thinking I would take the boys to visit her grave afterwards. I thought I could bring one of your carvings and lay it by the headstone. She would have liked that very much. It would be a nice gesture."

Hector began to sweat. He hoped she didn't notice. She would think he was running a fever and insist on staying home.

"It would have to be something really special, and I wouldn't be able to choose right now. I wouldn't know..." He stopped. He'd almost said *which one was safe.*

"It's okay, Papa. We can do it later. There's no rush. Momma isn't going anywhere." She put her hand up to her lips. "I'm—I'm so sorry. That sounded terrible."

"Always the comico, my daughter," Hector replied.

She laughed. "Okay, Papa. We'll be back in a few hours."

Hector heard the front door. And then he heard it again, and the quick clip-clop of shoes on the floor. One of his grandsons—he had no idea which one—stuck his face around the corner. "Are you sick, Grandpa?" He was very somber, his lower lip protruding like a large, shiny blister.

"I'm afraid so...um..."

"Xenon," he said, and smiled. "I have a freckle below my right eye. That's how you tell us apart."

"Why, thank you, Xenon. That's very kind of you to tell me."

Xenon looked serious again. "Are you going to die, Grandpa?"

Hector considered the question. "I'm afraid we're all going to die, child. None of us know exactly when. We live with the knowledge, or we pretend ignorance."

Xenon nodded. "I will pray for you today, in the church, and at my abuela's grave. I will pray that you find your way to Heaven." He left before Hector could thank him.

Hector forced himself out of bed a few minutes later. He dressed himself, although the trembling in his hands made for a poor job. His shoelaces became a mess of hard knots—no more lovely butterflies it seemed.

He stumbled out to the front of the house and collapsed into his old rocker at the edge of the field. It hadn't been used in years—he only kept it because it belonged to his father. But it had been left outside for so long—the slats were splintered and padded only with dust. It snapped and creaked beneath him as if it was disintegrating, but it held.

The explosions began a few minutes later. There were several of them, each one louder than the one before, and the rumble of hundreds of tons of rock giving way. There were lightning strikes as well—unusual for so early in the day. He wondered if the explosions might be causing the lightning, if maybe the noise and vibration might even bring about a storm. But maybe it was the other way around, the explosions the result of the lightning strikes, and with all that dynamite. More explosions, and a rain of dirt from the sky. Somewhere behind him he could feel the ground heave.

Another explosion, the loudest yet, loud enough—he

thought—to wake the dead. That's when he saw all their heads come up—their profiles rising out of his carvings, out of the crooks and warps in the cottonwood branches, and stepping out of the shadows, and walking out of the horizon where they'd been hiding, all those who had died over the decades and unable to move on because the way had been blocked. Too many of them, he thought. Too many ghosts to count.

It seemed he had been there all day. He had sat all day in this rocker without knowing. He'd watched the changes in the sky as that ball of white heat lowered over the ridges and became orange and then he was done.

The wind the dead made was but a whisper at first, issuing softly out of the broken down branches and sticks, the twisted hearts of the cottonwoods, shadows inside shadows, but it soon became a roar as they all exited past him, and the sun began its descent behind the mountain, and the entire horizon line burned with its fire.

The first forms that flew by him were long, and wooden, and almost expressionless, and then they became more expansive as the realization hit, and then they were practically screaming in pain or joy, when that one so familiar clutched his trembling hands and ripped him out of his chair.

WHEN YOU'RE NOT LOOKING

HOMAGE TO ROBERT AICKMAN

Blink your eyes, turn your head. Everything changes. It all goes away when you're not looking. Go on, look behind you, or are you too afraid?

Every morning Johnson was surprised to find the window open, the antique shutters pulled back, light flooding the room in sudden revelation. He would rise and go there immediately, gazing out at what lay beyond, almost expecting some dramatic change. He could have climbed out if the window weren't so far off the ground, but it had been placed at a dizzying height, so any exit would have been foolish, and permanent.

At night the management kept the windows closed, the shutters locked. Guests were not allowed to look out after dark. The establishment had so many rules—it often felt more like a jail than a proper resort.

He often attempted to get up early to see who opened the window, how they did it. But apparently he'd never been up early enough. Once he'd heard it creaking and leapt out of bed, ears ringing as if they'd been boxed, but the deed had already been done. The ill effect on his nerves had lasted most of the day.

He took advantage of the opened window as much as possible, using it as his last available portal to the outside world, and spent hours sometimes gazing out of it, not bothering with meals, until by force or trickery the staff pulled him from his room. He would always return to his accommodation as soon as possible, but every time he would find the window closed tight for the evening.

"Mr. Johnson, the others have gathered in the dining hall for breakfast. Best go down while they're still serving." The voice behind him was female and falsely cheery. He wasn't sure if he should read her words as a threat. He'd heard the door unlock but he hadn't heard her step into the room. Her voice was familiar, or similar to those he'd heard here before, as no doubt the entire staff had undergone the same training, but he'd have to turn around to see if he recognized her, and he wasn't quite ready to turn around. It was his favorite time of the day, gazing out this window in the mornings. He wanted nothing more than to extend the pleasure of it.

"Do you have an appreciation for antiques? By now you must have realized we have many fine pieces—the building is full of them! And the tapestries are—oh, you must examine each one closely if you're to understand what they are!"

If he stretched his neck and looked left he caught a glimpse of the battered concrete drive, permeated with potholes and other damage, which had brought him into the grounds a large number of nights ago. A hint of rhododendron just beyond hid the other drive, the older one. He wasn't sure what the appeal had been. Had he run out of gas? He couldn't quite remember. Perhaps he had simply been tired, and unable to go on. It was difficult to imagine coming here voluntarily, but he was sure people did, to avail themselves of whatever services were provided. He wasn't sure yet exactly what services—so far he had resisted.

"Remember, Mr. Johnson," she continued behind him, "food is medicine." She affected a slightly amused but scolding tone. As if he was a recalcitrant child. They scolded quite a bit in this place. It seemed an odd approach to customer service.

"You offer a great deal of food here," he said, still not turning around. "But it's really too much. I can't eat so much."

"But our food is good, I think, for whatever ails you."

"And what ails me, Miss? Perhaps you can tell me, because I surely do not know."

She left then, he thought. He never heard the door. Perhaps he'd been speaking in a forbidden area of conversation.

Eventually he would become hungry enough that he would

have to go down to their dining hall and stuff himself with their thick, substantial food. This was inevitable. At least he was better off than some of the guests who appeared to have no choice in the matter. They had to sit. They had to eat. He couldn't imagine what they had done—had they displeased their families so much they'd been sent here?

From his window the trees appeared dense, far denser than he would have imagined in this part of the country. You could not see past them, and traffic sounds did not penetrate.

He turned slightly to his right and was startled to see a woman's head protruding from the outer wall a few feet away, so like a mounted trophy it made him momentarily ill.

He stared at it, now thinking it might be some sort of large doll's or dummy's head, then saw the tears, and the eye blink. Of course, he'd been foolish. She was simply another resident like himself, her head also stuck out of a window.

"Excuse me? Are you alright?" he asked.

She turned her head slightly in his direction, but appeared to make no attempt at eye contact. "I don't belong here," she said. "I have no idea how I even got here," she said.

Behind him, the voice of that annoying young woman (Maid? Nurse?) came again. "You mustn't speak with her, Mr. Johnson. Here we respect the privacy of our guests. Really, there is nothing to be gained." He ignored her.

"Were you lost?" he asked his weeping neighbor. "I believe I was lost. I think I went severely off course. I'm not even sure where I was going."

"It's so very dim out here," she said. "So few lights. You drive for hours among all these trees and there are no landmarks, no houses, at least none that you can see. But you know they must be out there, the families safe inside and doing what families do, but you can't see them. Nothing makes itself apparent. It's all shadow and assumption, really."

"I know, you drive forever, and yet you pass no one else on the road, and the houses are all hiding from you, as if you're somehow dangerous. It's an uncomfortable feeling," he said. "I think I may be retired. It's the only explanation I can come up with. All this free time, and I can't think of anything I should be doing. It's sad, really. I wonder if I am even missed. It would be sad not to be missed."

"I really must insist, Mr. Johnson," the young female voice said behind him. "You mustn't speak to her."

"Really? Is this any way to speak to a paying guest?" He felt his volume rising, even though he suspected shouting would not be a good thing. Shouting would not be a good thing at all. "I don't understand you people."

He might have turned around and glared at her then to emphasize his point. But he could not bring himself to do so.

"Please remain calm, Sir. There is no need to upset yourself. Won't you please come down to dinner? You'll feel much better afterwards. I'm sure we can find you a plate of warm food."

"Please, please." He felt the whine in his voice and instantly regretted it. "Please just leave me to myself."

There was no reply. He tilted his face to speak to his neighbor again, but she was no longer there. He let his head drop, feeling a moment of dangerous despair.

No one had approached him concerning payment. Who was paying for all this? He supposed this benefit might have been part of his pension plan. He really should have studied his papers more carefully, but that had always been his problem. He had never, never studied his papers carefully enough. He never paid attention to anything he signed, and now his signature was everywhere.

Margaret must be beside herself. They'd told him there were no phones here, no way for him to call. A curious expression, "beside herself," as if enough trauma could split a person in two, until the world would be filled with one's multiples. Margaret, of course. Margaret his wife. What was she telling the children? He couldn't see how they could ever get over it.

Down below, the grounds crew busied themselves with a multitude of tasks. He considered how many workers must be required to attend to such a vast area of landscaping. He could not actually see them, however. He had to content himself with a glimpse now and then of legs walking by a hedge, hands bearing clippers, the sweep of a rake, someone pushing a mower or a garden cart of some sort, only their backs visible.

They all appeared so determined, so focused on the task at hand. He envied them. They hadn't yet learned that you were only permitted to do so much for so long.

Since his arrival he had rested badly. No doubt that was much of his trouble. Without sufficient rest, the mind functions poorly, cannot complete even a simple count without error. How many days, how many nights? Surprisingly for such an isolated location, every evening there was some disturbance or other, someone weeping out in the hallway, some thump or bump from the room next door, and all night long the arrival of lost automobiles, the knocks on the front door, the murmured explanations, the checking in.

"We have rules here, Mr. Johnson. Certain expectations. There have been inquiries concerning your lack of sociability, your absence from meals." The voice behind him might be from the same woman, but she sounded much older now, or perhaps it was simply that her patience had run out. No doubt she had superiors, just as he had once had superiors. And in every job there were certain criteria which must be met.

But Johnson still was not quite ready to turn around, not when there was still more outside to see. Even though the sun was still high in the sky the grounds crew had finished their work for the day, returning their equipment to some distant region of the grounds. Johnson could hear birds in the trees, and other sounds in the distance which he thought might be voices.

"Are you ever coming home? Is this your life now?" It was unmistakably Margaret's voice behind him, although it was possible they had a recording. They could do so much with technology now, things he could not possibly understand.

"There is a certain rhythm to the world," he replied. "We cannot stop what nature is determined to bring us." Was that what they wanted to hear? This could not possibly be his wife. She had no idea he was here. No one did.

Then he heard the wind coming up behind him, and the unmistakable fragrance of his wife's hair blew past him, lifting the curtains until they were like pennants waving from the window frame. He heard the door closing, abandoning him to his own silence.

A dark car wound its way slowly down the broken concrete driveway. By the time it arrived it was heavily laden in dust, the windscreen grimy, the wheel wells clogged. It pulled to a stop below his window, and the engine shuddered into silence. Johnson watched it for some time before a shadow stirred behind the driver's side window, the door frame cracked open, showering the pavement with fragments of caked earth, and the man in the rumpled suit climbed out.

The man wore mirrored sunglasses. Johnson could see fragments of the building reflected there, jumbled, confused. The man stared at his watch, then leaned back against the car looking exhausted, dejected.

Johnson wanted to shout down at the man and warn him away. He wanted to let him know that however desperate his situation might seem, stopping here for a night, or more, was hardly the best solution. But who was he to tamper with another person's destiny? And what consequences might be brought to bear for Johnson's interference?

The man looked up, his posture humbled. He looked like some pilgrim at the end of an extended quest. Despite his misgivings, Johnson waved. Getting no reaction, he waved again, more vigorously this time. He could feel the forces gathering behind him. He might be jerked away from the window at any time. But it was obvious that the newcomer did not see him, instead gazing up at Johnson as if trying to interpret some passing and peculiar cloud.

Then the man's face changed. Johnson felt uneasy as the fellow slipped off his glasses, and then there were the obvious signs of pain as the fellow stared directly into the sun.

BETWEEN THE PILINGS

The dark blue neon scribble was so faint he had to stare awhile to determine if it said VACANCY or not. Finally Whitcomb decided to take a chance. He went up to the battered screen door beneath the water-damaged sign: *Between the Pilings*, and in smaller letters *Innsmouth Beach*, and in even smaller letters, an afterthought, worn almost to illegibility, *Accommodations*.

A light was on inside over a small counter, no brighter than a nightlight, really, and he couldn't tell if the hunched shape beneath it was a person or the back of a chair. But the door was unlocked, so he went inside.

He didn't see the clerk. Indeed it was just a counter with a battered surface and the rounded top of a chair behind. He gazed around the shabby, antiqued room. The lichen green wallpaper appeared to be dotted with tiny pale flowers, but they were so faded they might have been random stains. The armchairs and the couch might have originally been of high quality, but were now so scraped and worn it was hard to believe a business would countenance their use. The rug sparkled, but he determined it was from the grains of sand worked into its fibers. There might have been a central pattern, but the design was thoroughly obscured in grime.

Because of the numerous faded rectangles on the walls, he decided a number of pictures had been taken down. He had vague memories that it had been a fairly full gallery of past patrons displayed here. He didn't remember this room being so dilapidated. But he'd been barely eight years old when last he'd been here, so how could he know? He'd had no standards. He'd been happy just to be alive, to swim and play and watch television. And to eat cake. Oh, how he'd loved his cakes, the strawberry ones his mother used to make, the slices delivered to him on sparkling white plates, with a kiss on the cheek.

"Room?"

The word was so low-pitched and faint it might have come from the floor. Whitcomb looked more closely at the counter, the door behind it. The bluish glow coming from somewhere below the counter's edge. Had someone just come through the door? But he still didn't see them. He moved closer, peering over the edge.

He didn't believe in staring at people with disabilities—people all had differences, and we were all better off for it, in his opinion. But because he couldn't quite grasp the young man's malady, Whitcomb's gaze was fully engaged in staring.

The body on the wide chair was relatively short, fat and lopsided, and he thought, collapsed as if the spine or a portion of the spine had been removed, allowing the rest of the young man to fall down in a clump because now there was too much flesh for the available height. The head was pushed forward by the swollen neck so that it was easier for the young man to look at the small computer screen in front of him than to look at Whitcomb above him. His too-fleshy fingers flapped against the keys. His skin was pale and oily, and poorly washed. Whitcomb thought of a giant frog that had once frightened him as a boy.

"Yes. I would like to rent a room. For three days, perhaps four."

"That'll be two days in advance then," the young man said, still without looking up. "Forty-five dollars on the counter please."

Whitcomb put his money down. The clerk used a pole with a hook on it to transfer keys from a pegboard to the counter, all without taking his eyes off the screen. "Number eight. You been here before?"

"A long time ago. I was a child."

"Won't have changed much, 'cept the beach is a tad closer. You have to leave your car parked up here on the street. Nobody'll bother it—Innsmouth isn't like other places. There are some steps at the end of the building. You take those down under the boardwalk and out to the beach. The rooms are built around the timber pilings."

"I remember that part. It's unusual."

"It's why we have the name. Number eight is near the middle. But you'll have to wait up here a bit while the maid sweeps it out."

"Sweeps it out?"

"We have a sand problem."

Whitcomb didn't remember a sand problem, nor was he exactly sure what that phrase meant. But children often didn't notice the things adults classified as disastrous. The opposite, Whitcomb thought, was also true.

He looked for a place to sit. The couch looked like it might sink and fold itself around him, and the seats of all the chairs were thoroughly, darkly stained. He picked the least objectionable one, closed his eyes, and sat down. It made a squishing sound, as of rotting fruit.

The room was silent for a time except for the flap-clicking of the keys on the other side of the counter and the occasional sigh or struggle of breath from the clerk. Whitcomb could see out the dingy front window and down the street: spare of street lamps or even the usual illuminations leaked from windows or car headlights. Still, a bit of parchment glow made the shadows deeper and fuzzy-edged and sometimes runny, as darkness flowed from door to door, from one side of the street to the other. Feet and fingers and faces turned away. It was probably just him and his softly dying memories, but they might have been real. Had it been this way when he was a child? But everything was some bright adventure in a child's eyes, especially on vacation. His mother had hated it, he remembered that much, right up until the end.

That summer, his mother had wanted to return to the Southern seacoast where she'd been raised, to the extensive sands of Myrtle Beach or at least Virginia Beach so that their son could have "a proper beach experience," but his father insisted they had to stay in New England—they couldn't afford to travel farther than that. His father had won—as he did all arguments in which money was involved. At that point Mother wanted nothing more to do with the planning.

He hated those old men who babbled all the time, who had

to fill up every silence with their voices, but there was so much to talk about, and no one to talk to.

"The billboards on the highway going in? I remember them as being so much brighter. That first one, *Visit Historic Innsmouth*, with a collage of quaint Victorian buildings. You can barely make out the details now."

The clerk said nothing. But even when Whitcomb had been a child and saw that billboard for the first time, the colors had seemed off, shaded into dirty greys. Far more bothersome had been the cartoon character who was supposedly speaking those words. Whitcomb had guessed it was meant to be a fish. But the eyes were wrong, the pupils appearing fixed and dilated. Perhaps he was editing it in the remembering, but he recalled them as the eyes of a dead human being. On this trip that figure was missing completely, that side of the billboard scratched out.

"The second billboard, well, there's not much of an image left at all, is there? I remember this lovely picture of the Innsmouth pier with a wide shot of the ocean. Now everything is so heavily graffitied—loops and swirls and all kinds of nastiness emerging from the waves."

"I've never been to the highway," the clerk murmured. "I've never seen them."

"Oh, sorry." Whitcomb thought perhaps he'd been rude to the young man, insensitive to his disability, whatever its specifics. He would not ask him, then, about the final billboard, now completely blank. Worse than blank, actually—scoured down to grey, flaking wood. He couldn't imagine how the damage had occurred—even a hurricane wouldn't have created such complete erasure.

He tried to remember what it had looked like before, but he had never understood what it had been intended to depict. It had been in the process of being changed at the time, he thought, newer strips pasted over older ones, or perhaps the newer bits torn off to reveal what lay underneath: the legs of a sun-bathing beauty married to a beached sea lion or something similar, a chaos of torn and frayed buildings collapsing over them.

He felt a cold draft and glanced at the front door. He saw no obvious gap at the bottom, but there was sand there, fingers of it flowing his way as if blown. Suddenly the door banged open, and a squat grey woman stood there holding the largest broom he had ever seen, the thick shaft of it filling her hand. "The Mister's room is ready!" she proclaimed, and glared at him. He came quickly off the chair and squeezed past her, dashing to his car to retrieve a small suitcase.

The trip down the stairs was long, and Whitcomb was glad not to have a steamer trunk to drag. It was also dark and the railing minimal, so he took the steps slowly. In fact, it was so deeply in shadow in places that the only illumination was a sliver of moonlight reflected off the damp edges of scattered timbers.

He remembered negotiating these steps as a child. Of course it had been daylight and mid-summer then. He remembered alternating areas of sunlight so bright it glazed the grey boards a brilliant white between shadows so dark he disappeared stepping into them. His mother behind him had been hysterical, sure he would kill himself flying down those rickety stairs.

Now at the bottom Whitcomb was confused. He remembered how it had been when he was eight: a broad strip of grass with a fountain and a bordering walk that shimmered from all the seashells embedded in the concrete, and beyond that the gleaming white beach. It would never look as good as it had on that first glimpse, and over the years he would wonder if his imagination had simply embellished it, because every day after that while they were there it had appeared a bit greyer, a bit shabbier.

Now there was no grass at all—he had stepped off into sand. And a few feet away were the piles of rubble, broken concrete, and other rubbish. And looking around him, he didn't see the rooms. Certainly the few closest to the staircase were gone, leaving only hollow dark cavities filled with more sand.

He started walking parallel to the pilings, peering into the darkness for some sign of the old motel and finding none. It was hard to fathom how the young man up in that office at street level could believe he could get away with such a blatant con, taking money for rooms which no longer existed, but Whitcomb had his own eyes and the memory of what had once been here. He even ventured into the deeper shadows beneath the boardwalk thinking the rooms might have been set back further into the seaside structure than he remembered, but the area was wiped clean.

Then he passed one of the thicker pilings and there was what was left of the old motel: a short stretch of rooms with battered screen doors and a single window each. He remembered the walls as a bright coral red, but these were a pale salmon color, repaired here and there with grey cement like disease spots or patches of dead skin.

A small light glowed above each door along with a number. The first he saw was number six. He paused in front of eight before trying the key.

He remembered following his father into the room all those years ago. He had no idea which number it had been—it hadn't been important to him and they had all looked the same. There had been a bright multicolored oval rug inside, some blonde furniture, and one large bed. He'd gazed at that bed in dismay until he'd seen the rollaway they'd rented just for him. He'd sat on that bed and bounced, declaring it perfect.

His mother had come in slowly, her face drawn. She was rubbing her arms. "This sand, the wind blows it everywhere. It's burning my arms."

"It's just ordinary sand, dear," Whitcomb's father had said. "You probably just have sunburn."

"We've barely arrived, how could I—"

"The drive in, all those miles. You had your window rolled down, remember? And your arm resting on the frame? I told you you should have put on sunblock when the trip began."

"I'm wearing long sleeves." She'd said it crossly. She hadn't wanted to come here at all.

"Lightweight fabric. You can practically see your arms through the cloth. It doesn't take much, a hot day like this."

His father had never thought his mother intelligent. That was why he'd always been explaining things to her, trying to explain why she shouldn't feel upset, why she shouldn't be disappointed or angry. Everything was always fine, the way his father had explained things, even when Whitcomb didn't understand the explanations.

Obviously his mother didn't understand them either, because as far as Whitcomb could remember, they had never helped. He'd resented that sometimes. She could have at least pretended to be happy. She could have been a good sport. Part of being happy, as he remembered from his childhood, was being able to pretend.

Whitcomb felt strangely hesitant to enter number eight. He was afraid to be disappointed in what he found inside. Sand as white, as pure-looking as snow, had drifted out of the shadowland fronting the ocean and up to the concrete step in front of each door. It required only the dim light above each number to bring out the sand's unusual brilliance, its eerie luminescence. He looked down at his feet—of course, he was standing in it. There was no grass or sidewalk anymore. From above it looked oddly liquid, milk-like, rising and falling around his shoes—nothing like sand at all.

But he was tired, and he was drunk with memory. He fixed his eyes on the door and stepped forward. It was late, and the world was always a different place in the morning.

The key made a scraping sound as it went into the keyhole. It felt like there might be debris inside. He turned the key and tiny particles drifted out of the hole and down to the threshold, joining the fingers of sand that had already blown onto the recently-swept step. He pushed the door open.

It was dark and chilly in the room, as if instead of going inside he'd actually gone out. He reached for a light switch and found it, coated in grit, so was not optimistic about the maid's cleaning job. But when the lights came on he was pleasantly surprised.

The room brought back vividly the one from decades before. The furniture was the same or of a similar style, blonde wood with clean lines, typical of the fifties. There was even a rollaway, although the mattress was greyish, the frame spotted with rust. But the floor was clean, and the rug, although it wasn't the colorful one from years before. The colors were more muted, as were the colors throughout, he realized, shaded toward greying pastels. The blonde wood duller. The ceiling white less white. But there was a comfort in all that. After all, if it had been exactly the same he might have been terrified.

But that was all quite enough. Whitcomb thought he could not bear to be awake any longer. He dressed into his pajamas quickly, turned off the light, and slipped into bed. The sheets didn't feel crisp, but at least they weren't sandy. He didn't bother to set the alarm clock—he hadn't even noticed if there was one. He was content with awakening whenever.

He had no idea how long he had slept when he first awakened. It was still dark out, according to his window, but he hadn't slept through the night in years, so that wasn't surprising. Wind scratched and occasionally beat on the door. He thought it might be raining because he could hear the spray against the glass. Surely the ocean was too far away for it to be the advance spray of a wave, but he could not bring himself to check. Better not to know if he was about to drown.

He leaned over the side of the bed to get a good view of the door—white had eased through the bottom, a few threads of it. Sand. But perhaps he'd just tracked that in when he first came inside.

His mother had complained of the sand, the way it burned, the whole time they had been here. Whitcomb hadn't understood—he'd loved it, couldn't get enough of it, the way it squeezed between the toes. It frightened him that she should have such a strong reaction. For years afterward he would think of her when he met anyone with allergies or peculiar sensitivities. Some people lived in an unfriendly world. Certainly, no one lived in his world, and he was uncomfortable whenever he ventured out of it.

"You're supposed to drive your life, not let your life drive you." Jane had shared that bit of insight the last time she'd consented to see him. "Do something spontaneous for once!" It was goodbye advice, but at least she had been sincere. She might have liked him more if he'd managed to be someone else.

He might have pretended to her that his return visit to Innsmouth was a spontaneous act, but of course it was not—it had been coming for years. He'd just been gathering his nerve.

Over the years, he'd tried to remember every detail of that

vacation when he'd been eight, and although he'd recreated much of it, a great many moments were still missing. It angered him, the way the bits wore off, and he could not decide if it was the mind's normal decay or the old realities themselves which were going away. Something about the process seemed deliberate, as if the universe didn't want him to remember everything.

He did not feel sorry for himself—he'd made his choices, but he realized not everyone had a choice. Eventually all the bits of a life wore off, and for some even the memories went away. His father had gone on with his life, using drink to wipe the memory. But Whitcomb would remember his mother until the end.

He must have dozed off, because when he opened his eyes again the window was burning up with sun. He dressed himself in the sweats he'd bought for the occasion—he'd never owned a pair before. The door refused to open. He supposed the dampness had made it swell. He kept pulling until it came loose with a pop sound. A rain of grit poured from the jamb.

He stepped out into an intense scouring of sky and sand, so much blue and white he had to close his eyes, opening them slowly again using his hand as a shield. The beach looked ravaged, a churning of tiny white dunes and pitted places, black timbers and rocks showing ragged edges as if chewed. Streamers of rotting seaweed laced the beach, gulls landing to snatch tidbits, swiftly leaving as if the sand were too hot or corrosive to touch. Large amounts of fish flesh lay in partially digested chunks, the reek of it so foul his nose refused to process the smell. He gagged and turned to go back inside, but deciding he would not be so easily defeated, struck off down the line of pilings again, thinking he would see what remained here from his memories.

There appeared to be no one else about, and given the unpleasant state of the shore here, he supposed that should come as no surprise. In bright daylight, he had a good look at what was left of the motel—eight units, with the last two missing numbers and doors. He couldn't imagine who might rent such lodgings, unless they were beyond desperate or ignorant like himself. Perhaps they did all their renting after dark, when the extent of the damage could not be seen. He was curious if he had neighbors, but wouldn't go out of his way to meet them.

The place hadn't been that busy when he'd been here before, when things were painted, in good repair, and at the height of summer. At best there had been five or six other family groupings, and a few isolated stragglers, tall figures in rain gear with large hats pulled down over their features, strolling the beach. And not all the family members made use of the beach— some, like his mother, made only rare forays past their motel doors or the grassy areas in front.

But vacations weren't for everyone, or so he had heard. There were always some who felt safer, if not happier, at home.

He gazed down the beach to where it narrowed, eventually disappearing into a tumble of stone. There was the main part of Innsmouth, the old docks, the church towers and the sprawling meeting halls. Several buildings near the edge had actually tumbled into the sea, leaving a slope of woody debris soaking up the ocean salt and a splay of broken uprights.

Surely he was mistaken, but he had a vague memory of the same ruins, the same collapse, present when he'd been here as a child.

A broken chorus of voices rose with a sudden flight of black birds as if riding their backs into the air. The voices dissipated with the scattering paths of wings. Whitcomb had no desire to venture into that part of town, thinking it a far more dangerous place than this poor strip of sand.

He caught sight of a familiar sign and, walking closer, caught himself in a tease of a smile. *By the Sands: Miniature Golf.* His family had discovered the place their second day there, and even his mother had seemed to enjoy herself. It appeared to still be in business. He found himself passing through the gate without considering.

At first he thought the fellow taking money was the motel clerk from the night before. They might have been twins. Then he saw that this one was a little taller, not as fat, and he hid one arm inside a voluminous sleeve. He handed the fellow a dollar and was pointed to a rack of balls and clubs beside Hole #1.

It was the usual layout of obstacles, ramps, windmills, passages through miniature buildings, and wide metal curves the ball could cling to for a left or right-hand turn. But there were local touches as well: a giant brass frog with a wide mouth—a ball entered the mouth and shot out the anus in some random direction. A water obstacle with leaping mechanical fish— periodically a fish would alter its trajectory by some mysterious means and snag the ball. An array of dilapidated buildings—he couldn't really tell if the destruction was cosmetic and faked, or actual damage incurred by the miniature buildings because of exposure and lack of care. He didn't remember many specifics about this miniature golf course from his previous visits decades ago, but it seemed that some of these features might be new to him—except for the frog. Now that he thought about it, the brass frog had been here before.

The last few holes had been invaded by sand. But that fit the golfing theme, did it not? Sand traps designed to defeat even the most professional of golfers. At hole fifteen the sand trap moved, and the ball dissolved amidst a swirl of greedy silvery grit, ending his game.

As he left the golf course, he found himself staring at the ocean, the endless repeating waves, the long curving edges of foam, that meandering line where dark grey sea met an only slightly softer sky. As a boy, he'd thought that line dividing the air and water impossibly high, an instability that threatened everything he held dear. Now it seemed worse, and he thought he could detect structures inside it, only vaguely covered by the water—long reticulating lines, horizontal and vertical edges, the boxy shapes of some lost city drowned beneath the waves.

It made him feel empty, void of substance, and he realized he hadn't yet eaten and had gone to bed without dinner the night before. There had been a few small cafés, he remembered, accessible only from the beach, and he continued walking in the direction of that denser part of Innsmouth, hoping one might still be in business.

He closed his eyes at one point, having walked far longer than he had hoped, and near to exhaustion. He did not remember finding the restaurant, or sitting down, or ordering. But the next thing he knew he was blinking rapidly, and he was holding a large spoon, and warm and slippery things were washing down his throat. He almost choked when he realized it, and had to down a large glass of water which tasted a bit too salty and whose color was less than assuring. His teeth felt unstable, his tongue sore, the inside of his mouth scraped.

He only vaguely remembered the meals he'd had when his parents brought him here as a child. He remembered feeling ravenous the whole time, and devouring hotdogs and something else—some sort of pita-like concoction—from beachside stands. His parents ate hardly anything at all. His father had been drinking, not as committedly as he would after that vacation, but enough that it made him quiet, grumpy, and without appetite. His mother—he was never sure if his mother ate anything during that trip. He vaguely remembered sitting with them in a small restaurant like this one, only cleaner, brighter, and watching her dab at her mouth with a cloth napkin, always dabbing, touching her lips with it, her teeth, and a redness coming away on the cloth.

He looked down into his soup, or stew. Very little was left, a small bit of tail sticking out of a thick, grey broth. He pushed the bowl away, looked around him. There were other patrons in the small café. This shouldn't have surprised him, except that he had seen no one except the motel clerk and his near-doppelganger, the golf attendant, since his arrival the night before.

There were five, no, six others, huddled over their food. Thickly dressed in layers, high collars, some with weedy mats of hair slapped on top their heads. Some with stocking caps, despite the warm day. All looked vaguely ill or hung over, here to recover, perhaps, from the night before. The fellow closest to Whitcomb had a similar soup bowl in front of him, filled with grey. Periodically he jabbed his fork into the liquid as if attacking.

The walls looked greasy, with large spots by the tables along the perimeter, as if people had rested their heads there, soiling the dingy green paint. He saw a tall man in a muscle shirt asleep at one of those tables, perhaps a sailor given the theme of his tattoos—fish and whales and frogs and waves and some things tendrilled, perhaps vegetation, perhaps not. His torso leaned against the wall, one arm pressed beneath his chest, his head lolling, cheek smeared flat.

The sailor suddenly woke up, startled, glared at Whitcomb, and pulled his head and arm away from the wall. Sticky pale threads ran from his flesh to where bits of him still clung to the wall, including part of a bluish anchor design.

Whitcomb stumbled out of his chair and went through the door. Had he paid? No one shouted, no one chased him. But he stopped himself out on the beach, thinking that if he hadn't paid, the proprietor would catch up to him and he could apologize, explain that it was a mistake, and pay what he owed, pay double what he owed. But no one came.

He looked back down the beach searching for his motel. He had no idea how far he had come. He also hadn't realized that he'd been walking up a slope, this part of the beach being noticeably higher than from where he'd come. From here he could see the entire stretch of it, hundreds of yards, and the way the waves came in, taking greedy nibbles. And all that had been ruined. And how the sand moved, minutely, but seeing it all together like this, multiplied, so that for the first time he could be sure, all that sand, everywhere, was moving.

He must have fallen quite hard, because he was suddenly on the ground, eyes and mouth gaping. The sand edged around him. He shut his eyes, trying to force it out.

He'd awakened that night, all those years ago, because of a noise or a dream of a noise. Someone crying, someone lost. Bits of his memory from that time had wandered off, but this memory, at least, he had found.

His father lay passed out on the bed. Whitcomb was on the rollaway, shivering—he'd always been so skinny as a boy, and easy to chill. As he sat up he'd realized it was because the motel room door was open, and the ocean breeze was coming in, and the sand. He'd looked around for his mother then, but she was nowhere to be seen.

He'd wandered out. His feet must have been damp, because he could remember the sand sticking to them. He remembered looking down, all that clinging sand making his feet look frosted, sparkling in the moonlight.

Out on the beach there was a tall, thin form. He'd recognized his mother's pale yellow gown. She was swaying, and the wind was lifting her gown, and he'd thought he should turn away because he shouldn't be seeing this.

She'd turned her head then, and her mouth was so red, and he'd thought she was looking at him, but it quickly became clear she was gazing at the ground behind her, the sandy beach, which was moving.

She'd tried to get away from it. She never would have left him if she could have helped it. She'd always been devoted to him, despite her flaws.

He didn't know where she was running. He'd only been eight, but even then he'd understood that the ocean wouldn't have helped her.

The sand trailed up and her gown began to fall away. He was embarrassed and closed his eyes, but forced them open again as the hazy softness of her went dark. Later his father would hold the empty gown and ask him if he had seen anything. And he would say he had not, because he had not.

Whitcomb opened his eyes and saw the drift of tiny particles on the beach in front of him; felt them float in and out of his mouth, in and out of his ears. Red bits and soft bits, and an endless streaming of sand.

A lifetime later he sat out in front of his room, taking in the ocean, taking in all the sand. He was missing pieces. He could not remember why he had come here, just that it had been a compulsion, beyond important, but that memory was useless to him now. As were all other memories, scoured and taken and blown away by the wind. But it was almost a relief to see them go.

He gazed down at his sweatpants, which were almost empty now. He began to smile, but could feel that even bits of his smile were gone.

THE ERASED

Some things you remember clearly, after but the merest glance: a spot passed on a journey to somewhere else, a woman who gazed long enough to make you wonder about a different life. Other things vanish for no reason, even though you hold them dear: a friend's name, a favorite souvenir, a beloved's life. Some days it feels as if none of these things ever existed at all, and you yourself, are no more tangible than smoke.

These events recur with increasing rapidity until one day you realize: this is how the world goes away.

On most days Roy could see all the way into downtown from his apartment window. Today there was a brownish haze as if some buildings might be burning. Downtown lay comatose, diminished, the taller buildings disintegrating into increasingly narrow threads until Roy could see ancient stretches of undeveloped land in between, while overhead the clouds dropped rapidly, chimneys and roofs and windows distributing into mist.

He thought he heard screams. The air was loaded with too much conversation. He kept watching, anticipating but not hoping to see streams of refugees.

He closed his eyes and did the exercise. The exercise consisted of recalling the world as it truly was: the clock-tower, that silver needle of an office building still under construction, the top of an amusement park's giant Ferris wheel, and the upper reach of the water slide, the gleeful or terrified children momentarily trapped within. And all the buildings in between, some he could recollect now and then, and the others he invariably forgot.

He was a committed realist, or tried to be. He did not get his hopes up. He did not look for the brighter side. His was a small life, easily countable, easily captured in a single photograph. He liked it that way, or at least he was acclimated to it. He'd never imagined more. He'd put himself out there early on as most people did, tried to do well in school, talked to women, applied to jobs and opportunities, and the things that came his way, came his way, and he had accepted that. He'd never married, but the jobs had been adequate, paying just enough for day to day, but not for what would come after. Unfortunately now he was living in what came after, and had to make do with what the government sent him until he, or the government, ran its course. But he was a realist, and so he managed.

He finished his juice and looked around the room. Bed and table and chair, a refrigerator, hot plate, sink, a few things left out, everything else tidied away into closet and cupboard. He liked to keep the things he could count down to ten or so, never more than fifteen. More than fifteen he felt sloppy. More than twenty meant that chaos had descended, and you were well on your way to death or at least ruin.

But where was his cereal box? It should have been by the bed to sate some middle of the night hunger. The dual use of breakfast food for snack satisfied Roy's appetite for efficiency. He suddenly had the disturbing notion that someone had slipped into his room while he was sleeping and stolen his cereal. At least he could know for certain—it was one of the advantages of having a life that was countable.

He looked into the trashcan beneath the sink and found the empty cereal box. He had no memory of having finished it—that memory had been erased. He would have to go out and buy another box, and somehow not think about how that memory had gotten away from him. It was one thing to get rid of some no longer useful recollection, yet another to have that memory stolen away.

He found the piece of paper he kept as a shopping list, a "To Do" list, for whatever needed recording so that he didn't have to count on his increasingly unreliable memory. Words had been scratched out, rewritten, and erased so many times the paper had achieved a level of transparency. When he held the paper up some words floated in the air as if stray thoughts. He could sense other things floating nearby: plans, memories, suggestions of people, hints of scenes, but he was hungry and had no time for this.

Outside, the sun burned from a definite place, high above and slightly behind his left shoulder. It seemed unusual to apprehend the sun so specifically, as if it were a lightbulb fixed in an invisible fixture. He couldn't remember having that perception before, certainly not with this much conviction. He had an impulse to weep. He wanted to raise his head and turn and look at the sun directly, but he'd always heard that was a very bad thing to do. Or was that an old wives' tale? He was old enough he could probably risk some permanent damage, but he needed his box of cereal so being struck blind wasn't part of the day's plan.

From here he had a broad view of this part of the city. Roy had seen this view almost every day since he'd turned fifty, but he hadn't always paid attention, and now it appeared broken, bits completely rubbed out or obscured by new bits. A missing building here and there, and other buildings discolored, polished, altered, the horizon line a damaged grin of aging and repaired teeth beneath a thick lip of smoky pollution. He started to reason it out, but hungry and impatient he made a dismissive wave and turned onto the next street toward the tiny local grocery.

But he apparently made a wrong turn, and was lost a scant block or two from home. He looked left and right and slowly began to recognize individual bits and pieces of buildings, a certain tree, a certain green-painted lamp post left over from an earlier era of electrification, but there was a blurriness where things rubbed up against each other, and right in front of him there was an enormous empty hole, enclosed by one of those floppy orange plastic fences meant more for warning than security. He walked slowly to the end of the block to get his bearings, and saw the grocery store on the next street over, and then he walked back again and stood before the gigantic missing piece. He was pretty sure he knew where he was now. The huge old Victorian which had been there all his life was gone.

He peered over the edge of the pit. It was all raw dirt down there—every last bit of the house had been taken. An ancient drain pipe rose out of the center of the excavation like a severed root. There was a clanking of traffic sounds behind him, a certain metallic clatter that might have been a streetcar, but they hadn't had streetcars in the city for years. He turned around. The street was empty.

Roy flopped down onto the thin grassy patch in front of the not-house. That house had been built long before he was born. He'd heard it had first been a hospital for poor women, and then the Clarksons had lived there for generations, and Will Clarkson still did. No, *did*.

"Pity, isn't it? They must have torn it down sometime during the past two weeks."

Roy knew the fellow walking towards him, but he didn't have his name handy. He ran through his catalog of names, but some were missing, some scratched out, and only an alarmingly few had faces attached. Roy did know that the man lived in that house behind the missing one, its visible outer wall a pale gray patch of stucco unused to direct sunlight. Further down the block—he wasn't sure how far—another house began to shimmer, as if the entire structure were under water.

William. No, Willem. Roy remembered now, the only person with that name he'd ever known. Dutch, maybe. But he detected no accent.

Willem had a big brown dog with him which Roy wanted to call a mastiff, but which was probably something far less glamorous. But certainly descended from big breeds, practically a monster. When the dog breathed it made the air around it tremble. Suddenly the dog barked so loudly it made itself disappear.

Roy closed then opened his eyes and it was back again. It barked once more and Roy shut his eyes again—he couldn't help himself. It was as if the air in front of him had suddenly frozen, then snapped into pieces, the dog's throat a passage into some other dimension of pain.

"Duke! Quiet!" Willem shouted. "Sorry, Roy." Still, Roy didn't open his eyes. In the darkness inside his head he still lived on a quiet street lined with giant trees and the same old familiar houses. No one in that neighborhood was a monster or owned monsters.

The dog was whimpering now and Roy opened his eyes. The dog moved behind Willem as if seeking protection. "He's been jumpy lately," Willem explained. "He doesn't like change, but then, neither do I. And neither do you, from the looks of you."

"What happened? Was there a fire?"

"Nothing so dramatic. Some men and equipment came one morning, and they tore it down, hauled the pieces away. I didn't see it myself. I'm not even sure if anyone lived there anymore. The older Clarkson brother—he was the last, wasn't he? Did he die? I don't remember him dying, do you? I live right next door, but I didn't know—I had to ask around. There was just this hole, as if there had never been a house. I just never looked out those windows." He gestured vaguely toward his house. "And when I walk Duke, I usually don't walk him on this part of the block. A family of cats lived here for a while—they teased him."

Willem's hair was wild and windblown and appeared to be on fire. Roy at first thought the sun was behind it, but the sun was still high over Roy's left shoulder. It hadn't moved—some greater power had pinned it to the sky. Willem's face was dark and opaque, and Roy couldn't see the man's expression, couldn't even see his face for that matter, which was disconcerting.

"Could you move just a bit to one side, Willem?" Roy was inordinately pleased that he now had the man's name correctly. "I can't quite see your face." But he couldn't tell him his head appeared to be on fire.

The dark face barked. Roy looked for the dog, but Willem's dog had apparently wandered away.

Willem stepped aside wordlessly. Was he angry? Roy looked up—Willem's face was hard and cracked like damaged pottery. He couldn't find the man's eyes—were they closed?

"What happened to your dog?"

"My dog? I haven't had a dog since ..."

"The big brown one. Duke."

Willem scowled unhappily. "Roy, have you been drinking?

Duke died years ago."

Roy shook his head. He made a decision to forget all about the dog. "This house, it was here just the other day. Someone was living here—I saw him looking at me from that window." Roy pointed to where the window had been, then dropped his hand awkwardly. His finger had pointed at nothing but empty sky, a faint trace of smoke.

Willem stared into the not-place. "They keep tearing down old houses, putting up three or four new ones in their place. I imagine they could put six units into a lot this size. Boxes, mostly. Urban industrial. Bolt a few panels of rusted metal or polished wood on the outside and then you're done." He stepped closer to the hole and looked in. The sun suddenly shifted and shadows flowed from under the bushes and out of the sewer grates. "I'm glad my Alice didn't live to see this." Dark regions spread through the raw earth and quickly combined, heaving.

Roy stared at the leash dangling from Willem's hand. Willem made that barking sound again and then the leash was gone. "Willem?" he asked, blinking his tears away. "Do you have some water? Water is...we're all one hundred percent water, I believe. Our faces, the rest of us, are just dreams floating on all that water. Could I have some water, please? And some cereal? Do you have cereal?"

A screen of variegated noise filled the silence between them, but as Roy's eyes searched the street he saw nothing but parked cars. Nothing appeared to be moving, and there were no people or animals about. And yet his head still thrummed from the noise of traffic, excitement, conversations so layered they were impossible to follow. He looked around anxiously, expecting to be overcome at any moment by the press of all that life and activity. He was aware of shaking his head incessantly, Willem hovering over him looking concerned.

Willem helped Roy from the grass, hooked his arm through his and guided him as if escorting his date to a ball. They went up the slight hill, staying on the narrow sidewalk until they reached the front of Willem's house, where they turned and climbed the steps to the porch. The porch was wide and spacious and covered with dead potted plants. "I need to water those," Willem said softly, "but I always forget."

"But they're already..." Roy began, but stopped. The tide of noise had risen again, pushing behind him, distinctive individual voices but he still couldn't make out individual words.

Willem inserted his key, wiggled it. "Sometimes it sticks," he said. He appeared to be pushing on the door, but something was blocking its swing.

Roy turned his head. They were all gathering behind him, the mass of them—men, women, children—some of them shimmering, some less solid than smoke. He thought he recognized a few, but of course he could not remember their names. They were dressed in old clothes or none. He wondered if they actually had names anymore.

Some stumbled on the steps and sprawled. Their necks grew long and snake-like, twisting their way across the porch, their heads like hairy fingertips, touching, tasting. Eager and inescapable. But perhaps Roy misunderstood what he was seeing.

The door gave way and Willem pushed inside, Roy close behind. Roy looked down—it was like shoveling—books and a debris of mail, clothing, and trash spilled around the bottom of the advancing door. Something struck him in the face and he lost his sense of smell, but he still had the wherewithal to back up against the door and shut it against what he imagined was happening on the porch, a frenetic confusion of memory and dream.

He gazed around him. Intertwined stacks of boxes, bags, the odd bit of furniture, layers of reading material, opened and unopened mail, food cartons, clothing, hardware, bottles, kitchenware, unidentifiable cloth objects, wires and lumber and even an odd tree limb or two, material knit together and leaned together, rising high over their heads almost to the ceiling. Snagged bits of brown fur accessorized some sharp corners of rubbish. He counted three, four, six dog bowls, their contents solidified, and threaded with green.

"Follow my lead into the kitchen," Willem said beside him.

Willem stepped into what appeared to be a solid wall of

collected objects, but although he struggled a bit he was able to wiggle and push his way through. Roy could see now that that section of material was less dense, and as Willem passed into it Roy could see more or less bare batches of floor beneath Willem's shoes. He was still reluctant to proceed, afraid that the entire conglomerate might shift and crush him, but he was even more apprehensive about the possibility of Willem leaving him behind, stranded. So he took the plunge. As he became enveloped in paper and dusty objects he tilted his head back in order to breathe. Behind him he could hear a rising murmur, and then a slow serpentine progression of arms and legs and necks and torsos, the backs of heads, swept over the ceiling and through the junk and trash alongside him. He did not know whether to be frightened or relieved that these figures would not show him their faces.

There was nothing substantial about any of these forms—they passed through Willem's treasures and the tiny spaces between these treasures without a resulting disturbance of any kind. They were like the dust that covered everything and filled every cubic centimeter of air: they made an unpleasant effect, and they weighed nothing. They were like a visible odor.

And as if triggered by that thought Roy's nose began to work again. Everything Roy touched, reeked. He felt trapped in the bottom of the trash can with the worst part of the garbage. He began to cough and choke and ran into more solid and less penetrable portions of the mass of Willem's possessions.

"Willem!" he cried, before stumbling into an open space. It was the kitchen. A light bulb dangled overhead: greasy, fly-specked, buttery. The air itself had a similar beige cast, like a vintage photograph. Willem sat in a chair at a small rickety table, an apple in one hand, a deeply yellowed newspaper clutched in the other. One of those skimpily dressed young female popstars of several years ago was on the open page, beneath the banner "Entertainment."

"So this is what passes for entertainment these days," Willem said.

Roy took a breath. The stench was weaker here, but still present. "That story is from several years ago, isn't it?"

Willem examined the page heading. "So it is, but it'll do. History repeats itself, after all. Today's headline is 'We Die.' No amount of gyrating or singing, no matter how many people you shoot down from your rooftop, no matter how much money you steal from the poor, no matter what higher office you hold, you will, eventually, be erased."

Roy looked for another chair. There was none. "But they believe their names will be remembered, and their deeds, their performances. And they're right in that, actually, I believe."

"It's just a desperate grab for some small taste of immortality. People forget names, the small details of history. They do it all the time," Willem said. Voices began to issue from the debris surrounding them, first whispers then declarations then shouts, often accompanied by weeping. When Roy glanced at his surroundings he could see their faces now, and quickly turned away. Willem appeared to pay them no attention—he certainly betrayed no alarm—but he was raising his voice, as if to be heard above the din. "I have your cereal here! I've filled your *bowl*!"

Roy took the offering, raising the bowl to peer inside. The wrinkled flakes looked more like wood chips than breakfast cereal. They were covered by the water he'd requested. There was no spoon, and he decided he wouldn't ask for one. At least it didn't smell, so he raised it to his lips and began to slurp. The flakes were stale, like bits of cardboard as they gathered in his mouth. But he allowed them in anyway. He swallowed what he could and allowed the rest to fall back into the bowl.

"How long..." Roy looked around at the walls of trash, avoiding the eyes scattered in the shadowed spaces. "How long have you been...collecting?"

"Mostly since Alice died. I'd always been interested in things, finding interesting stuff in the world. Often I would bring these things home. But when Alice lived with me there were limits, you know? Back then I couldn't keep everything. But when you're by yourself—you make your own rules. And most importantly, you don't have to explain them." An empty shoe box drifted off the top of one of the piles and fell at Willem's feet. A scurrying and a rearrangement occurred within the depths of the assemblage. "I'm partial to interesting containers," he continued. "Things that will hold other things. They mean organization, even when nothing is being organized. We all need that sense of organization, that ability to place parentheses, and a period at the end. Other things I like are things I know might be useful to someone else: a part, a knob, one piece of some ensemble. Everyone is missing something—I'd like to provide them with that missing piece someday."

"Have you ever given any of this away?"

Willem looked up at his stacks, his eyes sweeping the walls of objects. "I have to find the right people to give them to. Do you realize how difficult that is in this day and age? People just won't stop anymore to figure out what they're missing."

Roy felt the pressure in his gut, the impending disruption. "Could I please use your restroom?"

Willem stood up, reached for something in the corner behind him. "Out of order, I'm afraid. I can't get anyone in here to even look at it. So that room's just additional storage space for now. You'll need to go into the back yard." He held out a beige grocery bag and a handful of old newspaper. He gestured toward the small door in one corner of the kitchen, by an old stove whose top was buried beneath dusty pots and pans.

Roy ignored the offered materials and shuffled over to that door. The top half was glass, permitting a view of the back yard. Immediately outside there were grocery bags, paper sacks, garbage bags stacked everywhere, several feet high and barely contained by the sagging wooden fence. Several squirrels worked feverishly at a bulging, misshapen package recently fallen, its contents spilled.

Roy left the room, forcing his way into Willem's belongings until he found a soft spot, then pushed harder, wading through what appeared to be one of everything imaginable as he attempted to find the door to the front porch. Things crashed behind him and Willem cursed and screamed in offended rage or pain, it was impossible to determine or process.

Roy was close enough to those visiting forms—the turned faces and offered lips—to hear what they were whispering, but the noise inside his head was louder than all their voices. He pushed past them as if they were no more than added bits to Willem's collection.

Some of the stacks beside the front door had collapsed around it. Roy turned the knob and dragged the door inside as far as it would go, then climbed over the obstacles and squeezed himself through the narrow opening. He fell out onto the porch and felt a sharp pain in his knee as something gave way.

Everything murmured. Everything had something to say. But Roy wouldn't look at any of them. He deliberately ignored them all. He climbed to his feet and hobbled down the steps and out onto the sidewalk. He stank. He needed to get home.

A great noise suddenly swallowed him up as if the secret engine of the world had just turned over. The air exploded around him in an ecstasy of escape. It was all he could do to hold onto his thoughts to prevent them from being completely swept off the planet.

A snow of tiny fragments powdered his head, his outstretched arms, and his hands. He brushed them off: bits of yellowed newspaper, trash. When finally he turned around he confronted the hole, the freshly raw ground, the fact that nothing remained to indicate that anything had ever existed there at all.

Roy wandered the empty streets looking for some familiar landmark. Off in the distance the conversations continued, but thank God the uncomfortably familiar forms kept their distance. When finally he found his block of course his apartment building was gone. In its place the terraced squares of freshly turned ground resembled most those peculiar South American pyramids, the ones where human sacrifices were performed, and everywhere you went you knew full well you were walking on the dead.

THE WAKE

Philip had not felt well for a very long time. He was fatigued, and fell asleep frequently. His doctors—he switched habitually—said it was most likely some undiagnosed allergy, although they did not hesitate to prescribe new medications for what they could not diagnose. It seemed unlikely he would die from this, but he did not anticipate improvement.

He could not remember the last time he had sat through a movie, or an hour-long television show, without falling asleep. Often he would dream the endings of whatever he missed. He could have watched those shows again if he wanted, but he chose not to, thinking that the endings he dreamed were probably more than sufficient.

His father, that old drunk, would often fall asleep in front of the television when Philip was a boy. His father had an old dog, Duke, who would do the same. Duke would whimper and softly yip while sleeping, constantly moving his thin, white-haired legs. Philip's father said that meant Duke dreamed of hunting when he was just a pup. But how did his father know? Philip always wondered if Duke had instead dreamed of being chased, terrified that he was about to be eaten by that vast mystery which pursues us all.

Philip remembered trying to watch TV while Duke slept and dreamed on the rug beside him, and his father slept in the recliner behind him, chewing at some unspoken distress, occasionally shouting at things he would never describe. Over time it seemed Duke and his father might be having the same dream, and if Philip fell asleep at that moment their dream might overtake him as well in a tidal hum of image and sound, which might not be entirely undesirable.

Today Philip had hoped he could just slip in and entomb himself in the crowd, but somebody had locked the front door forcing him to ring the bell. When no one answered the bell—although he knew they were inside because he could hear them talking, and peculiarly, laughing—he was reduced to beating on the door. Which was humiliating—this was his family home, and the wake for his father was being held inside without him. He was considering breaking a window when his sister opened the door.

"Where have you been? You're hours late!" Her face was pale, but he was sure she hadn't been crying. Lisa hated their father.

"Are you actually considering not letting me in?" She didn't answer. "Sorry. I overslept."

She walked away, mumbling about his lack of respect. She was appropriately dressed in a crisp black dress with a layer of black lace on top. Philip still wore the casual work clothes he slept in.

The figure in the casket only vaguely resembled his father. It could very well have been a cleverly made-up mannequin. The old man's cheeks reminded him of painted plastic. The lips were much more defined than his dad's had been. The weight loss he expected—his dad had been ill all last year. The hair was perfect and nothing like his dad's characteristic and thinning, uncombed mop. He expected Lisa preferred this approximation—a hopeful vision, closer to some unrealized ideal.

The only empty seat was a folding chair propped up by the foot of the casket. Philip supposed no one wanted to sit that close to the body. People would come by for a visit, gaze at the face inside and half-smile or sad-smile or whatever those expressions were, but no one lingered for long. No one stayed. But he was the son, however troublesome their relationship might have been. So he took the chair and unfolded it and sat down.

The awkwardness was immediate. No one could come by for their near-obligatory visit to the deceased without dealing in some way with Philip. Perhaps they knew him and felt like they should talk to him, but he remained sitting out of some vague sense of respect (or was he worried about losing his chair?) and they had to contend with speaking with someone whose mouth was navel-height. Or they didn't know who he was at all and had to maneuver around this stranger as they exited their visit.

Philip himself had to decide where to look. When there were people by the casket he was staring at a number of butts and crotches. He thought he should probably be gazing at his father's face—that was what a wake was for, wasn't it? Safeguarding the body, or at some point in history he supposed making sure the deceased was actually dead or that the body wouldn't be stolen for unspeakable purposes. Or perhaps he had misunderstood all that.

He could almost see over the edge of the casket's lid, but not quite. If he raised himself up a bit, straightening his spine, he could see much of his father's face, but he couldn't hold that position long without trembling. When he thought no one was looking he retrieved a couple of thick phonebooks from the corner cupboard and added them to his seat, perching himself on those. Now he could see his father perfectly. In fact there was something about the angle which made looking at his father almost compulsory.

But gaze at a still body long enough and you can't help imagining that it is moving, if ever so slightly. Philip had to look away finally, convinced that his father was preparing his enhanced mouth to speak to him.

It was chilly outside and apparently his mother, who he hadn't yet seen, turned up the heat. He was still wearing a light-weight jacket he hadn't hung up because the coat tree was missing from the front hall. He could not imagine where they had put the thing, but for some reason it might have pissed off the old man and he chopped it up and fed it to the fire. The furnace, the crowded house, his jacket, his nervousness, all conspired to raise the temperature. When had his parents gotten to know so many people? Philip didn't recognize half of them.

He'd never been to a wake before. He hadn't even realized they still had such things, that you could have a body on display in the house like that without breaking some local ordinance.

The heat was baking his head. He closed his eyes to escape it, and nodded off.

Philip didn't know what the etiquette was for these affairs, but he presumed the deceased's son falling asleep was not acceptable behavior.

He opened his eyes and looked at his father again, who looked differently. His father's head had tilted, had been tilted, approximately an inch to the left. His father's nose was at a different angle.

It wasn't a boisterous event. There was some drinking but not that much. And people largely avoided the casket when they weren't paying their respects. So Philip doubted anyone had bumped it.

He waited and watched, and noticed no other change. He wondered if he'd just slipped in his chair. He rearranged himself so that his father appeared at least somewhat closer to the way Philip had seen him before. And then he nodded off again. He couldn't help himself.

Even in sleep he was embarrassed. What would people think? What would his mother think? He made some attempts to wake himself up, but this had always been problematic—whatever happened in his dreams was always far more interesting, and truer, than anything that happened to him awake.

Philip snapped his head around. His father had rolled his head completely onto its side. The dead slept restlessly, Philip thought, especially in the dreams of their children. He glanced over the room to see if anyone else had noticed. Philip snapped his head around again and his father had rolled his entire body completely over onto his right side, messing up his carefully combed hair. Philip could see where his father's makeup had smeared across the white silk lining of the casket. "Dad, hey Dad," he said as softly as he could. "You really shouldn't be doing that. It isn't appropriate."

His father mumbled something, then cursed under his breath. "Don't turn the channel," he said. "I'm watching that."

Something warm and damp rubbed against Philip's pants leg. Duke was licking his right knee. The old dog looked up, revealing a cataract over his left eye. His right eye looked slightly cloudy. Philip wondered how much the dog could actually see.

"Philip," Lisa hissed from a few feet away. "Some men from the funeral home are at the front door. I haven't told Mom— you'd better handle it."

Philip got to his feet, told Duke to "stay!" Lisa had already disappeared. He jogged to the front door. Two men were standing there in their colorful prom tuxedos. He wondered if his mother had decided to go cheap with the services, and that was why the wake was being held at home.

"So sorry to bother you," the one in the lime-colored suit said. "We simply wanted to settle our bill, then we'll be on our way." He handed Philip a small slip of paper. "Due: $16,750" had been scribbled across it in red ink.

Philip supposed the amount was reasonable, but how could he know for sure? "I think I need this itemized. Not that I don't trust you, but when I show this to my mother, well, I'm sure she'll want it itemized. She's a specific sort of person."

The one in the peach-colored suit spoke up. "Well, this is highly irregular. We don't normally expose our internal paperwork."

Philip felt angry, although he wasn't sure why. Maybe because he didn't think it was his place to be handling this. He wasn't suited for it. "Well, that can't be helped. If you want to get paid." He handed the slip back and stared at the pair.

The one in the peach-colored suit pulled an envelope from his jacket pocket and handed it to Philip. Inside was an itemized list concerning his father.

Philip's finger flicked across one of the lines. "Music? What music?"

The lime-suited man replied, "We like to listen to music while we work."

Philip's finger stopped on another line. "Books?"

"We have books available for the bereaved. Self-help books, I suppose you would call them. To help with the tricky emotions involved."

"You delivered these books to my mother?"

"She hasn't asked for them, but they're available."

But the bulk of the charges were under *embalming supplies.*

"Molasses, sodium chloride, magnesium, glass cleaner, forty weight motor oil, corn lotion, and there's more. You actually put these things inside my father's body?"

"Apparently. Those and more," the peach-suited man replied. "Formulations tend to vary with the individual, as one would expect."

"I don't believe you. We're not paying for half this.

What is this?" A woman's frail voice behind him. Philip's mother squeezed in beside him and took the itemized bill out of his hand. She stared up at him. "I'm glad you came. Your father would have been pleased. But you have to wake up now. A son has to watch over his father's body. What if wolves try to eat it? You'll never forgive yourself, son, if wolves were to eat your father."

Philip turned and ran back toward the living room. They must have remodeled the house after he moved out, because the hallway leading into the living room was much longer than he remembered, and lined with such a standing crowd of people that he couldn't see any of the passing doors or mounted photographs or other familiar landmarks behind them, so he wasn't quite sure where he was in relation to his father's casket. Who were all these people and were they really his father's friends? His father had always been so unpleasant Philip couldn't remember the old man as having more than one or two friends. In an earlier time they sometimes hired mourners. Was that what was happening here? Had his mother actually hired mourners to send the old bastard off?

He kept seeing these eyes among the forms—yellow eyes and red eyes, flickering like candle flames, moving rapidly in the shadows behind the standing mourners. These must be the wolves his mother was talking about, racing him to his father's casket.

And there was the casket, but a small child was climbing out of it, and now the wolves were chasing that poor child up the stairs. "Dad!" he called, because Philip thought he recognized the child from old photographs. Death had diminished his father, and now his father was being pursued by wolves.

The child, his father, didn't turn around—he was too busy

being terrified. He disappeared around the turn of the staircase, three dark wolves nipping at his heels. Philip raced up the stairs after them.

But once he reached the top of the stairs there was nothing to be seen, the corridor was empty, and all the bedroom doors were closed. He listened carefully but could hear nothing but the loud noises coming from downstairs, the wake now in full swing. He realized he was foolish anyway for coming up here without a weapon to fend off the wolves, so he made his way back down looking for some kind of bludgeon.

His father was back in the casket, turned over, his hands over his eyes to block out the light. Philip went over to him and gently tapped him on the shoulder. "Dad, that's not the way you're supposed to be. Your clothes and hair, they're all messed up now—you don't want to look bad today of all days, do you? You should look your best at your wake. I'll comb your hair, okay? Just let me comb your hair."

He gently peeled his father's hands away and there was Philip himself, hiding in his father's casket. "Get him out of there! Tell him he can't sleep there!" his sister Lisa said beside him. She reached into the casket and grabbed Philip by the hair and yanked. "Get out of here! You don't belong in here!" Philip wept and wailed back at her, his mouth impossibly wide and mobile.

Philip looked down at himself with shame. "Get out of there and back into your chair! You disgust me. Just get back in your chair and don't say a word—I'm going to go get Dad and try to talk him into getting back into his casket. Lisa is going to stay here and make sure you don't get into any more trouble."

He went into the hall closet and found one of his father's old golf clubs. His father had never played, but thought these were a bargain at some long ago yard sale. Philip went back up the stairs, determined to kill the wolves and talk his father back downstairs.

The situation was relatively quiet upstairs, but Philip sensed a vague restlessness stirring behind the closed doors. He'd done this before of course, gone to retrieve his father and get him to one place or another on time. His mother's birthday party.

His sister's wedding. His own college graduation. Sometimes from this house, sometimes from other houses or rundown apartments when Mother had kicked his father out and Dad had increased his drinking as a kind of resentful or rebellious gesture. Philip was tired of it.

The first bedroom was empty. It was pristine, decorated in the floral patterns his mother loved so much. He figured this was either the guest room or his mother's room when Dad was away. Certainly his dad had never touched it.

The second bedroom was a bit more masculine—browns and reds and some wood paneling. But still quite tidy which made Philip think his father had never used this room, or had his mother redone everything in the hours following his father's death?

But he found the missing coat tree. It was neatly tucked under the covers, its bronze coat hooks elongated and reaching out from under the sheets and blanket, wriggling in dismay. One of his father's ball caps was jammed over the top of the spindle. Philip shut the door without saying anything.

He opened the third door and was immediately struck by the odor. The rooms his father lived in always smelled funny: cigarettes and beer, sweaty T-shirts and something that suggested chocolate but which probably wasn't. Philip entered and shut the door behind him. In the front room the wolves lay clumped together on a battered old sofa watching a rolling static pattern on a small TV with a coat hanger antenna. Behind them white curtains stained with tobacco-yellow splotches blew out the window overlooking a raucous lower downtown. Trash layered everything except for a narrow, kicked-out path leading into the next room.

Philip crunched through the emptied beer cans and peered around the next room. The bed had a dirty white bottom sheet and matching flattened pillow but no other bed clothes. A variety of reading material including several romance novels was arranged in stacks between the bed and the dresser, whose clothes-strewn drawers had been pulled out at varying lengths on either side of a milk-clouded mirror.

He found his father sitting on the other side of the bed

leaning against the wall under a window covered by a stiff brown shade. He had only his striped boxers on. His face showed several days' worth of stubble. He'd been crying.

"Dad, you have to get dressed."

His father turned his head and gazed at him rheumily. "Son. You found me."

"It's never that hard."

"What am I late for this time?"

Philip had no answer for this. "Do you have some clean clothes? If so, where are they? I'll help you get dressed."

His father gestured vaguely toward the other side of the room. Philip walked over, examined the piles of clothing and picked up the clothes hanging from the open drawers. He found a pair of pants and a shirt which appeared untouched, and more or less folded in the bottom of a drawer. He started with those and a pair of underwear which looked relatively fresh. All of his father's socks were dirty and wadded up on various parts of the floor. He wondered if the old man could get by without socks. Philip could pull the pants down to cover the bare ankles. After all, all his father had to do was lie there and keep quiet.

"Did you hear that?" his father asked while Philip was dressing him.

"Hear what, Dad? I didn't hear anything."

"You'd know it if you heard it. Like a rhino charging right behind you, or absolutely the worst storm you can imagine. You think you've avoided it, but then you discover you've driven right into it. Like this dream, Son. You don't really want to be in this dream."

Philip paused and stared at him. "Let's just get you dressed, okay? We're holding everything up."

His father sighed and let himself go limp, allowing Philip to continue dressing him—not resisting, but not really helping either. Philip considered how it was a bit like dressing a dummy, or a dead body.

"I can't remember—did you ever get married, Son?"

"No, Dad. I didn't."

His father flopped over on his side. He'd become more stiff, and harder to dress. "You might consider it. It can help."

Philip pulled his father to his feet, wrapping one arm around his waist to support him, and started toward the door. "Are your wolves going to bother us?"

His father didn't reply, but they made it out into the corridor and back down the stairs with little trouble.

There was no sign of his sister, but everything seemed calm and unhurried downstairs. People continued to talk and drink as if nothing were amiss. Philip lifted his father as if he were a statue, or a rolled-up rug, and slipped him face up into the casket. Afterwards he arranged his hands and combed his hair.

He paused to study the effect—his father in the casket looked exactly as he had when Philip first entered the house. Then Philip awakened, sprawled on the floor, chair and phone books collapsed and scattered.

Lisa was kneeling beside him holding his hand. His mother was there too, crying. He tried to speak but could not. His father walked stealthily past his mother and sister, grinning, out of his box again. Philip tried to warn them, but there were no words, only this roar coming up out of the dream behind him, moving so fast, and sounding so loud, he couldn't hear, or think about anything else.

THE WEIGHT LOST

They'd started the diet together, Clyde and Marjorie. Marjorie had stopped after losing thirty pounds, and kept it off except for the occasional slip. Clyde didn't care either way, unless it helped her live longer. He'd always loved how she looked, however she looked. He adored her, although he hesitated to use that word in her presence. Marjorie had always presented to the world a hard, no-nonsense surface. She didn't trust most spontaneous emotion. What he considered a very little she thought too much.

"Are you crying? You aren't crying, are you? Are you putting me on, being sarcastic?" She'd looked genuinely puzzled, but there was more behind it, he thought. A kind of distaste.

They'd been watching *Tell Me That You Love Me, Junie Moon* on TV, Liza Minnelli's scream after Arthur dies. God, it was like her soul had been ripped out. How could he not have cried?

She'd patted his hand, later. Her version of an apology. Sometimes he thought she loved him because of an idea, but it was not an idea she completely believed in.

"Are you still eating whole grains? It says here not to eat whole grains."

He looked up from his fruit plate and stared at her. He thought they'd agreed not to talk about the diet while they were at the resort. The resort was his reward for having lost a hundred and twenty-five pounds. That was Marjorie's idea—he hadn't actually wanted a reward. He thought most rewards were traps that distracted you from what really mattered. Too much talk about dieting was just another kind of trap. The more he had to talk about it, the less he wanted to do it. He wanted it to be no big deal. The problem was, it had always been a big deal.

So he'd agreed to go to the resort if they wouldn't talk about food while they were up there. But it seemed he was constantly misunderstanding things, so maybe he had misunderstood their agreement as well. "I thought whole grains were good for you. That's why I stopped eating white bread."

"Well, *apparently*, whole grains turn into sugars in your body just like regular bread. And you already know sugars are trouble."

Clyde hated it when she told him what he supposedly already knew. He stared at the book she was holding. *Food!* and some other words hidden by her hand. It was a new one—when had she gotten it? And hadn't they agreed to no reading at the restaurant? She'd said herself, "Let's not bring any books into the restaurant. We can sit out at a patio table with a gorgeous view. Why would you need a book when you have a gorgeous view?"

But they were out on the patio, they had their gorgeous view, and yet she had brought a book out here. A diet book. And what she had read to him confused and upset him.

"Then I can't eat grain? I can't eat bread?" The tremble in his words embarrassed him.

"You can eat sprouted bread, apparently. It says here your body treats that like a vegetable."

"Sprouted? What's that?" He had a vision of damp, moldy bread emanating a green cloud that escaped when he opened the wrapper.

"I don't know, but apparently it's really good for you. I'll get some when we get back."

Clyde made an effort to ignore what she'd just said. He glanced at her salad, which she hadn't touched, apparently preferring to suck on a piece of bread dipped in yellow oil. Her poppy seed dressing looked vaguely suspicious. Some of the seeds might be moving, but it might be a trick of the light. At the table next to them a man was eating chicken. Oil glistened on his chin. He snorted when he ate, as if he could hardly breathe. From somewhere behind Clyde a woman was making choking sounds, but no one was looking that way, so he did not turn around.

He went back to his fruit, which looked far less appetizing than it had only moments before. The colors were too bright, maybe due to some unhealthy additive or other. He'd spent a couple of hours researching the resort's menus before they came here, but there was only so much you could find out. Eating out had begun to feel like a variety of Russian roulette. What had happened to food? Junk food was part of the conspiracy, as was medicine. Human beings had been turned into longer-living but unhealthier organisms. It was positively Kafkaesque that the things you loved the most might be the worst for you.

"What did you say, honey?" She looked at him over the edge of the diet book.

"I don't think I said anything." But he wasn't sure.

"You were probably just thinking out loud again. So what were you thinking?"

She was always pinning him down like this. He thought about it, then opted for honesty. "I don't know if I said it or not, but it's *unfair*, you know? Eating should be like breathing, automatic and natural. Thoughtless and worry-free. I *hate* it that it's not." *In fact, sometimes,* he thought, *it can be absolutely hideous.*

He looked down at his arm: pasty and trembling, months of hard exercise having managed only to imbalance it, so that some parts appeared proportionately too large and others too small, as if the muscle underneath had actually gone missing.

He stared out over the patio, trying to recapture that gorgeous view and the peace he'd been feeling before this past half-hour. A bad smell had come along with the last breeze. Something butchered and corrupt, like misplaced meat. A smell of disappointment, he thought, of futility. He glanced at Marjorie, but she appeared not to have noticed. *Then at least maybe the smell's not coming from me.*

He scanned the nearby faces for some signs of awareness or recognition. At the edge of the immense patio, a good ten yards away, a man stood by the sculptured bushes that obscured the steep embankment on that side of the restaurant. Clyde had a notion there was something wrong with the man. He wore a light weight, ill-fitting jacket, so large on him he looked draped in it, like a seldom-used piece of furniture. There were lumps here and there under the cloth, like casts, or inflatables. And balancing these were the absences, an apparently empty sleeve flapping in the wind, a shoulder appearing less than full, something gone from the rib cage on the left-hand side. Clyde glanced at the man's face—he was staring at them, yet his face was turned mostly away, the eyes shadowed. Something about the man's profile made no sense. But there was still a certain intensity in the way he held himself, targeting them.

"Did you hear me, honey? I said how is your fruit?" Marjorie shook his arm.

He looked across at her and grabbed her hands, pulling them firmly into his own. At that moment he felt an overpowering love for her, and he wanted her to focus on him, and he didn't want her to see the man standing at the edge of the patio. "Delicious, sweetheart." He smiled. "Maybe the best I've ever had. I don't know how they do it."

There was movement in his peripheral vision. Certain subtractions were taking place there, shadows dissected and scattered.

He stepped up on the scale, waiting, hopeful, nudging the weights. He had invested in the physician's balance scale when he'd started the diet. They were said to be more accurate, but mostly he just liked the way it looked. It had a sliding bar with weights, and he had to calibrate it. Supposedly you only had to calibrate once, or when you moved it, but he liked calibrating it every Sunday when he first woke up. You set all the weights to zero, then you turned a screw until the floating bar centered on the balance mark. Then it wouldn't lie to you.

Much of everything else about losing weight had been an exercise in shame and despair, but he had struggled through it. He had lost the weight and was intent on losing more. He would become a smaller person. He would learn what it felt like to take up less space in the world.

"So what are you shooting for?" Marjorie asked.

"I don't want to say, really. Losing a set number of pounds isn't supposed to be the point. Becoming a healthier person is supposed to be the point."

She nibbled on a celery stalk and looked at him skeptically. "That doesn't sound very concrete. How am I supposed to encourage you if I don't know what your goals are?"

"You don't need to worry about my goals, honey. I'd just like you to encourage me to keep at it, however I'm keeping at it."

"Well, thanks for telling me what I need and don't need to worry about. I'm just trying to be supportive." She left the kitchen.

Being a healthier person *should* have been the point, and he *wanted* it to be the point, but it actually wasn't. He wanted to be the kind of handsome that drew people. He'd never had that; how must it feel? Embarrassingly, at least for a brief time he wanted people to like him for the shallowest of reasons.

The exchange had made him feel clumsy. And when he felt clumsy he wanted to eat. He opened the refrigerator door and stared. They'd removed almost everything that would be terrible for him to eat, but there was that half of a "healthy pizza" they'd tried the other night. Of course it was full of ingredients he shouldn't be eating in any quantity, and even with all that it didn't taste like any pizza he'd ever had before. There really was no such thing as a healthy pizza—usually it just made you want to eat twice the quantity. It was just a cold lie on a plate.

But still, it had said "healthy" on the box, so how could eating it be irresponsible? He decided to gnaw on it cold, and reached in to grab it.

But another hand, and a bit of the attached arm, was already in there, stretched along the back of the top shelf. Pale and soft-looking, unmuscular. A portion of the skin had slipped to unsheathe the red meat underneath. The meat was heavily marbled, with scattered pockets of congealed fat bulging between the tendons. The arm was more than somewhat familiar.

"Marjorie! Marjorie! Come down here! Please!"

He sat while she took her sweet time coming downstairs. He really did appreciate that she cared enough to try to motivate him, but this? Of course it was fake, even though it looked so real. But where'd she get something so vile?

"Something wrong? My God, you look pale!"

"Could you just get that thing out of the refrigerator, please?"

"What is it? Something spoil? I swear, Clyde, why do I always have to clean up the mess?" She opened the refrigerator door and stared inside. Then she was moving her head around, picking things up off the shelves, smelling.

"What are you doing?"

"Trying to ferret out," she spoke with a cold echo, "whatever it is that has you freaked out. But I swear this food looks safe to me."

He came up beside her. "Excuse me," and nudged her away, perhaps not gently enough. "It's gone," he said softly, then wished he hadn't spoken aloud.

"What was it, Clyde?"

"I'm sorry. I guess I must have looked too quickly, mistook something maybe for something else, I don't know."

"I think you've been exercising too much. You're pushing yourself too hard."

He searched again for the arm, lifted a small bag of romaine out of the way. Nothing. "Maybe. I'd better read up on it. Obviously I've gotten something wrong."

"Maybe you've lost enough weight."

"But it's not about losing the weight, honey," he said patiently. "It's about becoming something, someone better."

The next morning he drank several large glasses of water in a row. All the nutritionists said to drink lots of water if you wanted to lose weight. His personal doctor said any liquid would do, an input Clyde chose to ignore—the conflicting advice only made him angry. He'd heard it was crucial to get rid of toxins—his doctor said the body had adequate systems already in place to remove toxins thank-you-very-much. Sometimes he just wanted to weep—all he wanted was to be smaller.

But not drinking enough water might have been the whole problem all along. Drinking water felt like drowning. Glass after glass—it felt as if his mind were floating away.

He put in his time on the stationary bike first. It was in the nature of such a machine, of course, that you never went anywhere no matter how vigorously you pedaled. Maybe the idea was not to get to a place, but to arrive at a prescribed level of pain. "No pain no gain." He didn't know where to begin pointing out the flaws in such a sentiment, but he also knew that transformation could be painful.

Afterwards he took a scalding shower—hot enough to take off any cells he'd just killed—and got on the scale. He slid the smaller weight across the upper bar, watching the pointer as it sought the mid-point. There was something beyond satisfying when he had to move the weight farther left than the time before, a precise indicator of the weight that had vanished. Ten pounds. That seemed impossible, although he'd had remarkable drops before. When was the last time he'd weighed? Weighing yourself too much made you obsessive. It had been a couple of days maybe.

Tempted to step off, then step back on again, he reminded himself that the numbers weren't supposed to matter. When he'd first gotten the scale he'd sometimes weigh himself four times a day.

A whiff of sour body smell had entered the bathroom, making him skittish. When he turned around nothing was there. The garbage cans were just outside—maybe he smelled that. He thought about jumping back into the shower into even hotter water, hoping to burn away any possibility that the bad smell might be him, but this was a cycle he was loathe to begin again.

The ill scent faded into the ambient aromas of moisture and multiple soaps, and for a few minutes he was able to relax. He got off the scale and went to the sink again. The mirror had steamed. But then shadow seeped into the moisture beading the glass, and he could smell that sourness again, closer, worst, filling the air around him.

What had he weighed today? He'd been so distracted that although he remembered moving the smaller weight satisfyingly to the left, as if actually making himself smaller by doing so, he hadn't focused on the numbers. That wouldn't do. He got on the scale again.

As the pointer bobbed he felt himself go light, as if he weighed nothing at all. Elated, he breathed in deeply, then exhaled fully, years of disappointment rushing out of him. He closed his eyes, thinking he might float right off the scale. But then the raw dead stench welled up and the scale shook violently as if more weight had suddenly been applied. The pointer clanged against the measuring frame and Clyde stepped off in a panic. Fleeing the bathroom, he had to push past a sodden resistance, and it felt vaguely like one of those days when he'd tried so hard to cheer himself up, but his heart had resisted all encouragement.

Marjorie was waiting for him in bed. She raised the covers to display herself. "Don't take a shower yet. Come into the bed now—I'm ready for you."

He fell into her and she curled around him. She smelled of damp breezes and distant flowers, dates they'd had early in their marriage, a summer mountain afternoon. After a time he felt himself ready to climax. Then the bed shook as if one of them had had a seizure, and the mattress sank a bit, as if someone else had just gotten into bed with them. He could feel her rising above him. He opened his eyes and saw the bloody meat begin to spill from above her shoulder, someone behind her not quite touching her skin but closing in for a terrible embrace, a skinless arm streaked in fat reaching over her belly, and cascading down what might have been a sweeping flap of torn skin, an appendage, a wing. He closed his eyes as he climaxed, tears streaming as he wished it all away.

Afterward, he went directly into the master bath and jumped into the shower. He was gliding his hand down his left side, soaping himself, when he felt the wound. At first he thought it was just some odd looseness or wrinkle in the skin. This line, this edge, felt more like a rip than a wrinkle or anything like that. And the edges had separated in some places and allowed something puffy to come through, and his fingertips could actually go inside these gaps and sink in. He looked down but he couldn't see the tear—it was hidden by his arm, or just around the edge of his side, moving, avoiding his examination. He stepped out of the shower dripping wet and approached the mirror on the back of the bathroom door.

His skin had split open in a long, wavering line from just below his right armpit to slightly above the outside of his right knee. He wasn't bleeding very much, but copious amounts of an amber-colored fluid oozed just inside the opening. Here and there the two sides gaped, as if he were wearing some ill-fitting covering, and he could see the loose layers of fat inside, unmoored from the tissues, turned a sorrowful yellow like old foam exposed to the elements. "Margie!" he screamed, jerking open the door and stumbling out of the bathroom. "Call an ambulance! I've *hurt* myself!"

She scrambled out of sleep to the side of the bed, groping blindly. "What? What happened?" He pulled back, afraid she might damage him more.

"Look! My side! Look!" And he was turning around and around, like some girl in a beauty pageant showing off her best angles.

"Stop moving! I can't see!" She was crouching beside him now, touching his skin, but her touch burned, his skin alive with nerves. He turned more slowly and she said, quietly, "I don't see *anything*. Honey, point to it. Show me what happened."

He stopped, gasping, his thoughts clouded. She had her hand on his leg now, turning him gently like some kid who'd skinned his knee and then cried too much. "You don't see *anything*?"

"I...not unless you mean this red place. It's like a rash, I guess. Or maybe you burned yourself in the shower." Now she was just being nice, trying to calm him with some rational explanation. He doubted she'd even found a rash.

"I must have...dozed off in the shower. You can do that, I guess. And dream." But he could still feel himself bleeding, and the air attacking the raw interior of the injury.

"I *told* you, honey. You're exercising too *hard*. Slow it down, you'll still get to where you want to be."

But later that night, after she'd gone to bed, Clyde slipped downstairs and got back on the weight bench. That was the way he'd been calming himself lately. He'd do several rounds of abdominal exercises, then work the dumbbells until his muscles were so exhausted he could barely make it back upstairs, but at least he'd be too tired for worry.

He was into his third set of reclining crunches, a forty-pound weight plate held against his chest for additional pressure, when he felt the cold slip of something in his belly, followed by the sudden painful tightness. He eased into the bathroom to examine himself in the mirror. A large knot had formed on the upper edge of his abdomen, just below his rib cage. It looked like a baby's head trying to push itself out through his skin.

"You've herniated yourself," the doctor said. Instead of looking at him Clyde stared at the candy jar on the doctor's desk. "It happens. See?" Clyde looked up. The doctor had made a crude drawing on a slip of paper of an abdomen with an area circled just left of center. "You had your gallbladder removed some years ago. Sometimes the incision site opens, the intestines poke through—that's what makes the big bump. But judging from this scar..." He poked at a small line he'd made. "You've herniated before, right?"

Clyde said nothing. Marjorie leaned forward. "Seven years ago. The last time he was exercising—so much."

"Well." The doctor frowned. "Here it is again. You'll have to cut out the strenuous exercise awhile, at least for a few months post-surgery. Of course it doesn't *have* to be fixed, if there's no pain."

"I can't stop the workouts," Clyde replied softly. "Then it would all be for nothing."

"You can lose weight in other ways. You can diet," Marjorie said.

"If you diet with no exercise, you lose muscle. The less muscle, the less fat you can burn," Clyde explained. She didn't understand. Neither of them did.

"Well, you don't want to hurt yourself, either," the doctor said. "You don't want that hernia to get any bigger."

Clyde hated it when people told him what he did and did not want.

Clyde took his time packing for the hospital. It was supposed to be day surgery, but he expected complications. He always expected complications. He'd have the suitcase in the car just in case.

He put clothes into his suitcase and took clothes out, then repeated the process. He had some new clothes, but he missed the comfort of some of his older, oversized garments.

He was about to close the case when he caught a glimpse of pale flesh beneath one edge of his stylish new underwear. The skin was puffy, stretched, squeezed into too-tight elastic. A faint bruise was spreading. He shut the case and locked it, and hauled it swiftly downstairs to sit ready by the door.

As they wheeled Clyde on the gurney down the hall toward the operating room he began to talk. There were three walking along with him—two lean, tall young men of athletic build, and an older woman at his feet, staring at him. Even though they all wore surgical masks he could tell that he was making them uncomfortable, especially the woman. But he couldn't help himself.

"I wanted to lose more. I wanted—well, to know how it felt to be small, to be skinny, you know?

"Oh, I know. I know. But the weight thing. I always wanted to know what it would be like not to have it in the way. Because it *is* in the way. When you're a kid you get out of the house and you get out in the world, you go to school, and you want to be one of those guys people are drawn to, the kind of guy girls are drawn to, even when they don't know a thing about you, even before you've opened your mouth to say anything. And later, people listen to you, even though they have no particular reason to, because they see you, how you look, and they're going to listen.

"I'm not saying you can't screw it up. They might listen to the face but if the face has nothing interesting to say a lot of people will stop listening. I say a lot of people, but not everybody. Some people will always listen to a pretty face, no matter what nonsense it's spouting.

"I just wanted, I just wanted, you know, to feel different than I felt. I wanted to feel good about myself. I wanted to be one of those confident people."

He was surprised when he woke up in recovery. He hadn't really thought about it, at least not consciously, but he supposed he must have expected to die, even with such a minor surgery. He was vaguely aware of his bandaged lower belly, and of the fact that he didn't want to move it, not for anything.

On another gurney next to him was a man, judging by the haircut, the shoulders, and the loose sprawl under the covers. The covers were terribly stained, and the gurney smelled bad, and from the little he saw of the man it seemed some important things might be missing, and Clyde thought the man might be dead.

He squirmed, wanting to alert someone that the man was dead, but it hurt to squirm, so he stopped. He moved his head around carefully, trying to better see the man.

The man was roughly his size, had an unkempt hair style and pasty, somewhat puffy features, although there didn't appear to be enough infrastructure to hold the features in place, so they had moved around a bit on his face—all fat, skin, fluid, and some gristle. And almost the exact same nose except slightly asymmetrical; there appeared to be not enough of it on this side.

From the drape of the sheet, Clyde thought the man might have a very large chest, with not enough in it. The sheet had slipped, and now something nasty appeared to be falling out. Disgusted, Clyde had a strange impulse to lean across and kiss the man on the cheek. But it would have been too far to lean, and it would have hurt too much.

Clyde turned his head and began to weep. The smell was worse than before. He made himself turn on his side. It was extremely painful—he thought he might fall apart—but he wanted to be as far away from the figure on the gurney as possible, but the best he could do was to turn his back and pretend the figure wasn't there.

He felt the sudden shift behind him, the almost-seamless embrace. He resisted with all the strength in his leaner, trimmer body, but it was clear the increase in gravity would quickly bring him down.

THE MONSTER MAKERS

This is all I can bear of love.

Robert is calling the children in, practically screaming it, how we all need to go, *now*. But I'm too busy gazing at the couple as they talk to the park ranger, the way their ears melt, noses droop, elongating into something else as their hair warps and shifts color, their spines bend and expand, arms and legs crooked impossibly, and their eye sockets migrating across their faces so rapidly they threaten to evict the eyeballs.

"Grandpa! Please!" little Evie cries out, but now I look at the park ranger, who has fallen to his knees, his face pale and limbs trembling, mouth struggling to form a word that does not yet exist. Because it isn't the way it is in the movies; human beings cannot accept such change so easily—at some point the mind must shut down and the body lose itself with no one left to tell it what to do. "Please, Grandpa, *now*," Evie wails, and the intensity of her distress finally gets to me, so that I hobble over to the battered old station wagon as fast as I can, which isn't very fast. Because Evie is that special grandchild, you see. Evie has my heart.

The car bucks once as Robert gives it gas too quickly. It rattles, then corrects itself. Alicia is safely in the backseat beside me, but I'm not sure if she ever left. She doesn't move as much as she used to. But it's amazing how young she looks—her long hair is still mostly blonde, even though she's about my age, whatever that might be. We agreed long ago not to keep track anymore. I've loved her as long as I've known her. The trouble is, these days I can't remember how long.

The grandkids are both on the other side of Alicia. They're small, so I can't see all of them, just four skinny legs which barely reach beyond the front edge of the seat, and the occasional equally skinny arm. They kick and wave, thrilled. Despite their fear—they have no understanding of what they've caused, or why—they're quite excited about what's happening to them. I suspect this is the way some addicts or athletes feel—something takes over you, as if it were a spirit or a god, seizing your blood and bones, your muscles—and it makes you run around or die. From this angle there's no discernible difference between Evie and Tom, but they are not twins, except in spirit. They sing softly as they often do, so softly I can't make out the words, but I've come to believe that their singing is the background music to all my thoughts.

As we leave the park I can hear the long howls behind me, the humanity disintegrating from those poor people's voices. My grandchildren laugh out loud, giddy from the experience. These changes always seem to happen around certain members of my family, although none of us have precisely understood the relationship or the mechanism. Why did the couple change but not the ranger? I have no idea. Perhaps it is some tendency in the mind, some proclivity of the imagination, or some random, genetic bullet. My grandchildren possess a prodigious talent, but it's not a talent anyone would want to see in action.

Up in the front passenger seat Jackie pats Robert's shoulder. I don't know if this is meant as encouragement, or if he even needs it. My son has always been sane to a fault. His wife's face looks worried, the skin so tight across her cheeks and chin it's as if she wears a latex mask. But then Jackie always was the nervous sort. She's not of this family; she simply married into it.

"Dad, I thought I asked you not to tell them any more stories." Robert's voice is barely under control.

They're both angry with me, furious. They blame me for all of this. But they try not to show it. I don't think it's because they're careful with my feelings. I think it's because they're somewhat frightened of me. "Telling stories, that's what grandfathers do," I say. "It's how I can communicate with them. The stories of our lives and deaths are secrets even from ourselves. All we are able to share are these substandard approximations. But we still have to try, unless we want to arm ourselves with loneliness. I just tell the children *fairytales*, Robert. That's all. Stories about monsters. Something they already know about. Monster stories won't turn you into a monster, Son. Fairytales simply tell you something you already knew in a somewhat clever way."

Once upon a time perhaps gods and monsters walked the earth and a human might choose to be either one. But not anymore. Now people grow and age and die and then are forgotten about. It's the "great circle," or whatever you want to call it. It's sobering information but it can't be helped. I don't tell Robert this—he isn't ready to hear it. He loves his poor, pathetic flesh too much.

"Why couldn't you stop? What will it take to make you stop!" Robert is howling from behind the steering wheel. For just a moment I think he's about to change, expand, become some sort of wolf thing, but he is simply upset with me. Robert is our only child, and I love him very much, but he has always been vulnerable, frightened by the most mundane of dangers, as if he were unhappy to have been born a mortal human (I'm afraid the only kind there is).

Robert always refused to listen to my bedtime stories, so he's really in no place to evaluate whether they are dangerous or not. The members of our family have been shunned for ages, thought to be witches, demons, and worse. No one wants to hear what we have to say. "Your children simply understand the precariousness of it all. And this is how they express it."

"No more, Dad, okay? No more today."

Whatever my son decides to do, he's likely to keep us all locked up at home from now on. The only reason we went out today was because he knows the children need to get out now and then, and he didn't think we'd run into anybody in that big state park. Besides, it doesn't happen every time, not even every other time. There's no way to predict such things. I've witnessed these transformations again and again, but even I do not understand the agency involved.

I can't blame him, I guess. Sometimes human life makes no sense. We really shouldn't exist at all.

Back at the old farmhouse I'm suddenly so exhausted I can barely get out of the car. It's as if I've had a huge meal and now all I can manage is sleep. The adrenalin of the previous few hours has come with a cost. I suspect my food must eat me rather than the other way around.

Alicia is even worse than before, and Robert and Jackie each have to pull on an arm to get her to stand. The grandkids push on her butt, giggling, and aren't really helping.

Once inside they take us up to our room. "I get so exhausted," I tell them.

"I know," Jackie replies. "You should just make it stop. We'd all be happier if you just made it stop."

She's like all the others. She doesn't understand. It happens, but I've never been sure we can make it happen. Perhaps we simply show what has always been. Her children are learning about death. It's a lesson not everyone wants to learn.

She must think that because I'm an older man I'm likely to do foolish things. But we have such a limited time on this planet, I want to tell her, why should we avoid the foolish? I feel like that deliverer of bad news whom everyone blames.

Robert is less courteous as he guides us up the stairs, his movements abrupt and careless. He's obviously lost all patience with this—this caring for elderly parents, this endless drama whenever the family goes out. He'll make us all stay home now, planted in front of the television, transfixed by god-knows-what mindless comedy, locked away so that we can't cause any more trouble. But the children have to go out now and then. An active child trapped inside is like a bomb waiting to go off.

Periodically he loses his balance and crashes me into a railing, a wall, the doorframe. Each time he apologizes but I suspect it is intentional. I don't mind especially—each small jolt of pain wakes me up a bit more. You have to stay awake, I think, in order to know which world you're in.

By the time they lay both of us down in the bed I'm practically blind with fatigue. Almost everything is a dirty yellow smear. It's like a glimpse of an old photograph whose colors have receded into a waxy sheen. Perhaps this is the start of sleep, or the beginning of something else.

Several times during the middle of the night Alicia crawls beneath the bed. Is this what a nightmare is like? Sometimes

I crawl under the bed with her. The floor is gritty, dirty, and uncomfortable to lie on. It's like a taste of the grave. It's what I have to look forward to.

I pat Alicia's arm when she cries. "At least you still have your yellow hair," I tell her. She looks at me so fiercely I back away, far back under the bed into the shadows where I can hear the winds howl and the insects' mad mutter. I can stay there only a brief while before it sickens me but it still seems safer than lying close to her.

I wake up the next morning with my hand completely numb, sleeping quietly beside my face. I scrape the unfeeling flesh against the rough floorboards until it appears to come back to life. Alicia isn't here; she's wandered off. Although much of the time she is practically immobile, she has these occasional adrenaline-driven spurts in which she moves until she falls down or someone catches her. She is so arthritic these bouts of intense activity must be agony for her. I can hear the grandchildren laughing outside and there is this note in their tone that drives me to the window to see.

The two darlings have the mail carrier cornered by the garage. We never get mail here and I think how sad it is that this poor man will doubtless lose his life over an erroneous delivery. They chatter away with their monkey-like talk at such a high pitch and speed I cannot follow what they say, but the occasional discrete image floats to the top—screaming heads and bodies in flame. None of these images appears in any of the stories I have told them, although of course Robert will never believe this. What he does not fully appreciate is that out in the real world all heads have the potential for screaming, and all bodies are in fact burning all the time.

On the edge of the yard I spy Alicia. She has taken off all her clothes again and now scratches about on all fours like some different kind of animal. The Roberts of the world do not wish to admit that humans are animals. We may fancy ourselves better than the beasts because of our language skills, because we possess words in abundance. But all that does is empower us with excuses and equivocations.

The mail carrier has begun to change. He struggles

valiantly but to no avail. Already his jaw has lengthened until it disconnects from the rest of his face, wagging back and forth with no muscle to support it. Already his hair drifts away and his fleshier bits have begun to dissolve. These are changes typical, I think, of a body left in the ground for months.

At first Evie laughs as if watching a clown running through his repertoire of shenanigans but now she has begun to cry. Such is the madness of children, but I must do what I can to minimize the damage. I make my way stiffly downstairs with a desperate grip on the bannister, my joints like so much broken glass inside my flesh, and as I head for the door I see Robert come up out of the cellar, the axe in his hands. "This has to stop...this has to stop," he screams at me. And I very much agree. And if he were coming for *me* with that axe all would be fine—I somehow always understood things might come to this juncture—but he sweeps past me and heads for the front door and my grandchildren outside.

I take a few quick steps, practically falling, and shove him away from the door. I see his hands fumble the axe, but I do not realize the danger until he hits the wall and screams, tumbles backwards, the blade buried in his chest. "Robert!" It's all I have time to say before Jackie comes out of the kitchen screeching. But it's all I know to say, really, and what good would it do to lose myself now? He would have hated to die from clumsiness, and that's what I take away from this house when I leave.

Out on the lawn the children are jumping up and down laughing and crying. There is a moment in which time slows down, and I'm heartsick to see their tiny perfect features shift, coarsen, the flesh losing its elasticity and acquiring a dry, plastic filler look, as if they might become puppets, inanimate figures controlled by distant and rapidly-vanishing souls. I see my little Evie's eyes dull into dark marbles, her slackened face and collapsing mouth spilling the dregs of her laughter. I think of Robert dead in the farmhouse—and what a mad and reprehensible thing it is to survive one's child.

But of course I can't tell these children their father has died. Maybe later, but not now, when they are like this. If I told them now they might savage the little that remains of our pitiful world. In fact I can't tell them anything I feel or know or see.

"Help me find your grandmother!" I shout. "She's gotten away from us, but I'm sure one of you clever children will find her!" And I am relieved when they follow me out of the yard and into the edge of the woods.

I have even more difficulty as I maneuver through the snarled tangle of undergrowth and fallen branches than I thought I would. I'm out of practice, and with every too-wide step to avoid an obstacle I'm sure I'm going to fall. But the children don't seem to mind our lack of progress; in fact they already appear to have forgotten why we're out here. They range back and forth, their paths cross as they pretend to be bees or birds or low-flying aircraft. Periodically they deliberately crash into each other, fall back against trees and bushes in dozens of feigned deaths. Sometimes they just break off to babble at each other, point at me and giggle, sharing secrets in their high-pitched alien language.

Now and then I snatch glimpses of Alicia moving through the trees ahead of us. Her blonde hair, her long legs, and once or twice just a bit of her face, and what might be a smile or a grimace; I can't really tell from this distance. Seeing her in fragments like this I can almost imagine her as the young athletic woman I met fifty years ago, so quick-witted, who enthralled me and frightened me and ran rings around me in more ways than one. But I know better. I know that that young woman exists more in my mind, now, than in hers. That other Alicia is now like some shattered carcass by the roadside, and what lives, what dances and races and gibbers mindlessly among trees is a broken spirit that once inhabited that same beautiful body. Sometimes the death of who we've loved is but the final act in a grief that has lingered for years.

I think that if Alicia were to embrace me now she'd have half my face between her teeth before I had time even to speak her name.

As mad as she, the children now shriek on either side of me, slap me on the side of the face, the belly, before they howl and run away. I wonder if they even remember who she is or was to them. How only a few years ago she made them things and cuddled them and sang them soft songs. But we were never meant to remember everything, I think, and that is a blessing. It seems they have already forgotten about their parents, except as a story they used to know. The young are always more interested in science fiction, those fantasies of days to come, especially if they can be the heroes.

I watch them, or I avoid them, for much of the afternoon. Like a babysitter who really doesn't want the job. At one point they begin to fight over a huge burl on a tree about three feet off the ground. It is only the second such tree deformity I've ever seen, and by far the larger of the two. I understand that they come about when the younger tree is damaged and the tree continues to grow around the damage to create these remarkable patterns in the grain.

Their argument is a strange one, although not that different from other arguments they've had. Evie says it'll make a perfect "princess throne" for her after they cut it down. The fact that they have no means to cut it down does not factor into the argument. Tom claims he "saw it first," and although he has no idea what to do with it the right to decide should be his.

Eventually they come to blows, both of them crying as they continue to pummel each other about the head and face. When they begin to bleed I decide I have to do something. I have handled this badly, although I can't imagine that anyone else would know better how to handle such a crisis. I stare at them—their flesh is running. Their flesh runs! Their grandmother is gone, and they don't even know that their father is dead. And they dream wide awake and the flesh flows around them.

What do I tell them? Do I reassure them with tales of heaven—that their father is now safe in heaven? Do I tell them that no matter what happens to their poor fragile flesh there is a safe place for them in heaven?

What I want to tell them is that their final destination is not heaven, but memory. And you can make of yourself a memory so profound that it transforms everything it touches.

My Evie screams, her face a mask of blood, and Tom looks even worse—all I can see through the red confusion of his face is a single fixed eye. I try to run, then, to separate them, but I am so awkward and pathetic I fall into the brush and tangle below them, where I sprawl and cry out in sorrow and agony.

Only then do they stop, and they come to me, my grandchildren, to stare down at me silently, their faces solemn. Tom has wiped much of the blood from his face to reveal the scratches there, the long lines and rough shapes like a child's awkward sketch.

This is my legacy, I think. These are the ones who will keep me alive, if only as a memory poorly understood, or perhaps as a ghost too troublesome to fully comprehend.

We try and we try but we cannot sculpt a shape out of what we've done in the world. Our hands cannot touch enough. Our words do not travel far enough. For all our constant waving we still cannot be picked out of a crowd.

My grandchildren approach for the end of my story. I can feel the terrible swiftness of my journey through their short lives. I become a voice clicking because it has run out of sound. I become a tongue silently flapping as it runs out of words. I become motionless as I can think of nowhere else to go.

I become the stone and the plank and the empty field. I am really quite something, the monster made in their image, until I am scattered, and forgotten.

ACKNOWLEDGMENTS

"Breathing" originally appeared in *Black Static 53*, Aug/Sept 2016.

"Apartment B" originally appeared in *Nightscript 2*, edited by C.M. Muller (Cthonic Matter, September 2016).

"Red Rabbit" originally appeared in *Borderlands 6*, edited by Olivia & Tom Monteleone (Samhain Publishing, May 2016).

"The Hanged Man" originally appeared in *Black Static 40*, May 2014.

"The Fishing Hut" originally appeared in *Black Static 45*, March 2015.

"A Sudden Event" is original to this volume.

"Paula Breaks" originally appeared in *Surreal Worlds*, edited by Sean Leonard, (Journalstone, 2015).

"Lost in the Garden of Earthly Delights" originally appeared in *Shadow's Edge*, edited by Simon Stranzas (Gray Friar Press, March 2013).

"Blattidae Wine" originally appeared in *Weird Fiction Review 7*, Fall 2016.

"Half-Light" originally appeared in *Uncertainties Vol II*, edited by Brian Showers (Swan River Press, Aug 2016).

"Mister Ainsley" originally appeared in *Black Wings VI: New Tales of Lovecraftian Horror*, edited by ST Joshi (PS Publishing, November 2017).

"The Long Fade into Evening" originally appeared in *Darker Companions*, edited by Scott David Aniolowski and Joseph S. Pulver, Sr. (PS Publishing, Sep 2017).

"Domestic Magic" (co-written with Melanie Tem), originally appeared in *Magic: An Anthology of the Esoteric and Arcane*, edited by Jon Oliver (Solaris, October 2012).

"The Secret Laws of the Universe" originally appeared in *Psycho-Mania!*, edited by Stephen Jones (Robinson, October 2013).

"The Man in the Rose Bushes" originally appeared in *The Ghost & Scholars Book of Shadows: Volume 3*, edited by Rosemary Pardoe (Sarob Press, 2016).

"The Night Doctor" originally appeared in *The Spectral Book of Horror Stories* edited by Mark Morris (Spectral Press, September 2014).

"The Enemy Within" originally appeared in *Something Remains: Joel Lane & Friends*, edited by Peter Coleborn & Pauline Dungate (Alchemy Press, September 2016).

"Stick Men" originally appeared in *Jamais Vu 3*, Autumn 2014.

"Too Many Ghosts" originally appeared in *The Dark 19*, Dec 2016.

"When You're Not Looking" is original to this volume.

"Between the Pilings" originally appeared in *Innsmouth Nightmares*, edited by Lois Gresh (PS Publishing, July 2015).

"The Erased" originally appeared in *Shadows & Tall Trees 7*, edited by Michael Kelly (Undertow Publications, May 2017).

"The Wake" originally appeared in *Nightmare's Realm: New Tales of the Weird and Fantastic*, edited by ST Joshi (Dark Regions Press, March 2017).

"The Weight Lost" originally appeared in *A Darke Phantastique: Encounters with the Uncanny and Other Magical Things*, edited by Jason Brock (Cycatrix Press, 2014).

"The Monster Makers" originally appeared in *Black Static 35*, 2013.

ABOUT THE AUTHOR

Steve Rasnic Tem's writing career spans over 40 years, including poetry, plays, short stories, and novels in the genres of fantasy, science fiction, horror, crime, regional fiction set in the Appalachian South, as well as a less-classifiable imaginative prose more than one critic has called "Temism." His collaborative novella with his late wife Melanie Tem, *The Man On The Ceiling*, won the World Fantasy, Bram Stoker, and International Horror Guild awards in 2001. He has also won the Bram Stoker, International Horror Guild, and British Fantasy Awards for his solo work. His novel *UBO* (Solaris, January 2017) is a dark science fictional tale about violence and its origins. Steve's southern gothic novel *Blood Kin* (Solaris, March 2014) won the 2014 Bram Stoker Award. His other novels include his YA *The Mask Shop of Doctor Blaack* (Hex, 2018), *Deadfall Hotel* (Solaris, 2012), *The Man On The Ceiling* (Wizards of the Coast Discoveries, 2008, written with Melanie Tem), The Book of Days (Subterranean, 2002), *Daughters* (Grand Central, 2001, also written with Melanie Tem), and *Excavation* (Avon, 1987). A handbook on writing, *Yours to Tell: Dialogues on the Art & Practice of Fiction*, also written with Melanie, appeared in 2017 from Apex Books.

Steve has published almost 500 short stories. His first collection of stories, *Ombres sur la Route*, was published by the French publisher Denoël in 1994. His first English language collection, *City Fishing* (Silver Salamander, 2000) won the International Horror Guild Award. His other story collections are *The Far Side of the Lake* (Ash Tree, 2001), *In Concert* (Centipede, 2010-collaborations with Melanie Tem), *Ugly Behavior* (New Pulp, 2012-noir fiction), *Onion Songs* (Chomu, 2013), *Celestial Inventories* (ChiZine, 2013), *Twember* (NewCon, 2013-science fiction), *Here With The Shadows* (Swan River Press, 2014), the giant 72-story treasury, *Out of the Dark: A Storybook of Horrors*, (Centipede Press), *Figures Unseen: Selected Stories* (Valancourt, 2018), *The Harvest Child And Other Fantasies* (Crossroads, 2018), the YA-oriented *Everything Is Fine Now* (Omnium Gatherum, 2019), *The Night Doctor and Other Tales* (Centipede, 2019), and *Thanatrauma* (Valancourt, 2021).

Visit his website at www.stevetem.com.

Curious about other Crossroad Press books?
Stop by our site:
http://store.crossroadpress.com
We offer quality writing
in digital, audio, and print formats.